"For wicked  *9:17)*

PREACHER:

"Go tell them that injustice has infected their way of seeing the world." Pope Francis on the US Border

- J.A. Wayne Hellman, *Professor of Historical Theology, Saint. Louis University*

Morgan writes with prodigious fluidity. At one point, we are hurled into the midst of a riveting account of the sensational 1962 protest at Indiana University against the US blockade of Cuba, where Morgan and his Trotskyist comrades faced down an outraged mob of thousands…a calculating narrative with a sweep revealing a protagonist full of contradictions. Although a Marxist in his political opposition to class and racial oppression, he holds classic Puritan ideas about [sex] and gender. Liberated women are a source of disorder in his world. Long stretches of this epistolary novel evoke a broken hearted country song mediated through the mind of an Ayatollah. He is a writer fond of short literary citations and compressed forays, but also one with a dark wit who knows when to shift modes to express the way tragedy and comedy daily intertwine. Most impressive is how threads laid earlier are picked up.

- Alan W. Wald, *Professor of Literature and American Culture, University of Michigan.*

"The dumbass illusion from bourgeois enlightenment that religion and sexual morality is fleeting superstition requires an abjuring ignorance of the loyalties, longings, flaws and work of ordinary human beings"

- Shotgun Preacher p.437

"Edgy in every direction. I hated I could not put this book down."

- John McFall, *Hitachi Data Systems*

"The Shotgun Preacher reflects a breathtaking life struggle for a higher ideal in politics and justice; and straighter path in religion and spirituality."

- Mohammed Elyassini, *Professor of Earth and Environmental Systems (Political Geography) Indiana State University, Author of 'Global Restructuring and Peripheral States'.*

"Shotgun Preacher proves Our Father in Heaven, Yahweh, and Allah is the same God who can love a Communist."

- Eliot Thomas Aquinas Morgan, *Creative Director Cosm Press, New York City*

Troubles, you see, is the generalized
word for what God exists in

Jack Kerouac, On the Road

To Sister Paula Damiano
whose work and Programs
Provide sign of Providence.
Respectfully,
Tom

Published by Mindstir Media, LLC
1931 Woodbury Ave. #182 | Portsmouth, New Hampshire 03801 | USA
1.800.767.0531 | www.mindstirmedia.com

Printed in the United States of America
ISBN-13: 978-0-9975435-3-7
Library of Congress Control Number: 2016909645

SHOTGUN PREACHER

*Where the Cold and Old political wars of the sixties
began to converge with the Culture wars of this new century*

THOMAS G. MORGAN

MINDSTIR MEDIA

CONTENTS

1.   Friedrich Hölderlin: "Much has man learned, much of the heavenly has he named. Since we have been a conversation."
2,3,4,6. John Calvin: Institutes of the Christian Religion volume I
5.   Ross Lockridge: 'Raintree County', the great Indiana novel.
7.   Ezra Pound: Cantos LXXI

For Pope Francis
As he reflects all the saints, especially
his countryman Che Ernesto Lynch Gueverra.
And the brave Fedayeen.

"I would not spend one hour in preparation of a book which had the ambition to perhaps titillate some readers. But I am spending many hours because the full story is the best way that I know to have it seen, and understood."

Malcom X,
Autobiography; One year before his death

"Adequate spiritual guidance can come only through a more radical [left] political orientation and more conservative [right] religious conviction."

Reinhold Niebuhr from 'Reflections on the End of an Era'

One of the sins against Faith is presumption, defined as "A foolish expectation of salvation without making use of the necessary means to obtain it."

Padraig Pearse from 'Peace and the Sword'

PART ONE:

SINCE WE HAVE BEEN A CONVERSATION

I

Sweeney drank a fifth of V.O. everyday. Sometimes more at night. He was obese and dying. But my… he was so very much more;…Bernard Sweeney was the most gallant of men and great company. He loved to tell stories about shopping for doctors. He'd seen many and they all said he had to diet, lose weight and quit drinking whiskey.

Finally he found old Doc Dire who said, "you'll have to diet, lose weight, stop the smokes…but how long have you been drinking that much V.O?"

Bernie would answer, "forty years!"

"Well, you might as well continue with that," the doc said, "but you're going to have to diet."

Bernie would then say, "I rose to my feet and embraced the man. Sir, I said, you've just become my family doctor!"

There was always laughter with Bernie before he terminally wrecked his car over the ramp of the Wabash River Bridge.

Bernie held to the Irish maxim that even if you were an acclaimed novelist, poet or philosopher…all was for naught if you were a failed conversationalist. No one could accuse Bernie of being a failed conversationalist.

One night late into our conversation of laughter and seriousness he counseled me concerning my parental custody problems.

"No father can get custody of his children in this state", Bernie said, "unless he is a Methodist Minister. They are Indiana's Moral Majority. They keep horseracing out and 'M.A.D.D. (mothers against drunk driving,) and the A.T.F. in. Except for da' region[1] and Terre Haute they dominate the bench from the Indianapolis State House to its every satellite county courthouse. It's like Moscow and Eastern

---

1   da' region: N.W. Calumet steel workers region

Europe. They've gone from the *Klan* to *Temperance* to *Timocracy* in a very short time. We have more Methodist Judges than the nations had Masonic Presidents." Bernie claimed the only non-Masonic Presidents had been assassinated…Kennedy, Lincoln and maybe McKinley.

I'd never thought much about Methodists, I had as yet to experience them as "Baptists who read."[1] I only knew they'd looked impressive riding horses to church back in 1965 celebrating the bi-centennial of their circuit riders. I watched them ride by from the porch of our student housing in Bloomington. This one circuit rider looked like the Kingston Trio's "Reverend Mr. Black." Mounted on a gaunt Saddlebred he rode tall in the saddle, a straight line between his shoulders, knees, and the irons of his English tack. A magisterium of balance he held his bible as firm as his faith for all the photographers to see.

Later elderly hoosiers would share with me that when they belonged to the Ku Klux Klan in the twenties they thought of it as merely a methodist saddle club.

Early spring…the car crash. My estranged wife and I were transporting our children home. She drove while I sleepily rode shotgun. The children fussed so I brought my six-year-old daughter up in the front on my lap. My four-year-old son stretched out in the back.

Our marriage was not irreconcilable but my wife was dead set on her own course. As that night she stayed at the speed limit, in the correct lane, unswerving to the destructive reality ahead. The head on collision knocked the three of us through the windshield. My soon to be ex wife lost an eye and severely scarred her face. My little girl fractured her arm and shoulder and at thirty is still retrieving shattered glass from her forehead. My boy in the backseat only broke his collarbone. I got a concussion, broken arm, leg, and ribcage.

Frantic as a half butchered bull I bellared from the stretcher for reassurances my children and their mother were safe. Then I saw their mother sitting sullenly in the ambulance beside a paramedic holding her hand. She gazed at me as hostile with one eye as she had with both an hour before. Out of my head, I kept ordering another paramedic I recognized to return to the wreck for her husband. They were neigh-

---

1"   Methodists are Baptists who read" A River Runs Through It by Norman MacLean

bors and she'd recently left him. Everyone in the ambulance except my children were as annoyed with me as I was with the Hindu Doc I first saw... coming to... in the hospital. He held my wedding ring with a forceps. It was stretched out jaggedly like a piece of barbed wire. His thick south Indian accent inflected, "Ahnd whot do you whant us to doo with this?" "It's shot", I answered. I thought he threw it away, somehow my mother retrieved it the next day.

The children and their mother were put in a separate hospital room from me. I had pervasive night terrors for seventy hours...waking every fifteen minutes embarrassed by my own screaming. Still, I was amused when the guy who shared my room suggested, "Tom... do you think you might have some mental problems too?"

Technically my problems were more emotional than mental and one of them walked past my room to my wife's every afternoon. He was a married gawky gaited white male colleague of hers at Rose Hulman[1].

In traction, adrenalin only gave me anxiety. I was having the typical cuckholds anxiety, but I think to about the tenth power. I couldn't leave my bed to see the children. They were brought into me everyday after gawk ass walked by.

On the fifth day there were two more discouraging arrivals. I was served divorce papers one hour before board members arrived with a termination notice of my job. They'd also come to arrange severance pay.

The board members were sympathetic. Bernie was one of them. I knew his old heart went out to me, but I was not amused he seemed more interested in eyeing one of the shapely nurses. Father Dietrich was also there and ashamed...as well he should be, I thought. Even though the new Archbishop was a bulbous idiot from St. Louis he would never have fired me without, at least a nod from Dietrich.

Dietrich... who was supposed to be my best friend... I was too whupped to be furious with him. We had worked together for nearly twenty years loyal to the old Archbishop... a prayerful, saintly man from Prague who tolerated our neo marxist patter about liberation theology [Helder Camara, Camillo Torres and how we were building

1   Rose Hulman Institute: College of Engineering in Terre Haute

Christ consciousness along revolutionary perspectives.] He had died the year before and was barely cold in the grave when we had to start dealing with the bulbous one. We'd retire in the evening with Bernie to the Knights of St. Peter Claver Bar off Fall Creek to strategize our survival. It had not been a good year. Alarmingly I saw Dietrich become daily more clerical and less comradely. More alarmingly I think, he saw me increasingly as canonically non-classifiable. Earlier I think he thought of me as a colorful notch for leveraging his ecclesial career. Our friendship like both of our careers seemed headed as far south as my marriage.

The severance pay was generous but I was not when Bernie insisted on speaking sensuously of my mother in law he'd just met. "I need to sleep, men." I adjourned our uncheerful meeting.

The next morning was Saturday and seemed providential. Winter sunlight in the window and no night terrors. After breakfast I had a surprise visitor. It was young Pastor John from the Methodist Parish in Freedom, the village near our farm. I'd counseled him regarding wounds from his own divorce some years back. Lean and serious he was studying for a PhD. in Religious Studies at IU. He had an almost caste like embarrassment that my wife was using a similar degree to wreck her family. After quick greetings he got right to the point, "I hear you're unemployed."

"News travels (incredibly?!) fast."

He touched my cast, "Man… have you ever considered the ministry?" Sun continued streaming in the window as I appreciated this young guys concern. I didn't answer him.

"You told me you were the second best speaker of the sixties after Malcolm. You are an intellectual Christian with graduate degrees. You could become one of C.O.C.U.'s new leaders.

COCU, the acronym for Church of Christ Uniting was the ecumenical fantasy of mainline protestant and liberal catholic ecumenicists. Conservatives pronounced it COOCUU.

Bankruptcy is still the leading motivator for consolidation. Mainliners were still celebrating Sydney Ahlstroms "definitive" (1973) *Religious History of the American People*. I'd read it. I liked reading church and denominational history. It reminded me of the flora and fauna of Marxist "tendencies". All those cans of factional worms coiling and recoiling in their struggle to influence His story. Ahlstroms thousand plus pages concluded that the post sixties, post modern American religious culture would be pre-dominantly 1. secular not dogmatic, 2. acutely aware of contradictions and 3. doubtful toward church and governmental institutions. He railed against the puritan ethic of "strenuous moral commitment to make the state responsible to enforce religious values."[1]

Gak! Isn't that what Martin and Malcolm and all of us Leftys were doing in the civil rights and anti war movements. Without a strenuous moral commitment to make the state responsible for peace against war, for justice against bigotry, murder, disease and exploitation is to concede state power to the free booting corporations who cultivate a religious culture of 1. (heretical) dogma 2. denial and 3. blind patriotism. American liberals (secular and religious) have been rehearsing for decades their destined role as a kind of Weimar Republic for the storm troopers to trample over.

I weakly, babbled on like this, but John just smiled, "Oh there'll be lots to talk about." He said, "at the State Conference this spring I can recommend you to the superintendents and I'm sure they will hire you. There are so many unpastored churches throughout Indiana's country-side. You can be a circuit rider. If one doesn't pay enough, do several."

I did not speak the obvious, that is to say, "John, I am not a Protestant. I am not a Methodist. I am Catholic." For John...all God fearing men were uniting toward the valued future. And that...after all, I thought was a decent notion. Even if Ahlstroms ilk...by dusting off the "unbiased" leaders of bourgeois liberalism were preparing the field for the next century's politically driven majority of mega-church morons. God forgive me the idea of being a Methodist minister was less inspired by young Pastor John as it was by old Bernie Sweeney.

If I could not reconcile my marriage then my children should live on our farm home with me. I knew they would prefer it and it was bound to be better than somewhere off to the liberal left of whoopee with their mother. She was enmeshed with her colleagues and other

1   Ahlstrom p. 1087-88

conferees of her career. Homemaking and parenting were clearly not her priority. Yet she was riding the rising tide of Yuppiedom (Y.oung U..rban P.rofessionals) while I was locked in the undertow of Aging Rural Something or others.

I'd become an unemployed ex archdiocesian. I'd hired on with the Archdiocese instead of the mental health establishment my first year out of graduate school. The truth is they were the only outfit in Indiana who would hire me because of my political background. Now decades later a canned red catholic… my career prospects were looking questionable. I was near the edge with thousands of others in the late Seventies of what was to be called the "culture wars." To survive these domestic conflicts would require everything and more I ever learned from the "political wars" of the sixties. First I had to get a job.

After two weeks of the warehouse atmosphere at Regional Hospital I was discharged home. I drove straight to my favorite Tobacco Shoppe, buying a contraband box of Cuban cigars and two dress canes. One had a polished greyhound head and the other was a sword cane, i.e. one with a concealed 26 inch blade. At home I had a black bull phallus cane and two hard hickory ones. I intended being a cripple with panache.

Within weeks I managed the March calving of forty some brood cows in my casts and with my hickory canes. Also in casts and with my greyhound cane I applied for jobs all over the place. At night with my sword cane I visited all the rough taverns. Early on I hurt all over, especially my right leg. After a car wreck even your hair hurts. I didn't think much about the leg until I stuck it in deep mud beside the cattle chute. Pulling it out I could feel it shift, give way, and pop in three places. The E.R. x-rayed it and found three more breaks. I got another cast and had to switch from canes to crutches.

My job interviews were disastrous. I had no references for the last decades of my "professional" life. The articles I'd written were all in…to them…"sectarian" that is, Catholic or Socialist publications. I think the "modern" mental healthers saw me correctly as a peculiarly depressed cripple. I imagined them scouring the new DSM (Diagnostic Statistical Manual) to more clinically categorize me. I did my best to disguise my opinion of them. For I thought the metaculture of so called mental health in the seventies was morally and patently insane. One clinical director actually looked at me with limpid eyes and said… "Here… we are into touching and feeling…" I promptly excused myself outside for fresh air.

In short, I was not offered work… anywhere! I accompanied John to the Annual Methodist Conference. We met with a superintendent at I.U.'s Auditorium. He was an older black man who seemed to know about me. Smiling warmly he took my hand and said, "I wanted to shake hands with a brother whose touched both Martin and Malcolm." John seemed surprised. I hadn't told him that. It seems this superintendent was pals with the A.M.E. (African Methodist Episcopal) Bishop Anderson in Indy. We'd worked together in the sixties and then later at the Interfaith Council. I'd written a grant for the (I.F.C.) Indiana Federation of Churches funding the Institute on Religion and Aging (or IRA) which Bishop Anderson favored. He would joke at public meetings that I was the IRA man. When I drew him aside to explain that I was a fundraiser for NORAID[1] he stopped publicly joking but I think was doubly impressed as well. I had a friend in Bishop Anderson.

The Superintendent offered me the pastorates of three country parishes in the Bloomington area near my farm. John would help me with the necessary paper work, but first I'd have to become a Methodist. The pay was lower than I feared. The hours were every weekend and Wednesday nights. I could get a regular five day work week job as well. But, first… I'd have to become a Methodist. C.O.C.U. (The Church of Christ Uniting) was still just an idea, the U.M.C. (United Methodist Church) was the present reality. Before long, I would hear those first three syllables rather preciously pronounced.

The good superintendent concluded, "Thomas, my job is to find rams in the bushes. I think the ministry may be your natural calling. But you take your time. Pray about it. Think about it. Talk to your family. Count your shekels. Whenever you're ready…you let me know and I'll put you in the cloth."

That afternoon I checked all the John Wesley I could find out of the library. I knew about Wesley of course, but wondered if he was some-

1   Noraid: financial aid to oppressed Catholics in Northern Ireland, chiefly administered by Sinn Fein, political arm of the Irish Republican Army

one with whom I could identify. "I mean...Christ!", George Corley Wallace is a Methodist, I thought, but then Hitler had been a catholic. It is the song, not the singers, I kept telling myself but some sympathetic singers would be nice.

I was still attending mass semi-occasionally at St. Benedicts, the Franciscan parish in Terre Haute frequented by my mother, aunts and cousins. I dodged anything diocesan, as it seemed like the company that had fired me. More significantly...all my friends associated with the archdiocese were avoiding me. My non-personhood from an estranged and/or embarrassed bureaucracy I could understand but I sensed there was something far deeper.

Responsible catholics wish The Church to loom larger than life and/or time... above human foibles. In many respects it does. But in so far as it achieves or fails this state is not simply due to its leadership. The secret I was learning is that the most remote hierarch is utterly dependent on the culture of its constituents i.e. the culture of those families that support it.

Cynically one could say it is the codependent relationship between parasites and host but that captures only a thin part of the truth. I think there is a core element in human nature on which it hinges. A metaphorical pact programmed in our genes.

In 1940, the year I was born the caves of Lascaux were discovered. Fifty years later in '91 and '94 the ones in Cosquer and Chauvet were found. Forty thousand year old evidence about the essential nature of our pre-tribal Pleistocene relatives has been decoded. "The Nature of Paleolithic Art" by R. Dale Guthrie and subsequent archeological digs completely negate the gender dysphoric idealism of Engels[1] and the ilk of Evelyn Reeds, "Problems of Women's Liberation."[2]

The prolonged childhood of human issue requires intensive co-parenting i.e. nurturing and cultivating qualitatively unique "cognitive

1   Frederick Engles, 'Origin of the Family, Private Property, and the State': brilliant indictment of capitalist property relations flawed by outdated anthropology and an aging bachelor's libido.
2   Evelyn Reeds 'Problems etc. etc.': Engles metaphors expanded meanly and madly by subsidized (i.e. kept) woman's libber of Socialist Workers Party.

and creative skills [that] were again and again selectively successful."

Perhaps the most successful of these Paleolithic notions was that of the supernatural. In Guthrie's view, "a necessary, universal human corrective to reason, cushioning us all against the distresses and disappointments of life... encouraging enthusiasm, good health, honesty [cooperation] and other noble purposes...creating beauty where little is produced from literal reason."

Acute and chronic co-parenting the distinct core of our [Species] nature and Supernatural supports of same our greatest need! Catholic hierarchs do not proselytize individuals they serve and are served by a culture[1] of parenting families best utilized if ethnically strung together. The Church had preserved this Christianized pagan; probably animistic notion where the bourgeois reformation had rationally thrown it out. Perhaps Islam has retained it in their tribal and pre-tribal connections, but Protestants haven't a clue.

Wesley's method and search finally took him to Ireland. There... I think his writing reflects he found that apostolic organicity he yearned for. John Wesley was not a cause of the Reformation but a casualty of it. "A separated brethren" trying to find his way back home. 'Maybe I could do this', I began to think.

I thought the core culture of parenting families seemed shot... seriously degenerated... in contemporary America... I thought. The divorce rate I'd become a part of accounted for the majority of Catholic, Protestant, Muslim, and secular households. These modern women were wanting each other in careers independent of men in something unclearly more...more than supernaturally ordained families let alone intensive co-parenting ones. Their men were becoming too sensitive to work or fight and following the lead of women were bitchily becoming second rate instead of first rate parents. Priests and Nuns seemed the same. Worse... a brutish lumpen reaction was already rumbling in the wings. Charisms of mega churched mindless militancy would soon supplant serious leadership as well as the mainliners' fantasies. It

---

1   "The synthesis between culture and faith is not just a demand of culture, but also of faith. A faith which does not become culture is a faith which has not been fully received, not thoroughly thought through, not fully lived out." Pope John Paul II

had gotten so bad that to attend mass or spend the night at our Major Seminary was to revisit Sodom and Gomorrah. St. Meinrads actually had a gay bar on campus called the 'Unstable Influence'. I think our old Archbishop died no longer denying that most of his priests at their best were fantasy fornicating someone's wife, child, or each other.

Father Dietrich thought my harsh criticism of priests came from some idealized notion of the priesthood. No idealist me... there were dozens of flesh and blood positive examples of good priests (regrettably to me usually the politically conservative ones) walking around among us. Tending their parish duties with sacrifice and good humor. Exemplary to the people they drew strength from. These men seemed to understand celibacy like poverty as a disciplined sacrifice not a pivotal life style. Intellectually curious but dogmatically strong; the party line strengthened rather than oppressed them. They seriously signed on for celibacy never expecting to marry or sexually experiment around. How un-American! Not even Elijah Muhammad's or Ebenezer Baptists could top the new world scandal of a truly celibate American catholic priest. For not since Ancient Rome has there been a more sexually indulgent people. The very idea of American Freedom has been reduced to; 'No one interferes with my economic and sexual selfishness.' Liberals wish to be as recklessly unregulated with sex as conservatives are with the economy.

It is common knowledge how the A.P.A. (American Psychiatric & Psychological Associations) had merely voted at conventions to drop most heretofore illicit sexual behaviors from their lists of psychopathologies and to reclassify them as alternate life styles.

What is not so commonly known is how they continued to medicalize all previous categories of moral and immoral sexual conduct. Their [A.P.A.s] D.S.M. (Diagnostic Statistical Manual of Mental Disorders) came out authorizing clinical thus educational, legal, and through private insurance corporations financial definitions of what has always before been privacy and/or sin.

Nymphomania, adulterous liaisons, promiscuity, homosexual panic, gender confusion, and other sexual hysterias have been eliminated as psychopathological. Instead a dozen "sexual desire disorders" are listed all relating to not getting it enough, adequately, or on time. Followed by another dozen "paraphillias" relating to sexual urges or behavior involving non human objects, humiliation, children or non consenting enough adults over a period of at least six months. It carefully notes "Gender Identity and Gender dysphoric problems must be distinguished from sexual orientation" which refers merely to erotic attraction to males, females, or both. Even sexual sadism and pedophilia is qualified in the latter especially to "at least six months recurrent sexual activity with a thirteen year old or younger which causes "interpersonal difficulty." Child Protective Service Champions were just beginning to feign surprise when the celebrated sexual revolution society spilled over to children. Even more stupid is the continuing politically correct denial that the 21st century priest pedophiles have anything to do with the 20th century blossoming of buggery in the seminaries. Slogans that gayness has nothing to do with pedophilia here denies even the reality of physical accessibility.

Something exceptionally American has been going on. As late as 2005 the Vatican instructed all diocesan authorities in the world not to ordain homosexual candidates to the priesthood. Several American bishops immediately and publicly... (many more privately) responded "they did not regard this as a ban on their ordaining gay men, and would continue to accept gay candidates on a case by case basis"[1]

The words of a rabbi on T.V. made more sense than all the so-called Christian ballyhoo put together. He said, "it is clear that God prefers us to be faithfully man-husband-father and woman-wife-mother begetting and parenting children to love and serve Him. In so far as we fall short of this through mateless, childless, unfaithful, separated, divorced or different orientated conditions...He forgives us." Likewise we should struggle to overcome, minimize, and forgive, but definitely not celebrate the falling short of Gods will for us. Parents should not present freedom of choice in sexual behaviors for their children any more than they should allow freedom of choice in what's for breakfast. That is, oatmeal is good, ice cream is not independent of which one you crave. As parents we lovingly forgive errors in eating and sex. It

---

1   NYT "Bishops Draft on Ministering to Gays" October 24, 2006.

would be insane to celebrate them.

Most of us have family members and friends who have struggled with and/or succumbed to adulterous, homosexual, or violent orientations. Only one of these however has a national caucus saying 'if its really you, you're not responsible.' Thank God I do not have to struggle with homosexual temptations. Mine are worse. A national caucus encouraging me to indulge my violent temptations might lead to the assassination of several politicians.

The (G.A.F.) Global Assessment Functioning Scale of modern America, records world wide cavalier sex is 'all for one and one for all' unless one is thirteen or younger for more than six months. And when did ones sexual preferences become the defining element in human beingness anyhow. It is cartoonish simplification to suggest sexual labels centrally define the complexity of a human being either as epithet or justification. My dear relatives homosexual preferences no more centrally defines them than my heterosexual preferences (i.e. I'm more of a pelvic width than mammary gland man) defines me. Neither preference is fit for civilized conversation.

Civilization is out the door in a "Culture of Narcissism." No one nailed it better than Christopher Lasch in his book with that title. Then he wrote one on family called "Haven in a Heartless World". I arranged for him to address an all diocesan 'Family Life Commission' for the Indiana Catholic Conference. He was brilliant and much appreciated by serious delegates. Lasch, Dietrich, many delegates and I spent half the night smoking and drinking in dialogue with his ideas and the political and moral consequences of family breakdown.

But... the bulbous bishop was offended. He *felt* some of his liberal counselors and all of his female fanatics (both feminists and foetalists) were insulted. Narcissists know when they are nailed! Dietrich was beginning to grovel. *Solomon, Solomon Gynaecocratumenos!*[1] I noted these lines of Milton when I gave notice to my board and to the Archbishop... the bulbous one... the unbright bulb. All diocesians, i.e. those who are employed by a diocese work directly for their bishop or archbishop. He is legally the proprietor of all property and the employer of all personnel in the bishoprics realm. The new bulb

1   * Solomon Solomon why are we ruled by Women?

personified the bishoprick.

The old archbishop was frail and saintly conducting his office in an exemplary and principled manner. This new fat ass was all personality.

In short the old archbishop liked me; the new one didn't. We rode different tides of HisStory. My days in the diocese were numbered. The board loyally accepted my twelve months' notice while he objected that a year was highly unusual. Over the years I'd stacked the board with solid family men and women, working people, and labor skates. They held fast. He did not overrule them.

With a years lead time I could reestablish myself. I thought of reconnecting with Bishop Shea of Evansville, a tall serious McBishop who made you proud instead of embarrassed to be Irish. (The bulb had taken to performing at wine tasting athletic club events. Sycophants from the suburbs encouraged a kind of ethnic stupor in him.) Evansville was about the same distance south from our farm as Indianapolis was north. Ray Rufo of the Indiana Catholic Conference had spoken of hiring me as a consultant lobbyist. My wife had always encouraged me to go into private practice.

New possibilities! There was new mental health money in secular community clinics. The farm was beginning to be profitable and my wife had just finished her PhD. I was supportive if she wanted to teach or just stay home research and write. (What she preferred was to attend conferences.) I got her a job on faculty at St. Mary of the Woods. The marriage had gotten off track. We needed time and different schedules, I thought, to get it back on track.

There was no going back for her. I was delusional to think otherwise. Our car wreck, my being canned, and her filing for divorce all happened within a month of my giving a years notice.

II

Father Conway phoned me at the farm. Finally, a caller from…but not exactly of the Archdiocese. He was a Benedictine Order priest from Minnesota who'd been temporary rector at St. Maurs where I'd taught a few classes a year ago. St Maurs was a poor little Benedictine Seminary in the heart of Indianapolis run by a marvelous mulatto monk and mad man named Mario Shaw. In spite of being libidinally lunatic he could still talk the socks off and charm the money out of almost any guilty white audience. Jerry Conway managed St. Maurs Graduate Seminary Academic Program with intelligence, imagination and integrity. I taught courses on Liberation Theology, Christian Marxist Dialogue and Victor Frankl. Yet we all knew the academic program functioned mainly as a front for Father Mario's financial machinations.

Jerry said on the phone, "Hey Tom… kind of an unusual call… we've reviewed some of our books and found that last year we significantly underpaid you… that is we failed to cut two separate checks for you… about $600 bucks. I'll deliver it if you'll give me directions."

I think he took up a collection from my students and friends. My severance pay had not kicked in and Father Conway was the soul of kindness. He was shocked I would consider the Methodist ministry. "No way Thomas," he said, "you belong in The Church. These dioceses and these protestants will never understand you. If you really want to be a clergyman and I can't imagine why (I never saw Father Jerry Conway in a Roman collar)…go for the real thing… go for the priesthood." "I'm committed to reconciling my marriage" I would reply. Then we'd settle into our old argument.

Father Conway not only thought but actively recruited liberal seminarians with the fantasy that soon priests would be allowed to marry. "Ultimately" he would say, "there is no canonical reason why Rome cannot allow the marriage of some priests." One condition of being delusional is while you cannot recognize your own… you immediately recognize the delusions of others. (Like Mendelsohn on Mailer.)

I knew the reality that Father Conway's liberals denied...yes, yes The Church could handle some married priests, what it could not handle was a mass of divorced priests...and that is exactly what we would very quickly get. We quietly finished our cold supper of lamb stew and Shiraz. I never saw Jerry again. I think he returned to Minnesota. My true friend knew that groceries were even more fundamental than thinking.

Like all Minnesotans I knew, Conway came from his states farmer-labor[1] background. Before things got silent at supper he'd look around and say, "Whatever you do Tom, don't lose your farm... you've got to earn enough to save this place." With that in mind I phoned my friend Mike, in California. He was the most business-minded guy I knew. The 'mercantile marxist' we used to kid him.

After hearing my long winded story Mike succinctly said two things; 1) Morgan, you're gonna have to start writing these stories instead of living them and 2) Come to California as soon as you can arrange it... I'll make you a full partner in my Real Estate firm and you can earn enough to pay for ten Indiana farms. The California real estate market was hot and Mike was in a position to sell parcels of ranch land in the Diablo range to bay area wannabee ranchers. "You know everything from horses and livestock to Berkely political lingo... you're perfect for the job," Mike flattered me. "Get out here and establish residence, you can live with us, and I'll help you pass the real estate exam," Mike continued persuasively. Finally, he reminded me, "You always said, you are as free under capitalism as you have money in your pocket."

Money!?! I'd always worked hard and made my fair share of it... but I never, not very naturally anyhow...ever thought much about it. Even as a fundraiser my specialty was rhetoric not collections. The top prices I got for farm sales I considered as recognition for quality live-stock not as some source of acquisitiveness. Now I was forced to think of money in survival mode. I'd never kvetched like so many church mice diocesians for being on a slightly lower pay scale. I saw that staff received good wages and benefits, for the thorough expectations I had

1   There is no 'democratic party' in Minnesota. There is a 'Republican party' and a 'Farmer-Labor democratic party.' See Charles Hiram Walker's book "American City" on the Minneapolis general strike.

of them. I appreciated and considered it just…my unlimited expense account for away from home meals, bar bills, staff car and gas. And I considered it an honor to work for The Church instead of the state or corporations. I had my mother's peasant view of economy. Now, I would have to be otherwise. I could probably arrange for neighbors to lease my cattle on shares and sell enough timber and sheep to pay ahead on my mortgage. I'd get Farm Credit Association to concede a once annual payment plan. Mike was always right when it came to money. My decision was congealing. It still left the problems of my children, my horses, hounds, and stockdogs, legal expenses, my marriage and my wife.

I cannot yet write… (at length) about my children. For they were the real life… I only lived vicariously in all other dimensions. I could not bear to be without them…and could not bear to see them…bear the injury of their parents not intact. They were with me every other weekend. Their genuine joy at seeing me was as afflicting as the pretense to be happier than they were. A shadow had fallen jaggedly across their confidence in being.

My four-year-old son had always been supremely confident and pleasantly spirited. Over compensating now he pushed it. Swaggering in false confidence yet becoming afraid of the dark and imagined monsters. We had always described my daughters first six years as the gentle *reign* of the Princess of Gloryville Farm. Her crown of confidence was replaced now by this shadow of agony across her brow and the shattered glass in her forehead.

We'd sit under the bell tree (a hard maple shaped a perfect bell…it rose from the hill, that rose behind our house) and look out over what had come to feel like the impermanence of our valley. In the growing season grass grew up the middle (of our frontage road, the Gloryville) from our gate all the way East to where a forest ridge enveloped us, two miles long and nine hundred yards wide. Half the year in multiple shades of green foliage; the other half as a stark black and white photograph. Ours was the only farm between fish creek (pronounced feeesh crick) and the horizon; the valley an outer hide for our nuclear privacy of one hundred twenty acres of the finest limestone pastures north of Kentucky.

When I would look long…at the valley in early summer… it would enclose my senses and speak to that part of my being unshared by others; no foster selves of official and public personas…I would leave that thinking on the far side of the old bridge before crossing home.

Prior to my children's birth the happiest day of my life was the one when their mother and I acquired Gloryville Farm. Sitting by the bell tree and looking out over the place… the brown gravel lane cutting through the coming Spring colors. With the divorce now pending it felt like a great green shroud.

My daughters face would glisten with tears when she looked out over the place. From the beauty of it, from its impending loss, and from just sadness in general, I thought. It fell to my son, to keep us defiantly cheerful.

When I could, I'd spend time with Bernie. His counsel was always too direct and practical for me but I still enjoyed his company. "Your wife's gone bad. Get another one. Get an annulment and get a better one."

A few "priest friends" from the diocese finally called and they all counseled the same… annulment! Sinatra had just bought another one. My response was always the same "Yeah… yeah… just what I need now… to make my children bastards. Yes my wife was an atheist…yes she had been when our marriage was convalidated in The Church… our pre-cana pastor had not pushed conversion he said "because she is objectively in principle and behavior more Christian than you or I." Yeah…and she'd also been a time bomb ticking I told him later.

The truth they wished to liberally and illiberally deny is that we'd had a good solid marriage for a decade and a half. It had been betrayed. Whatever my faults and errors I was not the striking vehicle here. No modernist heresey denying this reality would I tolerate.

I was becoming angry instead of sad and hurt. It was liberating. I was visiting Bernie in his penthouse perched on the roof at the nearly vacated relic of a hotel 'The Terre Haute House.' Bernie called his place 'the olde boars nest' and it was one of a few 'residences' left in the deserted old building. The coffee shop of late night conversations at the 'Crossroads of America' (7th & Wabash – intersection of old US 40 & 41the national roads E. &W. & N. & S.) was closed. The Marine Room bar shut down. Off lobby shops all boarded up. The grand lobby was maintained with one elevator man for Mrs. Hulman's[1] Suite, Bernie's Boars Nest and a few others. Six by eight foot tall paintings of Axtel and Nancy Hanks[2] still hung on the West Wall of the lobby by the wide no longer revolving doors. At dances throughout my youth I would escort girl friends from the decorative Mayflower ballroom across the lobby on a sort of pilgrimage to those paintings. Pastoral Icons of what I knew about. Safer haven from the improvised etiquette of the dance which I was never sure about. A few years later, my uncle Louis who worked for the Hulmans "packed up and shipped off" both paintings to the barroom at the Red Mile[3] in Lexington. I've been planning a pilgrimage there ever since.

Bernie liked to talk about his years as a fireman and fire marshal. "The great gasoline trail," he'd say. He'd led the investigations of several famous arson fires in Kentucky and Indiana. He liked to remember driving tandem hitches and repeatedly told a joke about tandem ladies of the night, but he'd be so overcome with his own laughter and never deliver the punch line. His laughter was so contagious that like everyone else I would laugh with him not needing a punch line. He loved telling the story about a joke of his he told to the new Prosecutor in town. I can't recall the jokes punch line about speech impediments if I ever heard it but Bernie's deft and dramatic delivery of the story is unforgettable. He was drinking with some democrat politicians at The Saratoga on Fifth & Wabash, after a late meeting. The group included the new Prosecutor and his wife. This new Prosecutor was a slight, kind of weasely, sweet catholic fellow with a not so slight speech defect. Bernie was a master in mimicking accents and speech impediments. The young prosecutor had been fairly successful at not revealing his own speech impediment all evening. With much banter,

---

1   More ubiquity of the Hulman family in Terre Haute. Tony Hulman owned Indiana's 500 mile race track.

2   Axtel and Nancy Hanks were famous harness race horses from Iams Farms of Vigo Co.

3   Red Mile: Historic race horse track in Lexington, Kentucky

camaraderie, and Canadian whiskey Bernie missed what the more relaxed prosecutor began to reveal.

Everyone urged Bernie to tell his famous joke about the bull with a trumpet enema and the toll bridge speech impediment. As he started the story all his fellow democrats began excusing themselves and leaving. Bernie barely noticed as he continued his performance. The punch line was delivered with gusto; Bernie's big red face wrinkled up into a knot to sound out the speech impediment. Silence followed with slight laughter. The evening ended according to Bernie with the Prosecutors words, "Fenk you Furnie. Fut we have to fe foing now." Hearing this tale we'd collapse (with laughter) in the cruelty of good-natured humor. Two years later this same prosecutor would jail me in California for kidnapping my own children. I value the joke even more now.

Bernie once mentioned when he was mustered out of the fire brigades he appropriated some out of date equipment including some second story ladders. I tactfully borrowed a ladder.

I was now legally advised that there was no way I could win custody of my tender aged children in the state of Indiana. My cousin and other lawyers charitably observed that I was too emotionally, physically, and financially crippled to care for them anyhow.

My children's mother rarely consented to speak to me. When she did, it made things worse. She had perfected a position of aggressive and oblique ambivalence, which made me crazy. Or dialectically... my craziness made her aggressively oblique and ambivalent. That she simply wanted nothing more to do with me was preposterous to the way I was programmed. Was she leading me on or could I not compute what I did not want to hear? She did speak of reconciliation possibilities after, but not before the divorce. She would say "between A) the certainty of divorce and B) certainly no reconciliation before the divorce there were lots of possibilities." My primitive concept of parenting did not allow for those nuances of the non-custodial 'Chairman of The Entertainment Committee.' I wanted my family back. She adamantly denied there was "someone else" and haughtily laughed when I suggested the gawky professor at the hospital. "Thatch and I have simply a collegial and eudaemonic relationship. He is a happily married man, friend and neighbor of your sister."

I always choked on the way academics use the word collegial and colleague. I once gave that name to a kennel sour hound pup[1]. It always seemed a fraternal assurance at being intellectually kept. But *eudaemonic?!,* I didn't even know what it meant. Looking it up I didn't believe the dictionary anymore than I believed her. I decided it was some variant of *demonic.* I knew my wife, or thought I did. I knew she was encouraging me to think of reconciliation *after* the divorce to cover up something or someone. She wanted me to feel OK and go away. Too many things still did not add up.

Within two weeks of getting her PhD. she walked different and talked different. Her voice went down an octave and her gait trebled in speed. My friend Mike didn't believe me until he phoned her. She answered "Hullo yes"… in basso professional profundo and then recognizing his voice exclaimed, "O, hi Mike" in normal soprano. I considered an exorcist.

I settled for Bernie's ladder. In broad daylight while she was "at work" and the kids in school I laddered up (casts and all) into her upstairs bathroom window. Then into her bedroom I rifled through her underwear and [desk] drawers. I found several notes and letters from Thatch, and her journal of their adulterous adventures together.

That night I confronted her. First I'd knocked at her back door. The children were with my parents. Unusually hospitable and cordial she invited me in for tea. Sitting at her kitchen table in my long coat, my hands on the letters and journal in my pockets I confronted her about their contents. Calmly, she refuted everything I said to the point I had to shift my hands around the letters and journal in my pockets to remind myself of their reality. I wanted to believe her calm lies… not the purloined perversities I clenched in my fists. I felt light headed as her voice droned off somewhere until I heard the 'eudaemonic' bull stench again and slammed the letters and journal hard on the tabletop. "You've busted my heart…and the children's, wrecked our home and probably

---

1   Colleague for kennel sour: one who won't hunt far from the kennel and feed bowl.

his... for what?! . some fem-flammed idea of yourself and society."

My last words I could not hear through her screaming... high pitched and unwavering...like a mechanical alarm. I took my leave. Opening the door I heard her scream turn into words. 'WHAT DO YOU WANT FOR US NOW?" Whether or not the US meant her and Thatch I imagined it did and said, 'DEATH BY STONING."

"The heat upon my temples craved the cold barrel of a gun," I'd written weeks earlier when pain and lack of sleep depressed my normal thinking. I thought of the Frankie Five Angels[1] exit in a warm bath and I thought about the gun. I thought a lot about the gun. Suicide is almost a compleat compulsion. As there is little or no previous experience of the way back from it. It bore down on me again like "the savage Demon Spirit" Alvarez[2] describes in his book On Suicide.

Not yet divorced...it was clear I would not handle it well. I was sure I'd be a better widower than divorcee and seriously considered arranging it. I hated...her behavior but I loved her. Biblical I thought! "Hate the sin...love the sinner.'[3] I was using homicidal thought to supplant suicidal ones.

And it was working as it had before... except I could not think long of killing her. Even killing him seemed a tad unjust. I decided kneecapping them both would make the proper statement. If I could see them together I am sure it would happen. Seeing them separately was problematic. I followed him from his house near Collett Park across town to Rose Hulman. Entering his office I was frustrated to find him sitting with his knees securely under his desk. I carried a berretta[4] and subpoena in one pocket, his letters to my wife in the other. I sat down and quietly stared at him. He wouldn't look me in the eye or even look up from his desk. Finally he lifted his head a bit, looking straight ahead and mumbled something gruff and unintelligible. I stood and walked to the front of his desk until he looked up and our eyes locked. That moment was almost as satisfying as a gunshot. I

1   Frankie Five Angels: The Mario Puzo – Francis Ford Coppalo character in 'The Godfather'
2   A. Alvarez: "Suicide: The Savage God"
3   Chapter and Verse: I've since learned the phrase is agreeable but not textual in holy writ.
4   berretta: a small Italian pistol.

pitched the subpoena on his desk, turned and left his office. He never responded to the subpoena but I'll bet he sweat it. We never went before the judge. I never hired a lawyer. My attitude toward the court was kind of Anarcho-Amish. My Amish friend Jonas had scolded me sympathetically for my violent intentions. He could understand them. The Amish are a lot more peaceful and a lot less non-violent than most people realize. He scolded me not from the perspective of high minded morality but from that of peaceful practicalities. "You'll help the ol' devil further wound your family that way. You're gonna have to see it through. You're gonna have to be a man and suffer it through." As for the court?…the Amish don't even recognize the magistrates authority. They won't stand for the Judge, take off their hats, bow and scrape your honor this and that or suffer any 'honorable' delusions about the court. Then… those communards can afford more independence than I could. Nonetheless I communicated to all officials of the court "I took marriage vows to God, not to a pack of lawyers." And like the Amish at the draft board I did "not recognize their authority." Now… I can only imagine their gratitude as they poured over the lists of my sins and our property.

She got physical custody, furniture, china, paintings, books, and the grand piano. I got the farm, livestock, and pick up truck. If you believe in divorce; it was a fair settlement. I only squawked about the thirty volumes of the Collected Works of Lenin. But she'd always claimed them for her work. She read them academically. I read them politically…as they were intended.

Still no job offers and I had too much unemployed time on my hands. I half vengefully yearned and hysterically feared coming across the adulterous couple together. I had lost adequate control of myself and the normal sense of time. I would draw water for a hot bath and then be surprised to find it cold, unaware an hour had passed. I was obsessed with my children's happiness but my sadness seemed to infect them. I was too depressed to appreciate … to enjoy even looking at my horses, hounds and prize livestock. It was time to leave. I made the arrangements, packed a bag, grabbed my saddle and left for

California to work for Mike.

My daughter wept and my son was confused as I nervously drove around trying to place Bethany's kitten in a new home. It was the same day my plane left and... we were not well.

III

Landing in California, libidinally revived, I considered marrying the first cocktail waitress Mike and I encountered. She said she was from Malta.

We stayed in Mikes digs that night; a small apartment on Geary Street not far from the Plow and Stars[1]. San Francisco was just now consolidating itself as the Sodomite Celebrations capital of the world. I saw men necking with each other at the airport. The next morning I was eager to leave for Mikes ranch. I read from my Spurgeon's[2] 'Morning and Evening' before breakfast. I'd left a hardbound copy for Bethany to read to her little brother.

That mornings reading was a great one about hieing to the hills. I took it as a good omen for Mikes place in the diablo range and read it aloud to him at breakfast. A pal of his, Jerry Keen had joined us. They both looked at me as if my mind had become a discarded reliquary of their grandmas Sunday devotions.

Mike had business stops that day before getting home to the ranch. The first was in San Jose which I found attractively Mexican, new… slightly plastic but clean. Next…was around the Altamont pass to Modesto, which seemed like Terre Haute in the San Joaquin. Urban but manageable populated by prosperous working people. I liked its canals, orchards, and dairies. The great San Joaquin Valley… reechoing with the words of Kerouak and Steinbeck. I thought of being Tom Joads revenge. But first I'd have to better understand Mike's realty business palaver.

Following his "realty talk" was as difficult and tedious as dissembling an intricate and recently used manure spreader. I trusted Mike to stand behind his business promises to me. I also remembered the country joke about never trusting the equipment salesman who says

---

1   Plow and Stars: an IRA sympathetic pub with Guinness on tap next door to a Teriyaki joint

2   'Morning and Evening': Charles Spurgeons' book of daily scripture reflections

he'll stand behind his manure spreader.

Mike and I loaded what seemed like a months supply of groceries and provisions into his Bronco and drove through the Palms of Patterson into Del Puerto's Canyon Road, and the Diablo Range. It took an hour of rough driving up those hills to get to Mikes ranch on what was called the San Antone range. He drove fast, flinging at the steering wheel a foot to the right and then to the left around blind mountainous curves. It was dusk and I was carsick. I could still make out radical changes in topography at the different phases of elevation we were driving through. At the bottom and lower elevations it was grassy and rolling, lurching upward to vertical brush and manzanitas, then farther up to stark red desert like terrain and finally on top more level range with gorges and high cliff faces. Some of the latter were chalked white and Mike pointed them out as abandoned magnesite mines.

We arrived at the ranch in darkness. Meikje, Mikes Dutch wife, came out in the house light and greeted us, as warm as the inside of her home; gezelligheid! Their daughter Jennifer was a bit older than my Bethany and their son Sean the same age as my Eliot. We all immediately took to each other, had a fine supper, and turned in early, I phoned my children before going to sleep. There was no answer.

The next morning was Saturday and turned into a fine hot day. We all stayed poolside. Mike took his business calls while he barbequed and there was plenty of beer for the constant stream of ranch neighbors he'd invited over for me to meet. They seemed good people and I got on well with them. Mike was making most of them rich by politicking the county planning boards allowing him to sell off small parcels for the ranchers to bay area people at huge prices. They saw me as someone to help Mike make them rich.

One of the ranchers I found particularly interesting was an older guy named Phil Statler. He had a glass eye and was legendary to the hill people for many reasons. One recent one was that he dragged the movie actor Slim Pickens off his horse at the Oakdale Rodeo to collect a gambling debt. Later that evening we retired with Phil to the Junction Saloon a few miles from Mikes ranch. Mike and Phil were planning to market some high desert parcels with a landing strip for private planes.

Cowboys at the table near us handed over a bottle of rye whiskey to share. "Awright!", I thought…just like Joel McRae in the movies. I expected it to taste a little like rye bread. It was awful. "It tastes more like cough syrup than caraway seed," I told Mike. About that time Phil Statler popped his glass eye out into his whiskey glass and Mike ordered a round of single malt scotch. We talked together a lot about ranching and real estate. The former I knew about; the latter I needed to know about.

Studying me closely, Statler said, "Son you seem to know about cattle but you're a dairyman aren't you?" "No", I replied, "I have beef cattle back home." "Umm?" he wondered aloud and went back to talking with Mike. I was sporting an Amish like (or farmers) beard then (no moustache) and figured that's why he thought I was a dairyman. Twelve months later by fluke I was working for De Laval Corporation and Modesto Dairy Supply at the Stanislaus County Fair. I hadn't seen Phil Statler since the Junction Saloon meeting when he came by my booth and said, "I knew you were a dairyman!" and walked on.

I studied hard with Mike for the Real Estate licensing exam but I was still depressed and found it hard to concentrate. I was calling the children daily but only reaching them weekly. Their mother would explain, "We're on the go a lot."

I took the exam and failed it after six weeks of cramming. I wasn't trying to ace it…just pass it so the failure did surprise me. Mike was reassuring. "It's a tough exam on stuff that's all new to you. I let you take it too quickly. Take a semester of Real Estate school in the city (the *city* is always San Francisco) and you'll pass it the first of the year.

I'd have to go home and sell more timber and cattle. I needed to check out my farm again before winter and see my horses and negotiate better communication with my children through their mother. And I was homesick.

I made a quick trip home, sold more breeding stock and timber than I should have and ransomed a better communication agreement with my ex… , tied up loose ends on the farm, spending all spare time with my parents and children. Especially my children. Reassuring them that Papa was trying to build a new economic base for the family. Maybe I'd come home and together we'd establish a Land and Livestock Company. I told them about California ranches, orchards, vineyards, and dairies. Maybe we'd visit there soon. They appealed and I promised not to give up hope for mama, not to give up hope for complete reconciliation.

I helped a neighbor put up hay after he helped me pop rivet a black steel ice hook to the cast on my left arm. My little son loved it and called me Captain Hook. My mother didn't like the look of it. She always worried I was being too reckless, too soft, and /or too poor. My fathers attitude always that stern antiphon that I was probably due to walk the plank somewhere soon. I loved and love them dearly.

I also retrieved Digger our Jack Russell terrier who was not adjusting to life without me. Back in California he became a great rattlesnake and jackrabbit dog.

Mike had pre enrolled me in Real Estate School and I only missed the first three days. It convened eight hours every Friday, Saturday, and Sunday. I'd go to the city Thursday night with Mike and stay in his apartment with or without Jerry Keen until Sunday night walking the ten blocks or so to and from the classes. Mike would take me home late every Sunday night. Jerry worked for him part time. According to them they were "trading paper with slumlords and the Vietnamese." Some of the bay area buyers would trade their slum rentals to Mike for partial payment of their ranchettes prior to Mikes reselling inflated priced paper to a network of Vietnamese families. Jerry and Mike knew all about juggling points and paper to become they'd laugh... California paper millionaires. I didn't understand it and didn't want to! When I'd ask Mike if I had to understand such stuff, he'd say," take it easy Thomas, you'll get it."

I never got it and I can't say for sure I wanted to. I did try. The only thing I can remember now about those classes is (a) real estate law is like poetry in that it requires describing a property in a way it can't be confused with anything else. That's what I was trying to do with verse. And (b) the incredible smallness of some Asian girls waists.

I would try to study in Mike's apartment that is unless I phoned

Indiana. If I phoned and couldn't get through I'd go to the liquor cabinet. If I did get through I'd keep going to the liquor cabinet.

One Saturday evening after class when I had learned very little and listened to less; suffering Sinatras old ennui, I came out on to the street where madness prevailed. The Forty Niners had just won the Super Bowl, and people were racing around revving their engines, honking their horns and screaming from their cars. Pedestrians hollered, screamed, and yelled back. Young, old, black, white, and Asian were all jumping, speeding, and screaming. Only me and a few illegal Mexicans were stunned into silence. Walking fast along Geary Street I thought to get away from the loud vulgar throng. But there was no escape. They were everywhere. In the Cathedrals parking lot, on the sidewalk in front of Rev. Jones old storefront, shouting from stately homes and cheap apartments. I passed a liquor store marquee where a probable illegal in a country straw and work clothes seemed afraid to come out. I paused long enough to greet him, "Welcome to modern America," I said. "Come on out and get run over by Buchanan's Navigators who want to save us from you." He smiled. I don't think he understood a word but knew I was hostile to what he feared. I have never felt more alienated by the nations culture of my birth than at that moment. God forgive me this athletic sports idolatry offended me more than its imperialist wars... or maybe I sensed they are ontologically tied together.

Finally at Mikes place I was opening the front door when Jerry and Mike came excitedly up the steps. "Where you guys been?" I asked. "We've been riding around cheering and yelling for the Forty Niners", Jerry deadpanned. I looked at Mike. He looked away. They grinned at each other.

Back at the ranch I felt better. Monday through Thursday I'd do some ranch work for Mike, study, and read. I read a lot. At night I read from the Jerusalem Bible, the Holy Koran, Sam Beckett, Gary Snyder, James Joyce, Christopher Lasch, Rudolph Steiner, John Donne, G.M. Hopkins, John Wesley, and Ruallah Khomeni[1] by lamplight. I read

---

1   I decided Khomeni was next to Karol Wojtyla (John Paul II) the most significant religious leader of the twentieth century. In his revolutionary leadership he posed the question all others avoid. Noting respectfully those who died

no Rilke. No Duinos while depressed. But I did adapt a line he took from Pope to think of the Diablo Range… "as that long convalescence which was my life there." In the afternoons I ran the fence line and checked their horses. In the morning I tried to study real estate.

I had moved into a 12 x 12 cabin at the end of blind horse canyon, a quarter mile behind Mike's barn. The blind canyon was rumored to be one of Juan Murrieta's[1] hideouts. In the mornings and at night I would walk the half mile or so to the ranch house for plumbing and kitchen privileges. Mikes sister Melinda, niece Debra, and brother-in-law John Davidson had moved from Indiana into Mike and Meikjes home and we all shared meals together. They were great company. On Wednesdays I'd go to the Patterson office with Mike and at night meet with Steve Walker and the San Joaquin Writers Guild.

One morning Mike was early out of his shower and towel snapped the real estate notebook out of my hands revealing the small penguin edition of John Donne I was really reading. He laughed first at me and then with me. He never railed. Hey!…but for the love of Mike. My friend Mike. That night I read from Donnes Sermons for Grace; Mike winked and brought me a beer. "You'll be O.K.", he'd say… just keep hitting it."

The holidays were arriving, the weather colder, my depression deeper. There only seemed to be real life outside of real estate. A young lion jumped Jennifer's two-year-old gelding in his corral by the barn. It broke the horses back but couldn't master killing the colt.

Mike had to shoot his daughters horse but the lion kept prowling and whistling around the ridges at night. I was going to hunt him with Digger, but ranchers with Plott Hounds, Airedales and a Rhodesian Ridgeback were planning to hunt him on the weekend. Damn! I couldn't afford to miss the real estate classes and even if I could it was bad faith to Mike to do so. They treed and killed the lion on Sunday

for their faith under oppression, the Ayatollah asks 'Why is it not as important or more so to cause the oppressors death?' That is, 'to kill, not just die for the way of God.' Jews and Christians have not historically hesitated in this practice, but even more militantly avoid responsibility for their mistakes.

1   Juan Murrieta: Old Californian raider and resister to the Anglo-Saxon advance.

afternoon not 200 yards from my cabin just hours before Mike and I returned. They spent the night. At least I got to see the hounds and Airedales. And the latter were remarkable. Big Oorang bred lion dogs. There are paintings that depict such Airedales at the Art Museum in Sonora.

On Monday the temperature dropped down and it was billy be damned cold by dark. I turned the lantern out early and crawled deep into my sarcophagus shaped sleeping bag. Digger slept beside me. Hours later I was slowly awakened by a low muffled growl becoming slightly louder. My first thought was another lion… but whatever the thing it seemed already inside and getting louder. Must be a badger or coon I thought sitting straight up with my sleeping bag flaps flying open. At which point Digger, the growling Jack Russell, jumped into the warmth of my sleeping bag. Ol' digger… what a pal.

The McNaughton household claimed Digger grieved and missed me when I was in the city. He was awfully glad to see me on Sunday nights. While I was gone he worked as a team with a Tom Cat called Radical. Before Digger, the cat would hunt rattlers around the ranch house. When he'd find one, Radical would pounce on it until its rattle went off or sounded. Mike would hear the rattle, come out and shoot the rattlesnake. Digger compressed the action. He'd hunt with Radical and while the cat pouncing distracted the snake Digger would dispatch it entirely. Not quite as quick as the cat he was frequently fanged. It was not uncommon to find the little terrier with his head swollen as big as a melon. Within twelve hours the swelling would go down and Digger would be ready for another rattler. Ol' Digger dog.

The holidays were near. Mike and Meikje had old friends visit them from Stockton and the Bay Area. Still blue… feeling restless and unsociable Digger dog and I took a break from the ranch. I borrowed Mike's Bronco and headed down the mountain. Meikje worried I was headed toward wild women and was comforted Digger was going with me. I'd seen few movies since the wreck. I loved movies but with Edmond Wilson I disliked the word. Yet motion or moving picture seemed awkward to say and cinema or film sounded pretentious or flat. Whatever we call those images of flickering light ('flicks' a good word) they are the true canon of American "culture". If honest...most Americans would have to admit they enjoy them as much as sex or groceries.

I stopped by the Junction to 'have one for the ditch' and scanned the Bay area and Valley newspapers. There are only three roads out of the San Antone range. Down the Del Puerto road to Patterson, and Modesto. Down the mines road came out in Livermore toward San Francisco. I'd discovered the Mines Road as my way out of the troubles I'd get into in town. The longest and most treacherous road was past the Observatory and downhill to San Jose. The flicks I was most interested in were in San Jose. 'Chariots of Fire' had been reviewed as the first positive image of a Christian Minister in a major film for more than two decades. 'Heartland' was reviewed as an overdue attempt by Hollywood to resurrect "The Western." If I hustled I could see both.

Digger always enjoyed the Junction. He would sit quietly on his chair or barstool with more balance than many of the patrons. He also loved riding in a vehicle. I would have to leave him in a motel room while I went to the movies, but a canine's sense of time is different than the way we measure it.

In San Jose I checked into a motel located between the two malls where my movies were playing. I left Digger in the room to guard my bottle of Merlot.

I saw 'Heartland' first, to my extreme critical frustration. My God...it was a feminist western! Kathy Bates in the country not only had to suffer muddy ranch chores and changing weather but also cows getting out and...worst of all... worst of all a husband who was not sensitive enough. It all struck too close to home. I was eager to briskly walk away three blocks to the next theater.

It was one of those multiplex jobs, housing several screening rooms. I found the proper entrance for 'Chariots of Fire' and ordered a ticket from the frowning young woman in the ticket booth. Dismissively she spat, "It's already started you'll have to see 'Raiders of the Lost Arc'! Respectfully...politely I responded, "Mamn, I do not wish to purchase a ticket for "Raiders of the Lost Arc'; I wish to purchase a ticket for 'Chariots of Fire'.

Gathering herself up to full authority she slowly and patronizingly articulated each word, "It started almost an hour ago...'Raiders of the Lost Arc' is just beginning!"

More formally now I replied, "Madam I have seen 'Raiders of the Lost Arc'. I do not wish to see it again. I wish to buy a ticket for 'Chariots of Fire'.

She stood her ground, looking at me the way Kathy Bates' character looked at bad weather.

I appealed, "If there is a problem I will gladly buy another ticket at the finish to watch the first part I've missed."

She just kept glaring at my bad weather, which at this point was more than overcast.

"Are you going to sell me a ticket or not?" I thundered.

Clippty clip the ticket emerged on the surface counter before her. Thanking her I reached in and retrieved the ticket with and on the point of my hook.

It was a great film and of course I identified with Eric Liddell the young Scottish minister. I knew and admired his denomination and Westminster Confessional background. I enjoyed the last half of the film immensely and looked forward to seeing it completely even if I had to buy another ticket.

PART TWO:

POETRY AND POLICE

IV

The lights came on and patrons began to file out muttering their curiosity about all the cops that had appeared. A dozen on the stage and groups of half that many scattered in the main aisle, by the doors, and in the balcony. I heard someone worry aloud that there's "probably been another fire." I began to worry ... "but no surely not"... I thought as the police directed my line upstairs toward the balcony exits. As I started up the steps all of the police started that way too. "Damn... it must be... well maybe not" I thought walking down the outside steps, seeing the cops mill about the parking lot..none of them looking at me.

I went back in line for my second ticket. All the police ignored me except one little Mexican cop. He stood fifteen feet away motioning for me to join him. I motioned and spoke I could not leave my place in line. He approached closer and said in careful, heavily accented Spanglish, "What ees et hu are doing?"

"I'm standing in line to buy a ticket to see the movie."

"Pero...but ju alreddy seed da movie." Raising one hand I began to explain... when suddenly I thought I'd been hit from behind by a freight truck. Four cops, (it felt like forty) took me down flat and two others stood hard with their boots on my arm and cast.

"Git thee hoook and loook out for projectillees." the little Mexican yelled.

After they'd taken off my cast and hook, and looked thoroughly for projectillees they asked me what was I driving, and where was I parked.

I answered both questions and they howled why had I parked three blocks away? "Where did I live?", they demanded. I told them "Freedom, Indiana, now visiting with my friend up on the San Antone" and that I was "checked into Motel 8 a few miles from here." "Ain no

San Antone I ever heard." said one cop. Another that there was "no way he live in Indyahna." "Who's in da motel with you?", they asked.

"Just Digger dog," I answered.

"Wat dee kind of dog is dot?"

"Jack Russell…Jack Russell terrier." I even began explaining the terrier breed to the cops when we were interrupted by the Theater Manager.

He was upset this was taking so long. It was "causing a scene", he said. "It's bad for business."

All these peace officers looked up to the proprietor as if he were the force Commander. He told them if they would keep the hook off of me I could go in and watch the movie without buying another ticket. He also told them in front of me like I was part of the pavement "to instruct this guy that threatening looks are not allowed."

They all went to their squad cars except the little Mexican. He blushed and was very cordial and respectful now. He gave me a card where I could pick up my cast and hook, shook my right hand and said, "Have a nice day." It was already night.

A family man may scowl in public and be perceived as a concerned partner or parent. A man alone doing the same thing risks being suspect for murder.

I finished the Merlot with some onion rings and drove back to the ranch at dawn.

Thanksgiving was rough but my friends were great. I dreaded the coming of Christmas without my family … without my children. It was difficult to ship gifts. I started having night terrors again. Poor Digger. He would whine and try to comfort me. I had long talks with the Davidson's evangelical daughter Debra. She thought I should be a minister. There was no church in the hills. She thought I should start one.

I was biased against cripples in leadership. Jack Barnes, a secular youth activist amputee had taught me that. Don Smith[1] said it was an Adlerian thing and I agreed. "A wounded healer[2] is one thing", I told Debra, "but a wounded leader quite another. I cannot purport to tend

1   Don Smith: YSA Alum. Attorney and Revolutionary Socialist
2   "The Wounded Healer": A counseling book by Father Henri Nouen

the souls of others while mine is so very wounded." "Tending your cross will help you tend the crosses of others", she'd say and then blithely, "We must be grateful for our crosses." "…Hadn't heard that since I was ten." Nuns would say such things. I didn't like hearing it then any better than I did now.

Then… I thought I'd thank God for my Dads new Oldsmobile but I sure wasn't going to thank him for my mothers breast cancer. I guess I hadn't spiritually advanced much in thirty years. Because I had learned so much more from the latter than the former.

There was still no image in the night terrors however a diagram had emerged like a small eyelet getting closer and closer in my field of vision until I awoke in voluble yelling. I concentrated on the eyelet. Not only as to the speed of its motion towards me; I also tried to peer into…to enter into the eyelet with foresight to see its full range of vision. When I did this…fully conscious, the brain an active partner with the eye there would be a slide like click and a color photograph would supplant the eyelet diagram.

As many times as I did this a different color photo would click in. They were all photographs of large unrecognizable Portuguese families. Dozens of them. All unknown to me. When I was able to click in or conjure up images of these families the night terrors were deflected.

I had yet met these people but remained abstractly grateful to the Portuguese.

Christmas passed. I held up. Bethany and Eliot phoned cheerfully about the Christmas tree at Grandma and Granddads and enjoying the holiday with their cousins. They seemed better. I was getting better.

I took the real estate exam in January…and got the results that I flunked it the first week of February. This time it had significantly more math questions.

Later, back home again in Indiana's custody court a a very very… very young female attorney would snarl… "and he calls himself a good provider. I happen to know he failed the California Real Estate Exam twice and the second time after a years study did not significantly alter his score." She moved around the court room in exagerated right angles; her tone and countenance trying to catch up with the conceit that she really was a laywer. I immediately objected saying, "Not true. After a semesters study my score was significantly altered. It was worse."

Unflappable as always,...my friend Mike encouraged me not to give up getting rich in Real Estate. "Just take 'er again. You'll get 'er." Meikje knew tearfully better as she looked at us. Two old friends who were destined to part again. Mike was unflappable not oblivious. He thought I was slowly coming out of the depression at which time "I'd get 'er," that is pass the exam. The truth was...I didn't tell Mike but I no longer wanted 'er. I didn't want to see the hills developed with new roads, new mobile homes, and new mobile people. In the last year most of Mikes new people (his client buyers) became intensive care units within weeks, knocking at his door at all hours afraid of the mountain lions, the coyotes, stray cattle, and/or the vast stillness of the Diablo Range. The wilderness was too much for these people. It was becoming a bit much for me. I am as solitary a type as there is but even I need my battery jumped from time to time.

Meikje's solution had been to introduce me to every divorced woman in the hills. I finally had to tell her I was opposed to retreads. I hadn't the heart to tell her that most of her retreads looked like racing slicks.

Over the year I had received few letters and responded to less. I wrote my children every week and their mother every month. I wore my wedding ring again. Mother Vi had sent its remains in the mail. Mikes farrier melted it back to wearable shape.

Christopher Lasch wrote me respectful letters requesting I write an article on the Amish for his new journal called 'Democracy'. Young Pastor John wrote encouraging me to contact the Methodist Bishop of Northern California. His letter included a Xeroxed article on 'Deliverance Ministry' (which is a charismatic protestant attempt at Exorcism). From his letter I couldn't tell if he thought I'd be interested in contributing or was in need of it. Deciding the latter, I came across a story about Deliverance Ministry in the Sunday paper. I'd grown accustomed to reading Mikes Sunday edition of the Modesto Bee on Monday nights. There had been a Veterinarian from Indiana doing

Deliverance Ministry at Vintage Faire Christian Center in Modesto. The newspaper story included phone numbers. One was in Indiana. That cinched it. Tuesday morning I phoned the Indiana Vet. We talked for a long while. I told him about my depression and night terrors as I might describe colic symptoms in a sick horse. He asked about my religious background, marital status and offspring. He asked about physical work and lastly what I did for a living. Then he recommended fasting and prayer under the supervision of a Deliverance Minister in Modesto named Joe Reyes (he gave me the phone number), that I burn my books by Rudolph Steiner, move away from any place called the Diablo Range, phone the Methodist Bishop, and forgive every sonofabitch who'd ever trespassed against me.

I phoned Joe Reyes, borrowed Mikes' Bronco [again] and drove down to the Valley late that night. Joe Reyes had invited me to his modest home "around 8pm". As I drove into his driveway, others were leaving. Inside Joe and his wife, Helen, greeted me warmly, casually, and politely. We sat at their kitchen table getting acquainted. I noticed a catholic calendar on the wall and asked "are you catholic?" Joe blushed and looked at his wife who was not Portuguese. "We attend Vintage Faire now but…through Joes family keep in touch…"with the church", Joe finished her sentence.

Joe and I retired to the living room with our coffee mugs while and before joining us his wife busied herself in the kitchen. They were nice people but I couldn't imagine their relevance to my plight. She seemed suspicious of the nuns at St. Mary's my ex taught with and he said my situation sounded like a curse from others. I was about to excuse myself and politely escape all this pious superstition when their daughter entered the kitchen from the rear breezeway. In her early twenties and stunningly beautiful she'd dropped by late to show them some new pictures of their grandchildren.

Like so many Portuguese youth she was as dark as she was pale. She looked like girls you see on the West Coast of Wales. Maybe that's where the Portuguese fleet went down, I wondered. She and her mother came into the living room to introduce me and show us the pictures.

As her mother and father introduced us she extended her hand. I took it gently in mine and she began to convulse. As if struck by lightening or some other lethal dose of energy she jerked and jerked and cried aloud.

Joe intervened holding her and my right arm saying, "its alright she has the gift of tears." I had no idea what he meant and pulled my hand away from his daughters. Her sobbing began instantly to subside. Her mother said, "when touching you she can feel all your spiritual wounds and injuries! ...her tears go straight to God... who will give you peace." Looking directly in my eyes as she slowly closed hers ... she took my hand again, tightly this time and began the sobbing and writhing again. God forgive me I found this embarrassingly erotic.

It went on for a full ten minutes. The girl twisting in tears; her parents volubly glossolalic in prayer for me as I grimaced at the hall clock. Some of the prayer language[1] sounded slightly Arabic to me. She stopped crying as suddenly as she had started. She rose smiling from her chair, drying her tears with a bordered handkerchief as she started back into the kitchen. Her mother drying her own tears quickly followed. Joe motioned me to stay with him. "Do you like pie?" he asked. "Sure", I answered, "without a wife I hadn't tasted pie for several seasons." "Lets have a piece of pie together and then I want you to fast ... no food, only water until tomorrow evening. There is a prayer meeting at 7pm in Turlock[2]. You should attend." He gave me directions to a place called The Assyrian Hall.

The pie was rhubarb from their garden and terrific. Pie can sing when proportions of crust and filling balance... when your tongue touches both at the same time. This pie sang. I embraced the Reye's, thanked them for their hospitality, and took my leave.

The next night I drove to Turlock and found the Assyrian Hall. Entrance to its parking lot was marked by Babylonian statuary and murals of hanging gardens and mythological beasts with bearded human heads. In the evenings tule fog[3] it was creepy. I don't think

1   Prayer Language: Pentecostal glossolalia; semi-conscious utterances in prayer.

2   Turlock: Valley town with significant Assyrian i.e. Iraqi population

3   Tule fog: "As if a canopy were lain over the Sierras to the East and Diablo's to the west capturing clouds all the way to the ground. The heaviest fog in the world outside London" from December to Easter in the San Joaquin.

that Vet in Indiana would approve. Inside it was brightly civilized and I instinctively turned toward joining some Iraquis at the bar when I spied a poster and arrow toward the prayer meeting. I checked my watch... maybe I had time for both. Fasting all day I'd acquired what the Irish call a terrible thirst. I could hear soft Arab Aramaic[1] voices and the clink of glasses coming out of the comfortably dark barroom. These Iraquis were interesting. Most of them Nestorian i.e. Chaldean Christians of one stripe or another... I'd read about their community in the Modesto Bee. A pastor had been shot over a dispute involving money from the Baathist regime in Baghdad. The Iraq-Iran war was just heating up. The paper implied the local killing had something to do with factional disputes regarding the war. I felt that was taking politics and religion seriously.

I really didn't have time but I was about to enter the bar anyhow when I heard Joes voice over the Aramaic whispers. "We're here, Tom," he said. I joined him around the corner to the meeting. The meeting was held in a huge bright room. The atmosphere seemed convivial with about one hundred people present. Children scampered about. There were few men, less youth, and a lot of unaccompanied middle-aged women. About half looked Portuguese. There was the usual Pentecostal hugging not quite humping (recalling Thomas Hardy's discription of certain fellowship as "way warmer then Christianity requires") and the holding of hands in the air, some glossolalia[2], and then began their singing in the Spirit[3]. It was incredible. It sounded like an Ivesian symphony without instruments. Discordant, polyphonic... beautiful. The first set was spectacular. The second fair. The third tiring to boredom. But they kept trying to crank it back up. The fourth and fifth degenerated into a kind of nonsensical cacophony. But throughout I could hear that Arabic sound that Joe made. Then I recalled those lowered voices from the barroom. Sure, and it is Aramaic, I decided...

---

1   Arab Aramaic: The San Joaquin Assyrian community are Arabs from Iraq who speak an ancient Aramaic i.e. Northwest Semitic dialect.

2   Glossolalia: Speaking in tongues; Pentecostal prayer language.

3   Singing in the Spirit: Glossolalia singing in tongues.

the dialect Jesus spoke.

A kind of break was taken and the Reyes; introduced me to the young presiding minister. His black suit matched his coarse hair and large eyes. And he seemed anemically pale. I tried to determine a denominational connection. There was none... exactly. Like Joe, he did deliverance ministry, attended Vintage Faire Christian Center, and maintained his membership in the local Portuguese parish church. He worked as milker for his cousin and was saving to operate his own dairy. Joe spoke solemnly to him, with a nod toward me saying, "this is the gentleman from Indiana."

Acknowledging Joe, the minister seriously invited me to "please join the prayer line during the healing services."

After some announcements the prayer line began to form for healing. I timidly trailed toward the end of the line. The young minister carefully instructed those in line to concentrate prayerfully on the condition they wished healing for. No one was required to speak...no testifying to the violation of their own privacy like Oral Roberts on T.V. The people remained quiet and so did the minister as he walked down the line and touched them...usually on the forehead. Earlier he had prayed that demons be cast out of everyone in line ..."That the demons within us be cast into the outer darkness" and that "healing angelic Spirits" replace them. During this silent "laying on of the hands" people began to collapse. I mean hit the ground hard like they'd been rabbit punched.

At first alarmed I would be the only person left standing I noted that most of the people falling were those pear shaped old girls who were probably altogether too attracted to the lanky young minister. "Libidinal manipulation", I thought but still hoped enough otherwise to stay concentrating on my night terrors and ever present anxiety about my wife's, that is, my ex wife's continuing sexual sin. Driving down into the valleys tule fog these last evenings I couldn't get the latter out of my mind. I concentrated now on getting it out and ending the night terrors.

Before I fully knew it the minister stood in front of me locked in on my eyes and said, "Ven Espiritu Sanctu, Now feel the power of God" as his right hand touched my forehead. I did not go down exactly. I was shot backwards like a human cannon ball, then went down my palms slapping my boots as my back slammed into a row of chairs six feet behind me.

Extremely embarrassed I immediately jumped back to my feet, puzzling how I had literally fallen for this apparent collective power of suggestion. Glad to see Joe and the minister busy working with others I took a walk outside the room to find a water fountain. When I came back fifteen minutes later, people were still lying on the floor. Joe approached me and I shook my head…probably a little cynically. "No!", he said, "that was the power of God."

I hung out with Joe and the minister for another hour until everyone was on their feet. Joe's wife had left. "Give me a lift home and I'll pop for pie and coffee at Percos." "Deal!" I agreed, more then ready to break my fast.

At Percos after fresh baked berry pie, cold milk and black coffee we both felt better. "Can you tell me what you prayed for during the healing?", he asked. I told him the truth. "I prayed for the healing of those night terrors I told you about and to get shut of my obsessing all the time about my ex having it away with others." "Good and specific," he replied. "Now… have you been obsessing since you were slain in the Spirit?"

I knew what he meant; yet I was reluctant to affirm all this…especially his interlinear interpretation which I sensed coming.

"You did say all the time didn't you?"

"Yes."

"Well … what about the time since you were slain in the Spirit?"

I had to tell him that, "honestly I haven't thought of that once. But," I added, "the real test for the terrors will be tonight's sleep."

Smiling, he said, "you're going to have to be grateful for the graces you receive if you are to be given more. And we have a lot farther to go. Remember all the unforgiveness you have in your heart acts like a seal preventing Gods grace falling on you. Forgive, forgive, and forgive… Forgive others and forgive yourself…after you've properly convicted both. Do not allow your heart to rule. Trust your god given consciousness and conscience. Remember holy scripture does not celebrate the heart, it warns against it. 'That the heart is deceitful above all things.'[1] Trust your mind. God will help you take charge of your injured heart."

I felt like saying "Yessir!," so I did.

Parting...Joe directed me to have a big breakfast in the morning before resuming my fast Sunday morning. He wanted to meet Sunday at the Vintage Faire Christian Center at 9:00am.

That night there were no terrors. Thursday night they returned... only slightly altered. I still abruptly awoke from the volume of my yelling. Digger would whine and try to comfort me.

I'd also received a Christmas card from the Federal Land Bank Credit Association reminding me I had an annual balance payment on June 1st. I needed income and fast. I'd heard Mike say many times California is the Golden State... realty gold in the hills and Ag. gold in the valley. If it wasn't to be realty, and I couldn't yet cash in my degrees, I'd better look for work in Agriculture. I poured over the papers and yellow pages using Mikes Patterson office to send out dozens of resumes. Responses came quickly.

I interviewed and was offered jobs in Poultry Genetics, Feed Company Sales and Analysis, Irrigation Equipment, Embryo Transplants for Cattle and Mules, Artificial Insemination Technology, and Dairy Consultant Sales. The Great San Joaquin. Everyone here wanted to hire me. It was the flip side of Indiana where no one wanted to hire me. By God I was getting better.

I was most interested in working for Curtis, the Artificial Insemination Company. They operated out of a spit and polish clean and fascinating farm in North Stanislaus County, including well kept pens of several of the most valuable bulls of every breed (dairy and beef) in the world. Training for the jobs regular accounts included selecting the best genetic cross, that is, the best bull family to cross with a particular cow family. It was straight commission and no vehicle provided.

I decided on the De Leval Corporation and Modesto Dairy Supply consultant job because: (1) it was salaried and commissioned, (2) it

1   Jeremiah 17:9 "The heart is deceitful above all things."

---

provided a vehicle, (3) the Dunker owner and Portuguese staff enthusiastically promised an advance by June 1st to cover my balloon payment back home and (4) the job was to head a new department called Herdmasters where I would be trained in California and Kentucky to be a general herd consultant in order to introduce and sell new computerized feeding equipment at $100,000 a whack.

Hey...I needed the money. Overnight I was hailed a technical expert and introduced as such. God forgive me I liked the deference of Valley farmers and dairymen to my being an "expert".

Dairymen of the San Joaquin were defying history. All my life family farmers were going bankrupt. A generation of my family had lost their farms. Back in the Heartland small family farms (the NFO's[1] Withholding Actions notwithstanding) were becoming extinct.

Throughout the San Joaquin there were thousands of new and prospering dairy farms. Portuguese fishermen from the Azores would come to California, lease twenty to forty acres near a canal and the Banks would throw capital at them for cows and equipment. They would soon show a profit, raise a family on beans and sweetbread, then build a fine house: and not only Portuguese! Ethnic diversity among San Joaquin dairymen included Swedes, Basques, Dutch, Italians, Mexicans, two Irish, and a few Anglo Saxon families. The Stanislaus County Fair was a diverse mix of "rooted cosmopolitans." But the majority of new prospering dairymen were Portuguese. Middle-aged Portuguese would touch their bay windows and announce "Aye Prosperity."

Stan the Dunker who owned Modesto Dairy Supply kinda mentored me in advising, "Get to know these people for a year. If they respect you, that is, like you and look up to your knowledge... they will eventually buy the thing [the Herdmasters Computer] or anything else we peddle because they'll know it's the latest thing. Just as they've come to know they needed improved pipe line systems, herringbone designed parlors, and stainless steel bulk tanks."

The De Laval[2] corporation men were less blunt and less agreeable. Both the Swedes and the Americans! The Swedes (mostly engineers) seemed like dazed hitchhikers in an Ingmar Bergman movie. The

---

1   NFO National Farmers Organization: militant Midwest farmers union.

2   De Laval: a Swedish based International Corporation.

San Joaquin sun hurt their eyes. The more good-natured Americans (both engineers and sales managers) also seemed along for the ride. Everyone was a consultant to someone else.

All of the Dairies used artificial insemination, few kept bulls of their own. Some were using bulls with penectomies to signal cows in season and ready to be artificially inseminated. That is they could point out the work but were impotently incapable of performing i.e. doing it themselves. I came to think of them too as consultants.

"Now Stan and the boys have built you up in the farm papers, magazines, and newsletters", the corporate consultants would advise. "However your importance will be maintained only if you prepare these dairymen to experience a lack of what you must impute they need, (the company men would laugh) *our product!*" And they meant impute! They figured the eager to assimilate new Portagee-American would actually blame his peers for being ignorant, or less knowledge-able of what we would professionally define they objectively needed.

In so far as we had competition; and we did mainly from 'Germania' and 'Surge' each corporation helped the other by collectively imputing the same basic need.

V

Mike and I had been in Morelos in the late sixties. We ended up at CIDOC[1] with Monsignor Ivan Illich. The De Laval Corporation men spoke like villainous cartoons from an Illich homily. I would have to be careful. Illich had written an essay for Le Monde entitled "Useful Employment and its Professional Enemies." Being partisan to his ideas practically prevented me from finishing graduate school. Prophetically Illich had said Professional Technocracy ultimately reduces politics "to adjudicating competing claims for professionally imputed needs." Later when I heard a poor dairy farmer say to his wife, "We have a right to access this computer stuff as much as anybody else", I knew he'd become a customer. Years later I've been more recently horrified to see poor unemployed or working mothers prosecuted and sent to jail for not accessing services provided by the Child Protective Agency[2] and imputed as a need by the Child Care Professionals of the welfare department. No parent in the U.S. today is free to refuse professionally imputed needs of their children nor to refuse services provided by so called helping professions.

In the ides of March Digger and I moved down to the valley near Waterford. I rented an old garage with bath and kitchenette way out in the middle of an almond orchard. Warning Trees the bible calls them and they were beginning to signal and bloom warnings for the new season.

Digger loved the Steep Creek bank on one side and we could walk twenty yards on the other to the main canal where we'd swim like seals in the forced current. I got a bed, mattress, reading lamp and old T.V. from Goodwill, bought a half pint of tequila and was in hog

---

1   Center for Intellectual Documentation: Ivan Illich think tank for ministering to Social Revolution from Cuernavaca in Mexico.
2   CPS: Original of many acronyms (OFS or CFS to name but two) frequently changed to conceal the welfare department Gestapo unit of 'Protective Services' rescuing children sometimes molested but always abused by not experiencing the lack of what Welfare officials blame them for not needing.

heaven by the weekend. I also bought a writing table.

I sped around in my new Ford Courier meeting dairymen and their families faster than my employers thought possible. The more Portuguese families I met, the stronger I got. No night terrors. Qualitative less obsessing about the ex.

Not a single family on my list [I had hundreds] refused me inviting myself into their homes and hospitality. I'd make my presentation about computerized feeding systems and the future of De Laval designated dairy farming. Afterwards…when I would sometimes even earn applause…they would interview me. "What was it like 'back east' and the rest of the country? Were there Portuguese or Mexican farms in Indiana? Were market prices the same or how different? How would I advise them on heifer replacements?"

Saturday mornings I would go to the Stanislaus County Library and read from cover to cover an issue of Hoards Dairyman (magazine) and an issue of the N.Y. Review of Books. Saturday nights I would drink tequila and watch Public T.V. Sundays I began to go to church again. First mass at St. Stanislaus where the post Vatican II night club patter from the podium underwhelmed any interest I had in approaching the Portagee Priest. Next the big and banal United Methodist church next to the library. Several uneventful visits to country parishes and finally to Joe Reyes Vintage Faire Christian Center. The latter was the most disappointing. A Pentecostal free for all that went on and on for three or four hours.

I'd first heard of the Orthodox Presbyterian Church from my friend Bud Wilson, the terrier man. I'd read about them in a novel by Morris West called sign of or something about The Red Wolf. I'd picked it up by mistake thinking it was about the hybrid red wolf[1]. Morris West also wrote "Shoes of the Fisherman" which I thought partly prophetic about J2P2.[2] I liked the "wee frees" in his book and how they were portrayed in the film "Chariots of Fire". Years before I'd spoken with a man called Phillips who was beginning a kind of mission in North Indianapolis near C.T.S. (Christian Theological Seminary) and

---

1   Red Wolf: hybrid wolf x coyote wild canid frequently called a brush wolf from Missouri to Indiana.

2   J2P2: affectionate diminutive of Pope John Paul II

Saint Maurs. He gave me a copy of George Hutchinson's "History of the Reformed Presbyterian Church." I cheered on the Covenanters, Olde Dissenters, and Cameronians. Heroes of the "killing times", (the 1680's) in Scotland. They disowned the king and elected to live outside the state as then constituted and governed. They were put outside the church which the State and Society had corrupted. Their prayer, war cry, and slogan; "Let Jesus reign and let all his enemies be scattered"...of course, appealed to me. They claimed they'd been fighting what The Vatican calls American exceptionalism or the modernist heresy since 1788. Sidney Ahlstrom barely mentions them. What Professor Warfield at Princeton called modernist seemed close to what Lasch and Illich called Narcissistic. Their J. Gresham Machen described retrograde anti-intellectual American pragmatism as the root of modernist attempts to apply Christianity to modern life. These attempts he felt threatened to modernize Christianity out of existence. "There can be no applied Christianity without a Christianity to apply, Christianity different from that to which it is to be applied." The modernist mood was as imperative as the Bulbous Archbishop of Indianapolis. Orthodoxy was indicative.

Clearly this was a thinking mans church. But I also saw them as kind of like hard shell Baptists who read. Calvinists whom Father Jean[1] would be proud of. They also reminded me of my beloved Trotskyist sects whose integrity was so historically correct it had guaranteed their making no more history. Providence promoted them to an unconscious conservancy of values.

When I finally attended the Orthodox Presbyterian Church in Modesto...there was God knows what dynamic of correction going on between Pastor and flock. He sported a Mickey Mouse tie and preached on the theme of Bob Dylan's lyric "You Gotta Serve Somebody." The congregation sulked. Upon leaving one asked me about my current theological preference. I replied, "Welsh Methodist."[2] He smiled and immediately made the remote connection.

Still impressed by the jaunty non-priest ridden family man ethics

1   Jean Calvin, founder of Calvinist Theology in the Reformation
2   Welsh Methodist: Wesley's method came to Wales via Whitfield who preferred Calvin to Arminius

reflected in synod photographs of R. P.'s.[1] I even thought about going to Covenant Theological Seminary in St. Louis enjoining the Cultural Revolution like Covenanters at Drumelog and the Bothwell Bridge. But even St. Louis seemed too far from the farm.

On the other side of some significant funds I planned to return to my children on our farm with their mother or not. A failed revolutionary I would withdraw from modern degeneracy entirely and write great un- American books. I needed a premodern and/or postmodern income to cushion farm operations. Maybe ministry for money was the ticket.

The famous story of William Foster, early leader of the CPUSA[2] when he returned from the 1928-sixth party congress in Moscow came to mind. It was in the middle of the Trotsky vs. Stalin conflict. Bill Foster told Jim Cannon, "Trotsky has the principled program but Stalin has the power." Foster followed the power. Cannon followed Trotsky. Cannon became an obscure conservator of revolutionary values. Foster hatched the New Deal.

The Orthodox or Reform Presbyterians were the only American church not regionally divided by 'slavery' and the civil war, or shifted into Pacifist neutral. They had been ardently pro-union without sucking up to the government. They were not two-faced 'prohibitionists'[3] or god forbid the real thing. They were for ecumenical unity if based on principle not expediency and they rigorously studied and applied their principles. They considered themselves Catholic, Protestant and Reformed. They were anti-modernist pro-marriage, anti-divorce, pro-life, pro-family, and they seemed pro-social justice.

These orthodox R.P.'s had integrity and they had the principled program. The Methodists U.M.C.'s had the membership and salaried opportunity. Like Foster I would choose the latter. In R.P. historian D.M. Carson's words I was suffering from "a weariness of difference." I was tired of being a Terre Haute socialist minority, a Trotskyist, Cannonite minority and even an anti-clerical Catholic in Owen County minority. I yearned to be a mainstream unsuspected non-minority. Within all that undefined ecumenical haze of the U.M.C. surely there

---

1   R.P.'s: Reform (Orthodox) Presbyterians
2   CPUSA: Communist Party United States America
3   prohibitionists: historical deniers of strong drink

was a place for me to be a catholic, covenanter, communist; to be the Reverend Mr. Black for my children.

Sundays in church had become unsettling. I needed church badly, but I spent too much time ranting and reframing what I found there. Perhaps it was time for me to try and do it in ways I thought right. I phoned Methodist Bishop Chang in San Francisco. Bishop Changs office referred me to Reverend Bill White, supervisor of the U.M.C. district in Modesto. Bill was a kind, and hip guy about ten years my senior. He liked me and he had empty pulpits to fill. He assigned some Senior Pastors for me to consult. They liked hearing me talk about everything except church discipline and my not recognizing the courts dissolution of my marriage vows. I knew the old Methodist Discipline supported me; the new did not. Bill sped up the approval process.

I met with Bishop Chang, Bill and the other District Supervisors in San Francisco that April. I remember the Bishop having difficulty understanding how the United Methodist Church and the modern Roman Catholic Church could be different in any significant way. I told an anti-clerical story about Mexico and how a jewish friend of mind, Bob Handelman, was mistakenly mobbed by peasants trying to kiss his large vulgar ring. They had mistaken his dark suit for that of a Priest. Laws of the Mexican Revolution still forbid the wearing of privileged attire i.e. the roman collar or other religious insignia in public. Bishop Chang seemed nonplussed by my story; the supervisors all laughed...some saying, "he'll not be kissing your ring Bishop," - and others "or anything else!"

PART THREE:

PASTORAL STATES

I was approved in May and assigned as Pastor and circuit rider for the Methodist parishes of Knights Ferry and Coulterville. Knights Ferry lies on the banks of the Stanislaus River next to the Sierra Foothills. Coulterville was in the High Sierras an hour up from the Valley.

Knights Ferry is an old historic town with a Saloon, General Store, Hotel, and scenic restaurant by a bend in the river. There is only one church. Ulysses S. Grant had been a member of the church and there are tales he organized buggy races from the old covered bridge to the churchyard guided by the sight of its steeple. A kind of Americana Steeple Chasing. More recently the writer Barnaby Conrad had written his bullfighting epics from here. I liked Knights Ferry. It was not quite quaint but getting there. There was a colony of retired Rodeo riders who owned small ranches in the surrounding countryside.

Coulterville is an old mountain town. It has a saloon. It's membership is larger…about fifty families. Knights Ferry had approximately thirty families. Both parishes were rich in diversity of backgrounds. Membership was as easily transferred as mine had been.

People would sign on if they stuck it out a year or so. Both churches were extremely isolated serving isolated populations. There were Catholics, Baptists, Pentecostals, Presbyterians, Lutherans, several unchurched types and at least one Christian Scientist. Ours were the only churches less than an hours drive for most of these people.

I doubled the attendance and membership in both places within six months. No one was asked to deny or in any way devalue their background or previous associations. I don't know if it was close to COCU or Coo Coo but it sure was working. I studied most evenings, prepared the sermons Saturday and preached in Coulterville at 8a.m and Knights Ferry at 10:30a.m. In all due modesty, I did not know what I was doing but it seemed to work. An increased consciousness of living began to build caring communities of conscience. "He just talks to us" was the favored compliment my people gave to my Superintendent who liked to report it to his Bishop. As a single celibate I was always one phone call away for counsel day or night.

I made housecalls… for my people…housecalls on my congregations. They liked being called parishioners. Congregant sounds odd and member sounds slightly sexual. My parishioners liked my coming by on Sunday afternoons. And it was the only day I wore a coat and tie in ranch country.

Too often I was left with the women and children in the parlor while the menfolk would tend to things outside. More times than not they thought I'd object to their working, drinking, or smoking on the Sabbath. What I objected to was this clergy as the third sex eunuch in the harem horse manure that had so harmed church history with feminist delusions and phallic protests. After a while I began ducking out with the men.

A little cussing, drinking, and smoking with the guys was currency in ranch country. But, I really won them over with *work*. As an old subscriber to Dorothy Days Catholic Worker; an enthusiast for the worker priest movement in Europe and always inspired by my Amish neighbors in Indiana I had tried for years to make work a prayer. My parents had been hard working people. My father…steady, thorough, and stubbornly unrelenting until a task was finished. My mother was a phenomenon of work. She'd attack dirt while cleaning like it was the divil himself. Work was more like war than prayer to her, but I guess war against the divil is its own kind of prayer.

I called at the Marzetti ranch one afternoon as they'd asked for a meeting about children's services. Bill's wife, Kit, and his mother, Mary, ran our Sunday School at Knights Ferry. Mary was catholic and Kit described herself as "kind of Pentecostal". Raised catholic but sick of all the androgynous priests, Bill preferred to stay home and watch the T.V. evangelists. Their three grade school daughters were beautifully behaved children and made up approximately one sixth of our Sunday School census.

I'd visited the Marzetti ranch once before and Bill had hospitably shown me his cattle, horses and photo trophies from his rodeo days. The latter included a picture of Bill riding the famous bucking horse,

'Bombs Away'. A retired bronc rider, he was small in stature and talked tough as a rattler.

"I got tired of all that Junior Bonner[1] bull," he'd say. "You know, drink 'e'm down, ride e'm hard and put e'm away wet. I'd git bullet proof on brandy, steal the prettiest girl in the place and fight anybody got in my way. I've chopped down lumber jacks in Oregon tall as trees just for sport…and others too…until I met them Cajuns down south… those guys go for the eyes…they'll kill you…makin the sign of the cross before you hit the ground." He pulled out his shirt tail to show a scar from his belt buckle up into his ribcage. "Meaner e'n snakes!", he'd concluded. "Those altar boys probly been molested by the same priests up and down the bayous."

Later when I knew him better I would josh him about glutting for punishment from Louisiana by staying away from church watching Jimmy Swaggert's ejaculatory prayer dance on T.V. Saloon keeper Mickey Gilley's other cousin, Jerry Lee Lewis's song "Great Balls of Fire" I suggested he rename his neighbors bull that kept jumping the fence. "Yeah," he'd laugh, "I could keep better company", and started coming semi-occasionally to church. Over time…we became good friends. But this second Sunday visit we still stood on formality when after pie and coffee he announced to me and his ladies that he had work to do in the barn. Taking his leave he shook my hand and touched his wife, mother and children.

"He's planning to muck out all those stalls by himself?" Mary asked Kit.

"Yeah", Kit answered, "it's too much for the girls to help".

I rose and asked to use their hall closet. I was still wearing oxford cloth 'Packard[2]' shirts heavily starched on Sundays. They stay stiff and look clean for months. I hung up my black coat, tie, and Packard shirt on a couple of clothes hangers and went outside to find Bill.

Working at the edge of a corral by the barn, he grinned when he saw me and without saying a word motioned toward several pitchforks and shovels propped against the barn wall. I examined the pitchforks

---

1   Junior Bonner: Steve McQueen's Rodeo Movie Moniker

2   Packard Shirts: exceptionally fine shirts made in Terre Haute. An industrial tragedy when they closed out the 20th century.

carefully. Some had broken or bent tines. I found a fairly new one with five strong sleek tines and joined Bill. "Good choice", he said. He'd already entered the stalls with one of the wheelbarrows. "This ain't your fancy automated dairy barn", he said. I nodded, as we looked out…over the work to be done. Sixteen stalls; sixteen of e'm. Sixteen 12 x 12 dark stalls, stretching out across the pale barn. "Got to git e'm all done before dark", he said.

And we did! For months Bill bragged on his clean stalls as pastorally blessed. "We invited our Pastor out to bless these stalls", he'd say. "Why he blessed every piece of excrement clean out of the barn!"

The first community dispute also occurred in Knights Ferry. Billy Graham had announced on national TV that the new STD's i.e. (Sexually transmitted diseases Herpes, HIV, Aids, Clamydia) were God's judgment visited upon a wicked people. Conservatives lined up with Billy while liberals thought his pronouncement arrogant and punitive. I was pressed to take a position. I did so by agreeing with both sides saying, (a) unlike Billy Graham I claimed no inside track as to the exact will of God but (b) in this case I hoped he was right. That kind of settled the matter. I felt like Trotsky at Brest Litovsk saying, "No War and No Peace" to the Kaiser.

Next the Prez… President Reagan made his Evil Empire Speech about the Soviet Union and I preached against it. Two Reganites feinted away in Coulterville. I met with them privately to settle their wrath. They had petitioned a list of people in and out of the church in Coulterville objecting to my sermon.

President Ronald Reagan far more than I or anyone else had lifted their Spirits connecting with the best in their interiority and giving them hope for their futures, their families and their sense of place in the world.

The Prez… Ronnie Reagan was a man I could understand if not politically approve. A fallen away Irish catholic maverick who went his own way. The only President ever who was a refused applicant to the (C.P.U.S.A.)[1] Communist Party of the USA. The official reason for his rejection being immaturity and that "Comrade Ronnie hasn't learned to keep his mouth shut." The Party was off on some ultra underground

1   CPUSA "Dutch" A Reagan Biography by Edmond Morriss

tendencies or they might have kept the talents of Comrade Ron intact. Instead of losing the cold war to him and his pure blarney about stars wars, decades later.

I've ridden his clans country above Ballyporeen in the conifered highlands of the Galty Mountains. It's hill country isolated and different from the green commons throughout Ireland. It is country where independence, individualism and sociopathy is bred. Natural habitat for Lorenzean[1] lambs to go their own selfish way that is so attractive for entire flocks to follow.

Ex governor of California Pat Brown said that no candidate could ever be as naturally charismatic and personally popular as Ronald Reagan. His wit, charm and ability to connect with the finest in others. His appeal to fathers and mothers as a communist in the thirties was to their utmost needs as parents to provide a secure economic living for their children. His appeal to fathers and mothers as a Conservative in the eighties was to their utmost needs as parents to provide a moral and natural cultural order for their children.

Parents in the thirties worried about their children's next meal. Parents in the eighties worried about their children's next moral crises. I hadn't the heart to tell them that G.E. was for their idealized Ronnie what Krupp Industries had been for Adolph. Reagan in the thirties and eighties spoke to what parents feel in their gut is true.

The Coulterville Reaganites had been, like Reagan… militant New Dealers. Their children were cultural casualties. One son had been "recruited to gay liberation in college… gotten better and gotten married, had children but still had boy friends." Their oldest daughter had been a feminist not quite long enough to succumb to the pressures of Lesbos. She had two abortions, married a black man and "they smoke dope in front of their children." The grandparents, my parishioners were worried about their son having AIDS and drugs ruining their grandchildren's future. Their third and much younger daughter was

---

1   "Lorenzian" from Korand Lorenz who studied sociopathic charisms in sheep. Finding lobotomized sheep whose natural flock instinct is destroyed and confidently go their own selfish way make the most attractive leaders for the other sheep to follow. Lorenz thought this explained a lot about human political leadership. 'King Solomon's Ring'

not allowed to see or speak to her siblings or nephews and nieces. The couples marriage under these family stressors teetered toward divorce. A mess!

Reagan's banner inspired these folks it need not be this way. A puerile and careless lack of boundaries in governance, conduct, and lack of hard work had allowed society to slip into the slime. It was temporary and could be sloughed off through rigorous hard work, solid parenting and liberation from a corrupt governments secular influence. This radical right wing analysis was not qualitatively different from radical left wing analysis of degenerate bourgeois society.

It reminded me of my interview two years ago with the Society of Soviet American Friendship. At Shubert Sebrees funeral in Terre Haute, several C.P.ers[1] had approached and said the Directorate of the S.S.A.F. was open and they were recommending me for the position. Shubert Sebree had been one of the last olde red veterans of the Terre Haute General Strike. It may have been his wishes even though... or maybe because I was a "Catholic Trotskyite."

He had liked my presentation and review of Socialist Labor films for the Wabash Valley Labor Council. We spoke at length together about the German film maker Pabst or "Die Rote Pabst" (The Red Pope) as he was called for his marxist catholic predisposition.

The SSAF was a C.P. front located in New York City that propagandized for peaceful trade and cultural exchange between the USSR and the USA instead of cold war. Their most recent claim to fame was assisting a multi-million dollar Soviet-Pepsi Cola contract. Most young Trotzkos had contempt for them. I was no longer young.

I wouldn't leave the farm, but maybe I could work something out. I'd worked for the Church one hundred miles from headquarters, maybe I could work for the Party a thousand miles from headquarters; like Heidegger in the hills die furorship would have to come to me. My real motivation was to provide a further New York corridor connection for my wife who was suffering an extended cabin fever from life on the farm.

At any rate, we went to Manhattan for my interview. After which it was reported to me... they were amazed. In partial complement,

1   C.P.ers: Communist Party members or followers.

critique,…and quite baffled they said, "he makes being pro-Soviet sound like the moral majority!" Indeed if the Soviets and their propagandists had concentrated on out moralizing the West instead of their bankrupted failures at out arming it the world would now be a safer place. Their loyal historian Eric Hobsbawm confirms in his book "Age of Extremes" that "demoralized cadre is what doomed the socialist dream in Russia."

I was not hired. I'm told I ran a close second to a business savvy engineer. Ahhh… the soviets and their engineers… the last industrial romance.

My Coulterville Regan Democrats were desperately struggling to save their marriage and parent their grown and growing children. I persuaded them to come to me for marriage counseling. I persuaded them that yes, evil exists and in multiple ways has harmed and is threatening their family. All of which has little to do with the Soviet Union.

The man was an IBEW[1] electrician who drank and buddied up with a younger couple who "did not like" and were disrespectful to his wife. The wife worked as a secretary in an insurance office where one of the agents "an older man" had taken what she thought was a fatherly interest in her. They "would do lunch" and he'd started coming by on her husbands bowling night, holding her hand and hearing her sad stories. Recently he announced he "had feelings for her." But their huge problem was husband forbid not only his youngest daughter but also his wife as well to visit or see their oldest daughter and her family. "They live less than two hours away in Pleasanton. My son lives clear back east in Pittsburgh. My parents are dead. My sister and brothers live in Florida. Next to Amey (the youngest daughter), Carol's (the oldest daughter) family is all I got."

I counseled them both to give up their disloyal friends. "You cannot have a friend who is not a friend to your marriage," I counseled them. They complied and did better.

The husband opposed contact with his older daughter because of her "past immoralities" and that they "smoked dope in front of their kids." He was not racist and had no problem with her black husband. "I thought he was the best thing ever happened to her until this dope

1   IBEW: International Brotherhood of Electrical Workers Union.

thing and the kids." He did say, "too many of them Oaklanders (his black son-in-law was from Oakland) use drugs."

I insisted we include daughter Carol and son-in-law Walt in the loop. "Impossible if he forbids seeing them, she said."

What about if we see them, I said, to negotiate their stopping the dope shit. Hearing a minister swear never fazed anyone in California. Back in Indiana it would later cause apoplexy. "You mean… negotiate their stopping the dope shit in front of the kids for my calling off the shunning treatment!" he said.

"You got it," I cheered aloud.

"Please"… she quietly appealed."

We agreed.

I phoned Carol and Walt in Pleasanton. She answered first. I got both on the line… you could hear kids playing in the background. I introduced myself and explained why I had called. They didn't know what to say and said so. I proposed we meet at the closer Knights Ferry Church that Sunday afternoon. It was about equal travel time between Coulterville and Pleasonton. They couldn't make it but said they could come the next Sunday.

I blocked out that afternoon. I wanted maximum time with Carol and Walt before bringing in her parents. We met at the Church. They were an attractive middle income looking suburban couple who said they didn't get to the country much. He was curious as to how close we were to Sonora, Groveland and Yosemite. She seemed shy. He did not. His dad was a duck hunter. He had a yearling Labrador named Miles. He was delighted I knew gun dog trainers in the area. I referred him to Sheldon Twer on Orange Springs Road.

Carol said very little but seemed to approve and encourage Walt's narrative, which was turning serious. "We both kept a lot of bad company in our youth," he said, "we promised each other to not let that happen to our children." She put in…"we have two daughters." "And a son," he said. I asked to see their pictures. She obliged with three school pictures from her wallet. Beautiful bi-racial kids whose eyes had that spark of hybrid vigor you don't see in dead end gene pools. A thirteen-year-old girl, a twelve-year-old boy and a nine-year-old girl.

The two oldest looked enough alike to be twins.

"We do everything with them. They are our life. Ball games, bowling, dance classes, school functions; we all do together. They're with his parents today. They could easily have been with mine. But… well, you know how they feel. Yet, I know that my babies will never have to turn to bad actors or gangs for family substitutes… because we do everything together."

"Sounds like today is kind of a reprieve. You know," I continued, "kind of a reprieve from child care … to have some Mom and Dad alone time together."

They laughed… especially him. "Doing everything together," I questioned, "includes… Drugs?". She quietly interjected, "Most everyone does some kind of drugs. All teenagers, sooner or later do pot. When my parents caught me they treated it like a crime!"

"It is a crime," I said.

"We've done very little weed since we've been married." he kind of weakly protested. "It's just that she feels strongly that…"

"You all should do it together?!"

"You know all teenagers smoke pot!" She no longer spoke quietly. "If not with us they'll turn to bad actors like I did. We see gang members at the bowling alley. Should we forbid bowling or just do it with them?! We bowl with them and they barely notice the gang bangers."

"I don't know that all so-called teenagers smoke dope. I do know it's a mistake to participate in anything you don't wish to approve or encourage. Has your oldest boy or girl been offered cocaine yet?"

"Don't think so," he said. She nodded.

"Are you going to use cocaine with them so they won't use it, abuse it, or use it with the wrong people?"

"We'll have to cross that bridge when we come to it," she spoke with significant complexity now; militant, reluctant, and defensively. "Sounds like a Ted Kennedy argument," I thought and almost said. "Come on Rev!" Walt protested and appealed at the same time. "We've not done weed with them that often and… you know… Carol's my Lady… you have to admit she has a point here."

"Have you told your parents about weed and the kids?" I asked him. "No, no," he answered.

"Why have you told your parents?" I asked Carol.

"Because I want them to know how wrong they were with me and how I'm going to be otherwise... with my children."

"That's a bit different than just protecting your kids... isn't it? What about Meth? Speed is becoming a popular drug. Will you do crank with the kids?"

"I don't worry about Meth and our kids," Walt thoughtfully said. "All that stuff is a white trash looking for receptive rectoms, biker project."

"What about Heroin then?" I returned. "You and I like Miles Davis and Heroin's got to him. That beautiful man's beginning to look like a gremlin, (I had guessed correctly about his dog). Will you chip a little H. with the children?"

Walt remained thoughtful and seemed put back a bit. Carol sighed... exasperated by what she thought was my absurd reach from teen pot to Heroin addiction. "I don't think our children will be tempted by that," she said.

"Will they be tempted by sex?" I shot gunned the question. "C'mon won't they be tempted like all kids to have sex with others? You know, have it away prematurely and/or possibly with the wrong other at the wrong time?"

"Spose so," he said. She nodded glassy eyed.

"Then why not fuck em?... ! Fornicate with your own children so they won't screw around with the wrong crowd?"

I thought I'd spread the shot too far for a second when Carol convulsed into crying. Walt had about sixty pounds on me. I was glad that after he got up he rushed to her not to me.

Her glassy countenance shattered she wailed and wailed. He comforted her. She looked remorsefully at me and said, "it's what I've done; it's what I've done!"

Walt explained that in her college years, an older – 'more mature' he scoffed, mentor had done just that. That is, persuaded her... to stick with him instead of bad acting peers... encouraged her drug use and ultimately persuaded himself into her loins... "For two abortions," she sobbed, interrupting Walt as he soothed her.

Walt's husbandry was phenomenal. He'd been wanting to change her mind about the whole business but had patiently bided his time. Patiently persevering with her, he could now stride above chance, to firmly, systematically lead his wife to a new perspective. Thorough and unhurried he seemed cheerfully resigned to suffering it through with his beloved,…his "lady" he called her. Never complaining, not at all passive or listless he was the soul of constancy and steadfastness. As we adjourned I tried to complement him accordingly. He listened, smiled, and said, "it was 'sabr'[1] My Uncle Patrice, my moms brother taught me. The muslims call it 'sabr'."

Whatever it was Walt was a master at it. Our meeting enabled him to arrange several with her parents and they visit back and forth regularly now.

Carol's parents reported to their Reaganite Committee; "We doan know what he is but he ain no milk sop liberal… not exactly a social conservative either, more like a socialist conservative. We asked him if he was more like a pastor, priest, or reverend? He answered back… more like what in the time of Jesus was called… a rabbi."

I studied carefully the elements of liturgy. Flaws in which I think drive people away from church services. I kept my services short, but not always sweet. My homilies or sermons averaged fifteen minutes. Personality expression was discouraged and put in low profile. Hymnody, psalms, and scripture readings were selected and coordinated thematically. I used the catholic calendar, collectio ritium, and Puritan Baptist Charlie Spurgeons "Morning and Evening." Announcements were restricted to print in the parish bulletin. Services were well organized, formal and over in one hour. After Services were concluded people could take the floor and refer to announcements in the parish bulletin. Fellowship i.e. personal interaction was engaged after not during the service. This was to avoid what Mary Baker Eddy called 'personal contagion'; which I thought so afflicted Protestant and post Vatican II priest liturgies.

My only Eddyite[2] (i.e. Christen Scientist) was organist at Knights

---

1   Sabr: an Arabic word from Sura 2:45 in the Koran.
2   Eddyite: Christian Scientists founded by Mary Baker Eddy emphasizing

Ferry. She was a tall intimidating Lady who tolerated her Methodist husband and the rest of us. Refusing to play on Communion Sundays she told me, "Methodists like Catholics restrict their imagination with this." In her early eighties my organist was also ethnically narrow-minded.

Many 'city people' from Sacramento and San Francisco visiting Knights Ferry would admire the church. It was pretty, made of brown brick and slumpstone, nestled in a hillside just above the town. Some would decide they wanted to be married there. At $100 a whack it was significant church income.

I told the parish council they could rent it out to whom ever they pleased but I would marry no one unless I thought there was a sound Christian basis and commitment for the marriage. We compromised on a policy that still encouraged weddings but would have to be approved by me.

A Basque couple from the bay area approached me after church on Sunday. They wished to be married. His family lived in Sonora, hers in Modesto. They were in their thirties and both worked in the city. She was a widow, with a thirteen-year-old daughter. He was divorced without children. Both were Catholics or as they said… "had Catholic backgrounds." Neither had attended any kind of church over the last ten years. Both had previously been married by J.P.'s. She had been widowed for five years. Her daughter had been christened at "Our Lady of Fatima" parish in Modesto.

I explained to them they could rent our church and still have a priest from Sonora or Modesto do the wedding. They said they would prefer I do the wedding. I told them I thought they could still convalidate their marriage vows later with the Catholic Church if they wished to do so. They had questions.

I explained the politics of it. We left it that (1) they loved each other and wished to make a lifetime commitment of fidelity to each other, (2) to raising her daughter and all other future issue (i.e. life they formed) in the straight path of Christian faith and morals as defined by (3) the Gospels and Gods holy and historic Church. I encouraged them

---

mind over matter.

to reconnect with a parish church in the city.

The afternoon of their wedding beautiful dark complected Spaniards and Basques dressed to the nines filled up our church. My organist was extremely vexed. "Did your parish council approve this mafia wedding?" she asked. Harrumphing up and down the aisle she tried to appear as conspicuously disapproving as possible. Thank God she was ignored completely. Finally she took her seat and began the introit (entrance theme). I didn't recognize it at first. She played well as always and the people were busily greeting each other. Ever once in a while I would notice someone pausing a moment to hear her organ music. Then I recognized it. She was playing 'Speak Softly Love', theme from "The Godfather" movie for the weddings introit and entrance theme.

Once old comrades came to call on Sunday morning. Jim Brigham from Madera, near Fresno. Rolphe Levin from Lafayette, near the bay. D.O. Smith from Chicago, near all the Heartland I loved and another comrade from Boston who was half irish and half jewish known simply as 'Dradle.' They all had convened at the Royal Oaks Bar in Oakland the night before to see Dradle and his Boston team compete in the National Trivia Championship. They were billed as the 'Natalie Wood Swim Team' and won the contest handily. Dradle was deferred to as the best trivia expert having memorized among other things a half century of ballgame and horse racing statistics.

Heavy bearded, they sat bulkily in winter coats taking up most of the back pew next to the organ. I thought they looked like the old Smith Bros. Cough drop box. They had come to church because (a) I had invited them (b) they had some comradely concern for me but mainly I think due to their (c) morbid and mordant curiosity about how I was crazy enough to become a country preacher.

My olde organist took great interest in my old comrades. She approached them after the service and said, "I don't know who you men are but there is something strange and historic (she may have meant histrionic) about you. I decided it is… you men have an apostolic presence!"

Best description of bad ass bolsheviks I ever heard!

Life in the San Joaquin was good. I had a sense of sunlight and providence there. It was not hard to think of God as prescient guide and guardian of human beingness. I tried to pray unceasingly, patiently, and gratefully. The Portuguese families befriended me at work through the week. I was bringing the radical intelligence of Christ's teachings to the people of Coulterville and Knights Ferry. Night terrors were gone completely, anxiety and depression was kept at bay. I dreamed again… mainly of deep peaceful time with my children. I phoned them several times a week. Their mother was sometimes encouraging sometimes not. One time she chattily suggested I watch an Elizabeth Taylor – Richard Burton skit to be rerun on network T.V. She was clearly recommending their humorous flirtations carrying on over to the other side of serious love for exes.

Elizabeth Taylor while attractively reminding me of Ann Ennis and ninth grade necking always seemed sparrow brained after her southern Suzanna role in "Raintree County." Richard (Burton) Jenkins, his real Welsh name, I regarded as the leading totem rep. of the Celtic mind, the sonorous socialist, irascible and intellectually political.

When Anne and I were in the Soviet Union in '73 (Burton) Jenkins and Taylor were also there and much applauded by Soviet citizenry and media. In a television interview (Burton) Jenkins announced he "was born and raised a Welsh coal miners son which meant he was born and raised a Communist." Then quickly added "but I'm not sharing any of my hard earned money!" He much amused the Soviet sense of humor. Whereas I usually failed attempts at it. In 1960 while riding the chandeliered Moscow Subway I told a then popular (back home) 'sick joke' about little Patty on success of the Cerebral Palsy Marathon eating and coordinating her very first ice cream cone. I demonstrated the punch line of little Patty planting the ice cream cone squarely into her forehead. My Australian comrades laughed so hard, some fell to the floor. Our Soviet comrades only grimaced as to the decadence of the west. As much as I admired Dick Jenkins, his left wing Welsh nationalism and acting ability (I thought his 1963 filmed 'Hamlet' was the best Shakespearian performance ever recorded) I could not watch his being an ex and jolly about it.

Another time she phoned me, late (even with the time difference) on a Saturday night. I think she was on a date or looking for one in a comparative shopping spree. Very,… very friendly she asked me what I thought was her best personal quality. She sounded like a marketing agent consulting satisfied ex customers. She hung up after I replied, "Your haunches."

VI

A year passed. De Laval liked my work. I was close with local dairymen especially in the Portuguese community. After my second Sunday sermon at Knights Ferry I'd retire to my pal Joe Da Silvas house in Escalon. Many Sundays he'd have a barbeque with other guys from work and their families. Other Sundays we'd all meet at the Fesht[1] Hall in Oakdale. A string of young equipment mechanics were (a team of) 'Forcados'[2] for the "Tourados" (bullrings and bullfights) held throughout the valley.

In a Portuguese bullfight the bull is not killed as in the Spanish moment of truth. Also then he is never killed badly as in the all too frequent and disappointing Spanish lack of truths. The Central part of the Tourodos is the holding not the killing of the bull. After the banderillas are placed from horseback by the Cavalieros and the bull has been worked with the cape on the ground… the forcados take center stage. They stalk the bull in single filed hubris across the ring while the bulls attention is distracted by capote work from behind the far barrier, until the forcados reach the center of the ring where they taunt the bull still moving toward the capote… as it is withdrawn.

If the bull sees these men afoot before they reach the center of the ring its lethal speed cannot be avoided. From the center and closer they can take the charge and survive.

They take the charge in single file; the first young man slender as an acrobat, the last endomorphic as a fullback. The first man whirls sideways between the horns taking the charge in his arms around the bulls' neck. Synchronized the second man supports the first mans arms. The third embraces the second and the fourth the third accordingly. The last man adds the final ballast, holding on with one arm free to sometimes catch (and sometimes not) the tail of the bull. Done correctly they

---

1   Fesht Hall: Portuguese Community Festival Hall with full bar, priests table and dance floor.
2   Forcados: Pega Forcados, the principal bullfighters in a Portuguese Tourado

will hold the bull still; "to hold death still."[1] Done well it is moving and very aesthetically pleasing to see. Done poorly or even with the slightest error it does not cause disappointment like a bad kill, rather it becomes the exciting and amusing entertainment of hubristic young portagees being knocked, flung and hurled all over the bullring. Either way I saw it as polemical pageantry against the modern complaint of control. I wrote about it later for Glenhill press [See addendum of Glenhill promotional piece] in 'Glimpses' p.305.

These forcado mechanics of Modesto Dairy Supply came to see me as their poet laureate and I rarely missed a Tourado. I became acquainted with Father O'Dwyer, Chaplain to Mexican and Portuguese bullfighters who was also the parish priest in Escalon. A great aficionado we would discuss Conrad and Hemmingway's books and the great El Cordobes we'd both seen in Mexico City. We talked about Americas Lincoln Brigade in the Spanish Civil War and the confused Irish who fought on both sides. A picture of his father, an IRA Commandant during the Easter Rebellion hung in an honored place on his rectory wall. Only once did he hear a bit of my checkered past.

"Ahhh… you're livin' in the plaid," he sighed. "I will pray for you."

Livin' in the plaid I'd wonder while driving the perfectly paralleled and perpendicular north-south and east-west roads of the San Joaquin. I'm a plaid cymric[2] and that's for sure, I'd sing while making my rounds to the dairy farms.

All these dairymen from the Azores[3]… they struck me as multiply archetypal; pastoral submariners steering under vast seas of modernity, surfacing successfully but never quite surrendering to assimilation. Practicing the ancient discipline of husbandry to beasts, crops, and family networked into catholic parishes of universal concern. Some had Celtic names (like Lowell or Powell?) and never knew why. A

---

1   "To Hold Death Still": See addendum (A Serugar Morto Imovel) in "Glimpses" p.308

2   plaid cymric: pan celtic nationalist

3   Azores: Nine islands almost as far from Europe as from America, rising from the Mid-Atlantic Ridge in rich volcanic soil, bathed by the North Atlantic Current (a branch of the warm Gulf Stream) inhabited still by sea-going farmers, fishermen, whalers and bullfighters. Rumored to be what's left of the lost continent of Atlantis.

Galician connection? Forgotten intermarriage? They'd laugh appreciatively when I'd tell them of the legendary black Irish, and black Welsh connection to the sinking of the Portuguese fleets. Many kept teams of draft horses. A few trained teams of Oxen. All reared lots of children and ate beans for breakfast. The men demonstrated a mastery of highly technical equipment ...pipeline systems to massive chrome bulk tanks, in herringbone-milking parlors. Their women were faithful, feminine, fertile and deferential. That is, like Amish, Muslim, and non capitalized women everywhere they avoid the direct gaze of unrelated men deferring to their husbands exclusive attention.

Separate as their Azorean identity was from the mainland they still staked a claim in the Fatima Story... albeit with a certain spin. Many were sympathetic with Lisbon's leftward coup in the early seventies (many were not!) and spoke of Fatima's prophecy of the conversion of Russia to be the Christianizing of Communism. All of which delighted me and inspired a more Maryological turn in my sermons. Joan Didion had recently complained that while the Gospels describe Mary's consciousness, she rarely speaks for herself. Her wish to know "why the Gospels had gagged Mary?" says more about Joan than the jewish virgin. The forgiven Magdalene, the contemplative Mary of Bethany, and especially the mother of Jesus Mary were all we needed to know about what we had lost or were losing in our dying cultures' free market. Free enterprising cultural decay is required for corporate profit. The mental health industry deliberately dodges responsible analysis... glad to bill for hand holding victims and justifying others liberating themselves from normalcy.

But these Portuguese stayed on course... Conradean...in the heart of modern darkness operating their intricate pipelines and gleaming dairy machinery like sub commanders periscopes...prevailing upon a present and future for all of us.

The only available Portuguese women seemed to be too old, that is widows my age or incredibly attractive young girls closer to my wee daughters' age. It was a bit discouraging and I said so to my pal, Joe Da Silva. He grinned like a mule eating briars and said, "I'll fix it."

The next Friday he invited me home to meet a girlfriend of his wife

Cheryl. I was not encouraged. She had an Anglo-Saxon name… not Portuguese, a youngish, divorced town girl with two kids. I weakly protested. "C'mon" Joe argued. "She's a looker! She needs a man. You need a woman don't you?" On the reverse side of a child's scolding "that you don't always need what you want", I was doing my best not to want what I needed. I still wore my jaggedly repaired wedding ring. Comrade Jack London[1] had warned that a great "weakness of the human mind is that the want is parent to the thought." I wanted to so overwhelm my wife, and family with moral integrity that anything less than complete reconciliation would not be considered. I wanted to so please God with marital fidelity that as with Hosea…He would form a dimensional hedge around my ex to keep her safe from whoring after others. "Who couldn't love someone who faithfully loved them back…", I preached to myself. "Beasts of the field do that…but it is major league love… loving the one who betrays you, takes your children and continues to straight arm your every expression of love and desire to restore your children's world. I thought it must be what Dostoyevsky[2] called "the harsh and dreadful love" Christ requires of us.

The Jesuit scholar John McKenzie S.J. in his book "The Two Edged Sword of the Old Testament", notes how human language lacks adequate resources to describe sin and the suffering caused by its resultant withdrawal of love. Yet Father John thinks that prior to the Gospels the Prophet Hosea comes close. Hosea "charges Israel with the supreme human infidelity: the faithlessness of one who has pledged love, has known love, and has withdrawn from love. The picture of God as the rejected lover pursuing His faithless beloved is too bold for any man to draw; only God discloses it."

Only decades later would I want to get over my ex and finally,… did! I trust God has gotten over Israel!

"C'mon…" Joe continued, you'll like this girl. Cheryl told her all about you. She's very interested…" He carried on and on, describing…

---

1   Jack London: Great American writer, pioneer socialist and founder of 'The Communist League of America' wrote intensely of the conflicting natures of man and beast. Quote is from The Iron Heel.
2   Fyodor Dostoyevsky: Brothers Karamazov

promoting this girl like a cerveza rubia Mexican beer commercial.

I met her that night. She stood to meet us in their parlor as we came in from the kitchen. She was stunning!

Glowing, like a reincarnated Jean Harlow in cowgirl clothes, she was long legged, slim waisted and full breasted… so voluptuous her endowments appeared eager to escape the strange western gown she wore.

After taking my hand and kissing Joe she turned to her friend Cheryl so they could celebrate her new dress. Walking away then slowly turning around like a model…Cheryl cheered the dress while Joe winked at me and the marvelous avoirdupois that moved in the backside of the gown. I required a drink.

And she was a major rubia alright…a peroxide rubia oxygenate. De tez Blanca as pale as her dress. The perfect anima for Mediterranean's (or for Joes crowd, Mid-Atlantic) imagination as dark as her mascara. The longitude of my loins were otherwise…however she did deserve ones attention.

That is, until we reached the Fesht Hall where I found the Portuguese girls even more distracting.

La Rubia had a soft childlike voice. She so wanted to be admired. She certainly wasn't ignored at the Hall. After applauding our entrance several of the young Forcados came by our table "to throw the glass" with us, nodding their appreciation of my beautiful company. I knew I was disappointing her. She had been asking to be loved since she first said hello. I was not prepared to love her. More naturally humid than cool around women my assumed aloofness was as uncomfortable for me I think as it was for her. And I was surprised…no amazed that such aloofness increased her aroused attention to me. She initiated a lot of touching, first holding hands on the way to the dance floor, next while laying her hand upon my knee and then upon the very point of my pants pocket, she actually said, "I like to be touched…" That touch, the *ratio objecti* St. Thomas[1] has noted "is subject to natural immutation, not

---

1   St. Thomas Aquinas: 13th Century Saint: author of the 'Summa Theologica.' Thomist philosophy distinguishes sharply between faith and reason. Reason not qualified to establish doctrines, which is a matter of faith, it can demonstrably show they are not contrary to reason.

simply spiritual ones, in regard to the proximate organ in accord with the quality that is properly presented to it…! ." or something like that.

Contemplating the evening I had consulted my pocket *Aquinas* that day…morally [and immorally] considering fornication. Following the Thomist rhetoric that…"given a woman free from husband, under no control of her father, pleased to consent the disposal of her own body… why is it folly for those who say such simple fornication is not a sin?" St. Thomas polemically answers his own question, "…because God has care of everything according to that which is good for it…and He is offended by what we do against our own good, that is, diverted from our *"due end"*.[1]

Then followed a lot of vulgar argument, I thought, about the proper emission of semen and great wisdom about sexual union and children.

I had counseled a hundred horny husbands against their delusions of adultery. They inevitably thought of 'getting some on the side' as if there were some amoral dimension outside the mainstream of their life. I counseled there was only one stream, one story to write between their beginning and their due end. Adultery always screwed up the story.

But, confoundit, this was not adultery… or was it?… I argued within while fingering the wedding ring I'd put in my pocket. At most it might be fornication… or not! What if we (Rubia and I) would enjoin a new due end together. And if we didn't… I explored a further justification…sexual union might constitute, an honorable if failed attempt *not* a deliberate sin. I warmed to the idea. I'd been slowly sipping 'Bagaco', a strong brandy when Joe passed a jug of "Portagee Diesel"[2] under the table. Soon I was warming all over and responsive to her loving attention. Appreciatively she nestled as close to me as two chairs would allow. She was drinking 'Angelica' and seemed as sweet and delicate as the wine.

It became late and the Fesht was closing. They began playing "The Shamarita" and I knew she wanted to try it. Loyally looking at me she refused several young Portuguese who asked her to dance. Together…

---

1   due end: Summa Against the Gentiles III *St, Thomas Aquinas*
2   "Portagee Diesel": ultra-strong fermented spirits distilled from dairy farm silage pits.

we watched Joe and Cheryl dance the Shamarita with all the others which seemed to consummate a kind of collective mating ritual. With further consummating notions we held on to each other following our friends Joe and Cheryl home.

At their house after shared coffee and sweet bread they retired leaving us alone in the parlor. We could see the light on in the guest bedroom down the hall. Framed photos of the Da Silva children were barely visible in the soft dim light. We spoke of them. She reached in her purse and brought out pictures of her own children.

My sap began to rise from its base toward the higher branches again. The subject of children never seems to de-erotize women the way it does men. I've seen women libidinally aroused while smooching an infant. Normal men go the other way.

She spoke of how her children would soon be starting school and how she was single parenting them. I asked about their father. She winced and showed me another photo from her wallet. It was of him and his/their admiring children on his lap by the Christmas tree. His name was Wendel.

"He is a good father," she said. "He sees them every other weekend. Sometimes he's too harsh…"

I was looking away.

"Now…" speaking my name she pled with eyes looking up as if she were already lying down…"Wendel and I have been divorced for a year and a half and we were estrained for twice that long."

I knew she meant estranged but felt estrained more poetically described that state I was all too familiar with…

She spoke my name again, "all that time…I have not been ready for love until now. Do you understand?"

God help me, I understood. She was very ready!

"In due time, I knew I would be," she continued. This is my first date.

At first I thought she said 'fesht date.'

"He…Wendel is due to find out, but I don't care. We need to get on with our lives." "And the children's?" I asked.

"What do you mean?"

"The children's lives are a central part of yours...yours and Wendel's lives." Nonplussed... she said nothing.

Motioning in the general direction of the Sierra Madres[1] I asked, "What do you think we'd get if we took fawns from the mountain range and tried to raise them down here with the Valley herds? Or vice versa?"

More respectful silence. She was even more attractive when she shut up. Thomistically answering myself, I exclaimed, "We'd get a lot of crazy deer. The due end of children cannot be met by one parent alone. They require decades not only of mothers nurturing, but fathers discipline and in tandem co-parental training of their souls.

"But Wendell's not a Christian like you and me," she countered. "He refuses to go to church like you and me." She belonged to one of the Vallys many mega-churches.... "and I told you.! he is harsh with the children."

What perversity! I was not going to be up for penetration by association and it sickened me to think that even churchiness could be used to justify coital home wrecking. I blurted out, "Wendell still loves you... doesn't he?" Quietly, she said, "yes." "Couldn't you still love him?" She looked down, saying "You have no idea how controlling he is!"

Gak! I had plenty of ideas about that! Have you read Melody Beattie's, "Co-dependency No More".

"No," She replied.

"Thank God. Never read it. It is filth... laying out the libertarian superstructure for free market narcissism.

In all due respect children need not only long-term instruction but also controlling and sometimes harshly controlling repression." And then finally I delivered my one memorized sentence from the Summa I had heretofore only recited to Child Protective Services and feminist mental healthers."

"For this purpose the woman by herself is not competent, but at this point especially there is requisite concurrence of the man, in whom

1   Sierra Madres: Mountain range

there is at once reason more perfect to instruct, and force more potent to chastise."

Sobbing a bit, she thought I was displeased with her. "No, no," I said, taking her hand and touching her face, "you are a beautiful, a wonderful woman..."

"I was going to give myself to you... ," she sobbed.

"I know,...I know you are now ready for love. For Gods sake make love to your lost husband, Reconcile your marriage with the only man who will ever be father of your children."

"Reconcile...just for the children?" she questioned recalling dozens of modern lousy counselors.

"What better bloody reason to start with," I shot back. "Go to church *and* love Wendell. Pray for him. With a woman like you... he's bound to come around."

"Yes...yes," she almost orgasmically gasped. "I can do that...", she wailed now convulsively crying. Her crying was not bawling but it was very loud.

Joe hurried into the parlor with Cheryl not far behind. "Wot thee blazes," he began to ask.

"It's OK Joe," I said.

"It's wonderfully OK," she said, tears streaming as she ran into Cheryl's' arms. The two friends cried together for another ten minutes.

Within the hour we all kissed goodnight with Cheryl's friend especially thankful and Joe shaking his head.

From then on Joe would joke with me in front of the other guys at work, "Keep your women away from him; he makes 'em cry."

Wendell's wife returned to him and I hear they have another child. I also hear he still doesn't attend church but prayerfully attends to his family in the happiness of their domestic church.

As is known, the line between madness and sanity is very thin. Similarly there is the line between ego strength and egotism. The latter is best curtailed by collective criticism of those who share the same cause. Whereas I had become a solitary outrider without comradely criticism in my very own cause. Can the error... the sin of self righteousness arise even in the just pursuit of a righteous cause? The utter arrogance of certain social refugees cum' revolutionaries always gagged me. Atomized individuals serving the presumptive masses always sounded moronic even when I was agreeing with them. Secular sectarians.

My friend Mike suffered no sectarian constrictions enabling him open hearted kindnesses. And disabled him in certain compressions of cruelty necessary to be a combatant. In short, there was no meanness in Mike for bad or good. He'd only fight if amused. He had no instinct for the jugular. I couldn't counsel with him re: custody battles. Nor anyone else it seemed in the next few rounds of custody disputes.

I'd heard that my ex and her Rose-Hulman Perfessor were planning a rendezvous in of all places… Havana. There was a government permitted scholars conference there and she planned to hook up with him after his lecture for the War College at West Point and fly together from Canada to Cuba.

I couldn't swallow it. Bourgeois adultery trysting on the shores of socialist hope for the Americas. I decided to sabotage it…if I could.

Years before when socialist Cuba emptied out it's trash in a ship called the Mariel, the last of her lumpen elements set sail for 'Freedom' in Florida. They ended up all over the place in 'faith based' immigration sponsorship programs.

Catholic Charities agencies were largely granted the task of resettling these 'refugees' for about $1,000 a head. It was despicable work but my agency needed the money.

John Epling was our staff organizer in Terre Haute. He had organized several parish sponsors. A dozen single male 'refugees' were to de plane on Christmas eve at Terre Haute's airport. John had arranged a welcoming committee ceremony including Spanish speaking faculty from St. Mary of the Woods and Indiana State University. As always he had also arranged plenty of press and T.V. coverage.

As cameras flashed and the welcoming ceremony began several non-Cuban, nonplussed, definitely not departing flight passengers approached me and asked with polite agitation if I was the person in charge here?

"No, no", I was glad to protest while pointing out John. They quickly surrounded him pointing to the 'refugees' being ceremonially welcomed to the 'Free World'. These lumpen 'refugees' had stolen their coats as they left the plane!

Seeing John and the faculty interpreters deal with these Cubans concept of the 'free market' was quite a sight and only the first of several episodes to follow. And there were different episodes... some including innocents swept up with the criminal element.

One involved a young twenty-two-year-old bi-racial medical student who left Cuba to punish his father (a high ranking military officer) who was divorcing his mother.

Parish sponsored by the Cathedral downtown he wandered into the effluvia of Indiana Avenue in Indianapolis. Within three weeks of unemployment he was shocked by "all the sexual freedoms and pornography" he saw going on. He also didn't like the drug dealing freedoms he saw or the freedom to deny such social evils through insular ignorance in the suburbs.

He sounded like one of my staff members. I thought they must have been speaking with him ... influencing his thinking. When I realized otherwise I was doubly proud of this parallel development... that is the developed consciousness of my social ministries staff. I would have hired him except he wanted to go home. He sought out our help. Due to this I became acquainted with the 'Cuban Interest Desk' at the Swiss Embassy in Washington. I spent many hours speaking with them and with him; his English infinitely better than my Spanish.

He liked his sponsoring family and he fit in pretty well there. He "just didn't fit in well with America", he said.

"You've been here less than a month", I rebutted. "Hell, I don't fit in well with the worst of America but..."

"...But you can afford a separate place,... a separate peace", he nodded toward my desk photo. "Even if I could afford a farm like yours or a suburban enclave like my sponsors I would miss fitting into a larger society, a nation, a national purpose. I know... I know", he'd say defensively "I left Cuba because my father's heart has turned as black as his skin... and that's the other thing... my sponsors (who were an African American Physician, his wife and two daughters) speak to me of black pride, and the black community's progress from segregation. In Cuba we are light years past all that and more. Before the Revolution even the dictator Batista's dark butt was not allowed in the racist American owned casinos. Now Fidel's women..." he grinned, "Fidel's *women* are usually dark as my Dad who you know is a national figure in the army..." he wept a bit, continuing, "I'll get back to that... last year before I left a European Magazine interviewing Cuban school children asked them what color Jose Marti[1] was ?... You know what they answered?"

"No..."

"They thought for awhile" he went on "and then they said Jose Marti was blue. Jose Marti was blue like the sky." With a certain oratorical like rising he declared, "We are all colors in Cuba...clenched like a fist against racism and injustice!" Catching his breath from what clearly was a previously memorized slogan, he gasped, teared up a bit more then barely whispered, "but we are *not* moral. We are not immoral. We are not amoral. We are simply...pobrecitos... todos *not* moral. Pienso, I think we are simply too busy with social justice... fighting class exploitation, providing education, medical care and a United Front against imperialismo that we neglect personal morality. We've forgotten... I've not forgotten the Ten Commandments, the Beatitudes, Prayer, confession, forgiveness, communion and the mass. The entire Magisterium of the Church must not be abandoned to the Gusanos.[2] Conscience and conscience formation is essential for social consciousness."

Blazingly articulate he continued... I sat amazed and taking notes.

"I thought...", he faltered, "that proclaiming the Revolution officially *atheist* wouldn't hurt much. I know many principled atheists... at most I thought it would discourage heresy and keep out those Yanqui Missionaries.

Ees not happenin that-a-way. Revolutionary power like all power presents más hards... more hardons, más hardon opportunities with extra más que *extra* openings of mujeres; muchas mujeres wide open

---

1   Jose Marti: Cuban poet and hero of Independence. Founder of Cuban Revolutionary Party in N.Y. 1892

2   Gusanos: Worms; Counter Revolutionary Cuban worms.

for infidelity and adultery. Morally just politicos becoming moraless sexual morons. Mi Padre is a good hombre…a good man who with the *barbudos* (bearded ones) became a great revolutionary steeling himself against personal indulgence and scornful of conventional behavior… including conventional morality, family, child rearing and religion… My friends think more of St. Che…God bless him" (I thought he spoke of Gueverra the way a Muslim would speak of Mohammed) "and his 'necessary' marital infidelity than the conventionally tried and true family man loyalties…like the fidelities of Raoul Castro… Fidel's brother. Mira 'Necessity ees not a virtue!' They ain't Che. They'd…We'd all do better to build socialismo by following Raoul's example. Mi Padre has had it away with everyone then settled on his young secretary. My sainted half white mother has always been loyal to heem and to the Revolution. She gave heem five children and raised us right in the church and for the Revolution. My younger sister and brothers cry in confusion every night with nuestra madre. Mi padre… my father embodies the Revolution and he has homewrecked us. I've run away from my life, from my mother's tears to get his attention and to save his life…porque I was theenking más y more of killing heem. But who is the counter revolutionary theenker. Me against my father or heem against the strong conventional morality of the Jente, the people, especially the disciplined working class and new peasantry. We can build on that strength if we don't condemn it as backward."

He muttered the last sentence like an inner tube losing air. His life was hanging out there about to be flattened by personal and historic tragedy. He was enmeshed in all the dangerous thoughts, loves, and hatreds I cared about.

Some of my staff wanted to help him hook up with one of the Doctor's daughters and finish medical school. I wanted to help him get home. I thought the Cuban Revolution needed him and told him so.

The 'Cuban Interest Desk' was staffed by young sounding female voices…all decidedly hostile to helping anyone from the Mariel. They uniformly resisted differentiating our young man from the Mariel's lumpen mob. When finally identifying him through his father's name they became more hostile and less cooperative. One young thing explained to me he would be considered betraying his father's position as well as his own country. Finally after hours and weeks... seemed like hundreds of phone conversations I found a sympathetic catholic voice who didn't like homewrecking especially if it was harmfully claiming the Revolution as cover. Repatriation would be slow and tedious but she thought it was possible. Ultimately we arranged his trip home albeit circuitously and very ....very unofficially.

Years later Socialist Cuba has explicitly dropped its official atheism.

I'd like to think we all... as well as Nicaragua and the Pope had something to do with that.

VII

I was considering the Cuban Desk again. Maybe I could convince someone to hamper the adulterous rendezvous. My old comrade and co-defendant Rolphe advised against it. "Cuba's just come through a rough period. The last of her old degenerate$ deported. Tourist trade gone. The embargo on – no money moving. They're not gonna be... you know...if your wife's consort... you know she *is* your *ex*-wife... if that academic fuck stick of hers is a raving anti-communist he'll still be spending some money in Cuba. There are rumors they're even tolerating young cadre turning tricks *for the money*. "Speaking of which", he said, "Are you earning any...if you are – go hire yourself a lawyer and get your kids while she's gallivanting around."

I did just that... that is, the lawyer part but only after this same weekend I got solitarily drunk and tried to talk to the Cuban Desk at the Swiss Embassy. An expensive phone call...I had to wait a lot. Finally a husky seductive female voice got on the line with me as I tried to drunkenly explain my situation to consult with her. Then I had to hang up early because she kept asking if I were making a terrorist threat!?!

Finishing my tequila I fell asleep on the couch watching Public T.V. A pattern of behavior to which I had become regularly accustomed.

The next week all my free time was spent on the phone trying to track down the right lawyer. I'd also decided to mount my last cavalry charge to win back my wife and children. The adulterous rendezvous...hey!, he was still legally married...would probably be scheduled around the 26th of July. Maybe earlier! It wasn't even Easter yet. The biblical "Warning trees" were ablaze with color and blossom across the San Joaquin... in full bloom around my place with dangerous possibilities.

My children Bethany, eight, and Eliot, six, were by Indiana Guidelines scheduled to be with me their "non-custodial" father for seven days of their Spring Vacation. I would offer to pay for their mother's airfare too. She could stay with Mike's family or wherever she wanted. We'd go places together with the children. I'd pour on the last of my best charm and seductive ability (God knows I hadn't spent any of it on California women) and woo her away from this Kenny Rogers jive assin Johnny cum lately homewrecker. She'd see me (us) again with the children. No man on earth can give her the joy of her children as I could. I was ordained by God and by nature to be with them beside her.

Back home in Indiana I'd fallen into the same error of most cuckholds and rejects. I felt if she could just see how she'd hurt me… how wounded and miserable I was without her…that would touch her heart with sympathy… move her…towards me, towards reconciling our marriage. That always does the opposite.

Sadness and pain in the 'reject' only provokes guilt and confusion in the 'perp'. The discomfort of guilt and confusion cause (a) increased avoidance and/or (b) demonization of the reject to justify the rejection.

But now, I could appear cool, strong, and independently attractive… after all I… "Bang"…I thought…after all… I was still an underfunded countryman who preferred talking about cows and horses more than how to get tenure; a reclusive revolutionary marxist without a party, a rancher without his ranch, a horseman without his horses, and worst of all according to her an "Amish-like, Islamic McCatholic, Calvinistic Methodist Circuit Rider Rabbi." Much earlier she had complained "I had just gotten use to genuflecting and you started hanging out with the Amish"! All syncretic categories aside I'd been…I was…a hard-working faithful family man who loved her and she knew it. That was going to have to be enough or not.

Consensus of all the Catholic priests and Orthodox Presbyterian ministers phoned came down to one man…a lawyer named Jack McMurtry. He was a tough Mick who had recently moved from Sacramento to the valley town of Oakdale. Clergy described him as radical, game and willing to fight to the death to save a marriage. I made a Friday morning appointment to see him. He was also described as expensive.

Inside his modest strip mall office was a huge oil painting of Jesus before what looked like a very ugly judge. The brass plate title read

'Jesus Before the Magistrate'. His secretary showed me in to a hard chair inside his inner office. This inner sanctum was more posh; half walnut paneled with some leather furniture.

McMurtry himself; burst through the back door (I thought at the time it might have been a bathroom door) strode athletically and long leggedly behind his desk, grabbing the back of his chair for balance leaned over it in his dark sharkskin suit and pensively peered in my general direction. Near sixty he was gray and wore small gold spectacles behind which peered that recognizable Celtic squint. His squint struck me as both sneering and caring at the same time.

"Morgan, is it?" he asked.

"It is"! I answered.

Then began the predictable 'let's pretend' Irish nationalism of so many American native born Micks…

"Your people are from?" he asked

"You mean the old sod?"

"I do."… his squint near closing now…

"Cork… from Cork."

"Near Bantry?" he asked

"No, I mean I don't know. I think Cork is where they got on the boat." "Umh…some of my people are from Bantry."

"Since the troubles?" now I was asking.

"Before. And yours?" he answered and asked at the same time!

"During! My grandmother Katey Dunne and her family; right in the middle of the British imposed Genocide;" at that his half sneer turned into a full grin and he, now kindly, almost affectionately spoke, "I hear that you were an Archdiocesian, a Director of Catholic Charities and Social Ministries, even an Extraordinary Minister of the Eucharist. What the brass you doin as a Reformation Reverend?" His sneer returned.

"I'm trying to get by (to go bye[1]… like a border collie. I privately thought.") to repair what the Priests have screwed up". McMurtry blushed negatively. He didn't approve of swearing even if it was at the clergy. Actually it turned out Jack McMurtry was more anti-clerical

1   "go bye": Stockman's order for a stockdog to go around to the left of the flock.

than me. Influenced by Bishop LeFebres[1] Tridentines he sometimes attended their latin 'underground' mass in Stockton. Jack definitely had more than his share of Celtic contradictions. A right wing Republican traditionalist subscriber to Buckly's National Review he'd also been a quarterly contributor to Noraid and the Sinn Fein whom he knew politicked for a Socialist Republic in Ireland. "Any political system that honors the churches faith and morals is worthy of support", he'd say. "Principled atheists in the IRA were preferable to liberal hypocrites in our pulpits". He distrusted the US government from all angles including World War Twos bailing England out of the mess her bankers had created. He equated Zionists with New Testament 'Judaizers' and thought Israel a front for British banking.

"C'mon Jack", I'd later argue, "the Jews whupped the Brits in Israel better than our people have done in Northern Ireland". His eyes would glaze and carefully shifting categories he would change the subject. He'd spent a lifetime collecting quirky opinions. The result of which was a very eccentric fellow. Sometimes when he'd present his 'social credit' funny money arguments carrying on like I imagined Ezra Pound after too much wine. Other times the very soul of gravitas he would brilliantly engage Toynbee's categorical "degeneracies of the modern west and the recalcitrance of human nature to the laws of nature and the law of God." We recognized in each other more than the Californians penchant for self-reinvention. In our different ways we had both psychologically seceded from what we experienced disintegrating around us. Our psychological secession shared mutual and opposite points of view. We concentrated on the former.

I detailed my marriages failure and betrayal. I asked him how he knew my background. He only replied, "I keep well informed." Guessing that to come from the gossip network of Priests I emphasized how I knew dozens of priests back home and none would step up to tell my wife that divorce was wrong, that it and her attendant adultery violated her marriage vows and the very life of her soul. That she should cease her homewrecking and return to the farm home of her husband with their children and reconcile her marriage. None would do this. None! They all wanted to be ambivalent counselors blathering

1   LeFebre: Renegade Swiss Bishop

on and on about "both sides," "not taking sides", "It takes two to tango" and recommending annulment, the cowardly modern Catholic answer to divorce. "I'm"… sensing his disapproval I was trying not to swear. "I'm…I am the…bleedin counselor, I was the counselor…I needed a priest."

"Would your atheist wife have listened to a priest?" (Man… he was informed.)

"I think so. She was Italian Catholic in background… she personally liked priest-counselor Father Ruffkidd who nearly seduced her"…I was swearing again…McMurtry was frowning but with an edge of sympathy toward me.

"She defended him and excused herself by saying he [Father Ruffkidd] was just so loving and…she just responded to him. Intercepting a lewd phone call of his to her… I responded by promising to cut his throat if he ever called again."

"Did he?" McMurtry asked with a sinister smile.

"I don't think so. I know my 'best friend' and womanizer Father Dietrich met her out of town at conferences several times. Probably just for counseling…" We both smirked looking at the floor.

"Why…" he began. "Why…" (he may not approve but I could tell he was tempted to swearing himself.)

"Why". . he continued slowly and coldly "Why do you want her back!?"

"Our marriage was convalidated by the Church. Our vows til death do us part solemnized by God Himself through the full authority and magisterium of the Church. And the best I can do for my children is to reconcile their parents' home."

"But not just for the children"? he tested.

"Hell no! (I couldn't help swearing) Hell no…not just for the children but by God the children are an extremely important element here, the most primary element. Yet, I do love their mother and I've been more celibate these last two years than most of the turned around collars you know."

Even though sour at some of my profane remarks McMurtry was strong in agreement with me and on taking my case. "You need custody of your children whether or not she comes back... don't you?"

"Yes!" I'd already thought about it. "Like you've explained", he explained... "When she brings the children out for Easter... prayerfully, sincerely try to woo her back. Failing that..." he continued..."if the kids will stay with you...say good-bye to her and we'll sue for modification of custody, that is, get it for you here in Stanislaus county where you are a beloved minister of the Lord and she is an out of state adulterous homewrecker". He was already trying out certain rhetoric for trial. He explained how 'out of state' was generally deadly in California as "Californians think their way of life far superior to the 'midwestern subculture' and the San Joaquin Valley was the common folks bible belt religious respectful section of the state and would be sympathetic to a minister like you. I'm even sympathetic; man... I'm extremely sympathetic because I know you're trying to set the priests job right. We'll talk about vocation later. I know you're trying to minister to people the teachings of Jesus... how God loves them and the constancy of His wrath. I will be glad to... I will be grateful for the opportunity to represent you."

He didn't mention a retainer. I asked about it. Not time to ponder he seemed to regret, looking down half prayerfully... almost contemplatively for a quiet moment...then dismissively waved his hand saying, "that begins when legal work begins...not until. Now our work is more political than legal or"...nodding at me "clinical." "We should *collectively* (he enunciated that last word knowing it would please me) and warmly welcome your wife out here like the lost sister she is. Loving her from several good family's who'll respect her motherhood, your marriage and wish her to stay. Will your parishioners help?" Not waiting for a response he continued, "My pastor, Father Ryan will help key in some academics from our parish...we could get her a job, her careerism would be intact. I'll convene my clan for a... She'd be here Easter right?" I nodded. "It's set..." He said, "Invite your Valley friends and congregation...we'll dine and *collectively* (he winked this time) welcome her home."

"Where?" I started to ask. "As my guests...at my club." he beamed. McMurtry owned a tennis and athletic club in Stockton. "The cost?" I started again. "No cost." he interrupted. "The chows on me. There'll be a cash bar. The distance to Stockton will deter all but the most helpful. And… it's the way I recruit new members…you know new customers."

I didn't know…I didn't know about any of this stuff except I'd been gagging myself from swearing for over an hour. McMurtry's enthusiasm *was* catching and it felt like I'd gained a new friend.

"One last thing now…" he seriously put in, without the slightest sign of that sneer. "You'd not be having any kind of an affair with madam Bottle?… would ya?"

"Definitely not…I drink, but only as Jesus did." McMurtry looked puzzled as whether I took him seriously or not. He said, "I know you've drank with O'Dwyer." He was quite serious.

"You mean Father O'Dwyer, the bull fighter Chaplain?" "The same," he answered sharply. (His face appealing to be friends but ready to fight) "He's from the old sod too and has a terrible whiskey nose."

"We drank beer."

"He drinks a lot of beer with Father Ryan," he reported. That's the connection I suspected and said, "O'Dwyer and Ryan are friends?"

"Drinking buddies," he spat…disapprovingly. I took my leave telling Jack McMurtry I'd keep in touch;…leaving him hanging between his boyish enthusiasms and olde cold blooded judgment.

VIII

As the Protestants say I got myself all prayed up for the fateful phone call to my ex. Long before *skipe* I could imagine her face as she first answered my call...misty morning languid beauty still receptive to my voice if I could feign the tone of a disembodied date seeker rather than that of a 'git ya ass back where it belongs' (ex) husband. I did pretty well. When I said Mike, Rolph, and all the admirers of our children's pictures were eager to meet her and greet us charitably for a great Vacation here in California's early spring with the Valley in full bloom from the orchard trees and warm pleasant weather. She responded with a pleasant kind of sound. I quickly added she could stay separately with Mike's family at his ranch or in the Valley hotel I'd arrange and pay for as well as her flight out. She sounded positive asking, "Can you afford this?" "Sure," I lied.

"Well, maybe so," she said. "But Easter week is pretty well booked and the week before."

"What had she become...a landing pad," I thought and almost said.

"What about the week between the 11th and 18th she went on... The children could be taken out of school. They're doing well...I don't think they'd miss much...Could we do it that week...?"

She was matter of factly agreeing to come out. Cavalier about their school lessons I thought was not the issue now. Jack McMurtry's reception party might be rescheduled or triaged... but, Praise be to Allah, she was agreeing to leave her colleagues, conferences, and conferees for a full week to be with the children and me. "WONDERFUL", I uncooly blurted into the phone..."By God that's wonderful!"

She laughed sweetly saying, "it's early you can call the children this evening. We'll tell them together." She sounded like the last three years hadn't happened.

I phoned McMurtry about the change in dates. He wasn't happy about it. I could feel his sympathy and sneering through the telephone.

Sunday I announced to cheerful, almost cheering congregations that in a few weeks I would introduce them to my family...that my children and their mother would be flying out for a week's visit. I could not restrain my happiness in sharing this and everyone seemed to *collectively* respond in kind. Although I did overhear one young mother's near cynical remark… "finally we'll be able to sing some happy hymns instead of all those old dark ones of his." I had preferred the melancholy welsh hymns in the back of the Methodist hymnal.

Blithe and brief passed the next two weeks. Only one more week to go. I'd purchased the tickets, made all the arrangements and was to greet and gather up my loved ones this coming Saturday at San Francisco's Airport. Wednesday evening I was enjoying yet another joyful phone conversation with Bethany about our nearness to see each other and a more serious conversation with little Elliot reassuring him that the large Wells Fargo prints I'd sent him of Stagecoaches stuck in mud flats and being stuck up by outlaws was more history than present reality…but if any outlaws threatened us while we were out west together I assured him his Papa could whup all of them and he was not to worry. Satisfied he cheered… then said, "Mama wants to talk to you." Mama got on the phone in a minor key. "You remember Sister Luncia?" She went on not waiting for my response for which I was glad. She wouldn't appreciate my reminding her this S.P.s[1] nick-name from her students was Sister Lunacy and that I had likened her general disposition to a yeast infection. "Sister has planned her entire radio program talk show next Wednesday around interviewing me about Historic Political Roles of Women and the Importance of Higher Education". It was a one hour local weekly radio broadcast.

"Next Wednesday…? Does it have to be next Wednesday?" I cautiously began.

"I'm afraid it does. It simply slipped my mind entirely until Sister reminded me this week. We can still come but not for the whole week. Would that be alright?" she asked guiltily. Careful not to lose my cool, I said nothing… an awkward silence followed, which she filled with a new proposal. "Why don't we just put it off until the eighteenth? It's just a week. I'll juggle my other commitments. We'll do everything the same just a week later".

I stifled myself from complaining, or explaining any difficulties

[1]   S.P.s: Sister of Providence; highly educated college teaching order.

to say nothing of my utter disbelief that I could trust her for the next week's plans. Radio programs could be pre-recorded and ol' Lunacy's frequently was but …she might prefer it live. My ex was usually not deliberately damaging but in her new condition she was consistently fickle. A straw in the wind. As her feelings changed, sometimes abruptly, she would rearrange physical reality to match them. For three years I had stupidly growled about the above making it worse. Who knows… if I kept my mouth shut maybe the roulette wheel in her mind would stop at keeping her word.

"You're upset with me", I heard her threatening a reactive payback.

"No, no…" I lied. After all, there are higher virtues than honesty. And the greatest ones in my life had to do with these plans…this trip. "No …I am disappointed but glad we can all be together next week." Yike! I knew the 'all be together' line was a mistake and stumblingly tried to recoup and dilute any such aggressive intention by rambling on about how Mike, and Rolph, and so many old and new friends were anxious to see her with the children.

Warily warming to my acceptance of her change in plans she became chatty about the classes she was teaching and the radio program for Sister Lunacy. She asked if I had any ideas for the radio program. Trying to be unnaturally positive about Sister Lunacy I cautioned her to not let the conversation go too GaGa over Golda Meir without saying something positive about the Palestinians. I also asked for her to send me a tape of the program. "They usually tape and sometimes pre-record the broadcast…don't they?" I neutrally inquired.

"Oh. Yes", she answered with a slight little gulp as if she'd made one of her many famous faux pas. I didn't hit her with it, only thanked her…I could tell she wondered why…and asked to speak to the children again…feeling false in assuring them their trip …our visit was just a week delayed.

I hung up more perplexed than angry. I needed to understand… not just love and fight this woman…this mother of my children. For decades she had been loyal, loving, intelligent, and hard working. What was to understand? That was plainly that. Deeper unconscious knots grown cancerous beneath her consistant good behavior?! She had integrity!? She brought integrity to our marriage. Solid as a rock constancy I admired and reported to Mike before we were married. "As if you'd settle for anything less!" Mike observed. "Whaddaya mean?" I'd slightly retort.

"Man, she worships the ground you walk on, and you think that's as it should be".

"You talkin about expectations?" I'd query.

"Naw", he'd laugh and joke about bending Goldwater to say 'extremeness in pursuit of moderation can't be wrong' any more than

'moderate pursuit of the extreme.' Or…can it? I was asking myself. Maybe I was now paying the tax for all that previous positive expectation. Extreme? I don't think so. People endure luke warmness because they fail to expect better and settle for less. Gene Debs maxim "it's better to vote for what you want and not get it than to vote for what you don't want and get it."

This didn't puzzle me. The fickleness did. Hell, she wasn't even consistent in her present loathing of me. Perhaps her fickleness was associated with her predilection for 'faux pas' that is, those false steps and social blunders she was prone to make in language. Her most famous one was in introducing our nearest neighbors when we first moved to the farm. They lived about one mile from us on a rise just west of the creek and trees of our valley. The householder, Rebecca or Becky, a tall gaunt, pioneer looking widow woman whose ectomorphic condition made her long neck appear longer, almost giraffe like in proportion to the rest of her skinny frame. She was usually accompanied by Nellie, her teenaged daughter. Nellie was unhappily and uncomfortably coping with an unwanted pregnancy. She walked with her hands and arms around her huge pregnant swollenness as if it were a melon she wished to pitch in the nearest ditch. My young wife introduced them as…"I'd like for you to meet our neighbors… Necky and Belly." Then she gulped in gaucherie and grieved embarrassment almost akin to shame until the laughter all around would re-brighten her mood.

Once we had a house guest whose brother had committed suicide and who had himself been recently hospitalized for depression and suicidality. Fully recovered, healthy and strong he'd help me sickle out an acre of thorn brush. We showered and came down for drinks before dinner. Our T-shirt sleeves not covering the long thorn cuts on both sides of our arms. "Hey, Dan", she greeted, looking at the cuts on his arm, "what's this…a desperate suicide attempt?"

The fairly immediate gulp, grief, shame, and apology quickly followed. No laughter that time. She brightened anyhow.

Overcompensating positiveness may require undue repression of negative feelings…which then pop out inopportune…I mean… we all have to express our natural negative feelings…especially toward those who have crossed us…the trespassers, otherwise we'll resent and never forgive them.

Is that what's going on now I wondered. All those years of positive love from her an overdone repression of negative hostilities now pouring all over us. All that 'worshipful' stuff Mike called it… largely faked? Blast…and double blast…I'd rather have it faked. If all her love had been totally insincere it beat all of this…this sincerity.

I dully got through the next few days. Even tried T.V. Evangelists! Rolphe called them sky pilots. I had called them pussy-positive peddlers. Warmed over Norman Vincent Peale. Populist Pealers. They usually gagged me. I watched them this week…desperately. Maybe I wasn't positive enough. Not for mindless idealistic certainty…but for increasing the odds in your favor. My bookmakers theology always placed bad luck, that is, when bad things happen beyond common odds and random chance it is the devils hand. Conversely, when good things happen beyond common odds and random chance it is a clear sign of the Holy Spirit.

I invoked the Holy Spirit in prayer every day for my children… and for their mother. Especially for protection of their mother from the devil's hand…that she cease her demonic, daemonic, Eudaemonic sin. Like the T.V. preachers I tried to rev up positive expectations to increase the odds for some kind of positive outcome against the odds for a dreaded one.

Calling around to cancel the reception arrangements yet again…I positively, if tentatively, without enthusiasm re-invited everyone to the new time. Lawyer McMurtry responded cynically, "Good luck on that...boyo!" "Yeah... the luck of the Irish."

Yet days passed... day after day the dread phone message to call things off did not occur. In my regular phone calls to the children they would both say, "Mama says we're still coming." Maybe, just maybe I began to invite the hope of my heart into my head. When talking to the children I'd always ask to speak to her and all this last week she'd been too busy to come to the phone. Their plane tickets were for next Saturday p.m. By Friday I was jubilant. Turning in early I said my prayers...thanks be to God ...the phone call I feared with dread certainty was not coming.

It came... Saturday morning. I was up early to straighten my modest household, sweep out and trash the empty tequila bottles. I answered the phone trembling like a fraidy cat. Her voice was taut and cold.

"I'm just not ready for this", she said. Strangling in something worse than anger I managed to say,

"Ready for what?!"

"The pretense. Pretending for others that everything's OK between us. Giving the children false hope..."

"Pretending good things never hurt anybody!" I spit out... and hope is never false. It's what's needed when life seems hopeless."

"Bethany and Eliot are not hopeless! How dare you imply that..."

(The storm had struck). "Your answer to all practical concerns is some self-righteous metaphor or philosophical schlock. You save that for your sermons Reverend!"

She pronounced the last word hatefully hard on its consonants, like it was a rodent not escaping the jaws of a carnivore. Her voice not falsely base, nor naturally soprano but falsetto-shrill as a banshee raiding my frail grasp of civility. I choked the phones receiver with both hands but said nothing. She said plenty.

"You've told the children I am an incubator mare. That their good qualities come entirely from your seed that merely passed through me to their birth!!"

"Yes it's true", I confessed. "People...me...People say terrible things in angry scrimmage. I'm sorry. You've done worse." I wanted to say "Incubator mares are preferred when bred to Prepotent sires". I didn't. I just lamely denied saying 'entirely'. That provoked her more. "You've said and done so much that has to be corrected before I'll be seen with you."

"Didn't you tell the children that I was an inherently violent man?"

"I did not! I said you are a pervasively and potentially violent man and you are!"

"Dear… dear (*I was* trying civil) I will be glad to tell them, to correct the record, I will tell them you are not an incubator mare".

"What you are not is…funny."

"All good and peaceful men are potentially violent when confronted with enough wrong… things."

"What current things are your excuse?"

I could smell a set up. The millisecond I stated my mind, "Denial of visitation for starters, you witch of a homewrecker", I would lose… I said instead…"Look I am not being violent. I need no excuses. I'm not looking for any."

"You always find something," she continued. "If it's not something at work where you had poor O'Donnel scared to death for years."

"Hopefully", I put in.

". . its total strangers. Yes I heard about that cattle buyer when you were back here only a few days and you couldn't restrain yourself."

Who? …

"The Brawlesons told me. I don't know why you've let them move into the farmhouse. They're terrible gossips."

I had arranged for the homeless Brawlesons to move in rent free to watch over the place as caretakers. I was curious how she happened to speak with them but I was more interested in setting the record straight re: the cattle buyer.

"That cattle buyer radically misunderstood the price, was worn out from a long drive, seemed very upset and said he was thirsty. I offered him a beer in one of our pewter mugs and he struck me – pow - on the brow with it. He bent the mug and went nuts…was all over our kitchen. I restrained him.

"You knocked him out!"

"That too."

Then in my faked civil tone, "Are you coming at all…please?" Next in a truthfully negative tone, "Are you not coming? then?"

"We're not coming." she said triumphally.

Still…still civil, "It is harmful for you to deny our children seeing their father. Check with your lawyer. I'll see you in court!"

Then, my foot off the brake I concluded, "I promise not to tell the children what a maedadic cadaver you've become and as for your consort…I've already called him out and would prefer to kill him first."

Of course, she hung up.

The day got worse with the mail. It included an audio tape of Sister Looney's radio program. I listened to it with raging sadness. My wife had been one of the most talented and versatile women of her generation. Intellectually and ideologically bright, feminine, beautiful and loyal. Whatever she said used to sound alluring. She now just sounded hollow. A Terre Haute Hardshell Baptist[1] Minister referred to the broadcast in his Sunday sermon. He called it the 'Papist and the Popinjay'. He was at least half right.

That she would voluntarily trade in her past personae for her present one was tragically stupid.

I phoned no one over the weekend. When I appeared at church sadly and alone the second Sunday of expectations to see me happily with my family parishioners 'circled the wagons' of sympathy and support for me. They had genuinely and collectively bonded close and vicarious to my faith, joy, and sadness.

I joked we would not be returning to so many of those old sad welsh hymns, but I'd be strong enough for them later. I preached on 'consciousness and sin' around a quote of Kierkegaard's. "Doubt cannot be defeated by reason. It can be overcome only by the leap of faith. Consciousness of sin is the driving force in that leap." And consciousness of sin, ones own and others, ultimately brings one to "consciousness of Gods will and Grace. God Consciousness!" I confessed that in my own life…faith in God had sometimes worn thin but the overwhelming evidence of sin and evil always brought me back to

---

1   Hardshell Baptist: "Primitive Separatist" Baptists who consider even 'Southern Baptist's as "modernist moderates".

prayer and faith… 'God Consciousness'.

I told of Simone Weil, the young Jewish girl studying at the Sorbonne in Paris. "She was arrested and dragged off by the German Army to a Nazi Concentration camp where she and her people suffered unspeakable horrors …more (I emphasized) than anything you or I have known…during which time she converted to Christianity… which pissed everybody off. The Jews were pissed because she became Christian. The Christians were pissed because she wouldn't choose a church. She survived and after the war wrote a book called 'Waiting for God'." In it she wrote, I paraphrase "We have to be glad things happen the way they do, and exactly the way they do, otherwise we wouldn't learn what we're supposed to learn from them… otherwise we wouldn't be who we are." This ol' life is a test … one test after another and we pray as Simone did the 'Our Father' to invoke Gods will…to bring it closer…to this sin ruled veil of tears…that His will be done on earth as it is in heaven.

After church I solitarily drove to Stockton to meet the McMurtrys at their tennis club. I had not phoned ahead. Driving under the freeway near Stockton's Federal Prison I was amused to find a large white farmhouse looking restaurant that advertised itself as 'Indiana Farm Fresh Cuisine' featuring fresh produce, mango peppers, cucumbers and tomato salad, Fried Chicken, buttermilk biscuits and gravy. Feeling like Ralph Ellison discovering Carolina Yams in Harlem I made a mental note to stop there soon, taste their fare, and suggest adding pan fried bluegill and cold raspberry pie to their Hoosier menu.

The McMurtry's 'Stockton Tennis Club' was an assortment of modest looking slumpstone buildings and tennis courts on four acres of asphalt, neglected lawn and impressive oak trees. Black and white magpies flew about the trees. I headed for the largest building and was directed inside and up the stairs to a large dining area and bar. This room jutted out with a kind of balcony effect over an olympic sized swimming pool. A small crowd seemed happily settled at tables and along the bar. It was easy to spot McMurtry and his family just sitting down for their early Sunday dinner. It was near 2 pm.

Jack stood, greeted me solemnly, while introducing his wife, four children, their spouses, and his grandchildren milling about the adjoining tables. He reigned as Patriarch over the place. His wife Kathleen seemed an elfin cheerful counterpoint to his solemnity. His family seemed informed about me; friendly and interested. Moira, Ted, Sean, and Shielah in that order were his issue. Sean and Shielah were not married. Sean was an ex-seminarian. None were college graduates; all were according to Jack… underemployed. He was doing his best to help them with the Tennis Club and had recently latched on to the AMWAY pyramid peddlers of hope enterprises. Yet another reason I suspected for his aggressive invitations.

Jack said a quick prayer over drinks as he sat me down beside him and then a lovely meal was served with Kathleen supervising the servers. Several bottles of chilled white Rhine was served with the shrimp and seafood. Father McMurtry kept a nervous eye on how much wine Sean and I might consume. Over…I guess more precisely…under the buzz of dinner conversation Jack whispered aside to me, "she didn't come?"

I answered, "She didn't!"

"The children?"

"The same!"

"You know what you have to do now… .?", his eyes asquint but his voice kindly and paternal, he led with a question already becoming advice. I was used to the question and had pondered upon the obvious answer all weekend. I needed McMurtry's advice on the legal implications.

"Would it legally be considered kidnapping? . I asked.

"Not if your divorce decree and 'Indiana Guidelines' grant you Easter week visitation."

"….the out of state factor?"

"Out of State would be arguable. But once you and the children were happily out here for a week we could sue for modification of custody. Most California courts are persuaded that children are better off here." If she came out here to live she'd have a case. Otherwise I think we'd win."

I was persuaded but still asked, "Legal penalties for kidnapping are about the same as legal penalties for murder, aren't they?"

"They are."

"Let's do it. It's worth the risk. My children are partisan to me."

"Now, if you would ever return to Indiana", he spoke

sneeringly as if that would be a counter evolutionary crime, she could counter sue but she'd have to prove a substantial change in your parenting. The more years you have with them here the stronger your case anywhere. "And Reverend," he finally said both sneering and respectful, "if she comes out here you might reconcile her!"

He said 'reconcile her' like one might say 'capture her' or 'lasso her'. My feeling fit the intention of his remark but at a deeper level I knew reality had moved on. She would have to initiate reconciliation if it was to happen. I was through being straight-armed. I gave myself permission for the first time to think of my children separate from their mother. The best thing I could do for them I always thought was to reconcile their parents' marriage. Since I could not get even close to that… I would get them a better custody arrangement. With custody I could allow generous visitation to their mother and still raise them right. She could not be trusted to allow me proper time… even the minimal non-custodial variety of time. This unjust situation had to be radically altered even if it meant risking prison. I'd risked six years in the jug under Indiana's Sedition and Subversive Act in my twenties for being a Socialist.[1] I would not hesitate to risk whatever for my children. Jihad[2] begins.

That night I had hideously confusing dreams. I turned in after much Tequila and Shakespeare. PBS was broadcasting a Shakespearian Festival from Western Canada. I love those labors of The Bard. Not from high brow hauteur or academic dramaturgy, but from low brow revolutionary labor recommendations. Jim Cannon counseled me several times, if I was to continue speaking for Socialism I should study the Bible and Shakespeare. The Bible boundaries our peoples moral and spiritual lives; their compass toward justice. Shakespeare crafts

---

1   Socialist: 1962-68 attempt to prosecute I.U. students with prison for their Socialist ideas under 1951 McCarthyite law.

2   Jihad: Frequently misunderstood Islamic term for 'moral struggle against injustice' whether from interior conviction to force of arms.

human conflicts within historic settings of injustice; blood, terror, privilege, betrayal, disloyalty, conspiracy, hypocrisy, and seduction that violate these boundaries. Revolutionary spokesmen knowing both, quoting both (The Bible and The Bard) can best represent the Socialist Solution; can best authorize their leadership.

Since then, I've seen Janice Rule in London; she was beauty as a dagger in Lady MacBeth, Richard Chamberlin's Dr. Kildare cool as Hamlet in D. C., the palpable chill of Olivier's malicious glare in the filmed 1955 Richard III, and Richard Burtons uncanny Hamlet (filmed in '64) skillfully playing consciousness interpenetrating the lack of it. I've seen 13 of the Bard's 37 plays. Plays should be seen not read. I've read all his poetry.

Tonight I caught most of Richard II and all of Julius Caesar. Unlike Richard II who described his schizoid temperament, "Thus play I in one person many people and none contended." In my dreams I was in one person many people and they all contended.

To break through the cacophony of their contending true and foster selves require centering down on permanent things…then ruthlessly acting to unify the soul. All of which is dreadful only to the contending factions. I remembered the Kantian "unity of act is to will one thing". A conscious act of thought and act of will over and above ones required economies. To seize a single solution from a roiling sea of possibilities with adiabatic dispatch.

Yet… the difficulty of such action even against tyranny is described by Brutus:

"Between the acting of a dreadful thing and the first motion, all the interim is like a phantasm or a hideous dream. The genius and the mortal instrument like to a little kingdom, suffers then the nature of an insurrection."

I knew about the nature of insurrection. My comrades and I seriously studied and thought about it for years… decades. Not against some crumbling failed state, but against the Behemoth of world states… since the British Empire and ancient Rome. That is, the late 20th Century United States of America's Imperium. To not only decry its injustices but study and know its terminal weaknesses. To patiently poise and prepare its revolution. To mine all the ore of contentious knowledge yet exercise the means to close all consideration except the unitive steel of action. Even martyrdom is not deliberate but collateral damage to righteous will.

All of which became re-complicated. She phoned early that Monday evening. Pert and chipper she got right to the point. "I spoke to an attorney this morning…you're right! *Your* state of Indiana (Everyone I know who doesn't fault Indianapolis for Indiana seems inclined to fault me) will fault me if they're not with you Easter break". She listed a few more school ground recriminations and then proposed. "Why don't you come here for Easter week? I have a three day conference in New York City beginning Easter Monday. After that I'd like to spend two or three days in the city and visit Uncle Ralph and Aunt Mary. You can babysit the children while I'm gone. I'll return the following Saturday, perhaps we can do something together then if I'm not too tired."

She paused, waiting I think for me to indict her probable illicit rendezvousing. I didn't. I said nothing.

Somewhat relieved, I think, she continued,

"I could have all of their clothes and things over to your moms. You'll have to stay with your parents, of course,…I can't have you staying here…not after you…"

Interrupting, I said, "I got it!" Emphatic but not hostile. I wanted to note I was no longer interested in getting into the drawers in her house or those on her haunches. Instead I said, "I would like that. We could visit the farm and our Amish friends to the south… if the weather held…"

"Oh, I think the children would enjoy that." And as I hoped she began to prattle on and on about weather forecasts. She knew that such weather talk usually annoyed me and she was now free to ignore how I felt. I appreciate weather; not chatter about it. The weather never changed in California and it was always changing in Indiana. Never bothered with it. Her weather talk gave me time to think things through. Feigning enthusiasm for her 'babysitter' plan, I said,"I'll take the whole week off…and then some. Re-book your flight for this Friday and save some money from the weekend prices. I'll fly in Thursday, visit my folks, be fresh and sure to pick them up from school Friday afternoon for our long week together." I gambled she would want extra time with her consort and I would need all the time I could get. She balked a little; "Are you sure you can get all that time off your jobs this quickly?..."

"I've never taken a day off. Not a single sick day. I have so yearned...I cannot wait to see my son and daughter. It'll be O.K." I could practically hear her mind whirring, as her speech faltered making her devious plans. Equally devious I figured she wouldn't even check the airlines for a flight change because "they" would have extra time wherever they happened to be. And so (heh-heh) would we...my kids and me. She signed off questionably, "You're sure you're alright with this in Indiana instead of California?"

"Wherever!" I emphasized. "I'm more than a little homesick for Indiana." All that was true enough.

Plans were made, I booked a flight for Thursday morning. San Francisco direct to Indianapolis with a return flight recorded for the next weekend. I then booked three tickets on a different airline for Bethany, Eliot, and me to fly from Indianapolis to San Francisco Holy Saturday afternoon. The die was cast.

My love has been a fever, longing still
For that which longer nurseth the disease;
Feeding on that which doth preserve the ill,
The uncertain sickly appetite to please.
My reason, the physician to my love,
Angry that his prescriptions are not kept,
Past cure I am, now reason is past care
And frantic – mad with evermore unrest;
My thoughts and my discourse as madmens are,
At random from the truth vainly exprest;
For I have sworn thee fair and thought thee bright,
Who art as bleak as hell; and dense as night

Shakespeare Sonnet #147

IX

I made arrangements at work and then phoned Jim Brigham. Brigham the Bull who'd been our maximum leader in the old days. He'd detail check the conspiracy. He raisin farmed near Fresno but he'd drop everything for a comradely favor. I was going to ask him to meet me halfway around Merced or even over west near Los Banos but he quickly said, "Sounds Important."

I answered, "Very."

He asked, "Can we talk on the phone?"

"Nope"

"Then meet me at the Basque Hotel tomorrow at noon."

"Done!"

I had to add Wednesday to the days off arrangement at work. They knew it was urgent and concerned my children.

I left late Wednesday morning around 9 am to meet Brigham at the Basque joint i.e. the Sante Fe Hotel on Tulare Street alongside the Sante Fe Railroad tracks in Fresno. It has the graystone appearance of a bank and locals still called it 'the Shepherd's Inn' because retired Basque sheep herders rented rooms there. As usual the place was full of prosperous Portagee farmers and Dairymen. There was a handful of Basque stockmen too. Mexicans were rare. It disappointed me the valley Portuguese and Basque do not consider them Hispanic. The ambience here (like Brigham) was masculine and noon-serious; hats, boots even bullshit muttered respectfully with daylight restraint. Evenings were another matter.

The barroom was smoke filled smelling pleasantly of tobacco and sweat. At Brigham's table, he was standing… apparently discharging two older dark complected fellows who might have looked slightly sinister even in their shirt sleeves except for what back east would be called their bay windows which here was considered the valley sign of prosperity. As I approached they dutifully left without introductions. Brigham held court here at the Sante Fe several days a week. At night

SHOTGUN PREACHER

he convened his business at the Primavera, a wilder kind of place.

Glancing at his watch, he seemed disappointed I was right on time punctual. He preferred to start our meetings scolding me for being late. Ordering his second or third brandy and soda he nodded at me as I said, "the same". The waiter didn't need details. Bartenders here would always see that Brigham got the select brandy.

Drinks served…we comradely toasted the olde 'back in the day' struggles and I narrated every tedious detail of my plan to; (1) fly to Indiana tomorrow, (2) "babysit" my children briefly while their mother did her multi-conferencing in New York, (3) then fly back with the children, (4) for their Spring break in California (5) and lawyer McMurtry filing for custody modification in Stanislaus County pre-empting the inevitable kidnapping charge.

Smiling broadly through the smoke, (we'd lit up the Cuban cigars he brought) Brigham indicated his approval and asked, "You trust this McMurtry?" "More than most lawyers," I replied.

"Time is the problem", Brigham announced like some Heideggerian professor. "You've allowed seven and half days (he'd been counting) make it nine with the same weekend. Not much time. California courts are clogged with custody modification petitions. It's a cottage industry within the states Publiocracy. It will take weeks not days for your petition to surface in court. She'll sic the law on you that week when she returns and you and the kids *ain't* there". He used the word 'ain't' like someone not used to it; like a BBC upper class narrator.

"I think…" he continued. "I know how to win you more time… a little more anyhow."

"Shoot!"

"We… I…have a comrade…lives along the Kentucky Tennessee border…you write a letter as if you're down there getting back late. He'll send it from down there to her around mid-week. That can get you a few more days maybe a weeks more time."

Luckily the bartender found me some plain stationery and envelopes. I scratched out a note to the effect we'd traveled to Kentucky looking at horses. That the children were fine and we'd be back to Terre Haute by next Saturday or Sunday evening. Brigham read it, said

---

it was "satisfactory", and sealed it into his pocket. "I'll take care of this...You git after your lawyer about the time factor!"

"Got it.", I said, realizing I was being dismissed after only two brandies. A balding, Anglo-looking guy was impatiently waiting to see Brigham.

"I gotta talk to this crop insurance guy. Can you stay for dinner... Spend the night?"

"Sorry. Can't. I had expected lunch."

"Yeah...order some grub at the end of the bar there...put it on my tab. I got these people to see. Take care. Be careful about the time factor."

Brigham always picked up the tab...paid for food and drinks. He could afford it. I ordered a steak sandwich with onions and Dos Equis beer. Upon leaving, the crop insurance man went out the door ahead of me. Glancing back I saw Brigham stand as he greeted a young couple coming to his table. Always a gentleman to the ladies he was adjusting a chair for the young lady as I gave a final wave on my way out the swinging doors.

Outside sunlight glinted off freight cars full of valley seed for the Springs planting. They were stalled in the middle of the streets railroad tracks. New life...seasonally negotiated. That Brigham... judge, jury, and bailiff in one man.

Homosexual necking at the San Francisco airport always bothered me. In truth heterosexual public necking bothered me more this trip. I wondered if she and her consort necked in public and how soon they would do it in front of the children. Conscious that such thoughts would drive me crazier I did my best to repress them. Repression is an inadequate defense mechanism but the only one I could afford.

Mike drove me to the airport. He just dropped me off. He was going to the Marina. Shopping for a boat to buy. He planned to set sail in the Sea of Cortez...maybe sail all the way to Cuba. Way this side of 1968 and 'No Revolution Today'[1] my old comrades were prospering into middle age. While...I was barely surviving. It could have been otherwise. We had one hundred twenty acres of the best limestone pastures north of Kentucky located half way between I.U. and the three

1   'No Revolution Today': poem from 'Not of Our Time' p.57

colleges in Terre Haute. With two incomes we could have rebuilt the farm house to what she wanted and we needed. Or… she could have led a quiet literary life researching and publishing. Instead she chose to splash around forever in the shallows of ego boosting consorts and conferees…harming, no, shattering the soul of our daughter and confusing the soul of our son. I had to quit thinking about this… Soon action would supplant anxiety. After takeoff I slept all the way home.

Arriving in Indiana twilight, deplaning was swift and I found my father at the gate smiling. He greeted me… throwing his arm around my shoulder. My family are not huggers. In so far as they are affectionate…tactile at all is due to the influence of my Italian wife. They remain reserved if slightly improved.

"How you Dad?"

"Fine, just fine." Not one for small talk he was quiet until we pulled away from airport traffic on to old highway Forty.

"You home for good?" he asked. Not knowing exactly…

whether that was a moral or temporal question… I thought for a while then answered,

"Not long. I want to be with my children during their Spring break."

I did not bother my father with details he did not wish to hear. I knew he basically disapproved of my situation. Men with failed marriages were to him failures. Men who left their families were scoundrels. Men who got left were… equally inadequate. Worse…he was partial to… that is against which ever parent in this case would complicate accessibility to *his* grandchildren. I was at least two thousand miles from his favor.

"O.K. if I sleep Dad?" I asked.

"Sure" he answered."

Both of us relieved I lay my head back and was out. I dreamt of my parents life. My father's life, in the main, was textbook Proletarian. Son of a teamster at the clothes pin factory in Spencer and a Kulaks[1] daughter he came to town from Owen County for industrial work on the railroad and at the glass factory. A militant union man whose personal responses… whose very instincts predictably squared with the International Working Class. Oppositional to all management; frater-

1   Kulak: Russian term for prosperous farmers.

nal to all fellow working men and hostile or friendly to government policy according to that class division. Critical of military brass, veterans braying, and wars for corporate profits, he was nonetheless proud of his training in the 'light field artillery'.

Similarly suspicious of my 'revolutionary politics' in 1961 he would peruse much of my left wing literature as dizzy designs on disaster. The Socialist Party press he dismissed as whining liberals. The Revolutionary Fourth International press he thought too radical. He preferred the Communist Party press because it had a Sports page. He was aesthetically conservative... wistful about the past and dreamed of having his own farm.

My including him and Mom as partners in the purchase of additional acreage...to our 'Gloryville' farm was partial achievement of that dream. And he was fondly proud of the corporate title '*Morgans* Morgans Inc.' we gave for the purpose and loan arrangement at the Bank. (We were raising Morgan horses) Strangely he never blamed the divorce for its progressive endangerment and later loss of the farm. As a father holds a son accountable I think he always accounted its loss as my failure.

My mother was different. She was patiently loyal to her son against all odds, against all others. She felt equally responsible to critically correct, scold, verbally and/or physically punish him for any mistake he made or imagined making. When first hearing of the divorce, that is, divorce action of my wife leaving our home with the children and that I was broken up about it... she phoned. In speaking with her my voice caught in a kind of sob. There was a brief silence, and then me sainted mother, gathering her full hearts sympathy replied, "You are soft Tom, soft as a Turd" repeating as if I could have missed it "SOFT AS A TURD TOM!! Now straighten up! Suck it up and git after your life! I didn't raise no sob sister. Git after things!"

I'd been getting after them ever since. But when she called I had to hang up laughing. I laughed til I roared and wept at the same time. What mother on earth could be so capable of such an outrageous attempt to encourage her child. What a hardass. Me sainted, tender hearted mother; hard as nails. Contrarily to Dad, Moms persona moved obliquely to historical expectation. A coal miner's daughter fresh off the farm she was militant about never going back. "Surround me with cement", she'd preach "how Godliness was close to cleanliness".

An archetypal peasant whose sharp wit could not conceive of capitalist profit or collective effort. When my father retired from the milk truck and bought a little neighborhood tavern she was adamant that he could not make money unless he was actually, physically there… there at the tavern… himself working. That he could hire a night shift bartender and still turn a profit was too abstractly suspect for her to try and understand.

"It's like a field without a farmer, a court without a lawyer" she'd argue against "giving any shifts away."

Dreams like conscious states are real only as long as they last. I woke abruptly as Dad bumped his big 'Suburban' into the carport of my parents' home. I always thought of it as their home. I'd only lived in it for months not years. Dad designed and began building it in 1957. Moved in October of '59. I was already away at IU in Bloomington. The house was impressively formed out of my father's interiority. He'd looked at smaller Danish modern designs and tripled the size. It was a flat roofed, redwood in some respects heavy version of the fifties vision of the future. But it was wainscoted with Indiana limestone and had that unmistakable mark of my father's solid consciousness. I called it, Morgan Soviet Modern. For three decades it would serve as the central home place for them, their children and grandchildren.

Mother met us at the kitchen door with her usual greeting of "wipe your feet!" She had warmed up, that is to say re-boiled their earlier supper for me. Mom had several variations of severely boiled suppers. They all tasted the same. Flavor and nutrients were boiled away. As a kid I used to butter my beef so I could taste it. During the British manipulated holocaust, the so-called Irish potato famine people died of scurvy even when eating a head of cabbage a day. I think I know why. But she had pie! Delicious black raspberry pie. Baked that morning and refrigerated all day. We ate it cold with strong hot coffee.

Mom talked about everything. Dad said little. I was falling asleep in my coffee. It was too late to phone the children.

"You guys still get up early?"

"At six on work days..." they practically answered together.

Week days were still called work days at their house.

"I'll rise the same", I said with some tired enthusiasm. "I can phone the kids before they go to school, so I'd best get to bed." Mother's eyebrows indicated the clean sheets issue and I assured her I was taking a shower first. We kissed each other good night.

Exhausted, I slept strangely. Not so much drifting in and out of sleep but... drifting none the less, from one dream image to the next. Similar to night terrors but without the terror, I was aware of being separate from the images and attempted a 'kind of prayer over' to mitigate the fearful ones. I was surprisingly patient. I was learning... impatience always escalates pain, fear, and unpleasantness. I was bringing my conscious faith into my unconscious dreams; training my consciousness to take charge of the unconscious.

Mencken's famous "faith may be defined briefly as an illogical belief in the occurrence of the improbable" is cynical. And cynics are those who know the price of everything and the value of nothing. I knew now with Parkhurst that faith requires "a kind of winged intellect" and with the Bard "that there are not tricks in plain and simple faith."

Waking to my mother's touch and gentle voice, being conscious seemed good before the first light of day. Dad was already up, dressed, and directed toward the door. He came in, looked me in the eye and asked, "Will we see you and the kids tonight?"

I answered, "Probly not Pop. We're visiting the farm today. I've got to check on things. We'll be back later."

Not approving of my answer, he quietly looked at me. When he saw I appreciated his not asking me 'later when?', he sighed. My father sighed not at me but...for me...taking his leave, kissing my forehead, walking directly...out the door.

Mother was typically flying about the house, hurrying me by example. Stopping for an instant, or as she would say "instamatically", looked with untold sympathy...looked lovingly at her only son and said, "Hurry and call the children. I expect you've got lots to do today." She spoke almost mournfully like she knew... But I knew she didn't... it's just... that she always, in general, thought I was headed for the cross...or the gallows.I phoned the children. Their mother answered sharply, "We expected a call last night." A sharp request for an apology... I wasn't up for it.

Coldly polite I asked to speak to the children.

"I'll need to speak with you after them. O.K.?"

"O.K."

Then Bethany's voice showered timbres of "Papa, papa" in sounds so dear to me it made the room radiant with a joy I cannot describe. An assurance that this is what life is all about... to be with... to be there... for my children whether or not I could reconcile... restore their parental home. Then Eliot's voice..."Hey pop. Hey Papa...I got so much to tell you," he started over and over "we goin to the farm? Gonna swim in feesh crick, catch some fish. Ride my pony? Hey Papa...when you comin here?"

"I'm at Grandmas! Didn't Mama or Bethany tell you? I'm getting you and your sister after school today..."

Mama got back on the phone! "Are you sure you will pick them up promptly at three p.m.? Not a second later! You are not on their parent list so you can't go in the school building. I think you should stay off school property too. Just meet them at the north east edge of the playground on Sixth Street. You know by the Deb's house."

"I know... I know."

"Don't be late. Promptly at three p.m.!"

"I'll be there early..."

"I've got to go...kids have to get to school!"

I could hear them yelling "bye Papa, bye bye" as she hung up. She was in a hurry for her future. She would get it soon enough. I would give it to her. Ordinarily she would require more details from me. Exactly where I was taking them and phone numbers accordingly. She was pre-occupied. She'd be twatterpated until we were long... long gone.

As per usual from our attempts at phone conversations I partially collapsed. Quietly my mother brought me more strong coffee. She served it in the moustache mug[1] I'd given Dad years ago for a birthday present. Noticing I recognized it, she said, "He didn't keep his whiskers for very long". She pronounced *whiskers* disagreeably while she looked at mine. She sat beside me at table; with a cup and saucer of coffee her eyes snapping in early sunlight, partially scolding; joshing as always affectionately accepting all the contradictions of her issue in life.

"Will you take the children to mass?" she asked.

"Yes...I will."

"Many preachers go to mass...?"

"Not near enough", I joked back.

In all her multiple disapprovals, my Catholic mother never disapproved of my being a Protestant minister. Her sister, my very Catholic Aunt Mary pronounced to my cousins, "I'll bet he makes a good minister!" It was my Protestant relatives who always disapproved of my not being the right kind of Protestant.

In the few quiet times we ever had there was an innate mystery around and about my mother. Something about all that harsh tenderness harkened back past the Hoosier haze of her life to Celtic mists and the ancient tradition of intuitive intellect. Not ignorant, but uneducated (leaving school at twelve), and unravaged by modernization, her mind intact for imaginative possibilities but grounded in natural boundaries before utter negation. Passionate thought never hindering thoughtful tenderness.

"You and the kids... be here for supper?", she appealed more than asked. Then meekly added... "Eliot loves my salmon patties." I remembered a million Friday nights gagging on the canned fish and cardboard Mother called salmon patties.

"Please don't cook on our account," I spat out quickly. "I tell you what. I'll pick up a tray of deep fried fish at The Bramble Bush. You fix the trimmins... you know salad... and"

"And pie!", she said. "Fresh blueberry pie." "Blueberry?" I questioned. "Where'd you get blueberries?" Blueberry pie...much hailed

---

1   Moustache mug: Coffee mug with crossbar to keep moustaches out of beverage

by hoosiers and not readily available in south or central Indiana. Michigan blueberries are the most desirable.

"Neighbor Georgia phoned yesterday. Her son brought her almost a peck of Michigan blueberries. The title *'Neighbor Georgia'* for Georgia Hauser went clear back to high school days. I'd had two different girlfriends...both named Georgia. Mom started calling her friend and next door neighbor... *Neighbor Georgia* to distinguish between them.

"I'll bake a pie. Maybe two of e'm today. Have one of e'm cold for you tonight (She knew I loved *cold* fruit pie) Your Dad will like this plan."

So, it was re-decided since speaking with Dad... we'd be there for supper. In an improved mood, Mom poured us two more cups of strong black coffee. It was turning into a leisurely morning. One of the few we'd ever had. She reported on her good health and Dads. And that they slept well. I reported how I'd finally gotten over the night terrors and was sleeping... and dreaming well. I asked about her dreaming. She answered instead about her mother's dreams and how "they portended toward things...not crystal ball bull roar pre-dictions but you know portended... toward the signs and shadows of things... Aw..." she'd joke about "Queen Maeve and the fairy spirits of dreams and when we were little we'd search for fairy rings, those darker rings of grass, in the pasture and Dad would tell us came from horses manure instead of fairies. Mother would laugh at that and say they probably come from a little bit of both."

I wanted to explain to her my interest in the Jungian concept of dreams and the principle of 'Synchronicity' when...I was dismissed with "I think you're thinking too much about these things," she said. "What exactly is your plan? Men have to have plans as well as dreams. Your Dad is never happy unless he has a plan. You know, something to look forward to..."

Neither one of us dared speak about divorced or destroyed dreams. She wanted to hear fresh new plans for and from her son.

"I have new plans Mom, I tried to assure her. I've been working hard on them for me and the children. They just have to be secret for awhile."

"Not political stuff again?", she feared.

"No Mom."

"Have those Bureau Bums been bothering you again?"

She meant FBI agents (Bureau Bums) who systematically harassed us back in the sixties. She'd turned the hose on the last one who'd come creeping around.

"No Mom."

"Well, that's good. Saying your prayers?"

"Yes Mom… " With that I knew I was finally and completely dismissed. When a kid at home, she'd say "Saying your prayers?…then "OK, go out and play." I half expected her to say that now. When I was seven or eight and seriously pondering the "Lord's Prayer" I had asked her about the tense intended in the word trespass, that is, 'as we forgive those who *trespass* against us' surely meant the past i.e. *trespassed* not the present i.e. who was still *trespassing.* I reckoned we were to forgive those who had wronged us not some trespasser who was still over on us. My busy and perplexed Mom thought about it for a few exasperated seconds and then said, "You're a wyrd kid Tommy; go out and play."

Looking forward to dinner now, I phoned the 'Bramble Bush' after taking time to admire the milk bucket of Michigan berries Neighbor Georgia had brought in. At Moms behest I took a 'clinical' look at Georgia; asking her how she slept, cried, and handled anger. Neighbor Georgia suffered major depression and was seasonally hospitalized. She complained 'they' were still overmedicating her. I advised her to consult her attending physician like she would the mechanic for her car, not like some exalted movie star. Imagine… the mechanic will see you now… do not question what he does or bills for. If you're feeling too doped by his prescription call him up and complain about it. Mother then reassured her friend, "You can trust Tom on this…he knows all about craziness."

The 'Bramble Bush' Tavern and Grill was founded by the Conroy family back in the twenties and catered to Irish railroaders coming from Michigan to Terre Haute. Until Vatican II it had been *the* place for Friday fish. The Twenty First Ecumenical Council of the Vatican was convened in Rome for liturgical reform and Christian Unity. Latin was replaced in the liturgy with "the vernacular". "Too bloody vernacular!" according to Mom. She was still extremely pissed that the requirement to abstain from, to fast from meat on Friday was dropped. "C'mon Mom", I would tease, "half the time you would forget and we'd be spared those awful salmon patties."

"I know... I know" she'd counter...eyes flashing..."all those years...all that guilt...for nothing."

On the phone I ordered a dozen fish sandwiches with onions, lettuce, and tomato and six cold bottles of Blatz to be picked up at 3:30p.m. at 'the Bush'. Also I phoned the rental car service in 'Twelve Points'[1] walked there around 1:30p.m. and rented a car I could return at the airport Saturday.

---

1   Twelve Points: Olde North Side business district in Terre Haute

X

At 2:45p.m. I pulled up to the northeast curb of Indiana State University Laboratory School. Originally the "lab" for would be 'educators' to observe the high standard education of children and youth. It also functioned as the drain and depository of poor inner city kids. My ex and the children lived closer to St. Patricks' Elementary. Her colleagues, and teaching nuns (Sisters of Providence) were all shocked I vetoed St. Patrick's because I knew the Associate Pastor there to be an active predator and pedophile.

My divorce decree had granted me "joint legal" custody, a term mainly given to make the loser of real, physical custody feel better but does concede veto power to school and/or church attendance of the custodial children.

Not yet 3p.m. some kids were getting out early, girls milling about, boys playing catch with a football. They all looked like tough little urchins.

I stood on the end sidewalk watching them. Then the bell rang and the far entrance steps flooded with noisy, skipping and running boys and girls. Mine walked sedately in the middle of the throng. Hyper Eliot was restrained by Bethany holding his hand. That is, until he spied the other boys throwing the football. Breaking loose from Bethany he ran at right angles from the boy with the ball, yelling, "Hey Eddy, hey Eddy, pass me the ball!"

Eddy, the ball carrier seemed taller and skinnier than the other kids, hollered back, "Hey Eliot, hey Eliot you red headed li'l sprout. You think you can catch it?"

"I kin catch it!" El answered. Eddy threw it over El's head and when he turned to chase it down he saw me...

"Pop...Papa!," he screamed. Running now Bethany joined in shrieking a high falsetto Papa --------- Louder than the milling crowd, all the other kids stopped for a moment to look at us. Eliot got to me first with a $2^{1/2}$ foot jump into my arms kissing me on the cheek while I kissed him over the top of his head. Then while embracing Bethany came this hissing sound from Eddy. Just ten feet from us he'd come to retrieve his football. "Kissy, kissy, kissy!" he teased. Two other boys behind him joined in, "Kissy, kissy Eliot. Kissy, kissy, kissy!" they chanted.

The exultant joy on Eliot's face was wiped away… replaced not by embarrassment or shame but by a nonplussed humiliated look of total confusion as to what he should do or ask me to do… Bye God, I knew what to do and took off after Eddy. I chased the loathsome little shit clear across the playground and half way back. Fast Eddy indeed!

The crowd of children were shocked silent to see a strange man chasing down one of their fellow pupils. I caught him by the back of his collar, swinging him down around on the ground; holding him by his ears I kissed the bejeezus out of him over his face and ears…I thought about biting his ears or at least pulling his ears but, I didn't.

The boys closest to us were first horrified, then quickly ignited with good and vindictive humor. Rolling with mirth they could barely chant but managed… "Kissy Eddy, kissy, kissy, kissy." Their laughter was contagious and caught on quickly with the other groups and clumps of kids. Soon it seemed the whole school crowd was laughing not so much at Eddy as with us. Eliot and Bethany were delighted at such appreciation as we sped away from what was sure to be an investigation.

XI

Picked up and paid for our beer and sandwiches, then circled back to Saint Benedicts…the kids glad we were going to church. St. Bens was open so we didn't have to go next door for a key. The altar society gals were working inside so church doors would be unlocked through the 5p.m. evening mass. Church doors used to be open all the time. Insurance companies! God damned parasites!

As always Bethany and Eliot asked that we sit back by 'the Jackstock'. Of all the splendid stained glass panels at this old church our favorite was back in the northwest corner. It was of 'the flight to Egypt'…Mary, Joseph, and their donkey. It reminded them of their pet donkey…a sweet roan jennet, born on the farm, they affectionately called 'Mary Blanche'. I'd named the ass after my mother in law.

We knelt and prayed together. Then we just held on to each other looking up and around… soaking up the sacred atmosphere of the place. All my cousins, my sister, myself all christened here. My parents, sister, aunts and uncles married here… soon to be buried here. Perhaps the only continuity of value… in this fractious life.

It is like a prayer just looking at St. Benedicts. I loved looking at it inside or outside. I used to drive out of my way in winter traffic just to look at it. The stone strip of its northwest cornice crowning an entablature above a frieze you couldn't quite make out in the falling snow. Then later an overhanging mass of snow kneeling above the precipice… drifting in to you the way a memory is formed. An architectural profile both convex and concave; dialectical cymatium of the Holy Spirit.

We stayed almost an hour absorbing through the very interstices of our being safe together at St. Benedicts. Early arrivals for 5p.m. mass were coming through the sacristy, past the Pieta, and sitting across from us. Eliot had wandered down front to help the altar society ladies decorate. He'd recognized one as a friend of his Great Aunt Mary. My Aunt Mary was the veteran, and accomplished altar decorator.

I whistled for Eliot, who came running and the three of us left through the side door. I belonged to, yet was never really a part of what I so yearned for in the Church and for my children. Like James Jones', Private Pruett and the army. In 'From Here to Eternity' protagonist Pruett is not rebelling against the army, he is mounting a one man revolution to be accepted in his vision of all the army can be. But... twas ever thus. In the 1640's poet Corneille was writing magnificently of the conflicts between love and honor. While love may be honorable, conflict remains inevitable. In his 'Polyeucte' the conflict is resolved tragically. Four hundred years later Jones is ending similar tales too similarly. His protagonists killed not in rebellion against community, but in their attempts to restore it. Sure and I liked reading about Corneille in 1640's Paris and Jones in 1950's Paris, (Illinois) and Terre Haute but I wanted desperately to write a different story with my life. No tragedian me, I wanted to win. The 'Way of God' to prevail.

We won a great dinner and evening at Mom and Dads. Bethany said Grace, and Eliot entertained us with cherubic conversation. Everyone loved the deep fried fish sandwiches. Dad and I especially...joked how we'd dodged those awful salmon patties. Mother Vi, always able to laugh at herself still asserted at least Eliot appreciated her salmon patties. We all looked at Eliot... who just grinned. It was Good Friday. We left in the dark.

Hurtling along old 46 at night was eerie for Beth and me as we passed the site of our previous accident... our wreck that past summer. "Is that it?" she asked. I nodded turning to look at my dear daughter's face still full of shattered glass. She scooted closer as I drove faster home.

And the farm... 'Gloryville Farm' was still home to all three of us... the kids wide awake as we pulled in the dark lane... my headlights on the stone marker I'd commissioned ten years ago. The 'Agnus Dei' image of a militant lamb and Pennant was carved in the stone face bordered by the letters O.A.M.G.D. for "Omnia Ad Majorem Gloriam Dei" 'All To The Greater Glory Of God'. It wasn't hard to think of the farm as a 'sign' for all of that in its best days. Poetess Bonnie Lind of Glenhill Publishing described it as "a sanctuary of work and intellection much sought out by known and not-so-known literati, art-

THOMAS G. MORGAN   127

ists, and thinkers in the late 60's and 70's. Ron Pickup, the Publisher of Glenhill Press, spoke of it as "that cultural haven of the complete pastoral arts, near Freedom, Indiana, was a poem of Tom's you could walk around in."

"A poem you could walk around in...", I remembered so many moments here...before and after the children. A seiche of memories in seconds...I had to slow way down to sort out before crossing the bridge my friend Max had built for us. I'm no carpenter, I thought, nor a lot of other things, skills, abilities, talents, virtues... that had collectively, contributed to the Gloriam of Gloryville Farm. There was *her* hospitality, warm abundanza for all visitors. The serious 'production research of quality livestock'; hybrid cross development of the 100 ewe sheep flock, importation and marketing of the first welsh black cattle in the country, which had grown to 70 head, progress in developing a Blackhawk strain of Morgan horses that would breed true to color, type, and size, early success at crossing large so-called English Shepherds (also known as American Farm Shepherds) with Border Collies to improve size, capability, eye, and calmness in stock dogs.

Gloryville Farm had also functioned as a center for coordinating church support for the (N.F.O.) National Farmers Organizations, their withholding actions and aid to inner city congregations and parishes. It had become a center for Marxist-Religious Dialogue. Amish, Buddhist-Hindu-Ashramic, Catholic, Protestant, and budding Islamic communities met here comparing their moral compass with each other in the fractious present with clear and not so clear designs for a Marxist informed communal future. All gone now... I pondered...I wondered.

More importantly I remembered a happy contented family with well behaved children and adults lovingly sharing an active concern for each other and others around them. Not all gone...bye God if I could help it.

Still too early to show early signs of neglect...the house, barns, sheds, and fence looked fine in the moonlight as we got out of the rental car and walked toward the gate. "Where's Gabie dog?" the kids asked. Our main family dog was 'Gabriel Oakes', a border collie farm shepherd cross. I'd placed him with an Anglican Priest I knew who had a farm in brown county and was a good dog man. I assured the children we'd get him back as soon as we all got back to the farm. Then there was growling from the porch as Clover (Gabie's x Kuvasz) daughter barked alarm at us coming through the gate. She ran at us barking until with embarrassed joy she scent recognized who we were. In canine celebration she jumped and sprang around us licking and nuzzeling the children. They begged she come inside with them as the Brawlesons met us at the door. I approved notifying Father Chuck Brawleson with a nod he agreeably returned. I had counseled Chuck when he was slightly homicidal after his wife had left him for another man. I'd helped him get the Town Marshall job clear up in Cayuga. He didn't move there and tried to commute. It didn't work out. Now he worked at semi-occasional rent-a-cop 'security' jobs. His kids Timmy 15, Sylvie 14, Butch 12, and Hank 7 were all inside calling out to Bethany and El. They'd prepared homemade ice cream and were eager to share it. I passed. Bethany politely ate little. Eliot tasted it…gaked! and said "It's terrible!" Everyone laughed and I frowned El into finishing his plate.

All the boys then set to…playing with Hank's hot wheels noisily under the dining room table. Bethany helped Sylvie finish their kitchen dishes while Chuck and I retired to the parlor. He offered me a snort from his jug of Kentucky mule. This white mule didn't kick so much as tear. As the jug reached your scent path, before you even taste it you could sense what felt like brain cells tearing off your occipital lobe.

Chuck said he wished we'd came earlier. They all had to turn in soon because he had to work in Bloomington this Saturday and they'd be rising early. He had to drop his kids off at their mothers in the opposite direction. He waited for me to offer taking care of them tomorrow. I didn't. I did decide …to tell him why.

"I've an early flight out tomorrow," I said making the sign….*that* was confidential. He nodded understanding and asked if there was anything he could do to help?

"You already have," I answered, "just keep looking after things around here." Almost surprising myself I added, "I might be returning this summer."

The plan was congealing to [1]win custody of my children [2]get assigned to circuit ride churches close to the farm and raise my kids and consciousness, however poor, here on the farm. I had arranged care of all the livestock until the grass of summer. The horses I had sent upon his request to Benny Williams. A good horseman he'd always admired my mares and had tried to buy them. A fine harness man he could show them at the spring horse shows, and bring them home to summer pastures. Benny was the nephew of ol' Russ Williams who gave me my first job, the summer I was eleven.

In order *not* to talk about my immediate intentions... to Chuck and because he said he was ready to move to a house his brother owned in Bloomington once school was out... I traded some tales with Chuck while we tore off some more of his white mule.

He wanted to talk about his prowess in bar fights which I found interesting but unclear toward any point. I was encouraging him toward union factory work instead of chasing cop jobs. He'd enjoyed excessively being an M.P. in his army years. It made him excessively hostile to rank and file folk and cop eager to serve the managerial class.

I told him the tale of my first experience with management. I'd hired on for the summer as a picker at Russ Williams Produce farm. Russ produced cherries, berries, and currants. He knew my Dad and was glad to hire me. I was eleven. At 7a.m. I'd ride my bike from 1810 S. 26th Street all the way east to Fruitridge, then north to Williams's farm. Russ was a sweet man with always an encouraging word... never pushing you in your work whether in the trees or on the ground. He became ill that summer, was ordered bedfast, and appointed his young nephew Rusty to be overseer i.e. to manage the farm labor. He was a pushy li'l punk not much taller than me at 15 years old going on 10. Afraid of the adult male pickers he'd be more whiney, than pushy with them. He was rude and pushy toward the women and nobody liked that. He saved his worst pushiness for those younger than himself. I was the youngest. Whether I was on a ladder in the cherry trees, workin' around the briars of a raspberry bush or hunkerin' down over currants he was on me. My pal Joey Withrow told him, "You're kinda Pushy, ain't ya?" Rusty replied calmly, "Of course I'm pushy. That's my job. I'm the Pusher. I am management." When I heard that, lines were drawn. I bided my time.

One day up in a cherry tree which I was being so careful to pick clean… We earned 50¢ for every $2^{1/2}$ gallon bucket picked full of cherries… standing on the ladder all day you might be able to fill 4 buckets full… Rusty jumped my tail that I was "hurrying through this tree just sos I could move to one fuller with cherries."

I climbed down two rungs of the ladder, bent down, looked him in the eye and asked,

"Do you want me to work slower, pick less, or completely clean the tree?!"

He abruptly turned aside and walked on… not owing me a reply. I told Joey at noon, I should have said, I wished I said,

"Of course I'm hurryin'. That's my job. We're Pickers. We pick the fruit you just frump around about." We all laughed it needed said.

The next few days Rusty made a concerted effort to be nicer to me, Joe, and the other younger guys. But he still pushed. In his way he wanted to be friends.

At the end of the day at 5p.m. we'd carry what was left of our produce downhill, (the dark Bing Cherry, we still called Chinese Cherries back then, and marvelous black raspberries before the big invented Boysenberry bollicksed up the berry market) that is, what hadn't yet been picked up by the farm wagon. The farm wagon was pulled by a team of mules. Russ kept two teams, that is, 4 nearly identical bay mules. He directed they be rotated on alternate days. One team was always resting while the other team worked. So there was always two mules whose fence was 110 volts directly from the hotwired fuse box forming a full quarter amp charge from their shed. We would routinely set down our buckets and baskets of fruit by their shed, get a long drink from the well, take a pee and then take our fruit all the way downhill past the house to the fruit stand. Mrs. Williams would tally our pickings and pay us cash daily.

One day after our long drink, we jokingly but literally were having peeing contests toward the shed. Seeing this, Rusty good naturedly but with great seniority announced "you little squirts aren't big enough to piss far…" Unzipping his fly he flung out his phallus which at first seemed shockingly equine in proportion until I realized he was uncircumcised, like my Dad. My own stream safely depleted I challenged Management by turning toward the mules and saying, "No way you can piss over the fence into their corral!"

Posing himself like some kind of crazed fireman dancer…he pissed way up and over the hotwire. The mules jumped as he guffawed at us… mistaking our vengeful grins for smiles of admiration… his stream of urine quickly weakened and fell upon the wire. Whack! Aiee… he was knocked back and down, his torso still churning like the voltage was still at him. Help…help he cried. Being farm labor we felt dismissed down the hill to be paid the fruits of our labor. We left Management to help itself.

He washed for an hour and was fine. Farm labor was not pushed for the rest of the summer.

Chuck laughed a little. He didn't get it. All the boys laughed a lot. They'd slowly come in to sit on the floor by us and they got it entirely. In the spirit of getting it, Timmy, the oldest Brawleson boy raised his voice to ask his sister… Sylvie and Bethany were now joining us… "What's the name of that big shot, big farmers kid on the school bus?" She answered,

"That's Billy Effingham, and he's a sweet boy."

Timmy harrumphed, "You're sweet on all the boys. I tell you that Effingham kid, he's 15 and acts like that big shot kid in your story."

Then deviously, "You know what he said about you Tom?" He had all the kids attention. His Dad had gotten up to go to the bathroom. "I don't know the boy," I told Tim.

"But he says he knows about you. He says he heard you
killed a man and buried him out back in the sink holes.

You know what I told him?" He was asking everyone. "I told him if olde Tom killed somebody I was sure it was somebody who needed killin." Then we all laughed albeit a little nervously. I patiently explained to Timmy with all the other kids listening that I didn't hold with killin.

That was a sin except in self defense… but I appreciated Timmy's loyalty under the circumstances…The kids laughed and cheered Timmy.

Chuck came out of the bathroom. I went in. Like the rest of the house it was being kept fairly clean. Eyeing the shelves I noticed a large jar which I examined. It was saltpeter. Gawd… potassium nitrate…he must be having colt trouble toward his young filly. They'd all be better off in town with neighbors…not way out here in the country… in our country. Before turning in I told Chuck we would be moving back the week schools out and wished him Godspeed and good luck in town. The Brawleson males slept in the two bedrooms. Sylvie had a bed in my old study and we bedded down in the living room. With fairly clean sheets I made the kids a bed on the fold-out sleeper sofa. With an army blanket I stretched out on the adjoining couch. We said our prayers and were fast asleep.

About 3a.m. I woke to hear someone slowly walking in the closed in porch. Lying still I listened carefully. The slow steps were sneaking up the stairs into the house. A lanky figure appeared in the dark between the dining room and where we slept. Then with a small step the ominous figure entered our room. Too dark to make him out it seemed he was being stealthily still 'to case the joint' to figure out exactly where he was. He continued in toward my children's bed taking tiny stealthy baby steps. There was only a coffee table between him and my sleeping children. Pretending sleep I planned to strike him over the head with the small telephone stand beside me…when his shin bone cracked into the coffee table. "Excuse me," the figure said aloud, backed up and then bumped into the table again. This time the loud "excuse me" was clearly in Timmy's voice. He was sleepwalking. I guided him back to bed.

After a few hours we all woke again to hear noise in the kitchen. Sylvie and Chuck were frying store bought 'mush' with black strap molasses cold milk, and black coffee for breakfast. We all ate heartily. Even Beth. Chuck growled a lot to get the boys ready to leave. We were glad to be alone by 7:30a.m.

Once alone, Beth and El just wandered about the house and asked to do the same outdoors… reclaiming the place. It was a sunny but nippy morning. I made sure the kids were dressed warm and we set out together.

I hadn't limed the hill pasture behind our house last summer so it was covered with high winter sage. Eliot wanted to explore this new phenomena i.e. run around in it. Bethany and I accompanied him up the hill. We paused a moment by the Belltree, then continued til we reached the high sage pasture. Eliot loved it, running in and out of the high grass over his head. This excited Clover who ran ahead of El through this neglected jungle of sage. Bethany was delighted. Now's the time, I thought. I will share with them…the plan.

We called for Eliot to come in. Of course he didn't. "C'mon El," I cried out, "there might be cinnamon bears in there!" That brought him running. Our Hoosier neighbors were always reporting the rumors of someone spotting a bear or a panther. Like the neighbors little El loved to speculate and gossip about these exciting dangers. It was all probable Hoosier hysteria and I would always assure him there was nothing so dangerous in our woods. He preferred to think there might be. Right after he ran back into my arms today… a huge and loud fracas broke out far back in the sage. Clover had jumped some kind of critter and was volubly barking her attack. Probably a possum or skunk. A young green dog she couldn't have roared louder if it had been a grizzly.

Whatever it was fought back enough to scare Clover who suddenly yelped into canine terrors of yelping, and yapping. I figured something had scratched her nose but turned to Eliot teasing and said, "Maybe there is a bear in there. You kids stay here where it's safe and I'll go try and save Clover."

Quickly disappearing into the sage, I ran about forty yards to where Clover came wagging her tail up to me completely unhurt. Calling her to follow me, keeping her close, I ran forty yards further up the hill to where I knew my voice would echo and carry clearly down to Beth and El.

"Damnation!"…I hollered, "it is a bear! 'For Sure!' And a big one at that. Look out Clover! Look out Bear. Get off my Dog! Why you damn bear…Ow…Ow… ow Aiee" I fell whamp! and Silent! Clover nestled with me on the ground. Silence. So silent you could hear a faint breeze through the top of the winter sage. Then it started. Such wailing. Bethany was constant without words. Eliot's wailing included words, "Aaaah aaah. Everything happens to me! Aaah. Now I got no papa! Aaah."

Clover and I came smiling down the hill. My children's tears displaced with oh so welcome laughter. Decades later we still joshingly remind Eliot of his grieving egotism that day. Or…for a six year old was it ego strength?

That day we just celebrated his words as humorous. Even at his young age El could laugh at himself as well as others. Back in the kitchen I found a canister of Ovaltine I'd stashed in the far corner of our cabinets last summer. I made hot chocolate served as Captain Midnight's favorite. My kids liked to hear about the radio programs we used to listen to when I was their age. There was 'Tom Mix', 'Captain Midnight', 'Gangbusters', 'The Fat Man', 'The Big Story', 'Mr. District Attorney,' 'Lux Radio Theatre', and the scary 'Inner Sanctum'. My favorite was the Monday night Radio Theater Movie. We'd (Mom, Dad, my sister and me) listened to all three of the classic John Ford Westerns with John Wayne. 'Fort Apache', 'She Wore a Yellow Ribbon' and 'Rio Grande', voices coming right out of our Stromberg-Carlson Radio and Record Player Dad had got at a closing sale with dozens of Tommy Dorsey, Artie Shaw, and Louis Prima records. John Wayne's radio voice was my favorite, that is, next to Ronald Coleman's. I practiced imitating their voices, all the while aspiring to act out in real life adventures which as mere actors they had to settle for in scripts.

As we drank the Ovaltine, I told Beth and El how I had saved Ovaltine wrappers as a kid to send in for a genuine Captain Midnight Secret De-coder. With this device you could enter numbers given at the end of the radio program and it would de-code them into the secret message Captain Midnight was sending directly to you, his listeners. After painstakingly applying this contraption to the numbers given and writing down each designated letter for each number… a discernible message began to appear… D . R… I…N… K…M… O…R… E… O… V…al T .. IN ..E . Damn! It only said DRINK MORE OVALTINE.

It wasn't a secret message! It was a damned advertisement!

The kids were enjoying their Ovaltine. They didn't laugh much at my 'secret message' story. I think they'd probably heard me tell it before. Probably several times. Eliot said, "Hey Pa, you remember when you told us Ovaltine had caused the ovals under your eyes?", he pulled his cheeks down under his eyes... at that we all did laugh.

"But seriously now..." I began... holding their hands I told them the plan. Their response was...both of their responses were partisan and matter of fact.

"Hey Pa, Eliot reminded, you'd already told us this before you left..."

"I don't remember...?"

"Yes, you did Papa," Bethany joined in. "Don't you remember? Right before you left. We were in summer Montessori School out at St Mary's'. You picked us up and were letting us take turns sitting on your lap guiding the truck around the back roads behind the campus."

As sharp and precise as a scalpel stroke was the diction of my daughters thought. She always amazed her brother and me...describing exactly what we were thinking and/or couldn't remember.

"You told us", she continued, "that as soon as you could arrange it you'd take us to see California before we resettled on the farm with or without Mama. And if she wouldn't come home to the farm we'd be able to visit her plenty anyhow."

"Did I say...?" foggy in the delirium of those days, I remember talking to them that day but I couldn't remember...well the truth must be...that plan of the many tearing at my brain back then had crystalized into *the* plan.

"Bethany, Eliot... my dear children. Are you solid on this? Mama won't like it. The police may not like it? Who knows what the courts gonna say? But it's high time [1])we had your California vacation, [2]) asked the court for custody, [3])and came home to Gloryville Farm."

Bethany followed Eliot with Hurrahs! They went out and found their donkey and Eliot's pony Rex in the northwest pasture...said hi, g'bye and see you later; kissed Clover good bye and we prayed our farewells to the farm once again by the 'Agnus Dei' stone. Bethany led us in the Lord's Prayer and told Eliot Thomas Aquinas about his namesakes prayer I'd mentioned earlier.

There are so many variables, so many details beyond our, that is, my mortal ability to see to...I'd said we should pray the Thomistic Prayer. St. Thomas Aquinas, centuries ago, I told them had raided Aristotle's thoughts on anxiety, Christianized them into a strong three punch prayer [1]It is *logical* to give to God what is beyond our best ability. [2]While upsetting to religious people busily trying to help God...He does not need our help...we need His...so, we should *Faithfully* leave with Him what we have *logically* given Him and not try to help Him out. [3]Then *logically* and *faithfully* we can center down with *certainty* that God will give us adequate temperament to deal with whatever the hell happens.

Eliot Thomas Aquinas Morgan and Bethany Kate Morgan understood most and would come to understand every nuance of that prayer in the months ahead. We sped on together toward the airport and our afternoon flight. We sang 'California, Here We Come' all the way there.

XII

On the plane the children chattered a bit about the magic of this flight…
that we'd actually step off of it into California…then settled into the
glow of our company together…then into sleep. Half on my lap and in
my arms, the soft roar of the 707's engine determined our delegated
direction, I relaxed into that direction knowing the flight of this big bird
was unlike the bird of Proverbs who strays from its nest as I had strayed
from where I belonged. I belonged beside my children wherever that
was…not two thousand miles nor every other weekend away.

Light was even different around them. It emanated from Bethany's
smile and Eliot's laughter through my perception out to… others. In
that light or just thinking about it I loved all children. Was that the
Christ light?, I wondered. The teachings of Jesus to love all others?
What Dostoyevsky called the "harsh and dreadful" teaching of love
when we think of the adults in this world.

I looked around at those adults I could see on the plane, and then
back at my peacefully sleeping children. Maybe I could do this. I
thought of the many human kindnesses I'd known. I valued them more
now having severely experienced their opposite. Human unkindness,
hatefulness, cruelties, vicious racism, selfishness, exploitiveness, rude
disgusting, betrayals of virtue and nature. To get past all that and love
others as sons and daughters of Our Father in Heaven. That was the
"harsh and dreadful" teaching that Dostoyevsky and the rest of us
struggle toward.

If the God like man from Nazareth in His humanness suffered every
temptation of our species…*not* just the ones we normally think about
but the outrageously, bothersome, obscene, repugnant, contemptuous
and abhorrent ones we've learned all too well are part and parcel of
Humanity without…*without* succumbing to any of them there is hope
for us all safe this side of human nature. Safe in loving forgiveness of
our human behavioral muck, trusting our intuitive insights and faith
for a better life, a better world against all empirical evidence to the

contrary. Compassion then becomes the core of God-consciousness.

I remembered Father Henri Nouwen, a priest from the Netherlands who spoke at a Conference I convened for the I.R.A.[1] at Notre Dame on 'Death and Dying'. He was developing the notion of "like to like" ministry and invited a dying woman from the audience to join the panel of non-dying academic experts on dying. He later wrote "The Wounded Healer"... *the* succinct book on spiritual ministry. How our woundedness becomes a source of life for others and in our helping them our wounds heal. "Compassion," Nouwen writes, "allows one to stand in the midst of people free from conformist forces, able to avoid the distance of pity as well as the exclusiveness of sympathy. Compassion is born when we discover in the center of our own existence, not only that God is God and humans are human, but also that [others] our neighbor really is our follow human being." "This compassion pulls people away from the fearful clique into the larger world where they can see that every human face is the face of a neighbor." Compassion "restores the hope for a future in which the lamb and the lion can lie down together". I went to sleep.

The three of us awoke somewhere over Saint Louis. Eliot had to go to the restroom. In our private language he said, "I have to bump." Inside the restroom, sitting on the commode he worried about 'bumping' over, that is to say, on to St. Louis. He did have cousins there! Amused but seeing the sincerity in his little face I assured him there would be no collateral damage.

Back in our seats I pulled a large photograph from my briefcase I hadn't yet shown the children. It was a picture of Bill Marzetti 'riding' the famous bucking horse named 'Bombs Away'. Eliot got it immediately. To this day he and I will laugh about bombs away over St. Louis.

Before de-planing a matronly looking lady called me aside. "I've been watching you and your children", she said. Then gave me the greatest compliment I'd ever received before or since, "You are a great father...a great parent. God bless you". I thanked her gratefully and authentically pastoral to all human love necessary or not.

De-planing, the kids were more excited than tired and wanted to see the city in evening light. I quickly rented a small car I could return

1   I.R.A.: Institute on Religion and Aging

in Modesto. It was so small Eliot called it a roller skate.

I'd grown accustomed to kvetching about San Francisco's degeneracy so it was refreshing to revisit it through my children's young eyes. I showed them and they saw the 'Paris of the Pacific'. They wanted to see the Golden Gate so we drove near enough for a spectacular view, then trafficed back to North Beach and Chinatown. We dined at Art Sharons[1] favorite place downstairs in Chinatown. For so many meetings I'd been here in the past. Comrades Dan and Mary Alice Styron first brought me here, "In happier times", I almost said to myself... then stopped... thinking when could I ever have been happier than now with my son and daughter.

After dinner we walked around and up the street to Ferlinghettis famous 'City Lights' book store. Bethany loved browsing through all the books. Eliot enjoyed studying all the people. Both of them would run to me when they found a particularly interesting one. I found and bought Ralph Manheim's new translation of Celine's 'Castle to Castle'. Louis Ferdinand's retreat from vanishing political illusions.

I am not broadminded about Fascists but had always admired Celine's skill with the pen. I was curious as to whether his desertion on the Right might be psychologically similar to mine on the Left. Upon leaving we stood outside the stores famous show window where so many literary careers were launched and I told my children that with any luck I would have a book in that window shortly. It was not shortly, and it was not with any luck but within a decade Bethany and Eliot were able to see my book, "Not of Our Time" displayed in the 'City Lights' window.

We bed down in a motel near the Bay Bridge, said our prayers and went sound asleep. Waking to a sunny San Francisco morning we had sweet rolls in the lobby, juice for the kids, and coffee for me before crossing the Bay Bridge and heading home toward the San Joaquin. The kids were eager to see the San Joaquin Valley I had so talked about but knew that today we were first going to Mike's ranch as he'd be home on Sunday. On 580...on east of Dublin into the Livermore Valley we took the Arroyo Road south through Livermore bearing east again to the Mines Road. The Mines Road would climb all the way up

1   Art Sharon: Senior bay area SWP leader.

to the top of the Diablo Hills. That's where Mike's ranch was in what was called the San Antone range. A few years back Mike had been elected President of the San Antone Range Association even though he traded more in land than cattle.

Bethany and Eliot enjoyed the 'out west' scenery. First a few vineyards and tank houses followed by the steep Morgan Territory of pastoral green open range with specks of distant cattle and wild flowers everywhere. The pastoral green stayed constant all the way to the top where the San Antone was lush with long grass. The beauty of the ride was breath taking to me and the kids. I had to remind them and myself this beauty would last only a few months. Most of the year these hills were what Californians call golden and we would describe as straw colored.

As we pulled in Mike's long drive up to their ranch house we first saw a few kids and dogs, then several adults, and finally the whole McNaughton Clan out on the deck to greet us. What a welcome! First came Digger Dog howling his welcome, jumping up and all over El and me. Then there was Mike and Miekija of course, their children Jennifer and Sean; Mike's sister Minnie (Melinda), her husband John, their two grown daughters and son – youngest daughter an evangelical missionary, oldest daughter a cruise ship torch singer, and son a medical student. Also Mike's dad and stepmother were there visiting.

These last years my children had not known many adults except for my parents who approved of their father, let alone were enthusiastic in fondness for him. It's not that their mother's milieu expressed explicit disapproval but children's radar don't miss much. They seemed amazed all these people really liked me. It's an important thing. Children need to see their parents appreciated as they appreciate them. It validates their sense of place. Cognitive assonance. Not cognitive dissonance.

"Hey Preacher!", Mike greeted me, "thought you'd be preaching somewhere on Easter Sunday."

"I intend to….if you'll listen," I quipped back. Everyone…the entire clan were the very soul of hospitality and kindness. Happy Easter greetings and responsory toasts of 'He is Risen'. "Everyone shook hands with me and the children. Knightly…Mike kissed

Bethany's hand. She blushed with appreciation. Eliot then saluted Mike as if they both wore visored armor. We had interrupted their Easter Sunday reunion. They had sat down for dinner. They cleared the deck for us and Miekija set a place for us at the table like she was our country grandma. Real skillet fried chicken, buttermilk biscuits and gravy, mashed potatoes, fresh sweet corn, and tomatoes. Hoosier fare…cut with sparkling California Wine, I thought and said aloud to much applause and more toast making.

I explained to Mike with all listening that there are seven Sundays in the Octave of Easter up to Pentecost Sunday and the return to Ordinary time. They were all invited to next Sundays Post Easter Service followed by a dinner party at Stockton's Tennis Club. More toasts and Mike made a serious one with a wink toward us Morgans. "Here's to friendship and the Holy Spirit. Here's to a quick and speedy… a peaceful return to 'ordinary time'!" He emphasized the last two words.

"How long… how long?" had we lacked the peace of just that… ordinary time. Looking at my little ones I knew they had… we had longed for just such a thing.

"Ordinary time… to poetically dwell…in the possible," I half remembered-imagined lines of Wallace Stevens.[1]

He wrote "It is the philosophers search

For an interior made exterior

And the poets search for the same exterior

made Interior"

I admire how so many Latin Americans recall and recite lines of poetry. I've been accused of writing fragmentary verse. Not true! - but my memory is fragmentary when I attempt to recall poetic lines. I usually remember mere shadows…sun spot glances of the actual line. But I knew Mike's sister Minnie read Stevens…maybe she'd help.

"Not the predicate of bright origin", I began…"not renewed by images of lone wanderers.

To recreate is to use the ancient light

that is , wholly an inner light that shines"

"From the sleepy bosom of the real and recreates

A possible for its possibleness", Minnie achieved, not missing a

1   Wallace Stevens: "An Ordinary Evening in New Haven"

beat she leaned on in to 'Credences of Summer'…

"Like the trumpet of morning

Visibly announced, successor of the invisible."

"Its substitute is stratagem of the spirit", I remembered. Minnie ended with "What is possible", she spoke softly now,

"Replaces what is not."

Whew! What a sister Mike has in that Minnie…tall, beautiful, spiritually wise, intelligent, fertile, feminine…and fun to be around. She tends to things…she tends to bout everything. John Davidson is one hell of a man to have wooed her. They were high school sweethearts. John a six foot tall son of an Irish cop from Indianapolis and a Syrian mother from Terre Haute. Hybrid vigor! He asked me to tell all at table how his mother's clan first taught me lessons against bigotry. John and I had spoken several times about the large Syrian Community in Terre Haute. I had worked for years with Father George Rados the legendary pastor of St. Georges Anitiochan Orthodox Church. We had raised money and spoken up for the oppressed people of Palestine. Father Rados was transferred from Terre Haute to Washington D.C. to preside over the building of a national Orthodox Cathedral. The children's mother and I visited him the night before Letelier was assassinated below our hotel window.[1] Later, he had helped us arrange "adoption" of a Palestinian orphan whose P.L.O. parents had been killed.

Like so many things since the divorce, that "adoption" was left 'blowin' in the wind.'

But, the Terre Haute Syrian story John wished to hear…again… went clear back to childhood days of the post war 1940's. I was a member of the YMCA. I was trusted to take a bus downtown to swim and play in the basketball tournaments. I had seen black youth brusquely turned away. It was generally understood that black kids or who the 'educated' called colored were not allowed here. It seemed reasonable to me at nine or ten years old that the darker than majority 'white'… the darker colored Arab Syrian kids might not be allowed in either.

One day an older white majority kid named Toby was showing me

---

1   Orlando Letelier: Former Ambassador from President Allendes Chile. Leader of resistance to Pinochet free market fascists. Assassinated by CIA-Pinochet 'Operation Condor' September 21,1976 9:35a.m.

---

the handbrakes on his new bicycle. I'd never seen handbrakes before and was very impressed with the knowledge and maturity of this older twelve or thirteen year old peer.

Suddenly a darker complected Syrian boy rode his bicycle into the bike park. Disdainfully, Toby shook his head saying to me, "Yeah, they let those nanner noses belong here but we can yell NANNER NOSE at them."

Sensing it might be a bit dangerous yelling such a thing at anybody let alone this kid parking his bike...I mildly objected, "Naah, why do we need to do that." Persuasively Toby explained it as "our duty. We're spose to yell Nanner Nose at them."

"Ok, ok. I", defensively "didn't know we were spose to... yell NANNER NOSE. NANNER NOSE", I yelled right along with Toby, the older more mature more knowledgeable YMCA member.

Well... the nanner nosed kid quickly parked his bike, ran over and beat the larval racism out of both of us. And he kept pounding... utilizing my smaller frame as sort of a club to flog Toby into the cement, leaving us both bloodied and whupped. I learned then it was wrong and dumb to use ethnic or racial epithets. I was also learning what the civil rights movement painfully learned i.e. the pivotal core of re-educating the miseducated, even when done non-violently is best enhanced by the threat of violence. Malcolm's threat behind Martin's prayers.

After the laughter and second helpings of peach cobbler Miekija, Minnie, and Mike's young stepmother ushered the children and Digger (For the children Miekija had made (for her) a grand exception to the No Dogs Inside rule. Digger appreciated same never leaving Eliot's side, not begging for food or biting and scratching anything.) into the T.V. room for recorded episodes of 'Little House on the Prairie'. Us men finished our coffee with a shot of 'Hennessey' and Marsh Wheeling cigars.

I could tell Mike wanted to announce something or quote somebody. To my great annoyance Mike would sometimes interrupt "marxist" political discussions by formally quoting Churchill. His deceased mother had been Norwegian, his church background, Missouri Synod

Lutheran not Roman Catholic. He didn't share my great bias against the Brits. Formally now he gathered up our attention but spoke more directly to me, "Far more than we have lost is left us yet", he said. John asked him to repeat the quote. Mike did so looking more at his Dad this time, "Far more than we have lost is left us yet."

Mike's dad, nodded, as if knowing both the quote and its general intention. John asked Mike whose quote it was. Mike said nothing. I guessed it was Sam Coleridge. Mike said, "Wordsworth." "From his 'Preludes'," I guessed again.

"I don't think so..." Mike replied. Then confessed, "I can't remember...but Thomas, Much...Much is left ...to build on."

"You bet!", I agreed. We all seemed to agree.

"Whatever the cost?!" Miekija had peeked in from the kitchen unable to restrain her native caution.

"Aye the cost...", Mike feigned surprise at Miekija's caution. Things got quiet. The girls had joined us at table.

"It may cost...", I said. "It may be 'costing not less than everything'."[1]

Then Mike in fractured Shakespearian[2] Realty told Miekija and the rest of us "How large the cost depends on how short the lease...?!... dudn't it?"

I remembered the original sonnets notion of *lease* as the lease on life and wished to avoid any philosophical wool gathering regarding our advancing age and the self of mortality. When cornered Sam Coleridge[3] rescues;

"Vain sister of the worm – life, death, soul, clod –

Ignore thyself, and strive to know thy God!"

"Preacher Thomas has the last word", Mike affably ended conversation.

We all went outside for a constitutional; kids, dogs and all. We walked back to see my old place in blind horse canyon. Bethany and Jennifer wanted to know why it was called the Yurt. Mike and I

---

1   'Costing not less than everything': T.S. Eliot "Little Gilding"
2   Shakespearian "Why so big a cost, having so short a lease" Sonnet 146
3   Samuel T. Coleridge poem: "self knowledge"

explained as best we could.

Everyone turned in early for school and work Monday morning. I could hear Mike reassuring his Dad and stepmom to sleep in…they were "on vacation" while Miekija, Minnie and I bed down Bethany and Jennifer in one bedroom and El and Sean in a second. Both the boys and the girls bedrooms were new. Mike and Miekija had them built on the separate ends of their long house. Their old bedrooms were turned into one guest room off the kitchen. I wasn't expected at Modesto Dairy Supply until Wednesday. Beth and El were happily invited to visit 'the Mountain School' tomorrow. For over a decade Mike had managed and his income supplemented by the entire budget for San Antone School; K-12 – the last one room school house in California. At one point, I think, Mike earned the entire administration, teaching faculty, janitorial, bus driver, and tutorial budget. Slowly he delegated most of the tasks if not all the income out to his family. Miekija and Melinda (Mike's sister Minnie) were doing all the teaching and tutoring. I think John was temporarily janitoring and school bus driving. That left plenty of time for Mike's real estate and range politicing.

As I settled in their new guest room that night it seemed very familiar to me. Many's the time I'd sat on the floor there watching Mike's kids watch "Little House on the Prairie" and wonder if my kids had seen the particular episode. I'd ask them about it in my letters and phone calls. I promised to drive them to a "Little House…" film sett up in the Sierras above Knights Ferry and Chinese Camp. Beth and El called our Gloryville Farm home near Freedom, Indiana "The Little House in the Valley." I suggested to Jennifer and Sean they call theirs "The Not So Little House in the Hills."

At first light I woke from sleep like Roethke and took my waking slow. We'll learn this week by going where we have to go.[1] I'd dreamt of children in trees, heard inland from the Seas. I thought it was more T. S. Eliot imagery from last night and took Mike's "Little Gidding" from the shelf. It wasn't. Not quite…but I did come upon

---

1   Theordore Roethke's 'The Waking' "I wake to sleep, and take my waking slow… I learn by going where I have to go"

"A condition of complete simplicity
Costing not less than everything
And all shall be well and
All manner of things shall be well"
I wanted to stop here but the poem continued;
"When the tongues of flames are in-folded
 into the crowned knot of fire
And the fire and the rose are one."
I'd grown tired of suspiring for the rose on fire.
"I woke to sleep and took my waking slow...
....I'll learn by going where I have to go."
....starting with coffee...in the kitchen.

I stumbled to find Mike's Dad sitting in the darkness, wearing an old Army shirt over insulated underwear. The French Market coffee I brought them smelled great from the stove."Hey, good morning, I thought Mike told you to sleep in."

I poured coffee for myself and freshened his cup.

"I'm still the parent", he replied, smiling, just a bit sternly. Mike often referred to him as 'The Major'. He was a retired Major in the Indiana Guard. He knew more than anyone how I had practically ruined Mike's life "in American Society."

Twenty years ago Mike had been an adjusted ΣAE Fraternity Council, Union Board, Mortar Board, Chairman of the IFC Fall Carnival, entrepreneurial gifted business major at I.U. We'd both been favorites of our Study Proctor Harry Gunther, considered a genius at banking *who never liked anybody* and that's the only thing I thought we had in common. While a freshman pledge Mike was an 'active' sophomore. I was generally considered an "abominable pledge". One afternoon I'd been hiding out from phone duty. Pledges were responsible for answering all phone calls in a professional upbeat manner. I hid in one of the dark phone booths studying with a flashlight. It was the last place angry actives would ever look.

As phones rang and rang I could hear Mike's booming voice yelling PLEDGE, Pledge...without anyone answering the phones. All afternoon the phones rang, Mike's voice boomed, and I made some progress studying maps for my geography assignments.

Exasperated…Mike and some other 'Actives' started looking in all the rooms and closets for the missing Pledge. Finally Mike flung open the phone booth door to find me and my flashlight amongst maps sitting on the floor. I shined the flashlight in his eyes, crawled quickly through his legs and was scuttling down the hallway to escape when this loathsome little scut named Horner piled on me. Knocked flat from my hands and knees I whirled around to face both of my upper classmen assailants. 'Sizing' them up, figuring I could take Horner with both arms tied while McNaughton, that is, Mike appeared big and strong, but there did seem a kind of menace-deficit about him. His loud voice seemed put-on and fakey. I about decided to take both of them down when I noticed Mike was smiling, not grimacing, but smiling while Horner was jumping up and down with the profound grimace of privileged outrage. One punch to Horner's gut and he hit the floor softly bawling. Mike turned away, motioning me to follow him into his room. I did…but then checked at his invitation to sit down as he locked the door. He insisted I sit as he stooped to his small closet refrigerator fetching two bootleg bottles of beer. (Liquor and women were still 'House Rules' illegal in 1959.) Mike church keyed both bottle caps off handing me one of the beers.

"I hear you're the Pledge who refuses alcohol?" he asked politely but still in a kind of authoritative right to know. Raising my bottle as in a toast, I replied "On special occasions …" We drank the beer quietly. Mike still smiling. Me…just waiting for what's next. A pledge striking an Active was tantamount to a layman striking a Priest. I could be excommunicated! Expelled after all the stress I'd put up with to belong. I'd joined because of Chapter President Mike Hartigan, a senior premed student from Schenectady, N.Y. Catholic, intellectual and Irish he'd invited me to pledge the ΣAE's . Dick Lonnigan from my hometown had sold me on the idea. Lonnigan was by far Chairman of the Board coolest guy from Terre Haute. He was objectively working class but coolly oblivious to it. That made him popular with all the upper class students. He appropriated their style, manners, dress, and ambition while retaining his own native toughness. He had all the pecking order points required for a successful personality kit. Acceptable to the Haute and petit bourgeoisie and *apparently* proletarian tough enough to whup anybody who objected. *Apparently* because he dodged fights with finesse and fierce intimidation. And with an Anglican mothers wise instruction he never spoke disrespectfully of women.

Those guys Lonnigan and Hartigan had asked me in...now this failed hazing stupidity would put me out. Where would I live? I worried the old and new I.U. Dorms average cost was $150 a month. I'd been sold on paying only $80 a month to live in a mansion with 'brothers' who assisted you academically and socially, throwing parties and dances Coeds wished to attend. No one had mentioned hazing, hell nights, lack of sleep and the ever present obeisance,...the obligatory obsequiousness "owed" the 'actives'.

Standing I looked respectfully at Mike McNaughton and then quizzically at the door he'd locked.

"We through here?", I asked.

Mike nodded and said, "Don't forget your maps."

Appreciatively but not apologetically I turned to add,

"And the flashlight."

I answered the phones correctly for another hour. Then it was Tom Rushes turn. I heard later that McNaughton had talked to Horner and shamed him into silence. "You don't want the brothers knowing a pledge made you cry ... do you? So shut up about it", he explained.

XIII

"You and Mike met at the ΣAE House didn't you?" the Major began.

"Yessir", I curtly replied.

"Frat life wasn't so bad... was it?"

"I never liked it."

"Now...I know that's what Mike says... now, but I remember how he loved it the first two years..."

Here we go, I thought drearily unprepared for some drama à thèse on the doctrinal influences in my best friend Mike... even if it was from his father. I said nothing unable to avoid frowning. Tangential to this grave and sullen direction, Mike's Dad tried to pick up the conversation...lightly.

"I'd always heard ΣAE's were the best on Campus... Scholars like the Phi Gams only...sexier", he grinned. "I always wanted to be a Sigma Chi."

"Why?"

"The song. Because of the song, you know
the Sweetheart of Sigma Chi..."

Interrupting, "Yes I know....the Σigma Chis have a 'White Christian'
exclusionary policy whereas the 'best on campus' ΣAE's actually had an 'Aryan Race' requirement for membership."

"I thought that had changed..."

"Yeah, in 1959 John Bawls from the Chapter Eternal[1] came to call telling us the Aryan race clause was being replaced by the words 'socially acceptable'. He wanted to make sure, with a wink and nod, we understood it meant the same thing. 'Socially Acceptable' were code words for 'Aryan Race'."

"Celts like your son, me and Mike Hartigan weren't Aryans!", I continued. "Aryan" or "Acceptable" just meant white as in "white racism". I knew Mike's Dad was not racist. Mike thought it had been pounded out of him in the army. The US Army has always been ahead

---

1   Chapter Eternal: Formal name for the fraternity's national office, in Evanston, Illinois.

of other US institutions in this matter. Gun fodder is too scarce to be otherwise.

Mike's Dad, the Major now smiled the McNaughton clan smile that he'd grown comfortable with our conversation. I pressed on. Complementing the "Major you raised your family right. To be honest, straightforward, loyal and not to steal. The Fraternity was a scandal to those virtues. Property, I growled emphasizing the r's in the word was never safe in your unlocked rooms from the foraging thieves of your fraternity brothers. I told him how the self-righteous blow hard Mark Willyams had stood up at Chapter Meeting berating those who complained brothers were stealing from brothers. 'False gossip!', Mark exclaimed. Why there's only one or two thieves in this house, this shrine of the Goddess Minerva[1] and we should have the Police Administration Department investigate and ferret them out. Fifteen minutes after the Chapter Meeting Jim McDonald a senior football player caught Mark Willyams stealing a freshly laundered pair of underwear from his chest of drawers."

Still the fiction of one or two thieves prevailed. My sophomore year, the Police Administration set a trap to catch *the thief.* They 'powdered' ten five dollar bills and left them in a money clip on one of the spare desks stored in the main upstairs hallway. The trap was laid by dark and all the outside doors locked. The money was taken by 10p.m. At 4a.m. everyone was forcibly awakened and submitted to a Police Administration ultra violet light check of hands guaranteed to light up the thieving perpetrator. After the majority of brothers had been checked no one's hands had lit up. Then it was time for the Pledges to be checked.

One pledge named Tommy Hereford was a particularly hickish fellow, a legacy[2] from Huntingsburg whose folks owned a hardware store. He'd been hazed particularly hard for not learning to say street instead of road. When placed under the ultra violet…his hands not only lit up…they exploded with light and so did his arms, bare shoulders, neck and face! "You son of a bitch!" they screamed and knocked

---

1   Minerva: Ancient Greek Goddess of Wisdom. ΣAE's patron goddess.
2   legacy: frat name for relative of members who were always shooed in and not blackballed.

him down, bullying and kicking him into his room. "You Scrooge MᵃᶜDuck; You've been rolling in it. Wallering in the money. Wallering in your stolen lucre, you filthy fowl, you thief." Fraternal genius and technology had solved the crime, had caught the one thief red handed to cover their collective guilt.

Tommy Hereford suffered a kind of nervous breakdown, muttering to himself, going from room to room asking forgiveness for what must be his sleep walking and envy of money. Weeks later his older brother and his roommates were able to demonstrably prove that what lit up all over Tommy was his pimple medicine.

Mike's Dad laughed hard at this story so I finished the first one. "At that meeting with John Bawls is where and when Mike and I left the fraternity. I knew the Major blamed me and the Y.S.A. (Young Socialist Alliance) for his son being banned from the Fraternity and most other forms of what he considered conventional life. That wasn't exactly true. There were other variants in Mike's story which the Major might think better of than me…and the bad Bolsheviks influence.

"Do you remember Frank MᶜKinney?" "I asked.

"Sure", he answered, "American Fletcher Bank; MᶜKinney's the Banker."

"Well he was the Bankers son, back then. The only rich Irishman I ever met. (Yet we commiserated our mutual heartaches for being in love with and rejected by Jewish girls. I'd figured my rejection was for lack of money so his rejection with so much money was a mystery to me.)

Well sir, you know he was called Backstroke MᶜKinney because he was an Olympic Swimmer and that was his special event. I think he'd set some kind of collegiate record. We all liked Francis Backstroke MᶜKinney. He trained with the I.U. swim team in Hawaiian waters every summer. Some of his Hawaiian team mates would invite him to their family homes for dinner. He explained this to John Bawls and qualifying his request that he was not asking to *rush* these Hawaiians for membership but he would like to feel comfortable in asking them over to the ΣAE house for dinner…some times.

There was a short silence. Then John Bawls leaned almost perpendicular to Frank and spat,

"Those people are not socially acceptable to me! Are they to you Frank?"

Frank did not respond with words. He just gathered up his things and left the meeting. Mike and I followed him out and just kept going.

The Major sat pensive and I think making peace with at least the anti-fraternity side of his son's life in the sixties.

Minnie and Miekija were up…getting the kids up. The Major and I shook hands. He went for more coffee. I walked toward the children's rooms. The women swept by me. "Watch the boys. We'll take care of the girls", one of them said.

I found the boys on their feet but moving slowly. Eliot was pulling on his britches.

"Not yet", I corrected him, "We've got showers to take, nodding toward Sean to get on his robe. Then I began to realize I hadn't enough clothes for my kids. I'd been thinking about everything other than the practical tasks of child care. I sheepishly started to call on Miekija when she appeared at the door with cleanly laundered underwear, socks, shirt, and jeans for Eliot. "They're a little big but they'll do." She reported Bethany well fitted in some Jennifer hand me downs. Handing me a belt, she instructed I tie it tight for Eliot so he doesn't lose his pants, she laughed. The sun was up and I could hear Melinda and Bethany laughing down the hall. Convivial, I thought. Conviviality.

Mike was up and moving fast for work. His Dad and stepmom refusing to sleep in were going down the mountain with him today to see his new offices. Before they left, the Major shook my hand almost gratefully, said again how he enjoyed our conversation and the chickory coffee. But next time he wanted me to explain what in the world we (i.e. Mike and me) were doing, leading those five thousand I.U. students to perdition. He was joking. Mike and I glanced at each other very neutrally. I would have to prepare for any future conversations with the Major. There had been two to five thousand student protestors assembled back in '62 but they were not following Mike and me. They assembled in order to destroy us.

Back from Europe in 1961 Mike returned to I.U. (Indiana

University) and was elected President of the F.P.C.C. (Fair Play for Cuba Committee) Finances required I stay in Terre Haute and attend I.S.U. (Indiana State) for a year, live with my parents, and work part time. After last year's hitchhiking and camping out I was more than pleased to stay in the creature comforts of my parents' home. To this day I am patriotic about American plumbing.

At I.S.U. I organized a student group called the 'Left (Liberal) Forum', and chaired a student-faculty committee that purchased the Debs house from the Theta Chi fraternity. We founded the Eugene V. Debs Foundation.

The year in Europe had radicalized us both. We considered ourselves experts on East Berlin; what was wrong with it and why it was better than the West. Brecht had described the two Berlins as a rude peasant girl compared to a flashy veteran of the oldest profession.

After the 'Bay of Pigs' Imperialist invasion defeat, and Adlai Stevenson's shameful denial of same in the U.N., Mike thought I.U. was ready to hear more than campus liberals chatting about self-determination for Cuba. He invited me to speak 'In Defense of the Cuban Socialist Revolution'. I remember sprinkling my socialist rhetoric with some political science categories of Bryzienski and Morgenthau's for the academic crowd. However, I did not in any way dilute my respect for and defense of Cuba's Socialist Revolution. I quoted Fidel's speeches reprinted in the S.W.P. (Socialist Workers Party) newspaper, 'The Militant' addressing the Socialist foundation for Cuba.

(1)Land Reform: to give land to those who worked it, (2) Industrialization, (3) Full Employment, (4) Housing, (5) Education, and (6) Health Care for everyone. Fidel said these Socialist goals would be completed by confiscating all capitalists' property "down to the nails in their boots."

My speech was well received by most of the students present. More important to me, Mike liked it. He adjourned the meeting by announcing (1) he too had become an American Socialist in support of the Cuban Socialist revolution and that (2) the Sergeant of Arms had scared off several fraternity boys trying to stink bomb our meeting.

In all due modesty, with some pride and some guilt I had influenced

Mike light years to the left of his previous Business School orientation. He changed his major to 'Latin American Studies', and started dating 'bohemian' girls instead of the sorority types. He married Janet Shagreen, a very 'bohemian type' that spring. She was from the suburbs of Louisville, Kentucky. I borrowed a tux from Bob Warren and hitchhiked from Terre Haute as far south as Jeffersonville, Indiana for their wedding. Staying on the "the sunny side of the river"[1] with pledge brother Bill Ryall and his parents we (Bill and I) drove into Louisville for the bachelor party, wedding, and reception. Bill's parents were gracious and southern. Originally from Mississippi they'd traveled wherever his dad's career (a sergeant in the army corps of engineers) had taken them. Bill was later lost to his confederate idea of the CIA.

Mike and Jan's wedding was in a suburban Anglican parish where a bent over negro church warden painfully rolled out the red carpet. Equally bent and painful had seemed Jan's insistence she attend Mike's bachelor party. This very bohemian lady was soon required to endure all of us straight edged socialist comrades of Mikes.

I returned to I.U. the following September in '62. Mike lived with his wife in a cabin he'd rented out on Lake Lemon. The week of my birthday September 13th we both joined the YSA (Young Socialist Alliance). I was elected one of its three officers. Jim Brigham, Rolphe Levin and me were the Troika[2]; the three horse hitch, a team of three to lead collective efforts to carry out the Program.[3] Jim, the maximum leader, Rolphe the second in command and I was just the third man, the wheel horse.

From that October until our May Day indictments we maintained our grades and were active in educating and recruiting others for civil rights work in Tennessee, Kentucky, and Indiana, pro-union work in Indiana and Kentucky including assistance to the miners' strike in Harlan County, Kentucky. We also began mobilizing opposition to the

1   "Sunny side of the river": a Hoosier conceit for the north side of the Ohio River.
2   Troika: Russian word for three horse (abreast) chariot type hitch. Common in Russia from sleighs to artillery wagons.
3   Program: Leon Trotsky's founded fourth International program for Socialist Revolution.

War in Vietnam.

On May 1st we were indicted for Sedition i.e. violating Indiana's Anti-Subversive Act which made the assembly of two or more to discuss or teach Marxism and/or other un-American ideas was advocating the overthrow of the States government and punishable by two to six years imprisonment. The Monroe County Prosecutor claimed we'd "practically had a running gun battle with the state of Kentucky" and that our National Secretary Leroy McCrae's speech at I.U. where he defended the right of negro communities to arm themselves was "a call for revolutionary overthrow of the states government". Our case was considered the first in legal history where American students faced imprisonment for their ideas.

XIV

Events between that October and beyond May... I recall like a skein of geese. A skein of wild geese flying hard across a sky wide Gueverrista smile; innocent and insolent!

We made several trips to Chicago for advice and counsel from the old Stevedores and Steelworkers of the Socialist Workers Party... and to meet with the Chicago Y.S.A. I was impressed with the former; not the latter. On the way back to Indiana, Rolphe and I liked to stop, get out of the car to see and faintly hear the wild geese...still rare but sometimes loud in cloudbanks then waning away in the wind.

Similarly, the skein of events began with the gaggle of that great mob...those five thousand student protestors Mike's Dad was worrying about. By October, all sixteen thousand students at I.U., like the rest of America were alarmed by what came to be called the 'Cuban Missile Crisis'.

On July 9, 1962 Premier N. Khrushchev announced "that the Soviet Union would defend Cuba with nuclear weapons, if need be... should the aggressive forces in the Pentagon dare to start intervention [again] against Cuba".[1] Operation Anadyr[2] was launched to dispatch nuclear missiles to defend Socialist Cuba. Fursenko and Naftali[3] note that Khrushchev spoke frequently at Presidium meetings of Operation Anadyr as a plan not only to defend Cuba but a means to negotiate and establish a strategic weapons parity with U.S. forces assuring his policy of Peaceful Co-existence to prevail. All of which would include a tactically negotiated (1) withdrawal of western and soviet troops from Berlin, leaving it administered by the U.N. and neutral nation armed forces, thus assuring the sovereignty of Socialist East Germany, (2) the end of U.S. financial and military support to the Phoumi Nosovan

---

1   Aleksandor Fursenko and Timothy Naftali ("One Hell of a Gamble") and ("Khrushchev's Cold War") access since 2008 to Soviet Presidium minutes and intelligence materials.

2   IBID "Anadyr": a river in Siberia flowing south and east into the Bering Sea.

3   IBID

anti-communists in Laos, (3) strengthening of soviet influence with Baathists in Syria, Iraq, and Jordan and finally an openness for negotiated withdrawal of U.S. nuclear missiles aimed at Russian cities from Turkey.

By October forty nuclear missiles divided into five nuclear missile regiments, three with medium range R-125 and two with intermediate range R-145 were to be established in Cuba. Protecting the missiles in Cuba would be four motorized regiments, two T-55 tank battalions and a MIG-21 fighter wing, some anti-aircraft gun batteries and twelve SA-2 surface to air missile detachments with 144 launchers.

The total deployment was planned to be fifty thousand, eight hundred seventy-four soviet troops with forty-two IL-28 light bombers, a submarine base and extended naval presence to accompany the submarines.

Anastas Mikoyan warned the Presidium there was no way U.S. intelligence would be surprised or fail to interdict the buildup. Khrushchev seemed to think otherwise.

Robert and President Kennedy's summer reading had included Barbara Tuchman's "Guns of August" about how casually the Edwardian elite had drifted into World War I. They stood up to the more aggressive hawks in the Pentagon who could have mustered massive support from the U.S. population at large stirred up by right wing war mongers quickly joined by liberal 'don't leave me out of the patriotic parade' cowards.

Edmund Morris' quotes[1] a fictional student in the People's Republic of Berkeley finding himself in the Free Speech Movement atmosphere of Sproul Plaza [circa 1964] "You know that feeling when a really big wave comes in and sucks up so much fore water you can see the sand beneath you and there's no way you can't ride it in right through to the beach, with all the power of the Pacific boiling around your ass? Well that's how I felt here today".

Two years before the 'Free Speech Movement' at U.C. Berkeley mobilized two thousand students to challenge administrative bans on the dissemination of political literature… five thousand student protestors at I.U. reported by the Peking Review (People's Republic of

1   Edmund Morris: "Dutch" A memoir of Ronald Reagan p528

China Press) "were mobilized to challenge U.S. policy" during the Cuban Missile Crisis. Other press services, especially Hoosier ones, picked up on this Maoist hype.

There *was* a great mob of two to five thousand student and townie protestors mobilized at I.U.'s Showalter Fountain. But their intention was to shred and destroy the two dozen of us demonstrating against U.S. policy. Much of the mob was recruited and motivated but not exactly organized and led by the Y.A. F. (right wing Young Americans for Freedom) and Fraternity Row. It was fueled by that well known Hoosier hysteria that always ends up bullying those who allow themselves to be bullied. Right wingers here in the Heartland *were* acting like they had more than the Pacific boiling around their ass. In both cases – engaging and enduring the wave of such enjambed events is viscerally described by de Karengal as *"into that twist of matter where the inside turns out to be even huger and deeper than the outside."*[1]

We, the Y.S.A. (Young Socialist Alliance) and F.P.C.C. (Fair Play For Cuba Committee) had convened an 'Ad Hoc Committee to Oppose U.S. Aggression in Cuba'.[2] We'd organized and announced (in the newspaper) a demonstration to be held on the steps of the I.U. Auditorium by Showalter Fountain. We saw the 'powers that be' grooming the American public to perpetrate an invasion of Cuba to stop its socialist direction. The Y.A.F. wanted nothing more than to stop any socialist direction. Tom Huston[3] was chairman of Indiana's Y.A.F. I had formally debated Tom several times and we shared a begrudging respect. Later he was Y.A.F,'s national Chairman and served as member of the Nixon Administration becoming infamous for his "Huston Plan" of concentration camps for anti-government demonstrators. The "Huston Plan" proved too draconian even for President Nixon given his relative weakness to enforce it.

The evening before our demonstration we met at Don and Polly

---

1   Maylis de Karengal "The Heart" ("celte torsion de la matiere")

2   The U.S. naval blockade was not until October 24th. We were concerned on October 4th about the pressures for U.S. invasion of Cuba. "Air Force Chief of Staff Curtis Lemay was telling the president how simple an invasion could destroy all Soviet missiles and bombers in a few minutes." (IBID Fursenko and Naftali)

3   Y.A.F. Tom Huston: See Mary Ann Wynkoop's "Dissent in the Heartland"

Smith's house convening a motley crew of ourselves i.e. YSA and our peripheral supporters, Y.P.S.L. (Young Peoples Socialist League) youth group of (to us) the discredited U.S. Socialist Party and Social Democratic Federation, several Quakers and religious pacifists around the S.P.U. (Student Peace Union). Collectively we projected a possible core of one hundred demonstrators whom we hoped would inspire others to spontaneously join us. We expected a few dozen hecklers; not thousands of them. We'd also expected trouble from the Y.P.S.L. when it came to the picket signs and placards we'd prepared. They were always inclined to "balance" anti-imperialist slogans with anti-communist ones. They spoke of their position as some kind of sacrosanct "third camp" above the fray of the cold war. We'd tease them with the apocryphal story of their leader the Reverend Norman Thomas being busted by a cop in Chicago. It was at a demonstration of the unemployed and the cops were breaking it up. After being called a communist and whacked by a billy club the Reverend protested, "But officer I am an anti-communist!" The cop replied, "I don't care what kind of communist you are" and whacked him again.

And then there was what I called the Mecca phenomena. Left wing groups with all their global criticism tended toward reserving at least one place on the map for their unwavering loyalty. For the C.P. (Communist Party) it was the U.S.S.R. (the Union of Soviet Socialist Republics). For Maoists like P.L. (Progressive Labor) it was the P.R.O.C. (Peoples Republic of China). For Fourth International Trotzkos and Fidelistas like us it was Socialist Cuba. For Y.P.S.L. and the S.P. (Socialist Party) it seemed to be the U.S. State Department.

Over and above these differences Fidel Castro spoke in terms of "the Socialist Cause". That was having an influence. We all (American Leftys) began to speak of "The Socialist Cause"... especially when it came to Cuba.

Throughout this evening and its fall out, the YPSL was not sectarian nor divisive. They had an emerging new leader named Lionweber... Charlie Lionweber who worked as a solid comrade with us. As I recall he was from a Bloomington working class family. He knew cousins of mine who were firemen and stonecutters. His local personal fame was that he had wooed and married Nona Bell, a renowned beauty of Monroe County. By 1964 Charlie, like my friend Mike moved with his wife to the Berkeley campus. And Charlie's wife, like my friend Mikes was lost to the salt air and sensuality of the "youth movement".

We had no trouble with the YPSL. We had trouble with the SPU (Student Peace Union). That is, we had trouble with Rolphe and the SPU. The latter wanted assurance that our demonstrations would stay non-violent even if we were violently attacked. Rolphe had been reading Bruno Bettelheim. He was historically critical of the non-violent lack of resistance to Fascism in Europe, especially the Jewish communities. His heroes were the brave Jews of the Warsaw Ghetto who fought so boldly against the Nazis.

The SPU leader was a guy called Graham whose last name I cannot recall because we all (amongst ourselves) called him 'the Mahatma'. Graham wanted to talk on and on about Ghandi and Martin Luther King. We (the Y.S.A.) admired them but looked more to leaders like Malcom X and VI Lenin.

The Mahatma, that is, Graham wanted a policy that we'd all agree to go limp if physically attacked. Rolphe exploded at the very idea of it. No way was he going limp to somebody putting their hands on him. Brigham reminded us the Y.S.A. policy for "United Front"[1] demonstrations was "inclusive" and conflicts to be resolved by majority vote.

Don Smith quickly reckoned that a majority vote on "going limp" was sure to fail and... we'd lose a third of our demonstrators. He proposed we vote on a non-violent response policy where individual conscience would allow for going limp or standing ones ground. Rolphe fumed that socialists shouldn't be indulging individuals... conscientious or otherwise. The Mahatma worried that "standing ones ground with violent looks" would be further incitement to violence but that he agreed to a majority vote. Don's proposal passed and Rolphe reluctantly agreed to it. He nonetheless complained about it, muttering around for the rest of the evening.

That October morning was a clear crisp autumn day. I walked to the Auditorium and Showalter Fountain from my rented room south

1   United Front: Trotskyist principle as opposed to Stalinist "Popular Front" which was inclusive only on the leading parties' terms.

of the campus. I was to meet Jim Brigham forty-five minutes prior to the demonstration. My walk required passing by the Phi Psi fraternity house on Third Street. Tom Huston was addressing a crowd from its portico roof. A crowd of several hundred frat rats spilling into the street. "That'd be for us..." I remember thinking... amused at how many pledge hours must have been spent raising such a crowd. They'd probably had e'm, up all night phoning and 'networking'. I knew all about fighting those bully boys; "jest separate e'm out and one on one they'd wilt like wallflowers". Trouble is...paper tigers don't know the truth about themselves in a big enough mob.

Walking through the autumn foliage and up the slope to Showalter Fountain I first saw dozens...no then hundreds of students headed the same way. "All right, supportive troops", I thought. I found a grim Jim Brigham sitting on the fountains retaining wall surveying the crowds increase. I looked more carefully with him. It wasn't clear whose side they'd be on. "How many with us?" I asked.

"More against...", he answered, then directed me to mix with the crowd to figure who was for, against, and neutral to us. He did the same.

It took us less than fifteen minutes to know the mass of students were hostile. A few neutral curiosity seekers. More than a few hostile townies began joining the mob. In twenty minutes the mob had swollen to several thousand and still growing. The few neutrals identified were leaving scared of the mob.

"What had I read in Elias Cannetti about Mobs?" I couldn't remember. While I was trying to remember Brigham got down to business.

"Its nuts to face a mob like this," he said. If we have a hundred people, it's still about fifty to one odds."

"But Jim," I lamely objected, "they keep bawling, they [i.e. we] won't dare show."

"We'll show!", he blasted back. "This mob will masturbate itself out hours from now...then we'll demonstrate publically unafraid but not martyrs to this beast of a mob".

"Brilliant", I thought and started to say so when Jack Mace drove up. The mass of people blocking the street barely parting enough for his old Nash (we called his car Jacks Kelvinator) to pull up to the side of the fountain. In seconds Jack jumped out, opened his trunk full of picket signs and started passing them out to Jim and me.

The mob exhaled, then exclaimed as one creature and we heard individual shouts of they're here! they're here! Most of the seething mob turned toward us. Brigham grinned, and said resolutely, "I guess *we're here.*"

The rest of our comrades, Y.S.A.ers and supporters began appearing to grab a picket sign from Jack and follow Jim and me through the mob and up the Auditorium steps. Rolphe was the rear guard behind Polly Smith and Paul Ann Groninger. Under these circumstances our numbers had decreased from the theoretical one hundred to approximately thirty demonstrators. When we reached the top of the steps, we turned around with our peace placards facing the mob.

It immediately made this low roaring UNGHHHH sound like a single beast but loud enough for a barn full of sick bulls. Fred Lyce a burly town pizza man charged Polly Smith. Rolphe intervened "non-violently", he stepped in front of Polly knocking Fred Lyce back on the ground. Jim, Jack and I rushed over to Rolphe and we all stared Lyce back into the crowd. Rolphe was very defensive, "I hit no one", he kept saying. "I kept to the non-violent policy".

Heh, heh, not exactly. We were all very proud of Rolphe. Mahatma never complained. No one else charged us on the steps. We can hold them off all day in this position, I thought. Within the hour, many of our people were assaulted, wounded, and one comrade (Otto Picassa) was thrown down cement steps fracturing his arm. The campus and state cops stayed on the far side of the mob as if they were there to protect them from us. We stood fast. The mob began swirling within itself. I reckoned we'd wait them out...out endure them right where we were. But Brigham's blood was up now and he began executing the original and announced plan to march through the campus. Head down and elbows out he led us directly up to and through the mob which parted like the Red Sea for Moses Brigham.

Then all of a sudden the mob discharged a guttural shriek as they recognized Mike McNaughton. Oh My God...Mike was Union Board, O.M.G. and Mortar Board former ΣAE rep on the Inter Fraternity

Council. Oh My God O.M.G. He'd even chaired the all campus committee for the Fall Carnival!! Their perception of the Y.S.A.s political treason was abstract but Mike was visceral proof of treason to their very life style. Almost coordinated as cheer leaders they began shouting his name and calling him traitor.

Several dozen fraternity boys and Y.A.F.ers locked arms three deep preventing us or any traffic to pass. Stymied, we couldn't move forward and the forty some cops and FBI agents kept way back to enable this free market of cowardly bullying to continue. Stalemated for just seconds, a lone tall official looking man in a black suit began breaking up the locked arms. I mean he was really whacking those locked arms with one hand while he held open his wallet for identification with his other hand.

I didn't recognize him at first. It was Don Smith holding up his official looking library card. It worked. The frat-YAFers blockade came apart and they quit chanting 'block that ship'. We marched on past Woodburn Hall and the Business School. The shouting of traitor at Mike continued. Other mob shouting began to particularize its targets. Our female comrades and all the women demonstrators were called whores or sluts. I was singled out to be called 'wetback'; (I presume for my black Irish looks). 'Wetback' was screamed at me until the end of our march which continued down past the old Field House and the large parking area for the Student Union Building. Several hundred more students came running from this area. Some came running to join the mob. Some came running to just watch. Like James Jones, "Some Came Running"... "they came again and again, and then again, and when you thought there could not be any more of them left... to come, they came still again, and then again." In Jones novel *they* were lovers, friends, foes, gamblers, and the Chinese Red Army to a dizzying effect. No proactive illusion could dispel how life comes at you ... whether fated or consequent and you are responsible for it all. That is, responsible to wield life's events according to code.

XV

I am and have been inclined toward what my people have thought to be the 'Way of God' code. Repelled by the moral relativism of laodicean liberals and unctuous conservatives I was like most young Marxists militant that meaning inhabits the universe. Unlike most I would not deny that God put it there. The 'Way of God' struggles against unjust "powers and principalities" of this wicked world. (Jn. 12:30) "Satan is the Prince of this world;" imposing sin, capitalizing on and corrupting common people before and after the crucifixion of Christ, murdering and martyring the saints and prophets, exploiting all who work. For it is those who work — who bring into being (with the holy spirit) economic and moral value, that uphold the dignity of our creation. The powers of sin must be fought and Inshallah! — God willing overthrown by them. ("Now the Prince of this world is to be overthrown." — The gospel according to Saint John)

From St. Augustine's 'De Civitas Dei' in the fourth century, then Father Jean Calvin's theology of the moral value and duty of work in the sixteenth century to Father Karl Marx labor theory of value for Industrial times. These values were instilled... no seared into my consciousness and identity. Their mutual determinist, that is, inevitable pre-destinarian views of personal and political futures I resisted. Like the Islamic ideas of Oismet it seemed mere historical cheer leading, "Possunt quia posse videntur"[1] (they can because they think they can). Calvinist and Marxist philosophy of work had inspired the revolutionary bourgeoisie to overthrow degenerate aristocracys and the proletariat to challenge degenerating bourgeois society. Ideologies Islamic, Calvinist and Marxist tend toward the promise of a predestined, progressive... with enough faith and work almost inevitable success in the future. All my life I've subscribed to the work and faith part. The certain rosey future part, I still find beattitudeinally preposterous.

Nothing on this earth, cept death seems or seemed inevitable to

---

1   "Possunt quia posse videntur" re Calvinism in 'A Study of History' by Arnold Toynbee

me, least of all the puerile progress talked about by liberals and vulgar Marxists. It's as dumb as the sanctimony of hyper Calvinists who think they are "saived but you're not".

The double pre-destination of Calvin, i.e. that Gods unconditional sovereignty and inscrutable will arbitrarily predestines the elect (good guys) and the reprobate (bad guys) is particularly loathsome to me. Reading Holy Scripture anew and unfiltered by catholic philosophy Calvin shuddered at this conclusion even while defending it. His prolonged attention to predestination is because he was appalled before the contradictory, mystery of it. Accordingly Calvin cautions regarding the very mention of the topic.

He encouraged "mature minds to reflect upon this high and incomprehensible mystery in thinking of which we should be sober and humble".[1]

A century later on the American frontier Jonathan Edwards soberly and humbly reflected on his Calvinist view of the soul and society. He thought pre-destination was less a mechanical inevitability and more an inclination as "Man has the power to act in accordance with the choice of his mind; but over the origin of that inclination for choice he has no power".[2]

Bearing in mind Albert Camus' continuum between freedom and justice, i.e., it is proportional. The closer to one; the farther from the other. We know that individual will for good is rare. Willful selfishness is not. Socialists of the sixties like those before us were inclined toward the former and decimated by the latter. For inclination toward good is both spiritual *and* collective. Spiritual in Gods sovereign will. Collective in conscience formation from others. The plethoras of presumptious individual choices is modern man's selfish illusion of freedom and cause of anxiety. Children are now "reared" in our decaying culture with the ideology that virtue, rewards, and maturity has to do with their getting to decide. I see grammar school kids who get to decide what they eat for breakfast, whether they attend school and where they spend their weekends. They are often negatively described

1   John T. McNeill Introduction to "Calvin: Institutes of the Christian Religion"
2   Jonathan Edwards: "Personal Narrative of Notes on the Mind"

as "brattishly independent". More charitably we see them anxiously overwhelmed by individual choices. In clinical treatment anxiety is significantly allayed by eliminating choices. "You don't get to decide becoming", "You don't have to decide" and "You don't have to worry about it." Young foals always search for a hole in the fence, but they are traumatized by a lack of good boundary fencing.

By 1962, to my knowledge Marxist thought had not yet received the humble and sober wisdom that Jonathan Edwards brought to Calvin. I think the olde Marx knew such was needed when saying on his death bed, "I am not a Marxist."

Marx and Marxists knew and know there is a vast complex of phenomena beyond economic determinants. They have chosen to militantly ignore them. Worse, they tend to presume the slightest interest in other cultural determinants might detract from the primacy of economic analysis. Our doctrinal response to what we considered philosophical wool gathering was consistently... "What does that have to do with the class struggle?!" A good question to begin with I thought. It was almost always used to end with, i.e. condemn non-economic determinist views.

When Clancy Sigal[1] heard Rolphe use the question in pivotal refrain, he rebutted, "If asked what is the answer to the mystery of the universe - these guys would answer...immediately." I am no liberal objector to dogma. I value it, but doctrinal dogma needs to affirm the basics not reach out all over the place negating what it is not. Especially when it comes to cultural psychology and religion. Revolution is no less a conservative enterprise then religion. "The true sense of the word revolution is the movement of an object in motion that describes a closed curve and thus always returns to the point where it has started." (G.K. Chesterton.) Hopefully in a qualitatively improved condition.

In Stravinsky's "Poetics of Music" he affirms the natural importance of "the dogmatic element" in creative thinking and on "any field of activity for which it becomes categorical and truly essential." He

---

1   Clancy Sigal: Jewish-Irish-American author of "Weekend in Dinlock", "Going Away", and "Zone of the Interior". Creative writer who wished to be and many looked to as "the Conscience of The American Left." Clancy befriended me in London 1960.

notes "the words dogma and dogmatics however sparingly applied never fail to offend certain mentalities richer in sincerity than they are strong in certitudes." And sincerity, he quotes Rémy de Gourmont "is hardly an explanation and is never an excuse." Dogma safeguards integrity, order, and discipline. Its excess however plunges one "without transition from the wildest complications to the flattest banalities."

Marx has been quoted out of context and ad nauseam for one hundred fifty years allegedly saying "Religion is the opiate of the people." In his "Toward a Critique of Hegel's Philosophy of Law" Marx wrote, "Religious misery is in one way the expression of real misery, and in another a protest against real misery. Religion is the sigh of the people, of the afflicted creature, the soul of a heartless world, as it is also the spirit of spiritless conditions. It is the *opium* of the people."[1] (i.e. a saving, conserving medicine)

If religion is illusory happiness, the Marxist demand is "to give up conditions that require illusions. Hence criticism of religion is in embryo a criticism of this vale of tears whose halo is religion..." His criticism of religion is more an affirmation of religions criticism of society, "hence the categorical imperative to overthrow all conditions in which man is a degraded, enslaved, abandoned, contemptible being..." I have known principled marxist atheists who lead lives of moral integrity. Certainly more so than religious hypocrites. It is however an extremely difficult path fraught with temptations of enlightenment arrogance and secular cultism; without transcendent leverage to be otherwise. The more recent anti-theism of Brits Dawson and Hitchens[2] are egregious examples of a more degraded, and I think more Nietzschean atheism. In his "The Anti-Christ #43" Nietzsche clearly positions himself far to 'the right' of the best in humanity. "That everyone...has equal rank with everyone else, that in the totality of living beings, the salvation of every single individual may claim eternal significance, that little prigs and three-quarter madmen may have the conceit that the laws of nature are constantly broken for their sakes – such an intensification into the infinite, into the impertinent cannot

---

1   It is the opium of the people. Karl Marx on Religion Moscow Publishers 1957

2   See "Christopher Hitchens: "God is not Good"

be branded with too much contempt. Christianity owes its triumph to this miserable flattery; it was precisely all the failures, rebellious minded, and less favored, the whole scum and refuse of humanity who were won over to it...The poison doctrine of 'equal rights for all' – it was Christianity that spread it most fundamentally. Out of the most secret nooks of bad instincts, Christianity has waged war unto death against all sense of respect and feeling of distance between man and man [i.e. class] that is to say against the presupposition of every elevation, of every growth of culture; out of the resentment of the masses it forged its chief weapon against us, against all that is noble, gay, high minded on earth, against our happiness on earth. Immortality conceded to every Peter and Paul has so far been the greatest most malignant attempt to assassinate noble and gay humanity."

Early on...I realized how wrong it was to concede i.e. yield anything of importance to the upper classes. I was certainly not going to yield or concede the practice of religion and/or the very idea of God to them. At best it was a grave error in thinking; at worst, the fatal flaw afflicting revolutionary success. The morally criminal upper classes had best fear the likes of Marx as they feared the Thomas Münzers[1] who'd inspired him.

By 1972 erstwhile historian and Marxist theoretician Eugene D. Genovese had published "Roll Jordan Roll". First received as yet another 'Negro History' work churned out by academics inspired by us radicals in the streets. We thought nothing new could be said here. W.E.B. Dubois had said it all and Herbert Aptheker had fleshed it out documenting a revolutionary tradition among slaves passed on to the "free" black communities. Dubois and Aptheker were both of the C.P.U.S.A. (Communist Party United States of America) and widely

---

1   Thomas Münzer: sixteenth century religious leader and communist revolutionary whose political theology demanded the immediate establishment of the "Kingdom of God i.e. a state without class differences where everyone would work without private property, and without superimposed state power against its members." "The man with the hammer, T.M." called on the people to destroy, scatter and overthrow the land owners. His peasant army in 1525 armed only with axes and pitchforks overthrew twenty-one fiefdoms and castles armed with rifles and cannon. See Frederick Engels "Peasant War in Germany" and Ann Ramsey's "Revelation and Revolution": Basic writings of Thomas Münzer.

respected by all who care about the struggle against racism. I met Aptheker with Boston comrades in 1963. We traded some political differences and then settled in to an evening listening to Aptheker. I was impressed with his careful Marxian analysis and commitment to black liberation and the socialist cause. (He also came across as a solid family man, husband and father. More recent accounts I suspect as fem-flam character assassination.)

Who was this Genovese? A high falutin Professor who'd taught in the sixties at Sir George Williams University in Montreal, Columbia, and Yale. He wrote articles in the Atlantic, the New York Review of Books *and* the Monthly Review. Rumored to be a Maoist, his 'Roll Jordan Roll', book seemed mainly to be about religion; Afro-American religion. But no paternalistic head patting of Preachers was this book. It was a marxist... (magic word) *materialist* analysis of how religion even in its socially conservative mode not only 1) enhanced survival of the oppressed but 2) built collective compression in legacies of resistance 3) developing revolutionary perspectives against the oppressors. Finally, the dialectic restored! Religion even as opiate provides essential healing for the leaven of the soul and society to rise...to rise in revolution against sin and oppression.

White southern slaveholders in their aristocratic posturing repudiated Calvin's work ethic. "Yet they operated in a capitalist world market, presiding over the production of commodities, having to pay attention to profit and loss[1] "Consequently, they developed a strong commitment to the puritan work ethic – but only so far as their slaves were concerned... Now it is not the easiest of tasks to live by one code and to preach another to people who live close enough to see the difference."[2] Basically Anglo-Saxonized Calvinism helped shape both the work ethic and fatalism of "Southerners in general and slaves in particular and yet simultaneously generated a profound antithesis".

Black slaves developed within their Calvinist religion a work ethic of their own. "The black ethic represented at once a defense against an enforced system of economic exploitation and an autonomous

---

1   Eugene D. Genovese: "Roll Jordan Roll" (The World The Slaves Made) p.297

2   IBID p.287

assertion of values generally associated with pre-industrial peoples".[1] Slaveholders tried to shape the religious life of their slaves to value quietist submission. They attempted this with the biblical books of James and the Gospels according to Mark, and Matthew. What were they thinking? "Mark in his account of Barabbas, refers not to *an* insurrection, but to *the* insurrection that Jesus on the eve of his arrest tells his disciples to sell their cloaks and buy swords; that all the Gospels agree on his having entered Jerusalem to the politically seditious popular cry of Hosannah"[2]

Generations of padded unreality is required to read Holy Scripture as anything less than God's wrath against injustice and the requirements of love to endure injustice. "And ye shall be hated of all men for my names sake: but he that endureth to the end shall be saved." (Matthew 10:22) "Think not that I am come to send peace on earth: I came not to send peace, but a sword. (Matthew 10:34)

Genovese understood that Afro-Americans then and now "see the bible, not as white fundamentalists do, as the repository of unchanging truths, but as a source of historical experience and a moral context for discussion.";[3] A moral code to wield in their own world. "Christianity's greatest bequest to Western civilization lies in its doctrines of spiritual equality before God, but even in its powerful conservative force of marital fidelity, renderings unto Caesar, and the patriarchal family based on strict submission of wives to husbands it upholds authority both above and alternately aside from the slave-owner." Indeed, from all corrupted earthly authority.

Even if the concept of God is viewed as cynically as Christopher Hitchens[4] (Thank God for his departure) i.e. a mythology to reconcile real life in the real world it must be conceded as Antonio Gramsci says in proclaiming "a single nature, endowed by God, for every man, [Christianity and Islam] proclaim all men brothers...illuminating the

---

1   IBID p164
2   IBID p164
3   IBID Eugene D. Genovese "Roll Jordan Roll": Time and Work Rhythm p289
4   ChristopherHitchens: Deceased British Trotskyist lost to Washington D.C. punditry of war mongering, public promiscuous homosexuality, and Zionism for the George Bush Administration. Author of "God is not Good"

chasm that separated the equality of men before God from the grim inequality of man before man."[1]

Genovese dug down into Georg Simmel's "Sociology of Religion", finding "Christianity, like other religions, grew out of and based its strength upon the collective." In early tribal religions Dale Guthrie's Pleistocene research affirms the same thousands of years before tribes "African as well as European; God is at once a supreme member of the family – a veritable *paterfamilias* – and an independent force above the family who embodies its ideal life and symbolizes its unity."[2]

Genovese further concludes historically that "Christian churches have fought to embody an acceptance of the dignity and sanctity of the human personality in submission to a collective discipline that alone can guarantee the freedom of the individual in a world haunted by the evil inherent in the nature of man."

We were in the midst of the civil rights revolution for Christ's sake! And it was being led by preachers (as W.E.B. Dubois would have forecast) and yet wee minded vulgar materialists didn't get it. Some are simply not *inclined* to get it. Bouchard's Minnesota "Twin Study"[3] of identical monozygotic twins reared apart in different families found 0.49 personally inclined toward religion. Which is to say about half were not. Individuals see horizons differently. Yet every shred of historical evidence and the archaeological record argues for the truth in there being an objective reality outside our beings, which was there long before we were and will be there after we cease being – as individuals and as a species. The historical...the revolutionary significance of religious values and cultural determinants cannot be denied.

"Imperialists dominate information systems worldwide attempting to impose their values and justify their social relations. This is why the Battle of Ideas is so important and so complex. Our ability to wage this

---

1   Antonio Gramsci: Il Materialismo storico e la filosofia di Benedetto Croce p91-98
2   Dale Guthrie "The Nature of Paleolithic Art"
3   Minnoesotas Twin Study: 1990 Bouchard et al One of the many human properties measured was inclination toward religion finding about half of the observed variability of scores on a standard test attributed to genetic variation and half from environmental influences.

battle rests largely on education, on instruction, on *culture*... We want to make culture, to spread [culture] as widely as possible to defend our socialist identity."[1]

The depersonalizing horizon of five thousand hostile fellow students invites 'mob effect' thinking on both sides of the picket line. "Depersonalizing individuals allow one to disregard moral value in order to follow the super organism's lead and prejudices."[2] I was beginning to see the hostile thousands as one great beast, one mob but I was also beginning to remember Canetti. "The regulation of time is the primary attribute of political power", he'd said. "Rhythm of the mob is beaten out within the pack like dancing." This was their dance but we were cutting in, causing an interregnum, which if we endured would claim the time. The animal force and imaginary rhythms of this mob erupting and gesticulating was as they say not a pretty picture. "Their countenance distorted into every shape...permitted by the muscles of the face; every new grimace instantly adopted by all the performers in exact unison."[3] Being called 'wetback' I considered an honor. I was trying to think out, work through... imagine a different time.

Time here...was torn asunder. Innumerable moments of sight and sound seethed together. The massive jostle of the mob threatened our balance. The expanse of Dunn meadow was appearing on our left to the south. The upward prow of the ΣX (Sigma Chi) house seemed giving us the bird from the north. Stumbling I stepped up to the higher ground of the tree row whence I began to imagine the silent strength of my father's composure. He'd walked picket lines. I remembered the Creamery Strikes in 1947 and '48. Dad's captaincy of the Teamsters Strike Committee...breaking the legs of scabs and not liking it but never confusing necessity with virtue. Feeling threats of betrayal from the ranks tiring, their children deprived, and their women complaining. Neighbors presuming we had dairy products they couldn't get; not knowing we had less access than they did. The Press, police, and

1   General Moises Sio Wong; Chinese-Cuban General of the Cuban Revolutionary Armed Forces. From "Our History Is Still Being Written", Pathfinder Press 2005

2   Elias Canetti: Crowds and Power p33

3   IBID

gossip mills against us. Solidarity a grim achievement. But we won! Across the Nation we won! Strikes won, Unions prevailed, the post war Working Class prospered; contradicting middle incomes outside the Middle Class.

Memory of my fathers countenance became a compression of defense for me, a barricade against the violent pressure and cacophony of the crowd. "Countenance has the structure of registering events in accordance with things."[1] I thought if I could just make eye contact with just one individual of the mob I might dispel the depersonalized mob effect. And then as if sprung from my thought this red faced, skull faced ΣX, Σcreamer appeared. And he appeared right in my face... screaming all kinds of drivel until he settled into the crowds regular chorus refrain of 'Wetback – Wetback Go Home!' Eye contact was not possible. His eyes were all over the place. I concentrated on remembering his face. I would remember every single detail of his profile. Some day – some way, separate from this mob we'd meet and I'd splain all this to him. Yep, I'd splain it to him...compleatly.

Confident that I would never forget his face I tried to think of other things. I was from and had spent the last year attempting to speak politically with my people; the American working class. My family; their friends and relatives. My father was planning to retire from a quarter century on the milk route. He bought a small family tavern located amidst all his old milk customers. He changed beverages more than customers. I worked as night shift bartender. Perfect place for proletarian political conversations. All year I tried to gauge the revolutionary potential, the practical possibilities of working class political consciousness and action. Of course, I found it distinct from (a) liberals cheerleading students and their pet causes and (b) platitudinous leftys who never spoke with workers cuz (c) conditions were wrong and would have to change for there to be a socialist engagement. We'd have to stake out that future and conserve a program for it.

Generational conservancy. Not unlike the churches with always more than a few muttering about revolutionary conditions aka the rev., the apocalypse or rapture occurring within the next five years. "We

1   Kimara Bin 'The Structure of Abnormality' Japanese Philosophy Sourcebook. Edited by James Hesig, Thomas Kasulis and John Maraldo.

never failed to forecast thirty of the last three capitalist recessions and economic crises."[1]

That skein of events enfolding now between and beneath the cloud banked blur of things and that reserve of my father's signal narrative to quietly strike meaning into and through the fescennine features of their loud decay; their noxious colors of sloth and parasitically patriotic privilege always busy but never working. We had quietly announced the discovery of their prominent decline.

They were the noise rudely screaming their individual hatred for our announced communal purpose. Their radar was not wrong. If we were wrong about Cuba our delusions would be easily dismissed. If we were right or even not totally wrong, The Left was in remission and their futures remitted to History. A new/olde moral demand system was threatening bourgeois vacuity.

Nineteenth (so-called conservatives) and Twentieth century liberals alike shuddered at their glimpse of our solemn, serious intention. No foo-foo- fem-flam colorful cabal of free speech activists posing like the smiles of Social democrats in 1905... we had that under the gun gravitas of black and white photoed Bolsheviks in 1917. We aspired to no less than that engraved significance for the sixties.

Skull face wouldn't look at me but he kept yelling at me and into the atmosphere...still aboil... but spluttering out soon after Jack Mace pulled his Kelvinator up on the edge of campus at Indiana Avenue. We handed in our placards to Jack who sped away. Then without placards or picket signs we were unidentifiable to the mob whose mass absorbed us. Yelling ceased; replaced by a singular question repeated thousands of times in the buzz of mob monologue. "Where did they go?" "Where'd they go?" These phrases quizzically buzzing the length and breadth of Dunn Meadow as the mob dispersed into smaller crowds, fragmenting into groups then grouplets going home.

On October 16th, the Secret Soviet manuals on the R-125 missiles delivered to the CIA by their agent Oleg Penkovosky[2] confirmed ear-

---

1   Marxist Economist – Richard Wolfe on Democracy Now T.V.

2   Oleg Penkovosky: Russian CIA Agent and deep mole in the Soviet bureaucracy.

---

lier U2 photos were of medium range ballistic missiles sites in Cuba.

On October 22nd President Kennedy announced a naval blockade, but no other military action. For the next six days terse words between Moscow and Washington rode massive waves of covert intelligence information and downright gossip. That same day (October 22nd) just before the Soviet Presidium met, Oleg Penkovosky was arrested by the KGB in Moscow.[1] The day after his arrest he signed a letter promising full cooperation with the Soviets; detailing his meetings with M16 and the CIA to entrap western intelligence services. This was a significant loss to the CIA of its only mole in the Soviet defense Administration... leaving them scour for information from the likes of bartender gossip at the Occidental Bar and Willard Hotel in Washington.

On October 26th a US-U-2 plane piloted by Colonel Rudolph Anderson was shot down over Cuba. A Soviet commander had used a SAM missile without specific authorization. Soviet commanders had received permission to use force against an aerial attack but not against an isolated U-2 flight.

More pressure was put on Kennedy by the Pentagon and Bankster MacNamara to do more. Similarly pressure increased on Khrushchev to do less. Anastas Mikoyan had correctly predicted their old diesel powered cold water submarines could never rattle through the narrow Cuban channel without being detected by US radar. Now with Kosygin and Suslov's support, he argued retreat.

Not bothering to consult with Fidel or the Cuban government Khrushchev negotiated a total withdrawal of Soviet armaments from Cuba in exchange for a US Pledge not to invade the place and a US withdrawal of Jupiter Missiles (then aimed at the USSR) from Turkey. U.S. propaganda was 'we went eye to eye with the Soviets and they blinked'. Soviet propaganda was their action and withdrawal protected socialist Cuba and conserved world peace. Khrushchev did not gain any new strategic parity for peaceful coexistence. I think the old slyboots may have gained an extravagant new twinkle in his eye. The U.S. concession of Turkish missiles was not made public.

I've wondered if and what "intelligence" coveting agents ever came across or did with Peking and Hoosier reporting "Five thousand

1   Interrogations of Oleg Penkovosky, Central Archives F.S.B.

IU students protest U.S. aggression toward Cuba?" The essence of this event like so many sixties events we witnessed was broken away by separate 'Towers of Babel' 'reports and (mis) interpretations.[1] Time itself seemed no longer generative from restful gap between 'til now' and 'from now'. Just innumerable nows, now, now, now unconnected dots irregular and incoherent. Sam Beckett's; 'somehow till nohow'. "Lost in the temporal facts of now away from the event of just being oneself."[2] A shattered sense of self in time. The pivotal present, grounded in partisan historical pasts with imaginative perspectives for the future... "polarizing and broken now beyond any sentiment of reconciliation, any minimally shared sense of verisimilitude".[3] The matter, rather any shared or recognized need for the matter of truth shattered by the de-realization of time; yet remains a 'requisite nowness' for poetic validation.[4]

Right wing contempt for Justice in favor of Order[5] causing all this unjust disorder. Our own, the Lefts contempt for the present in favor of the Future[6] resisting disorder. Both contributing to the Middles mangled and manured mainstreaming celebration of the Now. The latter overwhelming times fulcrum into dazzling frequencies of discontinuous *nows*. (The now generation indeed).

To recover from such alienation of the self in time requires a reconstituted focus in the pivotal present between perceived past truth and worthy goals. Worthiness would of course require admonitions as well as consolations. In fact "Admonitions are the expectable predicates of

---

1   The clear exception being Allan Wald's essay 'Indiana Subversive Case: The Audacity of American Trotskyists in Against The Current July-August 2013. And Mary Ann Wynkoop's esteemed 'Dissent in the Heartland: The Sixties at Indiana University'. (IU Press 2002)
2   Kismaru Bin "The Psychopathology of Self Awareness" Collected Works p383-90
3   See "Elizabeth and Hazel" (Black and White of Little Rock)
4   David Jones 'Anathamata':"the time factor affecting poetic signs is a requisite nowness"
5   Jacques Maritain "The Peasant of the Garonne" Chapter 2 Our Cock-eyed Times
6   IBID "The real is never beautiful. What is not is beautiful". Jean Paul Sartre ("The Pure man of the Left detests being; preferring what is not to what is.")

consolations".[1]

America's ship of state was beginning to pitch. Its culture was floundering, not its economy. Feverish righties ran to one side of the ship. Remittent liberals and all other associated centrists indulged themselves sexually, medically (drug culture), and artfully in one inter-personal rapture after another on deck. That left, the Serious Left to work hard from the other side with balanced sightings of an economic and socially just (i.e. Socialist) future. To responsibly organize life boats to survive the coming economic crash with and for the working class. We'd add our (socialist cadre) consciousness to their power (the proletariat) and build the Socialist order peacefully until the capitalist hired fascists to stomp us as they had always historically done at which point we (the socialist led working class) would stomp the fascists. Liberal centrists always whine that fascists and communists seem so much alike. The bitter truth is they are only alike in that it takes one to stop the other.

We considered ourselves Leninists. At best we were Pre-Leninist. Like young Vladimir Illich obsessively incensed about his brother Sasha in prison. In a cultural redoubt predicting economic conditions not responding to them. No worse...too often responding to economic conditions we only predicted rather than experienced. As Richard Wolfe describes, we forecast at least thirty of the last three actual recessions (always in the next five years). There may be nothing more pathetic than a revolutionary in non-revolutionary times... except perhaps a non-revolutionary in revolutionary times. Stuck for decades in the former we were militantly opposed to ever be the latter. Revolutionary intentionists!

There *was* the Cuban Revolution, and revolutionary conditions throughout South America and the so-called third world. With every anti-imperialist revolution (Cuba, China, Vietnam, Algeria, Angola, even Indonesia and India) another tentacle was lopped off our capitalist Octopus. We connected the dots, connecting the dots with dates and shades, sometimes mere shadows, and sometimes with direct depth charged significance... We experienced (however vicariously) a revolutionary consciousness within the culture of our isolated position.

1   See Philip Rieff 'Toward a Theory of Culture' p15

Sasha Ulyanov proclaimed throughout his trial "that every change in the social system is a result of a change in the consciousness of society".[1]

Consciousness raising is profoundly important. Brother Sasha's unjust imprisonment and his revolutionary "spirit" influenced Lenin as much or more than any explicitly material cues. In his "Materialism and Empiro-criticism" Lenin grants that "human consciousness and the human mind are rooted in the material brain, but we don't yet know how". One hundred years of neurological research later and we still "don't yet know how" is no excuse for the "moral indifferentism"[2] of Marxist's entrapped in mechanical, non-dialectical formulae as bad as the worst bourgeois atheist. Asserting they do know empirically what science does not know. Worse, all other cultural spiritual and psychological phenomena are held suspect or ignored.

Social-psychological studies of the cultures of organization[3] is the primary requirement to understand revolutionary organizations in protracted non-revolutionary times. The new twenty-first century has arrived with some of the worst economic conditions since the great depression. Where are the Marxists? Their non-attention to cultural determinants has crippled their ability to respond to economic ones. Without cultural consciousness they have fragmented into multiple cultic grouplets. Without culture i.e. cultural consciousness the cultic takes hold.

There can be no dialectical materialism without non material phenomena with which it is to be applied; i.e. a dialectical materialism different from that to which it is applied. Without cultural (superstructural) analysis, dialectical thinking is arrested in vulgar materialism going nowhere. Or... if reduced to ranchers rhetoric "Without the inner penetration of opposites there is no fucking production".

Bicameral brain function sacrificed to Anglo-Saxon empiricism. Conceptual imagination (right brain) crippled under (left brain) positivists exaggerations. Remember Bertrand Russell's panic that Lenin viewed the dialectic as theologians view the Holy Spirit.

1   Philip Reiff
2   "moral indifferentism" Phillip Rieff
3   See Allan Wald's "Winter's Tale" Unrepentant marxist.com 2012

Scorning dialectical synthesis, logical positivists, no less than super-
stitious idealists and mechanical materialists oppose the dynamics of
economics ↔ and ↔ culture.

Dialectical analysis is also negligently not applied to its applicants.
The nature and character of "revolutionary organization" and revolutionary cadre cannot be sacrosanct separated from objective analysis
or left to subjective suspicions of disloyalty.

"Communal purpose operates through organizing behavior, language, and symbols in a way at once admonitory and consoling".[1]
In 'Civilization and It's Discontents' Freud notes that... "the wildest
revolutionaries no less passionately than the most virtuous believers demand consolation." Lack of success in revolutionary politics
becomes inconsolable without principled admonitions to the contrary.
Cultic leadership is organized to restrict not expand collective identity
in participatory mystiques expressing fixed wants with incommensu-
rate gratifications. Limitations of possibilities being the core design
of membership. The consolation prize for this programed failure is
tired old "euhemerist soteriology".[2] That is to say, Salvation through
following the Leader.

"In a world gone decadent and meaningless, resentment masks
self-imposed helplessness, (in contrast to real helplessness) and an
attendant irksome submissiveness."[3] Cadre have behaved as variants
of Hegel's bondsmen who rather than find in their work sources of
liberation turn back toward the Master and abandon the object.

Life is complex with ancient and coetaneous rivalries. The essential
rivalry; the rivalry that matters to Marxists is class rivalry. Agents of
marxist politics are either partisanly engaged in class rivalry or atomized in self referent directions. The latter is best prevented through
their remaining engaged in the formative activity of productive labor
and/or morally identifying with the same.

Work plus consciousness naturally positions primal values for the

---

1   Philip Rieff "Toward a Theory of Culture" p15
2   "euhemerist soteriology". Philip Rieff "Toward a Theory of Culture" p16
Triumph of Therapy
3   Floud Hayes: "Fanon; Oppression and Resentment" Purdue University
Press.

Proletariat. Without developed conscience and consciousness (what Frey and Latin American leftists call Conscientiousization) moral commitment to the interests of the organized Proletariat may grow thin and objective truth not achieve subjective certainty. What Frantz Fanon calls an 'ontic relapse' occurs, afflicting consciousness back into self-deception. Failure of leadership to morally lead members through and to partisan working class struggles inevitably fragments...turning back toward organizational forms away from work and the substantive sources of revolutionary politics.

Ontogeny defies Phylogeny and multiply diverse, partially helpful, neutrally distractive, and outrageously negative issues abound for the "whole of humanity". Self-referent delusions are emboldened to speak for the wholes in multifarious liberal projects, youthful sexual issues, and other neuro-pathological behaviors.

The cultural redoubt is without flanking defenses against the worst of lumpen culture on the one hand and bourgeois liberal influences on the other. Rosa Luxemberg had warned that during long periods of labor quiescence revolutionary youth too often acquire the culture of the Lumpen Proletariat *not* The Proletariat.

Yet safe this side of abstract thought times prelude joined the great Fugue which was 'the sixties' in symphonic if not psychiatric atonalities. Key sequences grounded in as many voices... stand up socialists worthy of comradely trust and collective leadership. Happy are they who endured the sixties! To paraphrase Christ's beatudinal Sermon on The Mount; "Blessed or Happy are those who endured, doing the right thing, and are not surprised when it didn't work."

In the Y.S.A.-SWP we were associated with comrades from our grandparents generation, such as Rose Karsner, Jim Canon, and Vincent R. Dunne. They had known the Debs family in Terre Haute and worked with Jack London, Zinoviev, Bukharin, Sverdlov, Lenin, and Trotsky in New York, Moscow and Mexico opposing Imperialism and fighting for the socialist cause against Stalin's betrayals of same... holding out for restoring socialist realities.

Our parents' generation was led by Farrell Dobbs SWP leader who with Jimmy Hoffa of the IBT (International Brotherhood of Teamsters) were leaders in the Great Minneapolis General Strike. Many others in that age group were there for us. To name a few I knew were comrades Della Rossa, Oscar Coover, Sylvia and Nat Weinstein, Ann and Mit Snipper, Art Sharon, Frank Lovell, Clifton DeBerry, Mike and Ruth Geldman, Ruth and Asher Harer, Gusty and Larry Trainer.

Our generation of Y.S.A. leaders and rank and filers seemed equally impressive in those days. Barry Sheppard as National Secretary was a straight edged, clean cut, social engineer from M.I.T.... honest, serious, dedicated and hardworking; a principled friend of courage to his comrades. LeRoy McRae as national Secretary was passionate, affable, and patient with us young white militants eager to fight for Black Liberation and relatively ignorant of Black Culture. Peter Camejo, as National Leader, was bilingual Venezuelan-American radiantly intelligent, and articulate,... probably even a better speaker than me, certainly a more humorous one. (Peter later ran for Vice President with Ralph Nader and the Green Party). Then there was Jack Barnes... from Carlton College and Chicago, always a presence in the National Leadership. Known as a scholar and genius. I've never trusted Jack and still don't. Whether a police spy liquidator, long in the tooth campus politician, innovative intrigue cultist, and/or something beyond my best thinking he's still a genius, agile, cunning and thorough.

We were all proud of Barry, LeRoy, Peter, and Jack. We thought they stacked up superior to other youth organization leaders and I still think so today. Rank and filers were no less impressive. Melissa Singler, Ann Dorazio, Joyce DeGroot, Gus Horowitz, Ellen and George Shriver, Harriet Talon, Evelyn and Irving Kirsch, Maureen, Carolyn, and Madeline Jazinsky, Jack Marsh, Mary Alice and Dan Styron, Bill and Paul Ann Gronninger, Don and Polly Smith, Joe Henry, Steve Chase, Dick McBride, Rick Congress, Robin Hunter, Dave Saperstein, Lou Jones, Mike Tormey, John McCann, Barbara Gregoritch, Les Evans, Mitsy and Julio Snipper, David Fender, Jim Bingham, Ralph Levitt, and Bill Massey. David Fender from Green County, Indiana became a leader of the 1968 near revolution in France and served as secretary for Peng Shu-tse veteran of the Chinese near revolution of 1925-27.[1]

---

1   See Barry Sheppard's History of the Party Volume 1 p228. Barry documents the great mid-century achievements of the SWP-YSA in which he played a

David and I went into the cattle business together briefly before my divorce busted everything apart by 1980.

By the seventies the older generation began to die. When notified Vincent Ray Dunne had died I feared an irreparable existential gap was opening. Without the experience of severe economic crisis and labor radicalization… then losing touch with older leaders who had… the "revolutionary youth" would start reifying themselves. Their own experiences and issues would be increasingly exaggerated in importance to compensate as and eventually substitute for real socialist experience…real socialist thought and action with and for the working class in real time.

The 1971 Socialist Workers Party convention discovered "a new way"[1] for revolutionary Marxism. They would thread all the youths sexual, gender, and family issues together in "a new way". The role of the revolutionary party was by bankrupt fiat expanded beyond its bid for working class leadership toward socialism to now "lead all of humanity to freedom… against every form of oppression" [reminds one of Sarah Palins "all of e'm newspapers"] "leading not just the working class"… but the wholes of society-all of e'm. Thus allowing the passage to 'fantastic materialism', from 'vulgar materialism' barely passing thorough 'dialectical materialism.' In lockstep with bourgeois feminist and lumpen degenerates asserting against anthropological evidence the revolutionary youth discovered "in a new way" that after all is said and done it really is 'fathers fault'. Patriarchal authority and the nuclear family done it. Of course, Capitalism caused it. Surely someone should remind materialist Harry Ring that patriarchal and family life existed as "naturally in humankind and the more advanced animals as homosexuality ever did in history and in all forms of society."

The youth and their youth issues!? At the 1971 Convention Barry Sheppard reports[2] giving "a talk on the sexual revolution that was taking place among youth and contributions of the German psychoanalyst Wilhelm Reich." It would be unfair and uncharitable to reply to that

critical role.

1   IBID History of the Party Volume 1 p303 'The 1971 SWP Convention'.
2   IBID p.305

fact...Gak! Wilhelm Reich the nutcase convicted of selling Orgone boxes to catch the blueish sexual energy in ... materially in the box: as I said, that would be uncharitable. But *not* very. At least he *was* a materialist. And he had written sanely at one point on character formation analysis. Indeed it may be less absurd that comrade Sheppard recommended for discussion the ideas of Reich to the Revolutionary Youth regarding the "ongoing problems they face in relations to their own sexuality and the political issues of sex" as the fact they'd already walked a parallel plank. These youth were already stuck as much as old Reich in an antinomian tradition as old as the classical mystery cults. That moral law is not binding sums up the doctrinal cult of religious antinomians. Secular sectarian devotionals push it a cultic step further; 'there is no moral law'. Morality is imposed on humanity before we =have the wit to realize imprisonment inside walls of sentiment separating us from the elemental rewards of true living. Whatever is is right. If it itches scratch it. If it feels good do it. Not merely the state but the conscience should wither away.

Comrade Sheppard was just catching up with how their liberal professors had prepared them. "The primary function of the family is the inhibition of sensual sexuality beginning with the taboos against incest. Sexual freedom is entrapped in sentiments of love."[1] The old thunder of nineteenth century German literati and degenerati became the "new" social science of Anglo-American professors of the twentieth century.[2] The Kinsey Institute at IU probably the best example. I was a research fellow there in 1966. They didn't like Freudians who were hip to their lustful authority envy regarding the fathers and families of attractive (mostly female) students. A phenomenon perhaps applicable to horny socialist cadre. Dr. William Simon, of the Sociology Department and Kinsey Institute was an ex SWPer who perceiving my views said he planned to write a piece entitled 'Sexual Revolution and the Renegade Morgan'.

Since the "historic source of authority is in the patriarchal system, the chief institutional instrument of repressive authority is the family."

1   Wilhelm Reich: The Mass Psychology of Fascism p116
2   Reich's "Religion of Energy" p157 Triumph of the Therapeutic Phillip Reiff

Reich then concludes "the controlling dynamics of our inherited religious family culture must be done away with."[1] Rejecting Patriarchal authority is the principal banner of the liberal bourgeoisie. It underlies their position on all political questions allowing them freedom to criticize, regulate, but never operate, i.e. take charge and be responsible for the running of society. Proletarians and the poor sometimes support the Right who at least take responsibility for operating Capitalism rather than the disingenuous dialogues of Liberals. The Revolutionary Left should stand apart in Profiles that include a capacity to take charge with the working class...to take over and operate things...not just complain about them. To lead exemplarily the masses in collectively overthrowing and co-operatively leading society to build the socialist order. Termination notice for the failing capitalist owners and managers.

The Enlightenments inspired feet of clay fits not only liberals but too many so-called socialists and radicals. They concede 'the holy family' to the bourgeoisie...living lives usually bohemian beyond the norm of working class acceptability. Critically advanced and above (they think) the backward, socially conservative, patriarchal Proletarian realities; they adhere to an enlightenment ideal of gender roles at odds with working class realities.

This contradiction handily concealed by pretending sexual issues are the same as racial issues. That is, to say racism has to be fought and expunged from society at large; no quarter to racism within the Proletariat. Racism is not only an evil unto itself; its material existence is contrary to the interests of the working class. For lumpen-liberal influences to equate the patriarchal proletarian family with racism is contrary to the interests of the working class.

Would these enlightened cadre please explain to Malcom X and all those black and white usually stern, usually patriarchal proletarian fathers that their families are unacceptable to achieve or exist in the socialist order.

Imagine the famous 'sixties' recorded "Interview of Malcom X

---

1   Reichs ultimate feminist, that is, anti-Patriarchal heroines are "the whores, women who rebel against the yoke of marriage and insist on their rights of sexual self-determination."

by three young Socialists" (Barry Sheppard, Peter Camejo, and Jack Barnes) which collectively vocalized a synthesis of civil rights, black liberation, and revolutionary socialism... imagine if it had veered off track into the later lunacy of antinomian atheism taunting Malcom for his backward religion and fidelity to his religious vows in marriage and Patriarchal role of father and family man.

But, the revolutionary youth became adept at treating themselves exempt from objective analysis in order to subjectively idealize themselves in illicit communions' *not* collective communities, in cultic and pathological togetherness. They will be out organizing and expelling themselves while working men and women with children and mortgages make the Revolution. There has never been a socialist revolution led by anyone other than incipient or actual patriarchal fathers; and not likely to be. Raoul Castro's family man example has much improved Fidel and Ches. Liberal and Lumpen ideas otherwise are left dancing alone with the likes of Emma Goldman.[1]

From Lenin to Malcom we have learned to distinguish between revolutionary 'nationalism' and oppressive 'nationalism'. The same distinctions are required for 'feminism' and 'patriarchy'.

Leaving California in 1964, Anne Dorazio and I stopped in at the SWP-YSA summer camp to announce our engagement to marry. Our youthful comrades were more than slightly non-plussed and put off by such a conventional plan. They were mostly living together. Our marrying seemed a judgment against their co-habiting.

"Why not continue just living together?", as they leered...somebody said, "You don't need the Church or States permission!" Many others asked "Why back to Indiana?"

"It is my home country and I don't intend being run out of it any longer", was my response. Adding, "We're going to earn an Indiana farm, raise crops of children, and other livestock bringing revolutionary consciousness to Yeoman Farmers and the Rural Proletariat!"

Some scoffed "Rural Idiocy!" I retorted "You all will be at wine tasting parties when you hear of the Hoosier Soviet!"

We all laughed saying good-byes when George Novack tim-

---

1   Emma Goldman: American liberal Feminist and Anarchist. "I don't want Revolution if I can't dance."

idly approached. George was the officially subsidized New York Philosopher reporting on Californian activity. Blasphemous but meaning well he took our hands saying, "Whatever the Socialist Workers Party has put together let no man put asunder."

Driving away I thought, "By God we'll force the Church and State to recognize our issue.[1] I also thought about George Novack and how he had so casually counseled divorce to Don Smith back in Bloomington. Don's young wife had made a selfish...even treacherous political mistake. I thought it required forgiveness and political discipline not divorce. Novack had encouraged divorce saying "it is very common among our people in the Party. It is not a big thing..." I thought it was a very big thing! They had a yearling child together.

In 1963 Jack Barnes and I were required to share a long car ride. I can't remember where or why. I can remember it being relatively unpleasant for both of us. We spoke of his coming from Dayton and me from Terre Haute. The subject of family followed.

Usually cool and dispassionate with me I was surprised at the venom he brought to this conversation. Jack passionately and kind of teacherly said, "revolutionaries must totally disengage from their bourgeois families." I didn't have a bourgeois family and said so. I wasn't sure whether he did or not. I began to realize he saw all families as bourgeois, that is *of* not just *in* a bourgeois society. I told him "the kinship patterns of mine and others extended Proletarian families were the very fabric which larger collectives could build on. As a kid I looked forward to family reunions the same way I looked forward to Teamster Union Picnics. And in the Soviet Union I thought strong working class families were the backbone of the place.

No, no he snarled you've got to get away from all that and build the party. He may have said the Movement, but Movement or Party he said it several times and emphatically. The last time he phrased it I finished the sentence for him, making it a question.

"....you've got to get away from all that and build the Party..." I quickly added... "with stable families, or atomized individuals?!"

Jack liked the last word so he kept muttering as we got out of the car. I couldn't hear his words and quit listening to him...forever. We'd

1   issue: race horse term for foals.

joke…liberal members of SDS[1] seemed oriented only toward a revolutionary overthrow of their own manipulative immoral parents while Jack Barnes oriented toward being *the* manipulative immoral parent of *his* own revolutionary members.

By the twenty-first century Jack has expelled, suspended, run off, wore down or otherwise purged most all of the afore mentioned persons of merit from *his* organization. Gravedigger of the SWP, possible police spy liquidator, but certainly a successful cultic leader of yet another children's crusade enslaved to never see the promised land.

---

1   SDS: Students For A Democratic Society

XVI

A fundamental axiom of statistical protocol[1] is you cannot legitimately test a hypothesis on the same data that first suggested that hypothesis. It becomes a self-serving circular solipsizm; a specialty of Evangelicals and Barnesites.

Evangelicals begin: (contrary to scripture, tradition and/or sound doctrine.)[2]

Jesus is God and we invite Him into our heart.

As Jesus God is within us, we maintain a personal relationship with Him.

Then concludes, they speak for Him, confusing the idea of His existence with their own visceral selves.

Barneites begin:

Recruiting marginally undefined youth to a highly defined ideological membership to maintain personal and personnel relationships of "loyalty" through ad- hominem gossip and purges against those not obsequiously conforming to their ideological identities.

Thus confusing conformity with loyalty, identity with politics, then substituting one for the other.

Both processes become unconscionable, that is, violative of conscience formation. Conscience no less than consciousness thrives with admonitions and work not with fantasies and sloth wherein it is further displaced with organizational relationship management. Relationship engineering or management is always preoccupied with those judged outside the managers pleasure.

A combat party of children emerges; i.e. atomized individuals primarily relating to each other in a circle jerk of abstruse concerns and ad-hominem gossip. The original Pussy Riot of Puerilitarians!

By the end of the sixties, Barry Sheppard comprehensively reports in the first volume of his political memoir, "The Party"[3] how success-

1   'Statistical Protocol' McCabe and Moore 1993 p477
2   'contrary to scripture, tradition, and/or sound doctrine; The Christ's instruction: "When you pray; pray like this: "Our Father" etc. etc.
3   'The Party' by Barry Sheppard Volume 1 p228. Barry documents the

fully the YSA-SWP had organized, worked with, and amassed significant political force to (1) "destroy racist legal segregation south and north." (2) Secondly, we'd led "in mobilizing a massive anti-war movement persuading the American people their government was wrong and morally deserved defeat by the armed Vietnamese peasants and workers." We were all a credible part of that. We were also a culpable part of the larger 'youth culture' which provided a half century hen house for the likes of Fox Barnes.

Aging comrades scratching their gray scalps are now reflecting they began to be suspicious of Barnes around 1979. Indiana (Don Smith and the Bloomington Defendants) had called him out in 1963. At the 1965 YSA convention I proposed an open dialog on the 'organizational question' separate from political positions. Barnesites knew that would expose their chicanery and hooted it down. By 1979 those aging recollectors had significantly collaborated with Barnes purging of so many "disloyal" elements they set up adequate precedent for their own "disloyal" expulsions.

Philip Reiff writes that Religiosity is where secular thinking leads when tangled with the hope of personalities. After the fall of fascism a rather manicy Reich moved to a kind of sexual religiosity. Now, 'religiosity' is basically spiritual faith cut loose from all tradition and doctrinal integrity. Reich's religiosity rioted wildly with marxist and meta-Freudian rhetoric in search of goals "no longer formulated in credible ways or sustained without forming little cults from which nothing can issue..." It is the "modern cry of religiosity that parodying faith, fails to engender a sense of power or security against the forces of darkness from any conceivable institution (past, present, or future) and therefore poses against real dissolution a fantastic newness of everything a newness so new that in the minds of its members it maintains forever all vitality and no definitive shape."[1]

New and not so new loosey goosey morality strapped tight into conforming 'factualism'. The one intolerance worse than a blind dog-

---

great half century achievements of the YSA-SWP in which he played a critical role. Let's hope Volume 2 will document the fin d siècle demise in which he also played a critical role.

1   Philip Reiff: "Reich's Religion of Energy" p184

matist; that is the peculiarly modern intolerance of those Reiff calls the 'factualists'. I've referred to them as fact mongers or ultra-pragmatists. "Marx, Lenin, and Trotsky have provided all the theory we need. Now we just need to organize"...has been their twentieth century refrain. Organizational forms are facts. Criticism of organization is a denial of facts suspected to cloak political differences and disloyalties.

Sexual criminals are disproportionately illiterate. Inadequately sublimating libidinal urges highly probable in most criminal behavior; more so in sex offenders. Sublimation is deterred by lack of language skills. Cognitively crippled, radically concrete thus hindered to take charge of and/or rechannell selfish gratification. Similarly concrete ideologues suffer a preputial like concretion formed beneath their political foreskins through the accumulated smegma of devotion to the faultless empirico – 'factual' organization.

Worshipers of facts – be they Reich's fantasy facts, Jack Barnes organizational facts, (or shared clinical genital facts). "compose the most powerful of all forces inhibiting serious criticism. Of course, facts do not speak for themselves; they speak only when theory teaches them to do so, and then only in the voice and with the resonance that theory lends them."[1]

Without adequate theory, followers of the factual organization speak gibberish heavy with admiration for the successfully established, unchallengeable factual organization. Their arrogance based on the fact that facts are never critical of themselves.

These new cadre, the Barnesites offer a cultic brutalization of facts assuming because they oppose what remains of old cadre they are somehow more... more so. The latest revolutionary thing! Puerilitarians!

In his book, 'American Night'[2] Alan Wald distils from Richard Wrights critique in 'The Outsider' with what ease a hierarchical organization demanding military-like discipline becomes a device of personal power. How aspiring leaders mask their will to dominate behind the altruistic long-term aims of the organizations ideology, deriving

1   IBID Philip Reiff
2   'American Night': the third volume of Alan M. Wald's history of the U.S. literary left. The first and second volumes were 'Trinity of Passion' and 'Exile from a Future Time.' (University of North Carolina Press)

pleasure from the psychological perequisites of even a limited authority. I view the Barnesian phenomena more grotesquely. Underneath its interlocked order of rigid organization and ad-hominem gossip management lies a latrine of liberal lassitude into which every lumpen vice has flowed.

As Reich's faith was in youth…and perhaps more pathetic for it, 'The Party's' faith had switched to Barnesian Youth and definitely more pathetic for it. It was and is a constituency continually outgrowing its relevance. Over sexed and underpaid atomized individuals rarely capable of more than a series of one night stands in sexual or political commitments. Bourgeois liberals indulge. Proletarian Socialists admonish. Lumpen cynics slide around and sleep til noon.

As Reich's 'natural youth' and 'natural man' are spoiled left overs of eighteenth century imagination; liberal hostility to the socially conservative culture of the Proletariat lead both to the same sick place. Reichian radicals call for a destruction of the Proletarian family. Liberals use "sex education" as their main weapon to divest working class parents of their moral authority.

Socialists should be supporting, strengthening working class families, their parental and if Patriarchal their Patriarchal authority to wage class struggle against the bosses no matter the bosses gender arrangements. Rather than castigating them with some genderdized psyco-babble brush.

C'mon…is it really too simple for the sexualized politics of the sexually complicated, liberalized mind to comprehend? Parents need to be loyal to each other (materially, sexually, emotionally, and politically) to provide for and protect their offspring, disciplining children's behavior in family solidarity that can build class solidarity. Stressed out, spoiled, disobedient and lazy brats seem to me altogether too Reichian. Adulterous spouses, promiscuous teens, and brattish children are no help for the Proletarian home, workplace, strike committee, or picket line.

Illusions infect virtue as well as vice. The 'radicalization of the sixties' was a great tidal wave of moral consciousness containing an undertow of sewage. It burst through the bourgeois dam of racist anti-communist lies, buttressed by Stalinist betrayals. The civil rights revolution carried us forward, the Socialist Revolution in Cuba was succeeding as the entire third world trembled with revolutionary potential toward the same. Regardless of origins we were egalitarian; free from the Establishments class, race, and gender bigotry. Militantly against any kind of discrimination and partisan toward a socialist cause which would grant to working people who created all wealth a proportional share and control of it…ending the carnage of imperialist wars.

This 'great radicalization' was also a 'great cultural redoubt' whose soft flanks were vulnerable to absorb bourgeois narcissism and lumpen sloths immorality. David Thorstad of the "Militant' newspaper went on to become a founder of N.A.M.B.L.A. (North American Man-Boy Lovers Association). Only an extreme tip of the glacial anti-nomian corruption within the Party.

Feigning shock at David Thorstad, liberalized anti-nomian cadre continued to wreck homes and marriages with individualistic abandon, demoting their spouses to cyclical companions. "Since the sexuality of all of us is distorted in a class-divided and still Patriarchal society" unaptly persuaded "no sexual behavior should be idealized" then urged "none should be admonished."[1]

It became as bad as 'Mad Max Beyond the Thunderdome' where no rules were broken because there were no rules. None !…for sexual, personal, family, community, — human relations. Not unlike the rest of the country…but we were supposed to be better. We supposed we were in training to be vanguard leaders for a great socialist revolution. We were not.

And yet when a singular behavioral rule was asserted the YSA-SWP discipline was spectacular. From the college campus to the factory shop floor, so-called recreational drug use was growing widespread. Absolutely no drug use was tolerated in our ranks or leadership on pain of expulsion. I had recruited well known previous leaders of Berkeley's Free Speech Movement who were not accepted because of their avowed cannabis use. Bay area chairman Dan Styron explained to me that as bourgeois dominated society degenerated our duty to be

1   1970s SWP sex educational.

leaders of the working class was to stand separate and demonstrate the straight way, the straight path to Socialist Revolution. I would joke with Dan he sounded sort of Islamic. And we would laugh in Dan's unexcelled, one of a kindness good humor. It was later rumored Dan sucided from an organic depression. In my clinical opinion no deadly depressive affect was possible in Dan Styron unless it was a damnably depressive objectively experienced episode. Barnes killed him.

If our probity against drugs was applied against illicit sexuality Comrade Styron would still be with us.

The penultimate probity was loyalty to the party line on policy positions established by majority vote at National Convention. Leninist Democratic Centralism i.e. to close post-convention public discussion for unity in action. However, democratic CENTRALISM was becoming the norm.

Post-convention discussion was to be allowed internally. Then "internally" but not organized. Then "internal" was interpreted to not include other Fourth International groups.

"Minorities" were traditionally given proportional assignments to national committees. That stopped, as locals were being stacked by Barnesites. Ultimately "disloyalty" was decided by the incessant gossip mill force fed by Jack and his hench-persons.

If not formally purged-expelled-suspended sometimes for preposterous reasons like the "potentially violent" manner of legless veteran Jimmy Kutcher and eighty year old Asher Harer; veteran loyal socialist comrades were simply worn down and wasted away.

Three generations of militant Marxists awash in their anti-nomian relationships were no match for evil relationship engineering…no match for Jack Barnes and his lackeys. The best were dumb founded as island foxes.[1] The worst were (partial) collaborators who sooner or later got theirs.

Throughout the sixties I was loyal to the majority line, but critical of its organizational culture. While in and of the Youth Culture I was not less anti-nomian than all the rest of my copulating comrades.

---

1   island foxes: on remote Alaskan islands free of natural predators foxes are known to calmly enter the tent and lie down in the beds of hunters intending their destruction.

Perhaps worse.

I've written about losing my high school Sweetheart in "Badass Gentile" of "Glimpses". Unconsciously I think I still sought her out in others. I met a Jewish girl from Miller Beach near Gary, soon after the October Demonstration. She was lovely in every proportion. Her parents had belonged to the CPUSA[1] in the thirties and forties. She fell in love with me. I treated her badly. I've never jilted any other female in my entire life. She deserved it the least. For she was nearly perfect... loyal and beautiful. My parents and family immediately loved her... as I did. Her parents, I think, considered me a wild, troubled, ulcerated,[2] McTrotskyite, but they did not reject me. I did the rejecting. A wrong I will have to answer for...maybe forever.

One late night in L.A. in 63' or 64' I was at a party thrown by the YSA-SWP for SNCC (Student Nonviolent Coordinating Committee) with several CP (Communist Party) Youth in attendance. We were all slightly buzzed and arguing. We'd been in a demonstration together earlier that evening. A certain late week fatigue had set in. A few undulating dancers seemed as droopy as I felt tired. When...a delegation of black Muslim arrived. They had been with us at the demonstration. Three young black men came directly in and joined us at the bar. They ordered ice water. They turned and stared the hump and grind dancers down. A solemn, more serious ambience settled in and we collectively became more respectful to each other.

Revolutionary Puritans! These guys were who (at our best moments) we thought we were. There was a spiritual, no, downright religious non cultic power about them. The same spirit comparably reflected in twenty-first century Mujahidin.

One of my marxist heroes was Christopher St. John Sprigg. He wrote under the pseudonym Christopher Caudwell. He was English; a physicist and poet. He volunteered to fight in the Spanish Civil War. Slain by fascists in 1935 at twenty-nine years old he'd published five

---

1   CPUSA; Communist Party United States of America
2   ulcerated: At twenty-one I was diagnosed having duodenal ulcers.
Rough camping from the year before in North Africa, Spain, and eastern Europe.
I followed the treatment of the time; eating only Pablum and a concoction of
mothers called graveyard stew. I had to get married to heal up.

textbooks on aeronautics, seven novels, several poems, and short stories.

Thirteen critical essays of his were published posthumously called, "Studies In A Dying Culture" (1938) and then "Further Studies In A Dying Culture" in (1949). Finding the former back in the stacks at the I.S.U. Terre Haute library in 1961 was an amazing experience for me. His thoughtful essays on Religion, Love, Violence, Beauty, and Consciousness have stayed with me more than anything political in print.

On Religion he insists it be examined within social i.e. class relations like any other phenomena *not* held preciously or condemned hostily apart. Seeing Fascist serving priests shot down by penitent prayerful communist Republicans gave him pause to note its contradictions. Even religion that has "served as a bulwark of an exploiting class grown parasitic may finally find some of its content in direct antagonism to that exploiting class". Conversely if the religion embodies a significant constituency of the exploited class it "may as that class becomes revolutionary and creative itself grow vital and insurgent."

Religion, "because it is the opium of the people and not the pride of the exploiting class, may at some stage give rise to a Revolutionary Religion, the weapon of the people".

Marx no less than Freud ultimately deferred to the limits of biological reality. Infinitely more than their modern meta-followers.

The core of human biology include our evolved behaviors from interaction between our environment and our brains circuitry. The nature ↔ nurture issues are not resolved mechanically but dialectically. We are no less inclined toward anything from the (a) superstructual (culture) than we are from the (b) (material) infrastructure. The Idealist or Religiosityist insists the former causes the latter. The vulgar materialist insist the latter causes the former.

More recent neurology and paleontology assert both (a) culture and (b) material are mutually correlative. In every mammalian species there are innate behaviors that discourage incest or inbreeding. There are innate avoidances as well as cultural ↔ economic environmental adaptations. (Directed not dictated so there are occasional deviance even among apes and humans.) Exteriority enhances ↔ interior values expressed in morally approved ↔ exterior behavior.

If only externally imposed step parents would consistently behave the same as genetic parents. They do not. Daley and Wilsons 1996 study of same found stepfathers fifty times more incestuous and hom-icidal than genetic fathers.

Human nature is inhibited from incest not only by *superstructual* (superego - cultural – societal) pressures and *supernatural* (id-like religious) morality but both are predisposed and incorporated in one common biological *material* property.

The same case can consistently be made for monogamous, paren-tal, patriarchal, collective, cooperative, autonomous family units.

Whenever, the Left capitulates to Liberal or Lumpen culture Right wing populists exploit the situation. Culturally bereft the working class clutching its most solid collective unit, its families is misled by those angry radio voices of the Right. Like German workers joining the Nazis to ignore those cabarets of the quarrelling Left.

Twas ever thus. What the Left neglects, the Right exploits.

XVII

By 1970, at thirty years old I was *over* being a youth. I'd been drawn to Malcom like other YSAers but I was also drawn to Islam. I was drawn back to the church. And I was drawn to living on a farm amongst the Amish… real communards not just rhetorical ones. I was married to Anne Dorazio and looked forward to being a Patriarch like my Grandfather Abe.

I'd been his favorite grandson. He kept the model Sputnik I brought him from the Soviet Union in 1960 on the mantel next to his picture of 'John L. Lewis' and Grandmas picture of 'The Sacred Heart of Jesus'. Abe was a militant Union miner, farmer, and family man. Like my uncles he loved the Amish who seemed to be holding on to a past and future life we'd lost.

Both gaps filled by the birth of our children, Bethany and Eliot. Revelation with and from them as to what life is all about.

Our life on the farm together was what the Amish were telling us. It's what Pushkin knew[1] never attained, and died for. It's what all sources of wisdom reveal… the greatest good is the rearing of children up in ways pleasing to God. And by God we had it…for a while.

By 1980, pushing forty, my dear wife Anne divorced me, getting her PhD to rejoin the aging faculty youth culture. A predictable and probably unavoidable time bomb whose tragic rupturedness still haunt my children.

In the winter of 2012 Alan Wald has published ("Winters Tale") in Louis Proyects Unrepentant Marxist.com. It was a call for 'creative' Marxism to address the culture of organization to understand the debacle of Jack Barnes and his Barnesite takeover of the SWP. That provoked Mike Tormey to submit his ('Winter Musings') an insistence on return to basic marxist doctrine and history. I attempted a (Wintersett) synthesis of both called <u>Repentant Revolutionary</u> (During protracted periods of labor quiescence youth movements adopt the culture of the

---

1   "What Pushkin knew": Dying from a duel, Pushkin confessed; "The only bliss is domestic bliss."

lumpen. Rosa Luxemburg)

Barnes and the Barnesites have captured the Socialist Workers Party. Some of us predicted this event and process a half century ago. It is as important to theoretically understand how this occurred as it is to recognize the fact of its occurrence. Consciousness is prerequisite for political direction. Open discussion is prerequisite for consciousness.

I commend this site for providing accessible discussion on these matters. Special plaudits to Mike Tormey for his splendid piece, "Winter Musings". Alan Walds, "Winters Tale" apparently and creatively provoked Tormey's article. What binds us all together is our share in this strange history.

The best of Marxist-Leninist-Trotskyist, (1) philosophical, (2) economic, (3) political, and (4) "creative" variations have not stopped the Barnesite onslaught; the successfully destructive machinations and organized coups of Barnes and his henchpersons. Wald noted we need to understand the culture of organization practiced by political groups. In seconding that notion we may grow closer not farther from the Proletarian foundations, Tormey writes. Again, comradely thanks to Louis Proyect.

It is especially fine to learn that the Karl Fredrick I'd earlier read on this site being patient, kind, and nonsectarian to an evangelical fanatic was the Karl Fredrick Smith I'd hoped it would be. I knew your parents son and lived with them the day they brought you home. They were sure proud of you then. I'm sure they're proud of you now.

Gus Horowitz; good to hear you're still kickin'. I told Rolphe last week I thought you and Melissa Singler were the hardest working YSAers of the sixties. However, you are misinformed Jack Barnes was in Bloomington working hard for (CABS) Committee to Aid the Bloomington Students. The reason Barnes was in Bloomington more than anything else was to compromise the marriage of Paul Ann and Bill Gronninger. Just as he lethally compromised Mary Alice and Dan Styron. You were right to suspect Barnes in 1979. He'd been betraying us on the installment plan since 1962.

A slight correction to Mike Tormey; Don Smith never communicated to me that Barnes was "tainted". He went on voluminous record with our mutual diagnosis that Jack Barnes was an "Adlerian Personality Disorder; embittered and driven to cripple others." D.O. would quote Miguel de Unamuno's remark to a one-armed fascist officer occupying the University of Salamanca October 12, 1936; "The trouble with cripples is they want to cripple others".

According to Marx (Capitol volume 1 p. 603) "The absolute general law of capitalist accumulation is in proportion to the active labour army, the greatest is the mass of a consolidated surplus population, whose misery is in inverse ratio to its torment of labour". Or, as the rich get richer from labor of the working class, there is proportional growth of sub employed surplus populations getting poorer and tormenting labor from below.

During the last half of the twentieth century this "absolute law of capitalist accumulation was widely taken to be the weakest aspect of Marxian Analysis" (Henry Frankel Braverman: 'Labor and Monopoly Capitol' Chapter 17 p269). From the vantage point of the Twenty-First Century we know now it is statistically true.

Marx distinguishes three forms of these relative surplus populations:

(1) The Floating (2) the Latent and (3) the Stagnant.

(1) The <u>Floating</u> is that stratum with broken down ties to localities and/or communities moving from job to job hired and discarded randomly.

(2) The <u>Latent</u> is that residual labor force surviving the annihilation of most of the agricultural population in advanced capitalist countries. Most rural families 'set free' from traditional country work to be atomized in sub employed city life. This 'latent' form of surplus population now exists chiefly in the neo colonies and this regulated internationalization of the labor market is supplemented by the export of various industrial processes (outsourced!) to cheap labor areas in the countries which are kept in subjugation as undeveloped regions. [IBID p208]

(3) The <u>Stagnant</u> sub employment is marginal, casual, and irregular merging with the "sediment" as Marx called it of "Pauperism, the hospital of active labour...and the dead weight of industrial reserves... stagnancy pauperism forms a condition of capitalist production".

[Capitol volume 1 p604] "It enters faux frais into capitalist production. Faux frais literally means fake freshness; figuratively, "the incidental operating costs of keeping the proletariat in line."

The Barnesites milieu in origin and style, form and content entered faux frais into the YSA-SWP. During the last half centuries vast undertow of lumpen stagnancy these sub employed social refugees were metamorphed into so-called revolutionary youth by the Barnesian phenomena. After decades of keeping the Proletariat culturally and functionally remote, then purging comrades of Proletarian influence, factionalizing relationship management one against the other until no one remained but themselves.

Where the surplus populations and the so-called sexual revolution converged... there grew the Barnesites.

Will these co-morbidites of lumpen and liberal corruption be lessened as Barnesites are now workerist ordered into Proletarian jobs? Their identity complex merely entering an industrial phase (They now refer to themselves as *the* working class.) or might the power of Proletarian influence boomerang them around to something else entirely.

As the possum prophesied, "We have met the enemy and he is us." Last night I checked out the new online post workerist Militant and subscribed to it. Current coverage of nationwide strikes. No gas about GLBTers. Little fem-flam from bourgeois feminists. Barnes and Barnesites may be producing the best Proletarian oriented socialist newspaper in America. And, Barnes so-called epiphanous turn to emphasize Fidelismo en vez de Trotzkozmo, to focus on a Western Hemisphere International is not less attractive, including the propensity like Latin's to emphasize being communist instead of slightly cold war shy of the word.

Is it possible? Is it possible his predatory, adulterous, cultic, crippling ways are achieving such things? The Dialectic may move in mysterious ways... or is it possible as a police spy liquidator he is staking out advanced positions to discredit them?

Workers require a party that is more than politically correct and Proletarian oriented. Above all else the Proletariat requires a Socialist

Workers party that is trustworthy. Trust is not complicated. One cannot trust leadership that consistently over a significant period of time says one thing and does otherwise. Likewise, one cannot distrust leadership that consistently over a significant period of time does what it says it is going to do. Let's hold Barnes accountable from the outside. Grit our teeth and critically support him if he straightens up.

"Sorry Tessio. Nothing personal. Strictly business. (The Godfather Part I)

"Nothing personal Jack... strictly politics, you remember, the principled kind."

Grit our teeth and critically support his policies if Proletarian Socialist. (We did no less for Stalin) If not...lay siege to them electronically. Barnes cannot, anymore than Egyptian Colonels deflect an electronic siege of information.

Concede for the time being the Barnesites their organizational forms; ... it's what they most value. Concentrate and capture a just share of the revolutionary content! Organization follows program content, not the reverse; Trotsky understood better than Cannon, Dobbs, or Barnes.

Without exclusive authority of content organizations reorient or organize themselves into oblivion. Lou, why not further pick up on Bert Cochran's ideas and build the site into an open SNC Socialist National Committee toward a Socialist National Congress to critically enjoin or support the SWP and all the other red mastheads. This electronic thing might do it.

Toward an Electronic Soviet,
Comradely,
TGM

This time warp banging me back and forth in simultaneity across the centuries line and life lines in no place not fully experienced and enacted in images projected to evoke the difficulties of living His-Story collectively recalled in a single reclusive narrative.

The skein of geese but trebled notes in a cloudbank. We've called to them through March charred pines and campi columns from Berkeley to Columbia and terminally to Kent. From one hundred factory floors and defiant Yeoman farms. Like the geese frail presence we are but a fading scar upon the brow of tomorrow. Gone upon the droughts or possibly... to brake toward earths prevailing dreams.

XVIII

Meanwhile back at the Ranch. (Easter week in the early eighties)... Daylight was inescapable. It cheerfully and invasively filled up every nook and cranny of human structure or mood. Cold night...kept at bay, most of the time.

Totalitarian sunshine, I thought, as I heard the kids pile out of Minnie's van onto the ranch house deck. They loved the Mountain School, as they called it and Minnie, Miekija, Jennifer, Sean, and all the other kids they'd met.

Minnie showed me a form she'd had Bethany fill out. With my signature it would constitute an application for transfer to their school. The form also included some personal profile questions. To the question, "What name she'd prefer other than her own?" Bethany had answered "Faith".

I didn't sign the application for transfer. "I'm not sure exactly where we'll be."

"It's just for my records", she explained. "If things work out, I'll have it to process."

"No paper trails," I explained. "Could be cops."

Minnie folded the paper away with a very worried look. I kissed her and told her not to worry. My kids, Digger and I took our leave saying good bye to everyone... especially to Minnie. We would drive down the Del Puerto Canyon Road to Patterson, then on across the Valley through Modesto to my place in the Warning trees. Just past the Junction Saloon we stopped for a hitchhiker. In these hills you are expected to stop if you recognize them. It was Rodney, a half Philippino twin son of one of Mike's rancher clients. The kids also recognized him from school that day. He was a seventeen year old senior. He was hitching down to Patterson for his truck from the garage just off the plaza.

Rodney was a tall, handsome, well dressed fellow, who in his Stetson could easily pass for Mexican. Another truck full of teenagers coming uphill toward the junction passed honking, waving and slightly careening in their high lift carriage. Eliot asked why their truck had such high lifts. I reckoned it was a teen Anglo thing and looked to Rodney to answer. He didn't. Neither did I...shaking my head to Eliot that I wasn't sure, thinking to myself, "there's not much mud at this elevation". Fifty minutes later coming out of the hills, we saw a low rider truck full of young Mexicans kind of rhumbaed off highway five's exit ramp. It was a showy kind of vehicle that seemed to glide rather than wheel over the roads surface. Studying it for a minute, Rodney finally spoke...in an exasperated tone looking directly at me. "You see my problem, now, don't you?" he asked, then said, "I don't know whether to be high or low!"

As we crossed over the Delta Mendota Canal, the children gasped as I knew they would at the shimmering green expanse of the San Joaquin. I drove up on the shoulder and stopped as I've done many times just to look at it.

Bethany held on to my collar as the next scene rolled out over the first cuttings of alfalfa. As if by some cosmic cue for their education, three Mexicans came running across the alfalfa field toward the almond trees. Two border policemen with guns were chasing them. Gunfire in the air. The Mexicans quit running and were thrown to the ground. Bethany's instinct for the underdog created a long sounding non word which I responded to with the word "Illegals". Rodney nodded.

"Is that right, Papa?" she asked.

"I don't think so", I answered as much to Rodney's look as Bethany's question. Rodney seemed relieved as we all looked with sympathy at the arrested Mexicans being taken away. I wondered if his sympathy came from way back to the Spanish influence from his mother's homeland or just from his own existential sense of justice. Whichever...we shared a moment of solidarity together.

Eliot then guessed, "Is it political, Pop?" We all laughed and Bethany as Eliot's perennial agent encouraged him to recite some of our political lessons we'd taught him. Reciting for Rodney he said, "Communists want justice. Republicans want freedom. And Democrats want to get elected!" Amazed and laughing still Rodney asked, "How old is that kid?"

We drove through the orchards into Patterson, past Mike's new office in the old library building beside the Swedish Methodist Church. I slowed down so Beth-El could see the many Magpies roosting in the church yard trees. I had spent hours past watching them from Mike's office window. Bigger than crows, beautiful black and white birds, common in this part of California, rare for us Heartlanders to see.

As we slowed past the churchyard, my friend Brian Wilson waved us down. A local artist with a studio nearby, he was walking one of his several Scottish Deerhounds. As I parked the kids asked to get out and pet the big dog. I got out with them and Rodney said he could walk the block or so to the plaza garage. Digger was growling through the window at the big hound. I assured him it was O.K. and told him to stay. Patiently waiting for Brian's permission, the children then petted, skipped, and played around his big sight hound. Brian said it would be alright to let Digger out as well.

After some initial growling around the little Jack Russell, the huge Beowulf, and my two merry children ran and romped together in the large churchyard. Earlier this year Brian, Beowulf, Digger and I had coursed and killed jackrabbits together. We hunted the borderlands between the barren hills of the Diablo and the lush hayfields of the San Joaquin. I admired Brian's landscape paintings of the Valley and he liked my poetry. He was a master at the art of coursing wild game. Unjustly I think, he was also alleged to be the most successful poacher of Deer and Elk in California. Before owning sight hounds he owned and trained cheetahs when he lived up in six rivers country near the Oregon border. His deerhounds could catch and kill a large coyote the way a whippet dispatches a cottontail. That is, without much fuss, just a simple jerking catch would break the neck of its prey.

Brian teared up a bit when the children gave him a hug goodbye. I knew he was far from his children and it plagued him. California and its uprooted populations! I knew the feeling... then I recognized in Brian's tears that same feature I saw in Minnie's countenance...a prescient concern, a prayer-like affect that we, the children and I were somehow in harm's way. We said goodbye.

We sped off through the plaza, out through the palms of Las Palmas, across the San Joaquin River into the wide savannah between Patterson and Modesto. I enjoyed pointing out the goat and Holstein dairy farms as we passed them closer in to the canals of Modesto. Then east along the Tuolome River toward Waterford where along the way we bought strawberries near my modest digs in the almond orchard.

Bethany and Eliot loved the place. Arriving there they seemed re-energized...running inside and out. Bethany wanted to explore the creek running below the ridge and Eliot wanted to take Digger into what he called 'the orchard forest'. Bethany and I unpacked while Eliot and Digger dog took off. In minutes Eliot returned excited that he and Digger had treed a koala bear. We joined him to find Digger treeing one of the many California ground squirrels that scurried along the canal banks. Happily we retired to a simple dinner I fixed of salad, ground beef, and fresh strawberry shortcake. We watched Masterpiece Theatre and went to bed. The children in my bed, me on the couch.

I woke at dawn to the phone ringing. This early usually meant a 'time difference' call from Indiana. I sleepily answered to a soft, feminine voice I couldn't quite recognize. It was Jo-Ann Henderschott, a secretary at Catholic Charities (Archdiocese of Indianapolis). Jo-Ann was the sister of Father Anthony Spiguza, an irascibly traditionalist priest and Pastor of a blue collar parish in Clay County that totally supported his resistance to "modernism"...to anything modern. In my work for the Archdiocese, Father Spiguza and I always got along as we shared a mutual contempt for loosey-goosey liberalism and preferred the company of Proletarians. I was especially fond of Jo-Ann and had protected her, I think, from the worst tantrums of our employer (erraticus clericus) Father (Littlesmith) Schmidlin.

Jo-Ann laughed it was good to hear my voice after such a long time (not two years) and kind of apologized for calling...saying she got "this phone number" from my Aunt Mary. Tony (Father Spiguza) often saw my Uncle Louis and Aunt Mary. "Have you heard from the

(Archdiocesan) Financial Office?" she asked.

"No", I answered.

She continued, "They have insurance money there…from your accident. Your ex-wife has been calling about it.…I thought you should know.

"Hell yeah", I almost blurted but restrained myself saying "God bless you Jo-Ann. I owe you big time for this and Thank Father Tony too."

"Just pray for us", she said. "We're praying for you."

I immediately phoned the old Chancery number I knew by heart. They had moved to the Cathedral High School building but their number remained the same. Bypassing the Bishops office, I asked the secretary to transfer me to the financial office. "Who shall I say is calling?", she asked. I didn't answer. The transfer went through. I asked for Harry, the chief accountant.

"Hey, Harry." I greeted him. "I'm told you have insurance money for me."

Surprised he answered, "It's been awhile Tom, we didn't know how to reach you…"

". . and you weren't exactly pressured to do so by the new Bishop… were you?"

He didn't answer, but said, "Your wife has been calling about it…"

"Technically Harry, *she* is my ex-wife *and* I was the Archdiocesian, the Archdiocesan employee. I have the children now…I need the money! What is the amount?"

He never answered, but said, "We are prepared to send you $5,000. What is your mailing address?"

No sense quibbling with an accountant thousands of miles away…

He said, " a check would be sent right away."

Exultant…I felt like my Pentecostal friends when they exclaim "confirmation!" That is, Providence confirming your direction. Confirming you are on the right path of prayerful intention. With part of the five grand I could afford wheels to get us home. Just last night I'd seen a low interest ad for Nissan trucks in Sacramento.

The children awoke joyfully with my news that we were getting a new vehicle. "Consumerist' as it is we were still that part of America where a new car or truck feels like a new member of the family. My parents used to make special trips to relatives in order to introduce their new vehicles.

Bethany understood the idea of "Confirmation". Eliot inhaled his cereal and struck out into the sunshine with Digger dog. My more mature daughter and I breakfasted slowly on the porch above the creek. She had found an article on oxen in my bookcase she wanted to discuss. It was in the 'Small Farm Journal'[1] I'd gotten from the Heifer Project[2] office. Incredibly, I thought, she talked on and on about how 'a dropped hitch point on the yoke best rotates the bow into the shoulder to capture the power of both oxen.' "It's how you've described the yoke in marriage, Papa. It's not heavy if they work together achieving great tasks knowing how the other feels avoiding the splinters of pulling against each other to go their own way. But Papa, what does *"nigh"* mean?"

"I think it means *near, almost,* or sometimes to the left. Like… nigh on to forty years", I answered…thinking – not saying like you daughter are nigh on to adult intelligence before you are nine.

"Does that make Mama, the nigh Mama?"

"No, no…maybe the nigh wife" I answered, "….somewhere to the left of almost…"

Bethany had more questions about the nigh ox and showed me pictures of a father and daughter working with oxen in Ohio. "Can someday…we do this papa?" she asked.

"Shore 'nuff daughter"….changing the subject now to our catching up with Eliot. Going outside I felt a further confirmation to take my children permanently home. Maybe train a team of oxen there. I wondered if I could use welsh black cows instead of steers for a yoked team.

We found Eliot, loaded up for Sacramento, all three of us saying

---

1   'Small Farm Journal': large quarterly magazine published by Lynn Miller from Oregon, originally from Indiana.; steadfastly holding that the comfort, care, and fertility of the family farm is the most vital component of all agriculture.
2   'Heifer Project': San Joaquin office of National Council of Churches assisting third world farmers with donated heifers and other livestock.

good-bye to Digger who would dutifully stay in the unfenced yard until our return. We stopped at two farms near Oakdale and a third just east of Escalon. All three farms were considering a purchase of the computerized feeding systems.

We easily found the Nissan Dealership in Sacramento. The children were busily babbling about how Sacramento sounded like 'sacrament' or 'sacramentum'. I really didn't know if there was a connection but thought it 'good medicine' to think so. We found exactly the vehicle we wanted within fifteen minutes. Selecting a vehicle, like selecting a mate is never as complicated as people pretend. A little last year model but new, diesel powered black pickup truck with an extended cab suited us perfectly. It was black inside and out, had a small back seat, and boasted great fuel efficiency with the *then* cheaper diesel fuel. We agreed on price, down payment, I signed papers and they told me my dealer-financed loan might be approved within twenty-four hours. Bethany and Eliot were delighted calling the new truck "our little black buggy".

The next morning I went back to work *with* the children. Stan, my old Dunker employer was completely charmed by Bethany and Eliot taking them on a tour of the place while I settled into some serious negotiations with his second in command, Johnny Carvalho. In my absence the Callan Farm had bought the one hundred thousand dollar Herdmaster Computerized feeding program. I had spent hours with the Callans, father and son. The commission was of course mine and went far to pay back the balance I owed them for the January advance they'd given me for my annual farm payment. Johnny said that due to the other commissions soon to follow he would prefer to pull my salary and I'd do fine on commissions only.

I told Johnny there might be serious legal trouble ahead for me and I didn't wish to hurt him, Stan or the company with bad publicity. Straight commission suited me fine and I'd close the pending sales on two conditions (1)he dummy up about our new arrangement long enough to confirm my dealership loan and truck purchase he'd be getting calls within the hour about and (2) that he continue to provide fuel (diesel now) for my farm calls. I was planning to close dozens of farm sales throughout the spring and summer to prosperously return to Indiana for the new autumn assignment of circuit riders and Methodist Preachers.

Johnny waved his hand approving number (1) but rapped his knuckles on the desk objecting to number (2). Wagging his head back and forth, dragging his feet he objected "there was no way to be accountable for a private vehicle". I liked Johnny. Not many did. He was a solid Portuguese guy but frequently acted smuggly Anglo-Saxon.

He knew I knew he'd save money pulling my salary. I knew he knew I was the one most likely to close the pending sales. He also knew I knew he provided fuel for *his* private vehicle. I said nothing but looked at him thinking all the above. Feigning a little bit of anger he stared at me. I stared back. We were having a Mick-Portagee Mexican Stand Off. Suddenly he said, "So it's your ultimatum; take it or leave it?" I still said nothing. He stood, stretched out his hand and said, "we'll take it, but Thomas for the record, I don't like it." I stood, shook his hand and said, "Johnny for the record, you don't have to."

I found Stan and the children back in the mechanics section talking to the young men who were Dennis Borba's team of forcados.

The Portuguese word for bullfight, or corrida de toros was simply the Tourado. They were amazed Bethany and Eliot knew that and applauded Eliot when he strutted hands on his hips like a Cabo (captain of Forcados) toward the bull. Eliot's agent narrator Bethany explained (as if they didn't know) how the Cabo must keep his hands down even as the bull charges or it will charge his face. These forcados applauded Bethany and El as the children of Don Thomas, 'poet of our Tourados.' To their further amazement Bethany told them she had read Father O'Dwyer's book "The Art of the Matador". Actually we had read it together inspiring El's imitating the Cabo routine.

Father James F. O'Dwyer as I've mentioned earlier is an interesting fellow. One year older than me he was born in Cashel (county Tipperary) in December 1939, son of IRA commandant James Joseph and Bridget (Atkins) O'Dwyer. He was ordained priest at the Cathedral in Thurles 1965 and came to the States. (We noted he began his vocation in the priesthood the same time I began mine in marriage.

Conjointly we took both sacraments seriously) Soon appointed pastor of the parish church in Newman, then to St. Patrick's Church in Escalon; from east to west in bullfighting country of the San Joaquin (Escalon, Tracy, Gilroy, Layton, Crows Landing, Turlock, Gustine and Tulare) Tourados.

I would drop in on him from my many crossings on the plaid straight roads of the valley… and I would do it…god forgive me at all hours. Once at 11pm I saw his light on and he welcomed me hospitably. I was interested in visiting some of the Valley Ganaderios[1] and he knew all of the Ganaderos.[2] My cattle back home were of the Welsh Black breed. There are basically three branches or families of cattle breeds (whether dairy or beef). Most of the U.S. and European domestic stock are (1) 'Bos Europas'. Then there are (2) 'Bos Indicus' from India, like our Brahma-Zebu breeds. The third classification is (3) 'Bos Llongifrens' represented by only three remnant breeds from the ancient 'aurochs'[3]; (a) the Welsh Black, (b) the English Park and (c) Spanish Fighting cattle. My welsh black cattle looked like beefy docile variations of Spanish fighting stock. Father O'Dwyer was also a member of the California Marriage Counseling Association. He invited me to attend a meeting of theirs. I declined. I was more interested in attending his meetings of the Pena Taura-Sol y Sombra Association of Aficionados that met in San Francisco.

Father O'Dwyer was a serious man who caused me to drop most of my innate anti-clericalism. He had made pilgrimage to the statue of the Virgin of Macarena in Seville venerated by bullfighters since 1595. It was a spiritual experience for him. He took serious his obligation to pray with and for the bullfighters of the San Joaquin.

I told him of how I was hitchhiking from Berlin to Seville in 1960 to study with American Sidney Franklin the arts of the Corrida. I got as far as the Café de Toros in Granada. I spent the winter in Granada studying with my padrino, Manuel who was called El Electrico in the bullring. My first (and last) alternativa was in the Andalusian village of Berja. [See "Not of Our Time" p77 "The Bulls of Berja"

---

1 Ganaderios: Portuguese for ranch on which fighting bulls are raised.
2 Ganaderos: Breeder of fighting bulls.
3 aurochs: prehistoric cattle

and "Glimpses" p308 "To Hold Death Still"] Father O'Dwyer noted there was a Celtic kinship to the Corrida and Tourados; a Celtiberian connection. He spoke of Diego O'Bolger, a catholic school boy from Buffalo who took his alternativa (first corrida) in Tijuana in 1969. And we were both Irish proud of Robert Ryan who'd taken his alternativa in 1967 and was demonstrating his artistry throughout the world not only with cape and sword but with his poetry and paintings. [See "Vestiges de Songre- Vestiges of Blood" by Robert Ryan] We spoke late into that night about Hemmingway's "Death in the Afternoon" and Barnaby Conrad's writing of Bullfights. Barnaby Conrad had written his book "The Swords of Spain" while living in my village pastorate of Knights Ferry.

Father O'Dwyer showed me on the map, the precise locations of Ganaderias (breeding ranches) Borba in Escalon, Correia in Encino, Mendonca in Tulare, Sousas in Crows Landing and Rochas in Turlock.

He was entre to introducing me to Manuel Sousa and his phenomenal ranch, bullring (Pico Dos Padres) and bull fighters chapel built into the diablo hills and …to the Frank V. Borba family. Years later we'd become regulars in attending the Tourados of his son Dennis who Father O'Dwyer christened "El Californiano". Decades later on top of a water park slide Eliot would recognize Dennis on account of the many (touranados) 'wounds of honor' (gore scars) he wore on his ribcage. They shared some laughter remembering their fathers love of the bulls. When Eliot finally met Father O'Dwyer he dutifully impressed him with a torero quote from his book. "To fight a bull when you are not scared is nothing, and to not fight a bull when you are scared is nothing. But to fight a bull when you are scared – that is something."

I asked my friend Joe Da Silva if he would drive us to Sacramento after he finished his route. He said sure, but our friend Howard Mason was off today and he'd be able to take us sooner. I phoned Howard and he said, he'd finish his coffee and meet us at the car rental agency. Great friend. Great comrades and coworkers!

Howard drove us to the Sacramento Dealership, and hung around for a half hour to make sure we weren't stranded. Johnny kept his part of our bargain. They'd phoned him, did a credit check and we signed the final papers. We thanked and said goodbye to Howard, then fired up our 'li'l' black buggy' and headed back into the countryside. Driving home through Oakdale I detoured down the Orangeblossom Road toward Knights Ferry to visit the Marzettis. Bethany and I enjoyed Eliot's reveling in the sunshine to announce, "When I grow up I gonna be a farmah in da San Wackeen Valleee."

It would be a couple of hours before the Marzetti daughters arrived home on the school bus. My kids were hungry so I drove into the Knights Ferry River Restaurant. It was a small ranch house with a great open lawn located right on a bend of the Stanislaus River. I watched the kids run and play on the lawn and riverbank as we waited for our order of omelets and salad. I had a glass of Chardonnay which shimmered in the sunlight. We ate outside on picnic tables.

We got to the Marzettis not long before their daughters arrived on the school bus and had a great visit. Bill introduced Bethany and Eliot to his daughters, his wife, his mother, horses and dogs as if they were little ambassadors of an important country. All the children took turns riding a pony and playing tag around the barn. We hated to leave when it was time to go. Bill and Eliot's private greeting had become "Bombs Away".

The next two days were spent calling on Dairymen. The children continued to be a hit especially with the Portuguese families, in how well behaved they would sit and listen to my equipment presentations (i.e. sales pitch). Early Friday morning Stan called to say he had a gift for the children if I would stop by around noon. It was a toy model dairy barn with several black and white toy-model Holstein cows. Bethany immediately named her favorite cow 'Magpie' while Eliot named his 'Shark Attack'.

Friday afternoon I phoned their mother. No answer. I left a message, "Children enjoying their Spring Break. Please call." Saturday morning…received a very angry call from Anne. "How dare you," she began. "You have betrayed my trust once again. You're supposed to be in Kentucky."

"No, no we are in California. I have never betrayed your trust. You can trust me forever to be a loyal husband and father. We promised the children a Spring-break here. I'm seeing they get one!"

"You are a psychotic bastard! I'll see you in jail for this."

Then she hung up. "I'll give her the weekend to calm down," I thought. She didn't even want or ask to speak to the children.

For the rest of the day, like most Saturdays, I wrote my sermon for Sunday.

Brigham phoned….just "to check in" around midday. I reported the 'Kentucky remark' and thanked him for it. He took the 'jail threat' more seriously than I did. Since I'd missed Easter, he asked what my sermon would be on this "Low" Sunday. I took offense at his Anglican calendar term and scolded it was residual contempt for the Celtic church calendar term still kept in Eastern Orthodoxy as St. Thomas Day. So I would be preaching on Saint Thomas.

Brigham was rekindling his interest in Christianity. I knew it and delighted in provoking him about it. He gave me no credit for hours of proselytizing with the horses at my place or on tractors at his. However he did credit my mother for a significant pivot in his consciousness. She overheard me, Jim and several Y.S.A.ers[1] in her living room discussing 'dialectical materialism'. As always I was emphasizing the dialectic; others the materialism. Jim was especially assertive; poking fun at all 'pie in the sky promoters'.

Serving us pie and coffee, with perfect timing, she bid Jim join her in the kitchen. Taking aim at his young face she said, "You bleeve when we die we're just dead like a dog?!" Very respectful and politely Jim replied

"Well Mrs. Morgan as a materialist I think that when the material body dies, deceases, that is, ceases to function. *That's just all there is.*"

Silently…while slightly tilting her expression with a sinister twinkle in her eyes, taking on a tone of parental menace she warned , *"You're not gonna git off that easy!"*

Hundreds of other religious responses, Jim Brigham was prepared to deflect easily. But, my mother's words worried him the next quarter century.

He asked if my sermon would be based on the Apostolic "doubt-

1   Y.S.A.ers: Y.oung S.ocialist A.lliance members. Youth group of the Socialist Workers Party.

ing Thomas", the martyred St. Thomas A'Beckett, or the scholarly Thomist, St. Thomas Aquinas?

"Maybe all the above," I mused, then struck seriously "but mainly of St. Thomas Münzer!" His political cynicism set upon he ended our conversation. "You and McNaughton spent too much time in East Germany!"

XIX

St. Thomas Day Sermon

(Coulterville 8am)

(Knights Ferry 10am) In the spring of 1871, Ralph W. Emerson rode through here. He stayed in Coulterville on his way from Stockton to Yosemite. He had delivered his famous 'Immortality' sermon at the church of Thomas Starr King in San Francisco. Thomas King was famous in California as a Pro-Union Pastoral minister. The Sage of Concord was surprised to find David Clark, our Betty Keller's Bruschi family and others in Coulterville familiar with his work.

His work includes, by the way, four volumes of Ralph Waldo Emerson sermons as well as forty-eight of his collected essays and lectures. All LXXXIV of his sermons replete with exceptional skill and wisdom, I think, contain three clear threads running through them. 1) The value and dignity of work, that leads to the 2) responsibility of immortal life and 3) the hand of Providence which is Gods will in History. All of which I'm sure sounds hermeneutically tedious and academic to the ordinary lives we lead until... Until we apply these thoughts and the faith that inspired them to the contradictions and struggles of our own ordinary lives.

On this Octave Day of Easter (eight days from Easter Sunday) in Ordinary Time we've heard or read from holy scripture [John 20: 19-29] the incredulity of St. Thomas the Apostle. Most of us can identify with Doubting Thomas who was not prone to believe in the Resurrection until he stuck his hand in the nail marks and spear wound on Christ's side. Some have suggested this Doubting Thomas be proclaimed patron saint of the post enlightenment, that empirico egocentric time we are only now recovering from. Two centuries of ultra-rational thought "dethroning superstition only to enhance banality" (Jaroslav Pelican)

In Gospel accounts, the Doubting Thomas event takes place on the eighth day after the Resurrection hence the solemnity of today on toward Christ's Ascension and the Pentecostarion. Fifty some days

---

from the injustice of Christ's crucifixion preparing us to receive the Paraclete (or holy spirit). I say holy spirit parenthetically as there is controversy regarding translation of the Greek word *Paraclete* used here. If the apostolic writers had intended to mean *holy spirit* why not just say so rather than introducing a whole new word to translate. Islamic tradition interprets Paraclete as a coded Greek abbreviation (paracleytos: translates to Ahmed, the praised one) for the Prophet Mohammed who comes as an Avenger against Empire and Collaborating Crucifiers.

For indeed the very essence of the Easter event is the injustice of Christ's crucifixion. The messianic presence of Jesus, a perfection of being incarnate in his person and teaching...betrayed, falsely tried, humiliated, tortured and executed. (Whaddaya expect in this world) The majority of Christians in this world (not in this country) are drawn to church on Good Friday not on Easter Sunday. The events of Good Friday square with their experience of this world. The events of Easter Sunday require the hard work of hope and faith not just the morning matinee before the Easter egg hunt. I would argue that experience of Good Friday is essential to understand Easter every bit as much as the touch of nail marks and open wound was for St. Thomas.

Who here has not touched their own nail marks and the open wounds of loved ones with medical problems and medical bills? Some of you have even spent hours on the cross – God Bless you. I am speaking of human suffering... and no one here is a stranger to it. Most of you have known the threat of not enough income, of job insecurity, underemployment and unemployment. Some of you have had medical disabilities that disabled you and broke the bank. Some have been betrayed by a loved one. Some unable to protect your children from molesters. You all have been stressed from time to time worried about your children or others going astray with drugs or sex. Many of you have lost proper access to your own children through custody judgments of the divorce courts. Sometimes the "helping professions" just "help" your children away from you. Some of you are reaching the age where you worry if 'Social Security' will be adequate for retirement. Others are concerned about their older parents, no longer productive for capitalist economy.

Yet...here you all are on Sunday morning in Gods house *not* the crack house...or the cat house...but Gods House...say Amen. You've come here for todays pastoral imagery, *not* porn or commercial imagery. And by Christ we'll have it here! His imagery and message become His presence to sustain and inspire us.

The Reformation moving upon this land and this olde earth is more than that of Vatican II, the pontiff-envy of Luther and the multiple grouplets of Father Jean Calvin's self-election. These variants of "justification in grace through faith alone" degenerate too easily into who can imagine certainty the most. *Justified grace is coming to Gods people through their experience of suffering and the faith required to endure it.* That is the theology of another St. Thomas martyred in the Peasant Wars of the sixteenth century. Fearless leader of the downtrodden, Minister Thomas Münzer led a Peasant Army of eight thousand against the European princes of privilege.

Feudalism was dying in sixteenth century Europe much as we saw it buried in twentieth century China. Cruel aristocracies ruled unjustly over everyone else who did the work. As Pope John Paul II has recently admitted 'the historic church of that time was extremely corrupt' and 'the Reformation correct in its criticism'. He went on to say while Luther and Calvin were right in their criticism of that historical church they were wrong in their conclusions regarding its Universal Catholicity i.e. its supra-historical truth and importance.

Münzer held with the Catholic Church that Luther's *sola-scriptura* was inadequate, i.e. the Bible alone is inadequate without rigorous intellect and spiritually inspired interpretation. The interpreter however would not be the Pope, Luther, or left to the individual but would be the traditions... of Gods suffering people sealed by the holy spirit with new prophets...new Elijah's...new Daniels who would deliver the keys of David and Peter to the collective poor who are the true church.

One hundred years before the Paris Commune, revolutionary Christian peasants were called commonists[1]. Then later...commu-

---

1   commonists: word based on commonsality, from Mensa, the Latin word for "table". "It means the rules of tabling and eating as miniature models for the rules of association and socialization" (Farb and Armalagos "the Anthropology of

nists. History books describe one Thomas Münzer as an existential-ist-religious commonist. His was a ministry consumed by passion for holiness and a concern for the renunciation of privilege with a radical degree of social leveling. *He* sat down at table to eat like Jesus and other peasant revolutionaries without regard to class or social distinctions. Just as Jesus sat at table with other peasants, zealots (i.e. zealous guerilla warriors) women, heavy drinkers, tax collectors, and sinners. He was accused of being a drunk, whore-monger, and political criminal. He was only guilty of the last.

It is clear in the Gospels of Mark and John… as well as the newly discovered, non-canonical Gospel of Thomas that Jesus criminally broke both Jewish and Roman law in his attack on the money lenders in the Temple of Jerusalem. Their activities were not only legal they were necessary for the Temples fiscal basis (however collaborative with the Roman political economy) and for its sacrificial purposes.[1]

"In the temple he found those who were selling oxen and sheep and pigeons and the money-lenders at their business. Making a whip of cords he drove them all out of their temple; he poured out their coins and over turned their tables… saying, "Take these things away; you shall not make my Father's House, a house of trade." (John 2:14-17)

Hollywood always has some pretty actor push at a table and feint a shove toward the money-lenders. C'mon…Jesus closed the joint, overturning tables and whipping the banksters clean out of His Fathers House. The Galilean Peasant had come to town! "That was the bitter and revolutionary Christ model for St. Thomas Münzer and of our poor ancestors". Calling Luther out for his collaboration with Princes replacing Luther's 'justification by faith' with 'justification by suffering' T.M. must have heard Christ preach in his heart. "Hearing the

---

Eating") Prefiguring the word communists as opposed to class privileges

1   John Dominic Crossan "The Historical Jesus". Later John Dominic in his "Jesus: A Revolutionary Biography". "It seems clear that Jesus confronted possibly for the first and only time, with the Temples rich magnificence, symbolically [and physically] destroyed it's perfectly legitimate [if collaborationist] brokerage function in the name of the unbrokered Kingdom of God. Such an act, if performed in the volatile atmosphere of Passover would have been quite enough to entail crucifixion by religiopolitical agreement." Passover was supposed to celebrate Jewish liberation not Jewish collaboration with Imperial oppression.

bitter Christ preach the masses in our hearts, and preparing Preachers full of grace who receive their faith and vocation to be suffering with their people even to have known the torment of unbelief; for he must know how a man feels without the Holy Spirit and how to measure the drive for faith with faith."[1] "Thus sayeth the man with the hammer", he was frequently quoted: "Preachers have to arise leading the people to revelation of the *lamb* by way of suffering judgment; of the eternal word coming from the Father."

Münzers dialectic of internal (spiritual) ↔ external (infrastructural) would reach a synthesis of cooperation between human suffering and Gods Holy Spirit. The Bible is "that ancient record of those experienced in the Holy Spirit' [where] only time separates their experience from ours. At best the Bible is witness to the internal struggles of its heroes with whom everyone is linked in the timeless confraternity of sin and pride"[2] Words of faith to become deeds. Holy Spirit into souls into social and political action revealing Gods will for the world.

More Münzer…"God is your protection and will teach you to fight against his foes (Psalm 18:34). He will make your hands and minds skillful in fighting and will also sustain you. But you will have to suffer for that reason a great cross and temptation in order that the fear of God may be declared unto you. That cannot happen without suffering, *but* it will cost you no more than the danger of having risked all for God's sake… whether you want to or not – conduct yourselves according to the conclusions of Daniel executing righteous decisions…For the Godless have no right to live except we grant it to them, unless we feed them with our work. The end of their authority is drawing *nigh*."[3]

No schizmatic; Münzer yearned to unite Christianity in the cause of poor peasantry everywhere, whether Catholic, Protestant, Pagan, Jewish, or Muslim. The universal experience of humanity, suffering conscience and consciousness was to declare war on everything not bearing the marks of a true encounter with God. "Fighting on for life

1   Collected Works of Thomas Münzers' Peter Mather
2   The Revolution of 1525: Peter Blickle
3   'Basic Writings of Thomas Münzers' Michael G. Baylor

free from human misery and filled with the glory of God."[1]

Thomas Münzer was rediscovered in modern times as a great prophetic figure in history. Frederick Engels credited him with developing a more theoretically advanced political program than most so-called "revolutionary parties" in three centuries. "His was a genius anticipation of the conditions for emancipating the Proletarian elements that had just began to develop...demanding the immediate establishment of the Kingdom of God, i.e. the prophesied millennium on earth... understood as nothing less than a state of society without class differences, without private property, and without superimposed state powers opposed to the members of society. "All existing authorities as far as they did not submit and join the revolution, must be overthrown; all work and all property must be shared in common, and complete equality must be introduced." (Collected Works of T.M. by Peter Mather)

In his conception a 'secret union' on behalf of the peasants and workers was to be organized to realize this program, not only throughout Germany, but throughout the fallen world. Princes and Nobles would be invited to join in the work and "should they refuse they would be overthrown or slain by force of arms at the first opportunity". (IBID)

This "pre-enlightenment" commonist assumed man is the architect of his own destiny...but only upon a genuine encounter between the human and holy spirit. The 'Secret Union' was dedicated to eliminating all opposition to the social and political realization of Gods will. The meek and prayerfully gentle peasants and workers were elected by God to take that revolutionary action necessary to establish a social order safe for the human soul from immorality and injustice.

Two hundred years before the Communist Manifesto this Preacher was teaching communist virtues and leading Peasant and Worker revolutionaries into battle. Little more than a decade ago Frantz Fanon, a psychiatric physician assigned to a hospital in Algiers during the French-Algerian War, wrote a book called "The Wretched of the Earth". In it he details the psychiatric injuries, that is, the damage to souls of the oppressed rural masses of people in the poor parts of the world. The suffering peasantry is still with us! In the preface of

1   "The German Revolutions" Leonard Krieger

Fanon's book Jean Paul Sartre notes that "outside of Europe and that Super-European monstrosity North America it is the Peasantry taking leadership. In the heat of battle all internal barriers break down, the middle classes, the urban working class, the lumpenroletariat of the poor Shantytowns – all fall into line with the stand made by the rural masses, that veritable reservoir of a revolutionary army; for in those countries where development has been deliberately held up, the peasantry, when it rises quickly stands out as the revolutionary class." Will we have to sink below the poverty line to find sympathy with them?

This whole business started with the cultural clash between the Roman Empire and those God-fearing Pastoral People of Palestine. The Ten commandments vs. the cities of the Plain (Sodom and Gomorra). John the Baptist and Jesus vs. Roman Occupation and Herod's collaboration. The Christian Apostles and Martyrs vs. Roman "Civilization" which included oppression of the poor and enslaved who did all the work, and produced all the food for Roman gluttonous feasts and vomitoriums. A cruel civilization worshiping its own cruelties where homoerotic military cults contemned women as mere breeders, macho copulating with each other on their shields between battles. Advanced plumbing to bathe the filth between orgies! Completely diverted by action entertainments! Coliseums full of cruelties; pawns killing pawns, then feeding the faithful to lions. Sound familiar?

Twas ever thus. Collaboration with the sloth and toxic power of empire or faith in God whom Jesus and the prophets tell us resides with the poor in spirit whose work and produce feed the world. We must be like the plain roughhewn people of ancient Palestine. Loving Gods justice and fearing His wrath. Living simply, working hard with faith and courage to endure adversity, knowing Our Father in Heaven is with us, credits our suffering and will proportionally comfort and reward it.

Courage to live a God-Fearing life in the face of an Empires influence is not easy. Contemporary Imperial influence is in our politics, our wars, our sports, our workplace, our T.V., movies, and even the food we're propagandized to eat. In his California sermon on 'Immortality'; Emerson preached, "Courage comes naturally to those who have the habit of facing labor and danger, and who therefore know the power of their arms in work, and courage or confidence in the mind comes to those who know by use its forces, inspirations and returns. Belief in its future is a reward for those who use it." He quotes Goethe, "To me, the eternal existence of my soul is proved from my idea of action. If I work diligently til my death, I am bound for another form of existence, when the present can no longer sustain my spirit."

"The one doctrine in which all religions agree", Emerson asserts "new light is added to the mind in proportion as it uses that which it has." Quoting first the bible, "He that doeth the will of God abideth forever"; then the Koran, "Not dead, but living, ye are to account all those who are slain in the way of God."

Emerson warned against ignorance confounding reverence with egotism. Everything connected with egotism fails. "The soul stipulates for no private good." We have our indemnity only in the collective morality to which we aspire. "If justice live, I live", Emerson has all the olde saints saying, "and this by any man's suffering are enlarged and enthroned."

....Which brings us back to Thomas Münzer. Born in the Hartz Mountains in 1489 to working people he became known as one of the best educated men of his time, fluent in Greek, Hebrew, and Latin languages. Ordained a priest he worked and preached in the Frohse Monastery until 1517when he reputedly had a confrontation with Luther in Wittenberg. Luther was offended by his Catholic Maryology, quoting Bernard of Clairvaux that since neither Mary nor the apostles were baptized with water... spiritual baptism is superior and that the Magnificat is Mary's critique of the existing social order. In all his Marian views Münzer quotes scripture as its basis. He called Luther Dr. Easy Chair who only wanted to help the burghers not the peasants. It was Münzer, not Luther, who composed the first German language mass while he served as Father Confessor at the Convent of Beauditz in 1519. By 1520 he was Pastor of Zwickau and began preaching to Peasant families out in their fields. He preached they should own the land they worked. Civil authorities expelled him and he fled to Prague in 1521. There he was invited to speak and preach in Latin and

German at the many University Chapels. He wrote and published "The Prague Manifesto, an anti-clerical and apocalyptic work. He called on the working people of Bohemia's mining regions to revive the revolutionary traditions of the Taborites[1] inspiring many in the most resolute actions of the Peasant Wars.

On September 13, 1525, T.M. was indicted by the Lord Count Ernest of Mansfield to forbid his sermon at Alstedt. T.M. denounced the Count as a buffoon and heretic, when driven underground returning to iteneracy and preaching again to Peasants in the field. Traveling throughout central and southwestern Germany in 1523 Münzer preached the equality of Peasants and Princes, Priests and Laity. Between 1523 and 1525 Revolutionary Peasants began appropriating the land they worked; inviting the Prince's Court to work the land collectively, but not to lord it over them ever again. Every Lutheran and Catholic Prince responded by declaring war on the Peasantry.

Thomas Münzer organized and led a Peasant-Worker Army of eight thousand to defend their Revolution. They were surrounded by twice that many mercenaries bought and paid for by the Princelings around Frankhauser May 1525. Five thousand peasant soldiers were quickly slaughtered by mercenary artillery. Fatigued toward surrender until a rainbow appeared encouraging them to fight on until annihilation. T.M. was captured alive and tortured into an "alleged recanting to canonical authority". I've read his confession. He confessed being fallible upon death but that his revolutionary actions were canonical as was his faith. "Omnia Sunt Communia". He was immediately executed and beheaded. All this a dirty little secret of Protestant and Catholic history. Only the most wee minded vulgar materialist or establishment bourgeois ideologue would condemn this temporal loss as defeat. Thomas Münzer, he and his were the salt of the earth that has not lost its savor. Light for this world.

Their revolutionary policies were inspired by their religious conscience and consciousness. Defeat is deflected by his beattitudinal legacy. His transcendent commitment to the poor, the suffering meek without a voice who hunger and thirst for justice and mercy, pure in

1   Taborites: Bohemian fifteenth century Hussites whose militant and revolutionary settlement was fortified near Prague and christened Tabor City.

heart struggling to make peace and persecuted in the cause of righteousness. Indeed happy are those abused and slandered for doing Gods will. To compress all the beatitudes; happy (or blessed) are those who do good and are not surprised when it doesn't work. It counts!

(John 20:24 Jesus sayeth to him... Thomas, because you have seen me, you have believed. Blessed (or happy) are those who have not seen and yet have believed.)

The bravery of belief...faith in the best of life...in others...and in justice beyond life. The lack of justice on this earth requires love to endure its absence. The unwitting notion of God as Omnipotent Dictator is finally dead or dying in America. It was buried a century ago in Europe by Dostoyevsky's Ivan Karamazov who announced for a literate public that belief in the omnipotent all powerful God is "not worth one tear of a starving child". If he exists he is a tyrant to be ignored or opposed. Some six hundred pages later Ivan discovers the corruption of evil in his father's murder thus recovering...restoring his faith in God and morality. The idea of God however is left in a kind of Dostoyevskyian disorder.

A popular book in America this season is titled "When Bad Things Happen to Good People". It is authored by Harold Kushner, Rabbi of Temple Israel in Natick Massachusetts. It has been suspiciously applauded by such ecumenical company as (Catholic) Andrew Greeley, (Protestants) Harvey Cox and Norman Vincent Peale, (Clinical) Elizabeth Kubler-Ross, Art Linkletter and the American Academy of Psychoanalysts. Rabbi Kushner wrote the book while caring for his son Aaron as he died from 'Progeria', a degenerative and terminal disease. He calls on Talmudic wisdom to clarify the kind of prayers we should not pray. Not trivial prayers (for bets or ballgames) or mean spirited ones (for smoke from a house fire be someone else's instead of our own). The book discloses a touching story told by a loving father. I recommend it. But in addressing the problems of untimely death, disease and evil, frustrated by prayers not answered the book demotes the idea of an omnipotent Father to an Avuncular screw up.

[1]Reviewing the answers for unanswered prayer he lists: We didn't get what we prayed for; "because (1) we didn't deserve it, (2) we

1   "When Bad Things Happen to Good People" by Harold S. Kushner p115

didn't pray hard enough, (3) the opposite result was more worthy, (4) God knows what is best for us better than we do, (5) God doesn't hear prayers, or (6) God doesn't' exist. All of which lead to feelings of guilt, anger or hopelessness." Instead the book suggests it is because: God exists but screws up.

On the last page, Rabbi Kushner makes an appealing heretical plea.

[1]"Are you capable of forgiving and loving God even when you have found out that He is not perfect, even when He has let you down and disappointed you by permitting bad luck, sickness, and cruelty in His world, and permitting some of those things to happen to you. Can you learn to love and forgive Him despite His limitations, as Job does, and as you once learned to forgive and love your parents even though they were not as wise, as strong, or as perfect as you needed them to be?"

You know...like Uncle Jake of all those words and little follow through. I agree with the Rabbis conclusion that "the ability to forgive and the ability to love are the weapons God has given us to enable us to live fully, bravely, and meaningfully in this (to put it mildly) less than perfect world". However I think there is a stronger more orthodox explanation and guide for us.

It is the Gospel of Saint John which identifies Satan as the Prince of this world, in charge but already condemned. Whose sentence is passed and is to be overthrown. (John 12:31) The Prince of this world is on his way. (John 14:30) But so is The Paraclete after Christ to convict the condemned Prince [and collaborators] in the final conflict and judgment. (John 16:8-11)

The God of Holy Scripture in all His Power and Might is not in charge here. It's worse than the Rabbi thinks and better than he seems to realize. In some massive and mythic disobedience our species of being defied Gods turf to be under the gun of evil. The Satanic Prince of this World and his Princelings rule in a state of entropic chaos which they insist is Freedom. Our Father in Heaven whose love is as constant as his wrath about this arrangement follows us (as a distant parent) keeps company with us (through our God consciousness). Our prayer and righteousness are resistant sorties through Prince Enemy

1   IBID p148

lines. However brief the Glimpse of God's Grace it is accessible in His sympathy for our suffering here, our respect for His natural laws, our love and forgiveness for each other, our love for Him and our continued resistance to Evil. The Amish farmers of Americas Midwest are direct descendants of those Peasant Martyrs who followed St. Thomas Münzer into battle. And just as the Amish do not account for fiscal years but account in fiscal generations; we must amply measure beyond manifold science - material, moral, and spiritual graces to include the momentary and the millennial.

Work has no end. What we know is a point to what we do not know. To Emerson – most men and women die insolvent, that is, the promise of their life's endeavors is much more than they ever perform. However much admired their work…it falls short of what it could be… and that constitutes no less than the perpetual provident promise and goading ideal of our Creator inhabiting eternity. Jim Thayer accompanied Emerson on his trip through here and the Sierras. He heard his California sermon on 'Immortality' and thought of its words later at Ralph Waldo's funeral in Concord. "That the doctrine of providence and eternity dissolve the poor corpse of nature and gives Grandeur to the passing hour." He described Emerson as "agreeable, accessible, cheerful, sympathetic, considerate, and always with respectful interest in others especially the humblest, which raised them in their own estimation". Emerson seemed always attentive to the 'secret union' that glimpses the grace of Gods guidance, goadings, and gifts in an amplitude of what little time we're given here within the greater habitat of eternity. "Whatever limits us we call fate", said Emerson, "yet limitation has its limits." Deliberation and destiny dialectically inform an active focus.

The sacred rage for order that inspired Thomas Münzer endorsed by Ralph Emerson is the way of Christ and the Prophets… to stand apart from the rot of Empire, against the genteel swamps of collaboration. To work hard for our families, to raise children up in ways that are pleasing to God and fight as we must for a social order materially and morally safe for them and conducive to justice includes much suffering and always has. It "will cost us no more than the danger of having risked all for God's sake." We must be attentive to Providence interiorly and exteriorly. "Any fool can learn from his own mistakes", Bismarck said, "we must also learn from the mistakes of others." Others in History providently inform our story.

What happened to so many others?
What happened to ancient classical Greece?
What happened to the Roman Empire?
What's happened to the British Empire, the Napoleonic
Empire? the Empire of Czarist Russia? and the Third Reich? Moral decay and degeneracy! Carl Menninger of the Menninger Clinic in Kansas, in his book, "Whatever Happened to Sin?" asserts Sin is still the primary cause of individual and institutional degeneracy.

More to the point...what happened to the souls of poor families within the dying cultures?

What is happening today in the Soviet Union and Imperial America? Since Stalin and the disappointed attempts to De-Stalinize...Russian Communists are so demoralized the U.S.S.R. will never last the century out. And look out once that happens. If the Ruskys messed up running a Monarchy and screwed up socialism their next version of some kind of democratic capitalism will set records for the world's worst examples.

Not to be outdone. See how America is selling its soul to the Global Corporations. Our sacred rage for order...the freedom to do Gods will has long been confused with the freedom to enterprise over others.

It is temerarious to exempt America, to succumb to the "exceptionalist" delusion that its development is different from other empires. We cannot deny our governments' Imperialism until it zombies out in our own front yard. Until the moral damages become so great...so palpable in our own soul that the dialectic of learning ↔ living breaks down. Even then...in the heart of despair there is light that darkness cannot overpower. For there is not one thing that has its being, nor ever had its being but through Him. All phenomena, all being begins with God...even that which degenerates into evil. Its beingness as our beingness is through God, Our Father in Heaven.

As Jesus instructed the wise Nicodemus during his stay in Jerusalem just before his Crucifixion. (John 3:11) "I tell you most solemnly, we speak only about what we know and witness only to what we have seen, and yet you people reject our evidence. If you do not believe me when I speak about things in this world, how are you going to believe me when I speak to you about heavenly things?" And then that awesome verse children memorize in Sunday School, (John 3:16) "For God so loved the world that he gave His only begotten Son that whoever believes in Him shall not perish but have everlasting life." ... God sent His Son into the world not to condemn it but through him it might be made safe."

The condemnation is that too many of our species still prefer darkness and reject the light in and of His word. But everyone who works (the Hebrew word ergazomai means not just to do, but to work)... everyone who works in, of, and toward the light — their work may be clearly seen and is of God.

Our greatest work... (beckoning Bethany and El to join me down front) is to raise "young beings, young sprouts... [laughter] fillies and colts, daughters and sons... in ways that are pleasing to God. Not according to the magistrates but according to Gods word. One Sunday after the love offering of this congregation to God, and to each other... my hand and eyes fell luckily upon the book of Jeremiah. I had turned not consciously to Chapter 31:16-17

"Refrain your voice from weeping
 And your eyes from tears;
For your work shall be rewarded
sayeth the Lord
That *your* children shall come
back to their own border
their own country."
[Applause]

Our services ended that day with Bill Marzetti and his new guitar singing 'Peace in the Valley'. Bill knew it was my favorite hymn and we'd talked about how great it sounded when Johnny Cash sang it. Bills Italian tenor was not Johnny Cash but it still sounded great that morning. "There will be Peace in the Valley…someday. There will be Peace in the Valley…for me."

We said good-bye to Coulterville's stern handshakes and collective respect. We said good-bye to Knights Ferry amidst tears of brave happiness. My children contained and continued this mood…merrily chattering all the way to Stockton for our meeting with the McMurtrys. I drove the back roads through Oakdale, Escalon, and Manteca. Oakdale was celebrating their annual rodeo and parade. Bethany read Eliot the sign that described Oakdale as the cowboy capitol of California. Eliot loved that and I told them we might make the evening parade on our way back toward Waterford.

When we reached McMurtry's Racquet Club in Stockton a young Mexican greeted us to park our vehicle. I spoke Spanish with him in my limited grammar which greatly impressed Eliot. Weeks later Bethany told me he was bragging to his cousins that "My Papa can speak more than just Englush."

Inside the clubhouse the entire McMurtry clan and their friends made a great fuss over the children; both of whom basked radiant in that limelight.

Jack was less tense and more pleasant this visit. He was less concerned about anyone's alcohol intake as his wife Kathleen seemed angelically lit enjoying her role as maximum hostess and chief celebrant of this family and friendship gathering. She took charge introducing all her grandchildren, children and friends. The friends all seemed to have German names, lived in Lodi and came from the Dakotas. I learned that Jack McMurtry and his mother's family all hailed from the Dakotas. Bethany had many questions for them about the Dakota country. Both children were delighted to hear that "Sacajawea", Lewis and Clarks Shoshone woman guide was commemorated there. Before I could conversationally add that the Wounded Knee massacre was also commemorated there, Eliot held forth about 'Sacajawea'. He knew that name because it was what Bethany wanted to be called as she led him around exploring the forest glades of Gloryville Farm. Getting them lost several times Eliot started calling her "Psychojawea". Slightly perturbed by Eliot's joking at her expense Bethany said she thought "names were important especially the stories about them." She asked if they'd ever heard the song, 'When I Take You Home Again Kathleen'. Kathleen McMurtry slightly disconcerted replied, "Why…Jack used to sing that to me. It's about Ireland isn't it?" Beth smiled at me to tell Kathleen the Bernie Sweeny story about the song. Expectantly the McMurtrys and their friends turned toward me.

Unsure how the story would land I abbreviated it into one long sentence. "According to our friend Sweeney the song was written by an Irish widower in Terre Haute planning to take his post funeral wife's corpse back to Ireland to be buried in the olde sod."

"Gak!", somebody blurted "you were being serenaded by a second hand song for a corpse!" There was nervous laughter. "By a man who loved his Irish bride", Jack gently touched the hair of his wife. Their son Sean put in, "I don't think John Wayne and his Regimental singers knew that songs intention when they serenaded Maureen O'Hara in … in…which of the Ford trilogy was it?" Jack knew precisely it was 'Rio Grande'. Conversation turned to a "collective" I thought, admiration for the John Ford – John Wayne black and white magnificent motion picture trilogy, 1)'Fort Apache', 2) 'She Wore a Yellow Ribbon', and 3) 'Rio Grande'. There was some difference of opinion as to which picture was the best. "I'll bet, Rev. Morgan is a cinema critic", Jack said. "Yeah", said Sean, "let's ask the Hoosier McPeacher…Hey Rev whaddya think?"

"It's like Matthew, Mark, and Luke", I said. "No favorites".

"What about John?…" began Jack's withering cross examination.

"You got me. Johns the best. I guess I do have a favorite".

"Aye you're cornered, now what about which Ford –Wayne classic is the best?"

"I'm cornered counselor", I clowned. "It would be the last.

"Why?" he asked.

"The Terre Haute song", I answered. "Rio Grande *is* about estranged parents…a good father and son saga *but* with a contemptible confederate friendliness. It concludes, I remember with a disgraceful display of

Dixieland, you know "the look away..." from southern slavers ditty. Yet I also remember Maureen O'Hara's smile brightened even that ugly tune." Jack drew me aside smiling, "I will file tomorrow a petition for your custody of the children." I had not paid him a penny.

We returned home through Oakdale again in time for the evening parade. Coming through Escalon I drove around the bullring off Bellota Road to show Beth-El where we'd later attend the Tourados with Father O'Dwyer. They were tiring but not sleepy. The Oakdale parade re-energized them as they caught candy thrown by mounted riders into the side line crowds. Eliot squealed he'd caught ten tiny tootsie rolls in mid-air.

"Don't eat e'm all at once," I warned. "Just a few. We'll save e'm in the glove compartment until we get home.

The parade was interesting. It included several dozen African-American riders from the Tracy area and three packing outfits from the Sierras. I spoke to one outfitter who said the preferred pack animal in the mountains was by Mammoth jacks out of Standardbred X Percheron mares. He had a long trail of pack horses and pack mules in the parade advertising his mountain trekking tours and hunting and fishing trips. What pleasure available, I thought, if you could live around here and be prosperous at the same time. The parade over we headed back toward our little 'warning trees' home.

XX

Pulling off 132 on to the long county road across the canal bridge and then into our orchard lane we were stopped abruptly by a county sheriff's squad car. One officer approached my window while a second walked around to the shotgun side where Bethany and Eliot shared the seat. I immediately checked all windows were up and the doors locked. Barely cracking my window I was asked for my driver's license and vehicle registration. I passed these papers through the barely cracked window. While the lawman surveyed the papers I surveyed the possible routes of escape. There was a footpath up the berm from where we were parked that went along the canal all the way east for miles until it came out on a north-south pavement. Our little Nissan truck was just small enough to fit the trail where the wide shot Deputy's car could probably not follow plus there were dozens of orchard tractor paths in hundreds of acres of almond trees where we could be hidden.

As the deputy on my side slowly announced he had a warrant for my arrest, the other deputy smilingly pantomimed for Eliot to roll his window down. Compliant…Eliot innocently obeyed. That deputy threw open the door, plunging over the children, stuck his big revolver into my face ordering me to open my door and get out of the truck…I sat still and politely asked the pushy rat to crawl off my children as I got out on my side.

Once out, my children came running around the truck to hold on to me as I was handcuffed. We were loaded into the back of the squad car and driven the hundred yards home "to pick up the children's things." The children and their things were to be taken to meet their mother at the Police Station. She had spent the night at one of the policeman's home waiting for them. I was to be taken to the county jail.

The cops, me and the children went inside to gather their things. Digger, sizing up the situation, in his canine mind… couldn't figure it out. Guns on me, captive to the cops, kids crying he roared alarm growling and coming after the cops. I commanded him down. The kids loved on him. He wagged his tail trying to reframe the situation as a friendly one. At that point Eliot picked up my old Stetson and proclaimed to the lawmen, "If you're gonna take my Papa, I'm gonna take his hat!" Eliot's defiance cued Digger he'd been right all along and he roared at the police again, I was afraid they might shoot him and commanded-cajoled him away from them. The confused concern on the loyal little terriers face would haunt me almost as much as my children's tears in the days ahead.

Another squad car arrived and took my children tearfully away. Assuring me they'd be fine and were going straight to their mother, I began to receive the good cop/bad cop treatment.

The bad cop who'd stuck the gun in my face continued to sulk menacingly. The more quiet cop began sympathetically to ask me my side of things. Fully conscious I was being played... I was too angry for caution. I told them how I'd been refused and my children denied their court ordered spring visitation. I objected to the arrest prior to any opportunity for reasonable explanation. And if the warrant came from Indiana – two thousand miles away how could Indiana know what was going on in California! I told them I'd been on the phone with their mother and she knew the whereabouts of (her) our children.

"Jest what do you plan to do?", the bad cop quipped, as the good cop gave me long faced encouragement.

"I guess I'll have to go a lot farther next time", I said assuming an authority which irked the bad cop and amazed both me and the good cop. That uncautious statement hurt my present situation and defined the future one.

In jail, I was booked for kidnapping, given one phone call, and told my bail was set at $250,000. My one phone call was to District Supervisor Bill White whom I asked to notify Bill Marzetti in Knights Ferry, Ted Harbinger in Coulterville, and Jack McMurtry in Stockton. Supervisor White suggested maybe it would take something like this for me to let go of my stubborn hope for marital reconciliation. I already knew it. He couldn't believe my bail was so high. I told him it was in the Hoosier tradition of high California bails. Mine was almost twice that of Charles Manson. He laughed a little. I tried to...

The deputies avoided my gaze. The jailers stared. The trustee janitor with a mop stared. I was stared out…glad to be locked up away from them. My cell was on the corner of a totally empty cell block. A strange open seclusion without company or privacy in a dingy dim light that never turned off.

My mind was racing with adrenal images of my children suffering. I could take this. I knew the risk. I hadn't factored in the children being traumatized by seeing me dragged off. They'd probably blame their mother… but that wasn't good for them either. I began anxiously fearing the consequences of my conduct harming my children. God knows it was not my intention. I prayed. I prayed a kind of shotgun, ejaculatory prayer about everything including comprehensive forgiveness of my sins and/or errors. Then rifled in prayerfully on why and what I'd done. Finally prayed the Thomist prayer logically giving it to God, faithfully leaving it with Him and settling into certainty that He would give me adequate temperament to deal with whatever the hell happens next.

Hemmingway had preached a kind of stoic bravery that requires restricting the imagination. My imagery was constant but with a little help I could displace fearful images with the consoling kind.

Thank God for the Gideons. Just the help needed… I fairly lunged after the Holy Book that lay on the hard bunk. Turning toward Jeremiah 31:16 I stumbled upon Chapter 12:7

"I have abandoned my land
left my heritage
I have delivered what I dearly love
into the hands of its enemies
My heritage has become
a lion in the forest
it roars at me mercilessly…"

"Gripped in anguish like a woman in labor…" even I began the existential whine. "Why me? Why is this happening to me? Has this last week been a Münzers rainbow? Hold on! I *know* the answers to these wretched doubts and all the other questions that Jeremiah pelts upon the problem of evil…like…Why does the way of the wicked prosper? And, why are those happy who deal so treacherously? Jeremiah was a major Prophet sent to "tear up and to knock down; to destroy and to overthrow" (Jeremiah 1:10) the evil and banality of this world. This man of peace was forever at war, with his own people; "a man of strife and of dissension for all the lands" (Jeremiah 15:10) Jeremiahs suffering purified his soul of everything unworthy and made it open to God"[1] His conception of Gods law, his respect for the function of love and how both can be experienced as an inward force (Jeremiah 31:29-30) make him dear to Jews, Christians and Muslims.

The whining why me? to a dictatorial tyrant is always a pathetic and stupid question. Providence is always symbolically instructive. The Prophet Jeremiah knew (10:23) "the course of a man is not in his control, nor is it in mans power as he goes his way, to guide his steps"

(La illaha el lill Allah)[2] I had committed my cause to Him (La illaha el lill Allah) who pronounces justice and rules over kindness and integrity wherever it touches this earth (Jeremiah 9:24). I prayed He probe my mind, heart, and loins and if fit let me know the vengeance He will take on my enemies. The jailers, cops, even so-called socialists entangled in the genteel swamps of borgeois liberalism and lumpen life styles... who dare to violate the Ancient Natural Law. With Jeremiah (13:26) I called on Him "to pull their skirts up over their heads and let the shame of their adulteries, the shrieks of their pleasure be punished" to the last consort of all the unclean harlots... including..."my love, My Love...where are you?" Memory of Ferlinghetti[3] was interfering with memory of Jeremiah... "Where are you?"

If you only knew
the huge emptiness here
that "stares from all the faces
All that is lost must be
looked for once more"
Ferlinghetti heard Segovia in the snow on the night road to Moscow in an old bus.

---

1   Commentary on The Prophets p1126 The Jerusalem Bible
2   "La illaha el lill Allah" Sufi chant to God - Yahweh – Allah
3   Lawrence Ferlinghetti "Segovia in the Snow" in his collection, "The Secret Meaning of Things"

"Traceries of the Alhambra
in a billion white birches
born in the snow"
"Where of a sudden, Segovia's hands"
grasp steerage through the radio
of the dark bus he drives
past John Reeds grave
and the stares of Mayakovsky
He strikes the strings softly
Sound melts in the snow
His guitar plays a longing sound
"He yearns and yet does not yearn
He exists and is tranquil
in spite of all"
In spite of all
he has no message.
He is his own message
Strumming…"saying
I am your ruin,
unique and immortal.
I am your happiness unknown…"
"After fifty Octobers
and fifty strange springs
From the dark heavy light"
in buses, churches, and jails
the sound of "Segovia
comes on like the pulse of life itself.
Segovia comes through the snowdrift
and plains of La Mancha"
through the bars of the jail
and its sad gray cement
Segovia sounds and drives the bus radio
through the night land of Moscow
Granada, and Seville

In Bloomington too... you'll remember he played for all of us including the late couple... whom he stopped to stare at until they were finally seated. Magnificent olde Republican...will we live long enough to hear and see sketches of a Socialist Spain or as Fidel secretly visits his family[1] "we'll know life flowers in the windows of the sun"[2]

But where is the sun...? The sun seems only to set...¡Seems, seems! Autonomic Nervous slop...Begone heart rending untrustworthy delusion. Faith in sunrise is daily met!

"Disequilibrium is a general objective rule... Disequilibrium is *normal* and *absolute* whereas equilibrium is temporary and *relative*."

Chairman Mao wrote that in "Sixty Points on Working Methods"[3] in 1958, the year I graduated from High School. Since that time to this jail nothing has been more true. If like Celine[4] I had journeyed to the end of night...I would like Mao mount a rear guard assault toward dawn.

Around eleven my fellow prisoners filled up the cell block. They'd been downstairs watching a T.V. movie and the local news. They were all very interested in who the hell I was. Variations of the question, "Who you?" "Whadidudo?" "Whatchyainheerfor?" were fairly precisely pitched from different lengths of the cell block. From their cell to mine. This created a cacophony...then quiet.

"For kidnapping my own kids", I answered loud enough to be heard. "Damn, he's the dude the T.V. just talked about". "You the country Preacher?", somebody asked I couldn't see. Around the corner a gaunt black man angled his gaze into mine and asked, "You the Preacher man?" "I'm the man", I answered. There was a lot of "he's the preacher man mutterings" but also more than a few, "Bet he's done more than that!" and "For sures" thrown in. Some raucous cackling followed but soon died down.

Then the gaunt man spoke respectfully saying, "We used to have church here Sunday nites as well as Sunday mornins. It was good...I

1   Fidel Castro secretly eluding the CIA regularly visited his extended family in Spain.
2   More Ferlinghetti
3   Mao Tse-Tung: "Sixty Points on Working Methods" 1958
4   Celine: pen name for Louis Ferdinand Destouches; author of 'Voyage Au Bout de la Nuit'

guess anything is good to go…away for awhile to git out of this lit up shit hole for awhile. You reckon you could have or do church for us tonite? Just some prayers and readin of the good book to comfort us git a better sleep in this half gassed light."

"It is an honor to be asked", I replied, "I am obliged but only on one condition." "Whazatt??" came from several cells.

"No sermon critics!" I said I couldn't get my hands on a critic behind these bars! There was laughter settling toward ease when a guy named Gus blurted out, "Not me! No more demerits bullroar for me. I'm against anything done up here without Shorty's approval."

"And I've just been ease dropping for that!" said Shorty our rotund jailer for this cellblock. "I don't think a little more church would hurt you girls. Just keep it quiet. I doan wanna have to splain anything noisy up here."

I prayed with them aloud (but not too loud) the 'Our Father'. I asked how many men here were fathers? More than half responded they were fathers. We prayed the 'Our Father' again with that in mind and louder. Gus and Shorty could fret about it. Then I prayed the Al-Fatiha; the seven opening verses of the Holy Koran:

1. In the name of God, Most Gracious, Most Merciful
2. Praise be to God, Cherisher and Sustainer of the Worlds
3. Most Gracious, Most Merciful
4. Master of the Day of Judgment
5. Thee alone do we worship and Thine aid we seek
6. Show us the straight way, the straight path
7. The way of those on whom

Thou has bestowed Thy Grace,

Those whose portion

Is not wrath

And who go not astray

"If we pray aright these prayers it means that we have some knowledge of God and His attributes. His relation to us and His creation which includes ourselves. We can glimpse the source from which we come and that final goal which is our spirits destiny. Under Gods judgment we offer ourselves to Him and seek His light especially from this insidious half assed light. At least I came close to saying as best I could remember from the Yusuf Ali commentary in my King Fahd edition of the Koran which concludes; "And we know the straight from the crooked path. By the light of His grace that illumines the righteous."

Through the dim light somebody interrupted that they didn't like praying in somebody else's words. They "liked talkin direct to God with their own words." There was some collective grunting in agreement with his remarks.

I replied back that was fine but they should realize that God doesn't really need our prayers of any kind. He does not need praise as He is above all praise. He needs no petition for He knows our needs better than we do ourselves. His bounties are accessible without asking to the righteous and the fallen alike but ... prayer is primarily for our own spirits education, to console and confirm our direction. That is why the revealed prayers of the good books are given to us in the form in which we should utter them. Or more bluntly, whoddaya gonna learn from your own words!?

We had closing prayers the rest of the week at around 10pm. After the Our Father and the Al-Fatiha I would ask for petitions and my inmates learned to reply respectfully and succinctly. Even Gus.

Wednesday afternoon I received my first visitors. It was Rolphe and Brigham. They'd heard through the grapevine and T.V. The San Joaquin and especially Modesto had the reputation of being California's Bible Belt. It was Sacramento and San Francisco news when a Valley Preacher was arrested for kidnapping. Both my old pals were comradely and solicitous. Rolphe wanted to whisper about a kibbutz he knew about near Nazareth that was both Christian and Jewish. He thought next time I should take my children clear over there and hideout. Israel?! I joshed with Rolphe that Indiana had been hard enough on me and Jewish girlfriends. In Israel they'd be illegal. Rolphe was patient with my jail house irreverence but he would never laugh about anything near the Jewish question.

Brigham had brought me two books. He clutched them with his fists during most of the visit. He asked what they could do to help. I told them I was sure my neighbor Jerome or my landlady would be seeing to Digger. I had him on a self-feeder and was still thinking I'd be out in hours or days...not weeks. Brigham said he'd see about him today. I thought of the bail money but said nothing. I did ask them both to phone Jack McMurtry and he'd advise them. Israel! I couldn't believe Rolphe. Against Gehennas Pit, we were P.L.O. supporters. I decided he was at least identifying with me in this trouble. Brigham fumbled with the books upon leaving. They were Freidrich Engels, "The Peasant Wars in Germany" and Abe Friesen's "Thomas Münzer: Destroyer of the Godless". Rolphe picked up the latter, looked at it, then looked at Brigham quizzically. Brigham said, "....he thinks he's Thomas Münzer!" And they left. Cheerfully and sadly.

That night me and my inmates were allowed two and a half hours of T.V. movie and news. There was no mention of the "outlaw valley preacher" and the movie was both silly and interesting. I love movies and was ready for one that night. To watch...to visit someone else's trouble; not my own.

It was a 1950's anti-communist drama called, "Conspirator". Robert Taylor was cast as Michael Curragh, an Irish revolutionary who trained in the Wicklow hills with Michael Collins to drive the British out of Ireland. Hollywood has this character absurdly presented as having become a Major in the British Army and a Communist spy devoted to his cause *and* to Elizabeth Taylor, his patriotic American anti-communist wife. The plot sickens as Elizabeth Taylor discovers his politics, betrays him to the British High Command and abandons her marriage. Robert Taylor is then left in a movie manufactured cold war quandary whether to abandon his life long career as a Communist Revolutionary or kill Elizabeth Taylor. Cognitive dissonance? I didn't think so.

Afterwards we could hardly follow the news there was so much discussion and argument about the movie. Many inmates took Elizabeth Taylors side. A few stood fast for Robert Taylor. Most wouldn't take sides saying it was just a Hollywood mess with your mind movie. Back in the cellblock the argument stayed hot for a half hour or so. Shorty kept sshhing the volume. I've always enjoyed cinema discussion. And I enjoyed this one. Nothing gets to the viscera of Americans faster than a really good or in this case really bad film.

Arguments exhausted, the inmates turned toward me. Gus spoke, "O.K. Preach, which side you on?" Then rather stiffly…"Of all possible options what would be the best moral choice for Michael, the lead character? What should he do?"

"….Forgive and execute betrayal," I answered.

We all retired that night in prayers, thoughts, and dreams of the women who'd loved us, reared us, abandoned us, scolded us, left, betrayed us, and given us the gift of life in our lives and our children's lives.

XXI

The next day Brigham was back. He'd stayed over, barged in on McMurtry, talked to McNaughton, seen to my Jack Russell Terrier, talked to my neighbors and phoned Anne in Indiana. He told me Digger was fine but howling all night in my absence.

"Your place was open," he said. "I went on in. It was a mess! Bachelor Squalor!!"

"You the housekeeping police?"

"I had to pick up and throw out all your old tequila and beer bottles!"

"I never learned to drink from a can."

"More than one thing alarmed me about your place. It had the smell of death about it."

Brigham thinks he can smell danger like a horse. I half believe he can.

"You're becoming some kind of primitivist!?" He managed to accuse me and ask me at the same time.

"Did you reach Anne?"

"Yes"

"What was said?"

"She wouldn't talk to me… much. But, let's get back to the primitivist thing…"

"What thing!? Primitive communism . ? you knew I think it is misunderstood."

"You're not misunderstood. You're understood only too bloody well…dragging your wife by her hair out of her classroom. Bloody cave man behavior!"

Of course *that* had not happened but it perversely pleased Brigham to fantasy that it did… I let him believe it and said,

"That probably should happen to more professors and it certainly should happen to more wayward wives."

"Did it work?"

"No."

"Did it make things worse?"

"....yes"

"But you think you made a statement."

"... I guess"

We were both silent for a long while, Brigham was in the habit of providing long comradely scolding. His previous political position as Maximum Leader seen to that. Although decades ago I still deferred... not so much from habit but from respect for our past which he seemed hell bent to forget.

"What's with all those cave paintings you've got up at your
   place?" he asked, more curious than scolding now.

"Most from Lascaux," I answered. ". . discovered in
   1940 the year we were born."

"Nawggh," he arrogantly replied, "I think they were discovered a half century before in northern Spain."

The most annoying thing about Brigham's thinking he knew everything was that he did come close... at least to facts. He and Levin were encyclopedic.

"Both! I sighed...both sides of the Pyranees."

"Why've you gottem all over your walls?"

"I likes e'm!"

"Not good enough."

"....cause its Pleistocene man. It's Pleistocene!"

"!??!"

"Marxists have misunderstood it. Even though some
   traditionalists like the Amish have not. The cave

paintings are the creative window to our past errors and the futures idiocy of the entire Lefts capitulation to 'pathological togetherness'. A historical (or worse-false- historical) enlightenment idealism displacing the historic dialectic of material (objective) ↔ and ↔ (subjective) existant conscious realities. Lumpen influenced imaginings for an effortless express lane to utopia dodging the hard work and moral responsibilities of material reality. The material history and objective reality of community building begins with the dyad of two human beings intensive co-parenting nucleus cooperatively related and structured socially with others of the same socio-economic interest. Collectively connecting in greater concentric circles class solidarity and moral agreement. Communards who wish Communism to pop out of their ideological egos remain atomized individuals. Then eventually lumpenized social refugees who barely conceal their contempt for working class realities i.e. their dyadic marital, parental, and patriarchal kinship relations. The very fabric which requires revolutionary struggle to conserve. Conservative family archetypes are the moral and material realities Revolutionary leadership should engage and defend which capitalist empire threatens to destroy. Instead the 'cadre', the social refugees lead lives of wanton contempt for the dearest form the proletariat is struggling to conserve. Conceding the field to bourgeois politicians full of populist rhetoric for working families as their corporations continue to cripple them. In short, the idiotic enlightenment of the Left romps right where the right wing wants them."

Brigham was quiet now. His intellectual curiosity always overcame his rude brashness. I continued...

"That cave art man, is the oldest evidence of the naturally preferred habitat of our species. The first 'art for life's sake'[1] where the intimacy and isolation[2] of monogamous autonomous intensive co-parenting families is both... "both the outcome and the original means of a lifeway"[3] we still yearn for. A lifeway where cognitive and creative skills selectively prevailed to cooperate not compete... under supernatural notions, that backed unselfishness and noble purpose."

"Are you saying —..."

"I'm saying these primitive Paleolithic parenthood families were the Eden... Morgan, Marx, and Engels missed. These closely associated autonomous families were communards with other sometimes isolated families under the authority of their shared supernatural agreements, not tribal coercion. The supernatural sharpened human thought vs. the stressors of life creating beauty where little is produced by

---

1   'art for life's sake': The Nature of Paleolithic Art by R. Dale Guthrie; Paleolithic art is the first clear spoor of advancing Creativity in human life... not art for arts sake, but art for life's sake.
2   IBID
3   IBID

literal reason. It was tribalism that first took children from Paleolithic parents and put them with "peers" that violated natural law and universal kinship with tribal patriotism – specialness, tribal obedience to privilege, tribal rank, and power. Universal notions of the supernatural were replaced by tribal 'organized religion' which gave us the first day care center".

"Are you saying…We didn't go back far enough?"

"Not going back far enough is cause for not getting ahead enough. Primitive communism was not the tribe but what preceded it. This paradigmatic flaw has given us Stalin, Polpot, and Jack Barnes; petty tribal chiefs and witch cultic tyrants. Forget all coercive tribal crap. The Amish have it right. The Portagees around here are ripe for it. We…"

"You're hanging out too much with that Virginian, …what's his name Walker?… with the San Joaquin Writers Group.

 You're talkin Jeffersonian Yeomanry."

"Nothin to do with Deists or masonic stuff but even…by the way they weren't completely wrong…Neuroscience and paleontology have greatly expanded what Lenin could only call the material outside ourselves."

"Later, later…" Brigham held up his hand to end our conversation just as Shorty was waving his arms saying "times up" for visitation.

Outside my cell Brigham shouted back, McMurtry and Mike will visit you soon.

I'd talked too much. Brigham presses a button and I can't shut up. If I'd talked less I might have heard more of what McMurtry thought and Anne had said. She probably influenced his "Caveman" suspicions… but deceitful as she is…she's not naturally a liar…more likely she subtly suggested something and Brigham was guessing. He'd figure it out. Brigham always did. I need to talk to McMurtry. Without bail… how many Sundays of Eastertide was I stuck here?

On Friday I had visitors from Modesto Dairy Supply; routeman Joe Da Silva and mechanic Howard Mason. Both were angry at Johnny. He'd pressured them to try and collect what I still owed of my cash advance. While they were pissed at him for sending such a mercenary message to a man in jail, I was saddened that it meant he didn't want me back to work. I'd counted on those imminent sales commissions to pay back the advance plus finance my return to Indiana.

"What about the De Laval men?" I asked about the Corporate guys. "Dick, Dennis, and Don are all for you, they kind of stammered in unison." "They appreciate you not mentioning the company", Howard whispered. Volubly, Joe said, "They're just glad they ain't in the papers."

"And Stan?" the boss, I asked.

"Stan's just given things over to Johnny", Howard answered.

"And you know Johnny!" Joe huffed. "You ought to git out of here and hide out in the Azores. I give you plenty of contacts in St. George. No one can (goddam) kidnap his own kids in the Azores."

What good friends and fellow workers! They'd gladly risk their own necks for me. Where is McMurtry?!, I wondered. And my friend Mike and Bill White the supervisor. Joe belonged to Father O'Dwyer's parish. I thought he might visit.

Saturday Kathleen and Jack showed up. While Jack thumbed through his briefcase, Kathleen assured me how upset he'd been when he heard I'd been jailed. He'd told her, "That man has done exactly what I told him to do. I am partly responsible for this." She went on, "he has given priority to your case and has good news for you today."

"First the bad... (which was always McMurtrys style) That Mike McNaughton friend of yours cannot be counted on in this fight. I contacted him because the police report included a raid on his ranch and school last Friday. The cops terrorized his wife and sister while he's away from home and still he wants to speak well and make nice with your ex."

Dear Mike, the unrepentantly 'moderate' marxist friend of my deceased marriage. I am sure he made sympathetic excuses for the mother of my children. I was equally sure he would never oppose my custody efforts.

"Not partisan enough!", was Jacks litigated militancy. "You need witnesses to objectify your responsible parenting and loathe hers. She's on record as saying she loathes you. You must out loathe her...

at least as far as her parenting is concerned. We can count on your parishioners. Bill Marzetti from Knights Ferry phoned and I met with him in Oakdale. They are loyal to you and loathe the way she's treated you and the children. And that Brigham your farmer friend from Fresno, what a character – he walked right past my secretary, interrupted my meeting… announcing he didn't have much time. He'll be a strong witness."

Now Marzetti talked to your people in Coulterville and Knights Ferry about bail money. I told him it would not only get you out of here (he looked around disgustedly) but impress the judge. Impress him you were no fly by night and had resourceful…

"And bourgeois…" I interrupted.

"Yes, yes…" he continued…"resourceful supporters. You know the Sinclair family?" I remembered them as prosperous small ranchers east of the Stanislaus River who had a son back east in Seminary. They were registered members of Knights Ferry church but rarely attended. "We will foot the full bail if he needs it", they'd told Marzetti and McMurtry. "But I don't think we'll need it", Jack said. "Because the main news is I've communicated about the judge. He thinks those cops over reached themselves because of the Indiana Prosecutors message that you were suicidal and homicidal. You'll be charmed that your daughter told the police her Papa would never be the former but after all this might be the latter. Also your ex actually stayed in one of the officers' home and convinced him you were and would be a violent and dangerous man. They charged into McNaughton's with guns pointing and he's still wishy washy about opposing your ex. However the main thing again is I think this judge is wanting to drop your charges from the 'criminal', to the 'family law' category. He'll probably keep you locked up until your hearing – bail or no bail – just to placate the law and order crowd then hear you in family law court where at worse you will be fined instead of getting life imprisonment."

"Much better!!!" I thought and said but worried "can he do all that?"

"He can do whatever he wants in so called 'family law'. No real statutes, case law, or applicable precedents. Just one phrase, one criteria. His decision must be in the 'best interests of the children'. Not in the best interest of the children according to Judao-Christian ethics, tradition or any other criteria. It might as well be what's in the best interest of the children according to what the judge had for breakfast!"

My hearing was convened the following Friday at 9am. My supervisor Bill White had spoken with McMurtry early in the week and finally visited me Thursday. He was generally supportive and was he said, "knocked out by the congregations… how encouraging and eager to stand up…to go to bat for you" he said and laughed "….for their pastor, their minister. Too bad you'll not stay here…will you?" He was actually wanting me to stay instead of worried that I might. He said he would none the less be glad to write Bishop Armstrong in Indiana who would pass on his support to the appropriate regional supervisor. I wanted to get home now to my farm, my children and whatever court action I could sic McMurtry on.

Monday morning I was allowed a Saturday shower early, a clean orange jump suit, and put into leg irons, arm shackles and hand cuffs for court. A string of us similarly shackled prisoners were brought along the side rail of the court room. When my people saw me there was a collective groan heard throughout the crowded room. Being sixth or seventh in line…I waited my turn. There were some rough customers in line. None I could recognize from my cell block, but crimes of rape, and robbery were noted as well as drug trafficking. I expected gasps from my people but didn't hear any. How was this going to be a non-criminal law proceeding for me?! McMurtry was there and smiling but I didn't like it.

I took my turn like the other guys; dragging my chains to the dock. McMurtry asked me all the questions we'd rehearsed last week in my cell.

What he called the Boy Scout questions. Had I ever been convicted of any misdemeanor or felony? Did I have or owe any outstanding traffic tickets in California, Indiana, or any other state? Did I have a current California driver's license and what was its number? The same for Social Security. Did I hold undergraduate and graduate degrees from Indiana University? Did I own property in California or Indiana?

Had I ever sued for bankruptcy in California or Indiana? Were my parents living? And where did they live? What had been my employment history in Indiana and California? What was my current employment? Rev. Bill White was there to answer that. I was asked if my pastoral congregations were represented in court. He then asked for them to stand... over a hundred of them. Some small cheering began. The judge's gavel came down. The judge then rather apologized to them saying he knew this situation was mighty unusual and was sorry if the court had caused them any undue stress... at that point old Sophie our ninety-four year old parishioner shook loose from her niece, standing frailly first on one foot and then the other to announce with a demonstrable shudder, "Why It's been just like the crucifixion." There was laughter; sympathetic and the other kind. Much shushing, of course, the judge's gavel reminding everyone of their responsibility for order.

"I hope it wasn't quite that bad mamm, but I can see you folks love this man. And I think he must love his children. How in thunder a custody scheduling quarrel ended up in my criminal court is... literally beyond me. I am remanding this case back east to Indiana... where it came from...the Prosecutor in Terre Haute where the mother and children reside." He then looked stolidly at McMurtry and his Prosecutors; they both looked down and deferentially away. Further addressing his audience the judge concluded, "I am releasing your Pastor on his own recognizance to report to the Indiana District Court in Terre Haute, Indiana. There was a standing ovation. No gavel. The judge nodded to the bailiff who announced a recess until 1pm.

It took a couple hours of signing papers and waiting to sign more before I could be released from jail. There had been a sharp turnover of inmates in my cellblock, I said good-bye to those who were left. A new young Mexican had been moved into the cell next to mine. He appealed for just a moment of my time. He said he'd heard "You know things." He showed me a book he was reading on Nazism. He said he wanted to be active in something more than just another lousy job. He said he wanted to serve in a human stud farm if I knew where any were located.

Only a bit dumber than most young activists avoiding work, school, and reality… I told him they were located in hell… exactly where he was headed unless he got to mass more often and had a long talk with his father. I could not in good faith refer him to just any priest. Most I knew in Modesto were libidinally licentious. I asked if he knew old Father Starret at Fatima Parish. He said he knew where 'Our Lady of Fatima' Church was but he didn't know the priest. "Father Starret lives there; go see him. "About what?", he asked. "About your studly delusions!!", I answered. He blankly said, "O.K."

So much misinformation, so much misunderstanding. The lumpen proletariat were almost as ignorant as the petit bourgeoisie. I picked up my impounded truck and headed home. Digger dog was delighted to greet me. I let him inside then showered the final stink that stays like a stain of jail off and away. Dressed in clean clothes I lay on the couch with Digger phoning McMurtry and others.

Jack was disappointed the judge didn't rule on the criminal category and just dropped it to family law status. Our case will never look as good as it did with all those people there for you. We may face criminal charges back in Indiana. I thought he was using the editorial "we" to merely comfort me, his client . He was, in fact, planning to defend me in the Indiana court. I knew his law degree was from Notre Dame; I didn't know that gave him privilege to the Indiana bar. I also knew he owned and flew a small piper cub airplane. He told me he would fly to Terre Haute whenever the court scheduled my – our case. "How soon can you wrap things up here and get home to Indiana?"

PART FOUR:

HOME TO THE HEARTLAND

XXII

Jack had dropped all reference to my staying and/or returning to California. Rev. White had formally transferred me to Indiana's Methodist bishop. I needed a day or two to properly thank my people and two days to drive to Indiana. He said he would move on requesting a court date the next week in Terre Haute.

I phoned Marzettis. Kit answered bright and cheerful to hear I was out of jail. She said she wanted to be the first to tell me what song Bill had wanted to use for the Introit last Sunday in my absence. "He asked the congregation if they thought 'jail house rock' would be appropriate. Of course, he was joshing and it lifted folk's spirits a bit who were so sad for you". She also noted the Sinclair family would probably not be in church tomorrow, as they rarely came, but I should be sure and thank them for being on the ready with that bail money." I phoned them next.

Mrs. Sinclair answered. She had a soft Georgia accent. Her husband was a heartlander from Ohio. She invited me for Sunday dinner tomorrow. She said her son would be home from Seminary and was eager to make my acquaintance. I could hardly refuse.

Next I phoned Mike. After gladness expressed I was out he complained "... your spud lawyer accused me of being Pontius Pilate the next sentence after hello. When I tried to say something conciliatory for the two of you including a kind remark about Anne, he called me Judas Iscariot. Under what pile of fanatics did you find this guy. He strikes me as a cross between a crew cut stalinist and the John Birch Society. Dogmatic and scary."

"Not a bad description, I'll hand it to you Mike, but unmoderated 'dogmatic and scary' just might be the 'principled and fierce' qualities required here." As Mike began moderating his view of McMurtry, I had to take my leave to hastily prepare my last California sermon.

But... I couldn't start without one more phone call...to Brigham. His was long distance down to Fresno so I'd have to be brief. Typically solemn at first even to my enthusiastic gratitude he brightened into good humor saying, "I thought sure you'd be Chief Joseph... and if you're not careful you could still be thirty miles from Canada.[1] Come on down...we'll tie one on at the Primavera and celebrate."

"Can't do...got to prepare a sermon for tomorrow."

"Don't you have any in the can?"[2]

"A few, but this will be my good-bye to these folks. I'll mention you in the sermon."

I think he liked that idea. There was a knock on my door. Digger exploded like the cops were back. It was neighbors including Jerry the next door professor who was an ex to my landlady. Jerry insisted we all come to his house for dinner; beer, steaks and one of the women brought a berry pie. My sermon was stillborn an outline, and a few notes for good-bye.

God bless them; both congregations knew I'd be pressed to prepare for Sunday. At 8am in Coulterville Ted Harbinger announced that "we can all do what he calls the liturgy this morning but for the message... the sermon today he gets to rest and hear from us. It'll be the same... down the hill at Knights Ferry. I've talked with Bill Marzetti. After what you've been through (he directed at me) just lead us in prayers, then sit down and listen to us."

Glad...and grateful to comply I led through our brief liturgical prayers and was shown a seat in the front pew. Sister Marie came to the pulpit. Marie Clark was a mainstay for the Coulterville congregation. She was sometimes called Sister Marie because she'd never been a Mrs., was judged not young enough to be a Miss and was far too conservative to be a Ms. She was retired from being a school teacher

---

1   'Chief Joseph (our inside tragic joke) of the Nez Perce' Indians who exchanged their native lands for a large reservation in Oregon and Idaho which the US government took back after Gold was discovered there in 1863. Chief Joseph led his people against a much larger US army defeating them in many battles retreating north attempting escape into Canada only to be captured thirty miles from the border.

2   Pre-organized sermon

somewhere down in the valley. Living alone in a modest cottage at the edge of this mountain town, she kept a horse, three dogs and a cat. Never married nor visibly attached she was considered mysterious. She *was* noticeable. A kind of sexually appealing spinster.

Between no longer a young maid and not yet an old maid, she cut a figure like Professor French's daughter Gwen in James Jones 'Some Came Running'. An Emily Dickensonesque sequel... beautifully obscure... unloved or not adequately so... her over the hill maturity registered not so much unaccompanied injustice as scarred lines of sacrifice and wisdom. She kept her figure clothed away like nuns used to...moving carefully in avoidance of appearing voluptuous, she struck up the band of men who looked at her as an 'older but wiser' habitué of the place...of these hills.

Not quite responding to her like Dave Hirsch did to Gwen French, at least like Sinatra[1] played him, I had consistently matched her restraint to our mutual attraction. But, today as she rose up taking charge of the podium I loved her, at least for an hour. Welsh pale, her silver streaked black hair, shaded strong grey eyes reflecting a serious woman with something to say.

"We are saying good-bye", she began, "to our Reverend Thomas today." She used the word 'reverend' (which I never liked as a title) more like an adjective or endearment. "We are saying good-bye to one who helped us hear revelation from above and cheer insurrection from below. His revolutionary thinking and prayers have broadened our imagination to how the world might be built up anew and differently into Godly cooperative commonwealths. Armed with the Holy Spirits premonitions unthought-of fundamental unities he's renewed our respect for Natural, Ancient, Scriptural truths that are old and imperishable. Our Christian souls share many kindred promptings and ideals with others... that are unrealizable in our individual...our particular circumstances. We've listened to his voice every Sunday in constant refrain that with God's love in our imaginative thought we can work and struggle for good against evil in this old world, and

---

1   Sinatra: Frank played Dave Hirsch in Hollywood's production of 'Some Came Running'.

finally rise above it.

He's preached to us as an olde Puritan or modern poet might. A poet whose pleasure is sharing images to others through his words and life to seek Gods love and fear only God's wrath. Through his love for us, and especially for his children he has taught us bravery, constraint, and frigid (I think she must have meant rigid) conscious consecration of purpose."

On the question of good and evil; that is, what theologians call 'the problem of evil' he has not been seduced by Eastern denials of dualities. No Haight-Ashbury hypnosis of harmony to ignore injustice and suffering. No liberal loitering about in the cheap grace of mindless mysticism which never defines evil but merely files and forgets it; not curing it but condoning it.

American Philosopher George Santayana has written regarding modern liberal religion: 'We have surrendered the category of the better and the worse, the deepest foundation of life and reason; we have become mystics on the one subject on which, above all others, we ought to be men!'

Our Pastor is a man! [She actually got 'here here's from the men and some 'amens' from the women giving me the second most complimentary moment in my life] He's the man… who helped us appreciate our men…our fathers, brothers… and others. (At that point she smiled the most languid, libidinal, yet nonetheless wholesome feminine smile ever seen upon a pulpit)

His moral vitality", she countered quickly "is manifest with us… awakening an elevation of mind to more fully comprehend our worship. To apply our spiritual insights displacing our lower passions and servile forms of intelligence."

Hurrah! What a sendoff. Leaving… I embraced 'bout everyone except Sister Marie. She approached tentatively and held out her hand. Thinking a hand shake was far too little and an embrace far, far too much…I took her hand tenderly and kissed it! That, was appreciated.

More surprises down the mountain. Harbingers daughter Carol, her husband Walt, their children and his Uncle Patrice had come to Knights Ferry. "Coulterville was too far up the mountain", they said.

The Marzettis had introduced them all around. I was particularly proud of my olde, slightly xenophobic pianist who glowed describing this racially mixed family as "more wonderful people our pastor has healed and helped."

Walt spoke to the congregation formally saying, "the Preacher made us realize 'tough love' not as a tactic but as the essential element in family life." Informally, Uncle Patrice called me, brother, taking me aside to say, "the mark of the Prophet is upon you."

Many of my parishioners spoke individually but all seemed a solid collective unit of what the Christ called love. Agape… for sure.

The loving farewells of Coulterville and Knights Ferry were as one. These loving communities touched the far corners of my soul to know that communism i.e. community, family, marriage, the dyad itself… (two lovers alone) cannot rationally be sustained. Only through the supra-rational existant phenomena of love can those human relations be sustained.

Revolutionary Marxists do not hate too much. To hate injustice is part of love. They do not love the revolution and the souls of their comrades enough. They do not collectively share an adequate active concern for their fellow cadre…collecting evidence of all that's good with each other. *Not* delegating that singular universal commandment of the world's most famous peasant-proletarian-revolutionary Jesus, the Christ who commanded we love each other and our enemies, even as we fight them and forgive them. *Not* to delegate, pervert and project that commandment into an idolatry of tin pot leaders.

The socialist order cannot proceed to be built by the best efforts of atomized individuals. Only a mass of loving, dyadically faithful, married, parental, mortgaged, farmers and workers organized to appropriate the power and profits from the capitalists' class for the greater good of their community of working families will be adequate for this historic task.

Extant love is stubborn reality opposed to the lies and spooks of fleeting unreality. In time it prevails. Usually too much time. Unless properly confronted… then the spooks of unreality will finally flee. Aiee ….it's what life's up against. Almost unutterably true. One experiences love from others paradoxically in deepest solitary comportment. Plato spoke of such knowledge in his Seventh Letter; "as when a spark, leaping from the fire, flares into light — so it happens, suddenly, in the soul, there to grow, alone with itself."

Alone with oneself, safe from the divertissement of togetherness *agape* builds community within the work of co-existant souls.

I hated to leave them… to leave sight of the place. As ordered I drove on to the Sinclair Ranch.

XXIII

The Sinclair ranch home was located on a high bluff overlooking the Stanislaus River valley. A sea of grass pastures below was cut through by a lane that wheeled around the bluff and up to the west end of the garaged side of the house. Thirty some head of Santa Gertrudis cattle grazed in the pastures. They were fine looking cows; dark red Bos Indicus.

Mrs. Sinclair greeted me at the door, with her twenty-five year old son Gary. He was sandy haired, plump...and had a serious look about him. He told me he was studying at O.R.U., back east. At first I didn't get the acronym. Upon brief reflection I thought...surely not... but when 'back east' was clarified to mean Oklahoma I knew it must be... Oral Roberts University! That ol ". . put your hand on your condition" T.V. evangelist and healer, Oral (so very) Roberts.

It turns out Oral was (or had been) some kind of a Methodist. (They had churches to fill) Pentecostals usually claimed him. I knew dirt poor country people who tithed to his T.V. shows for which they'd receive a little framed saying, "Expect a Miracle". Grandma and Grandpa Keller, the old folks we'd bought Gloryville farm from had such a frame hanging on their poor parlor wall.

I'd always thought the likes of Oral Roberts a great embarrassment to the faith. That he could actually "found" a University even in Tulsa was its own kind of miracle. Yet the following, that is, the faith of all those poor country people was quite something else. Yet...this prosperous California ranching family? "Must be the southern connection", I thought – maybe even muttered to myself. With the exception of Orthodox (Reform) Presbyterians, Quakers, and the Amish all American denominations had failed the civil war. That is, split to confederate loyalties. Even Catholics. Remember 'Gone with the Wind'.

Mrs. Sinclair considered herself a 'southern Methodist'. Mr. Sinclair was a retired manager from the railroad in Oakdale and militantly somewhere else. Our luncheon turned into a kind of Hollywood consolidation like the last meal in Lionel Barrymore's 1941 picture

'You Can't Take It with You'. Mr. Sinclair even looked a little bit like Lionel Barrymore.

Quite a few guests were arriving. Gary motioned me into their Den and shut the door. "For a little privacy", he said. This Den was well appointed with Viking Oak and leather. No T.V. "This is where I mainly live when home", he motioned now at the fully stocked, built in book cases as he sat down. I stood in order to examine the books. Amazing! Paul Tillich, Rhinold Niebuhr, Dietrich Bonheoffer, Jaralov Pelikan, and an entire section of modern poetry; W.C. Williams, Larkin, Stevens, Frost, Pinsky, Milosz, Corso, Ginsberg, Snyder, Jeffers, Pound, and the collected works of Eliot.

I was impressed and said so, "Best damn library in Stanislaus County." He blushed a bit at my swearing but said, "I'd planned to study English Literature in grad school but Dad insisted I go for an M.B.A. Mom thought Ministry, a proper compromise.

I wanted to ask him 'how the hadean heresies did you end up with Oral Roberts!" He sensed the question I didn't quite ask and he didn't quite answer it. "I'm minoring in drama and would like a career in teaching." He showed me pictures of a campus production of Eliot's, "The Rock" he had directed. Alright! I shared with him I was a great aficionado of Thomas Stearns Eliot and that I had named my son Eliot, after him... Which was a super compliment to the poet whose anglophilia was so contrary to my Celtic anglophobia. I always felt a little like Sweeney Among the Nighthawks even talking about it. We agreed that "Waste Land" was the greatest poem of the modern age and the most difficult to understand.

Gary had studied the biblical and Shakespearian referents. He didn't wish to recognize the tarot cards influences. He spoke a lot about Frazer's book, 'The Golden Bough'. I noted Frazer also credits the tarot cards imagery. He spoke chapter and verse from Ezekiel and Ecclesiastes but resisted the idea of Baudelaire's influence even when Eliot speaks from him in French "mon semlable – mon frère!" We agreed on Verlaine's French line from Parsifal and neither one of us liked his old possum's sapphic paeonic paean to Pound through Ovid. Yet we concelebrated his syncretic use of the Buddha's Fire

Sermon, Thunder from the Upanishads and the Dantesque frames of St. Augustine's Confessions.

"Finally…" I said, "From Carthage thence we come." We laughed together as he handed me a copy of Eliot's choruses from 'The Rock'. "We may need these", he said.

Then pensively, "Analysis aside I experienced 'The Waste Land' as an individuals breakdown; aloneness without intimacy, seeking the balm of an imagined but also…actual Christianity away from the confusion of being away…from my father's authority as the poet wrote in exile from Our Fathers authority."

"I think…I'm with you on that", I said…knowing he knew we both meant more than the poem. "My aloneness is…yeah without… and I feel like my fatherhood, my own fathers authority has been exiled. It is the glimpses of God-conscious community, the 'Agape' that's kept me goin."

"The thing with my father", Gary explained "is very normal. A normal part of life," he seemed trying to assure me and himself, "very normal", he repeated subtly, "but nonetheless very hard for me. Dads always harping about practicality and the practical end of things. I'm not very practical… but you know he likes poetry. He'll actually shut up and listen to me read from Eliot or Larkin. He likes Emily Dickenson. He thinks poetry is some kind of coded revelation."

Yeah… well, maybe it is."

"Maybe… when it gets bad I read poetry to him or recite it. He's impressed if I can recite it, but he listens carefully if I just read it. He tries to bend the poem to his meaning…you know, what he's trying to stress. I guess I do the same. But the cool thing is…the poems dimensions of meaning and primarily its intention usually envelops both of ours and we find some peace about it. About our own selves intention…our selfish intentions."

"Did you get that from ORU or on your own?"

"On my own, I guess."

"Son, you're using poetry as spadework for the Holy Spirit."

At that, Gary grinned like a country boy gone fishin. Glancing at those scripts of 'The Rock' we held, he said, "We'll definitely need these in there." He motioned toward the dining room.

Twenty some guests had convened. Mrs. Sinclair and Gary introduced me around. Mostly neighbors with some aunts and uncles. No children. The Marzettis came a bit late explaining they had to get grandma situated with her grandchildren. Gary's mom placed us at the end of the table, and the Marzettis to the right of her and Mr. Sinclair. The latter sat unsmilingly sober and judgelike as Champagne was served.

We all lifted a glass. "To our reverend guests of honor", Mrs. Sinclair announced in our direction. I guessed Gary hadn't been home long and issues between him and his dad were palpable as his mother asked him "to return thanks." Gary spoke a perfunctorily protestant prayer of grace, longwinded and chatty; thanking God for 'bout everything and blessing 'bout everybody, the weather, and safety traveling home... finally ending "thanks to Gods bounty, through Christ our Lord..." adding "and Mothers lovin hands." His Dad smiled briefly, at his mom as we all said Amen.

Dinner was served. Pure Hoosier delight. "The Marzettis joked about how you 'coveted' a meal at the Hoosier Country restaurant in Stockton. We love that place. Well, here is our imitation of it." Garden fresh tomato, radish-scallion salad, sweet corn on the cobb, creamy mashed potatoes with Sunday gravy (what Mrs. Sinclair called Riverbottom gravy) and golden flaked skillet fried chicken. Amply served up with more Champagne and yeasty dinner rolls. There was also green beans which I noticed the men largely ignored as the women did their second or third glass of wine.

Gary's Aunt Mildred noted, "This chicken is from our free ranging yard birds. White Rocks from the last hatch." "And..." Uncle Ned added with a flourish, "this all natural country cholesterol (he held up the butter dish) is from Ada our Ayrshire cow." I tasted the butter. It was phenomenal... that deep country taste of sunshine and shade I'd missed like most moderns stuck with citified creamery butter since leaving Indiana. I raised a toast to Ada in particular and to the great breed of Scottish butter cows, the Ayrshire from whence she came.

Then Uncle Ned and I became animated in conversation regarding dual purpose, that is, beef *and* dairy breeds of cows. We both loved the curved horn Ayrshire but we also liked the Red Poll and Milking Shorthorn. Ned didn't know about the Welsh Black so I was carrying on about my favorite breed, its hardiness and versatility. This sparked interest in the rancher neighbors. There were questions to Ned and me about the Galloway and if we thought they were related to the Dutch Belted breed. One neighbor said he was thinking about buying some, Irish Dexter cattle from Canada. He asked if I knew anything about them. I'd never heard of them. This neighbor had been to cattle sales in Calgary and seen Welsh Blacks and the miniature sized Dexters. "They look like little miniatures of your Welsh Black cattle." He thought "they just might catch on in California. Instead of selling sides of custom beef…you could sell the whole custom carcass that would fit in the freezers of suburban buyers."

This notion aroused great interest and more conversation from all the ranchers around the table. Bill Marzetti however remained unusually quiet, until he timidly asked Mr. Sinclair about his Sante Gertrudis cattle.

Mr. Lloyd Sinclair was not a talkative man. He grunted something about, "….you all probly know the breed is based on Zebu (what the Rodeos call Brahma) and Shorthorn crosses. Mine came directly from the King Ranch in Texas."

I'd been to the King Ranch, on my way to Mexico once. I told Mr. Sinclair his cattle looked like the foundation herd. He smiled, a little. I admired the King Ranch and all their Mexican vaqueros. The King Ranch had basically developed the quarter horse with Mustang, Thoroughbred, and Morgan horse crosses. I'd read a livestock book by Travis Rivers, a King Ranch foreman whom I quoted as near as possible regarding the art of animal husbandry. "To fix type and improve it requires endless observation and study of the animals involved and then finally concentration in the pedigrees of those animals whose characteristics are the most desirable and most complementary to each other. While the art of breeding requires intense attention to detail, endless study, observation and application of keen artistic sense, the rewards are great and I know of no task of such consuming and lasting interest." I added, it is sculpture of living tissue.

These old stockmen and their wives grew more reverently silent hearing the Rivers paraphrased quote than they did during grace. Lloyd Sinclair sensed this approving sentiment of his guests toward me and wished to test it further. First to his son he said, "I guess your old man is an artist too." There was some chortling then…"Scuse me Preacher," he began "but does your church belong to the National Council of Churches?"

"Yessir it does", I answered.

"Dudn't that bother you?", he asked kind of carefully.

"No sir", I replied, just as carefully adding, "Some of my best
friends have lived through liberalism."

"Didjaever belong, you know when you were a student?" he
asked while glancing at Gary, "to the SDS, you know the Students for a Democratic Society?"

Mrs. Sinclair had reached out to touch her son. They both looked aggrieved. The Marzettis looked suspenseful even though Bill kept grinning.

"Never did," I answered, "although I thought about it in the spring of 61' at the 'Turn Toward Peace Demonstration' in Washington, D.C. The Demonstration was prompted by the Kennedy Administrations phony missile gap, the U.S. military sneaking into a wider war in southeast Asia, and the governments systematic stalling of civil rights demands. SDS seemed a national organization to tie e'm, the issues I mean, tie e'm altogether and address them nationally as well as regionally. I talked to many SDS members and read their literature carefully…. Had to decide against joining."

"Whyisthat?" Lloyd now spoke for the entire table, "Whyisthat?'

"Well…", I slowly explained "I had no quarrel with Students *For* a Democratic Society but too many of them thought they already lived *in* one. I knew better! I believe in rendering to Caesar what is Caesars, that is, what Caesar deserves. Our government is *not*, is no longer of the people, by the people, or for the people. I reverently render to it, as to Caesar my life long opposition."

"I subscribe to the National Review", Lloyd now announced almost defensively. I was surprised to hear it...hadn't seen any evidence of it in their den library. Usually National Review subscribers leave issues of it lying about like land mines for anyone not in business school. There was an expectant lull. Everyone as quiet as Lloyd had been... expecting a response to him.

Guessing his age, I began, "My first year out of High School, Bill Buckley's first book was being heavily promoted on college campuses. 'God and Man at Yale'...Do you remember it?" "Sure do!", he answered. "I read it and agreed with Brother Buckley's two major points: (1) "that the duel between faith and atheism is the most important in the world" and (2) "that the struggle between individualism and collectivism is the same struggle reproduced on another level."

"Except!...I see God on the collectivist side. Gods omnipotence belongs to no individual or corporation and is alien to the very idea of capitalist property."

"You really are then, he asked more than accused...a kind of communist?"

"Yes I am."

"You're the kind that bleeves in Marxist-Leninist Revolution?"

"Yes I am."

"You want South America led by the likes of Castro?!!"

"Especially like Fidel... God bless him. Faithful and true to the words of Jesus; putting interests of the poor first. Essential Fidelity to farmers and workers who produce the wealth others merely consume."

Mrs.Sinclair covered her mouth and a very lady like burp.

"You're the kind that wants our government overthrown?"

"By the ordinary hard working people of this country.

Yes I do. Yes I am."

The latter repeated three words were militantly avoided by all the guests. (It reminded me how my mother would choose to not hear the f. word when Bethany and Eliot's mother would slip and say it.) But not by Lloyd. He was not angry but thought he ought to be. A life long anti-Communist, imagining their infiltration in Government,

Education, Churches, and the Movies yet he'd never met one. Now he'd met one as an honored guest in his own home, nearly revered by his family and friends. Worse!, he thought and later said, "I was beginning to like the S.O.B. myself."

With thoughts of stifling all this he turned on himself not blurting out a single sentiment...gagging himself into as much civility as he could muster asked, "I suppose you've read Russell Kirk as well?"

"Yes..." was my reply "but not as much as I'd like to... what of his writing would you recommend?"

"Why... just all of e'm..." Lloyd now blurted positively. "He's the brightest thread throughout the entire 'Library of Conservative Thought'."

"We have all thirty volumes of it", Gary put in.

"His best book... I think (Lloyd emphasized the last two words) is his one on Taft."

"The Political Principles of Robert A. Taft", Gary helped his Dad remember.

Both father and son looking at me open eyed and hopeful in a kind of recruitment mode. Knowing all ideologues of the Left or Right require recruitment of not so much agreement with others as approval of their own views for themselves. But, what could I say of Robert Alphonso Taft, that Buckeyed Brownnoser of Corporations who with Fred Ass Hartley had railroaded over Presidential Veto the Taft-Hartley [anti-labor] Act... outlawing the closed union shop, authorizing government eighty day injunctions against strikers and binding all unions to file evidence that their officers were not communist. I shifted back to Russell Kirk.

"He was a heartlander like us," I said to Lloyd.

"Bob Taft...?"

"No, no Russell Kirk. He was a Michigander and the son of a Railroader," I said to Gary. "Early on he'd been a lefty with James Burnham in the Socialist Workers Party"... I'd heard. Then quickly remembering some titles of Kirks I'd found interesting asked if they knew his 'Enemies of Permanent Things' or 'Beyond the Dreams of

Avarice'. They didn't. I thought I remembered his writing about Eliot.

"Yes…" Gary responded with some enthusiasm, "Kirk had written, 'The Conservative Mind: From Burke to Eliot'."

"I thought he'd written something on just Eliot and the morality of his verse."

"That's right," Gary said "it was Eliot and His Age: TS Eliot's Moral Imagination in the Twentieth Century."

Now I wanted to blurt…to blurt how by 1963 Kirk had converted to Catholicism and was campaigning for Gene McCarthy against the War in Vietnam. I didn't . Instead I remembered and spoke that one clear line of Eliot against all ideologues attempt to avoid morality, "By dreaming of systems so perfect that no one will need to be good."

"That's from 'The Rock'," Gary said; pulling out his script while his mother announced to her guests it was a play that Gary had directed back east at college.

He read, "The world turns and the world changes. But one thing does not change."

With seniority I read the next two lines, "In all my years, one thing does not change. However you disguise it, this thing does not change." The last verse of the stanza we read together, "The perpetual struggle of Good and Evil."

Then Gary led us back to, "Why should men love the church? Why should they love her laws?"

Answering, I read, "She tells them of Life and Death, and all they would forget."

"She is tender where they would be hard and hard where they like to be soft."

"She tells them of Evil and Sin, and other unpleasant facts."

Gary again: "They constantly try to escape From the darkness outside and within."

Together we read: "By dreaming of systems so perfect that no one will need to be good."

Before I could conclude with comments on how liberal, right- libertarian, and leftist ideologues all dodge moral discipline when peddling dreamy utopian systems, Uncle Ned was leading some loud rapping on the table as strawberry shortcake was served.

Gary laughed, "Is that for the strawberries or the poetry?" "For both, I reckon", Ned answered smiling so infectiously the entire table lit up with good humor. Even Mr. Sinclair, who asked, "How does it work? I couldn't imagine the meaning of Gary's play until you guys read it aloud."

"It is the power of suggestion," Gary replied. "Instead of the traditional procedure of poetically describing something to suggest its meaning, sort of, between the lines Eliot goes directly at it."

"Modern poets from Eliot to Neruda," I added, "directly describe the poetic sense itself. It's how Isaac Babel described the thoughts of Lenin like a hen going right at a kernel of grain. A direct seizure of that core understanding, no matter how nebulous, how cloudily we begin to perceive its larger context." Gary quoted Pasternak as saying, "metaphor in poetry is spiritual shorthand for those with overfull mental plates to move in leaps rather than walk like other mortals."

"Read us some more boys," Mrs. Sinclair requested and even Mr. Sinclair seemed to agree and nodded accordingly at Gary who began…

"The Word of the Lord came unto me, saying;
O miserable cities of designing men and women
O wretched generations of enlightenment
I have given you hands, which you turn from worship
I have given you speech, for endless palaver
I have given you my law, and you set up commissions"
I have given you words to hoard and exploit

I realized Gary was taking some liberty with the text i.e. poetic license with a wink and a nod I did the same…reading.

I have given you fidelity, for betrayal after betrayal
"I have given you hearts, for reciprocal distrust"
I have given you power of choice, which you dupe into freedom of

"futile speculation and unconsidered action"I went on:

> A cry from every direction
> "Whence thousands travel daily to the timekept cities
> Where my word is unspoken,
> And the wind shall say: Here were decent godless people;
> Their only monument the asphalt road
> And a thousand lost golf balls."

Gary rejoined:

> The god-shakened stranger has asked
> What is the meaning of this place?
>
> [Silence]
>
> "Do you huddle close together because you love each other?
> What will you answer? We all dwell together
> To make money from each other? or This is a Community?"
> Men in their various ways have struggled toward God
> "Now Men have left God, not for other Gods, they say
> but for no God; and this has never happened before"

Back again:

> "For man is a vain thing and man without God
> is a seed upon the wind; driven this way and that,
> finding no place of lodgment and germination"
> except in Usery, Lust, War, and Exploitive Power
> "Let us mourn in a private chamber, learning the way of
> penitence
> And then let us learn the joy of communion" with
> Our Father in Heaven in true community with all
> His children, our brothers and sisters

Together we finished our embellished Eliot, in staccato his reading a verse and my nailing it down.

> "Our age is an age of moderate virtue"
> And of extreme vice "Like Nehemiah, we have enemies with-
> out to destroy us and spies and self-seekers within"
> To rebuild upon the Rock of our souls a temple to God in our
> hearts within the faiths conviction and Community of others,
> We must work "with the trowel in one hand and the gun rather

loose in the holster"

Amidst appreciative table rapping coffee was served by Mrs. Sinclair and Gary's Aunt Mildred. In the adjourning convivial mist Mr. Sinclair drew me aside, in a fraternal almost comradely spirit asked, "So, you are not a pacifist?'

"No sir," I deferred to his tone. "It's not that I don't believe non-violence preferable but I've never seen any evidence of its existence. Not in nature or in the best efforts of our species in history."

"I've heard you favor the Amish."

"Sure I do...they're holding on to a life we've lost."

"You mean Pastoral and traditional?"

"Yes, that too...it is their primitive communism which allows them to conserve traditional life."

"Are they not pacifists?", he asked both sincerely and polemically.

"They are militantly non-violent against all pimps of war from athletic coaches to military industrial brass...but I would not call them pacifists." I referred him to 'Witness' the Hollywood film with Harrison Ford's character being protected by the peaceful Amish who surround violent predators and disarm them.

"You say their primitive com... com ..."

God help him, he couldn't say, couldn't bring himself to say the C word in a non-pejorative sense. Charitably, I began to pronounce the C word as communitarian or communal in order to spare him what seemed like real cold war pain from groin to grimace.

"Their traditional-conservative life and values are governed with communal-collective discipline. A violent predator might get loved or hugged to death. Not very pacific...not very pacifist."

We laughed a little...together; then Lloyd Sinclair spoke very seriously...

"You know...I got a lot more out of that Eliot, hearing you guys recite and perform it than my reading of it myself. But a couple parts I read you and Gary passed over." He held up one of the scripts we'd left on the table looked through the pages then read:

"Men have left God not for other Gods, they say, but for no God, and this has never happened before. That men both deny God and worship Gods; professing first Reason,…And then Money, and Power, and what they call Life, or Race, or Dialectic."

Lloyd like Eliot made a legitimate point. I wanted to speak to him about how young Bertrand Russell was 'shocked' how Lenin referred to the dialectic the way a Priest might refer to the 'holy spirit'. It seemed to me the dialectic could be the Holy Spirit and/or it could be otherwise. But Lloyd Sinclair read on:

> "The Church disowned, the tower overthrown, the bells upturned, what have we to do
> But stand with empty hands and palms turned upwards
> In an age which advances progressively backwards?"

I stood beside him my empty palms turned upwards. I was going to pray but Lloyd Sinclair read on as free with Eliot's verse as we had been:

> "O weariness of all turns from God
> to the minds glory and human schemes – thoroughly discredited
> turning vacancy to fevered enthusiasm
> for nation, or race, or what you call humanity."

His argument strengthened our positions in prayer he led as the others joined us. He read into prayer:

> Forgive us for seeing only strangeness in the stranger
> Prepare us for him who cause us to ask questions
> "Though we forget the way to Temple
> There is one who remembers the way to our door;
> Life we may evade, but Death we shall not
> We shall not deny that stranger."

Behindhandily I got it. Lloyd Sinclair was dying. Liberal pap at the pulpit and his cancer had kept him from church. In this afternoons newly non-estranged communion he now asked me to pray for his son's ministry, his sons remaining witness to his parents values and his fathers near departure. We all embraced loving good-byes. Lloyd asked me to walk with him to the bull pen so he could show me his prize Santa Gertrudis bull.

Evening was on. So was the continued creation of life. As he stroked the huge red bulls neck with an old hockey stick Lloyd spoke of the creatures generative power. The stamp of improved potency and production he was giving to his offspring. An improved quality and power that would last well beyond Lloyd and his bulls last days. For an hour or so we spoke, stopping occasionally to say good-byes again to company driving down the hill away.

This well-read Railroad Man had internalized Russell Kirks priorities of Religion, Tradition, Community, and Art. He valued others in so far as they served the same *safe* (he would probably say *saved*) path from the portions of wrath that come to moral relativism and crimes of chaos. He had worked as his father and mine had as a brakeman in Midwestern railyards. He respected the railway union and knew it was founded in Terre Haute. He knew Gene Debs had led the Great Pullman Strike in Chicago. He knew his social mobility was "in spite of", not "because of" the system of things. He had read most of Ring Lardner's short stories. He resisted knowing much about Ring Lardner's sons. I recommended seeing them as examples of conservative, that is, conserved values generative from father to sons.

James Lardner served and fought in the International Brigades for Republican Spain and Ring Lardner Jr. was the great screenplay writer of our time leading the blacklisted 'Hollywood Ten' against the criminal chaos of McCarthyism. "Have you seen the Steve McQueen movie 'The Cincinnati Kid'?"

"Well sure," he answered with a broad smile, "Ain't I, a Buckeye? I loved that movie. Made in the mid-sixties, wasn't it?"

"In sixty-five", I remembered the year I was married Ring Lardner Jr. wrote the screenplay. "Communitarian wasn't it? The primary value and perils of marriage and family up against the individualistic myths and chance of freemarket poker."

"Heh…I'll have to think about that", he said so sincerely you knew he meant it.

Gary came by the bull barn to say g'bye again and to check on his old Dad. We exchanged phone numbers and mailing addresses. I wrote down what I'd earlier recommended, Father John Crossen's 'Dark Interval' book, 'The Theology of Story' and wished my very best to the lady of the house, their mother and wife. "And special thanks for that great Sunday Dinner!"

Gary said, "she sent her thanks to you for coming". Surprising myself I said, "Gratzacham!" They looked puzzled.

"It's Irish brogue for 'Gratias agamus' thanks be to all.

It's from one of the oldest parables about Saint Patrick, 'The Hill, the Horse and the Fawn'[1]"

"We'd better hear this one before you leave", said Gary.

"If you'll assure us it's not propaganda", added Lloyd.

"O-Aye Father Sinclair it's the sort of propaganda which you'd approve." We all leaned on my little truck.

"Missionary Patrick," I began, "besought a rich man name Dairi to bestow upon the Christian community a hill property for religious uses. The rich man was unwilling but did give over another place on lower ground. Saint Patrick dwelt there with his companions.

Soon afterwards Dairi's groom came leading his horse to feed in the meadow of the Christians. This annoyed Patrick that a beast should disturb this small spot set aside for God.

But the groom ignored him leaving the horse there that night and went away. Coming the next morning the groom found the horse paralyzed and almost dead. Returning home sorrowfully he told Dairi that Christian has killed your horse for the trespass on his land annoyed him.

Then Dairi said: Let him be killed; go now and slay him. But as they were going out, death swifter than words fell upon Dairi. His wife claimed 'This is on account of the Christian; go quickly and bring his blessings to us which may save my husband.'

Two men went to Patrick, and hiding what had happened said to him: Behold Dairi is sick, please send us your blessing that he may recover.

But Saint Patrick, knowing what had happened, blessed water and gave it to them saying: Sprinkle your horse with this water and take it with you.

And they did so; the horse revived and Dairi too was brought back alive by the sprinkling of the water. Forthwith Dairi went to pay honor

1   Ancient tale told by M.M. Machteny (about 700AD). Translated from the Gaelic and Latin by Reverend Albert Barry, CSSR

to Saint Patrick bringing with him a wonderful over-sea brazen caul-dron, holding three measures. And Dairi said to the Saint: Behold let this cauldron be yours."

And Saint Patrick said, "Gratzacham."

"Returning home Dairi was annoyed at Saint Patrick. This is a foolish man, he thought who said nothing good save 'Gratzacham' in return for the wonderful cauldron of three measures. Directing his servants, go bring back our cauldron to us!

And they went and said to Patrick: We will take back the cauldron.

Saint Patrick said this time also, Gratzacham, take it.

After they carried it away Dairi asked his followers, What did the Christian say when you took the cauldron?

They answered: He said Gratzacham.

Dairi thought, Gratzacham at receiving, Gratzacham at losing; his saying is good.

And Dairi himself brought back the cauldron to Patrick, saying to him, Let this gift be returned, for you are a steadfast and immovable man. Moreover, I'll give you that hill portion of property which you asked for before. Dwell there in peace. And that is the city which is now called Armagh.

Then Patrick and Dairi both went forth to look at the wonderful offering and friendly gift. On top of the hill they found a doe with its little fawn lying in the place where the altar of the church, to the left at Armagh is now.

Patrick's companions wished to seize and slay the fawn, but the Saint was unwilling, and withheld them. Nay, more, he himself took the fawn on his shoulders, the doe following like a pet sheep until he lay the fawn down in the field just north of Armagh where... (I winked at Father Sinclair) as the learned say, some signs of his power remain to the present day."

"Gratzacham", we all three said in our third goodbye.

And yet again Gary waved me over as I started my drive down hill. "Of all the verse you know Preacher, what one poem would you recommend I read my father?"

"John Donne's 'Eternity Prayer', of course you know...about our last awakening and the gate of heaven."

"I'm not sure…"

"Where there's 'no darkness nor dazzling but one equal light. No fears or hopes; one equal possession'."

He remembered, "No ends or beginnings; but one equal eternity."

"That's it!"

"I got it, that is, I'll get it. Thanks Preacher."

"Also…", probably feeling more insular in my truck…heading out, definitely not disrespectful, but more than a little worn with all this conservative comfort, I recommended "Pablo Neruda's 'Love Song to Stalingrad'."

XXIV

Monday morning I'd stashed my few belongings, terrier and writing table into my Nissan truck and was headed home. The little diesel engine gasped and coughed its way through the Sierras and Yosemite into and across Nevada. I was "east bound and truckin' listening to country music; 'Hammer down and truckin'; truckin on down the line." Around the great Salt Lake into the evening of Wyoming, I stopped to record, to write down the lyrics I was hearing Don Williams sing "I Believe..." I wanted to share these words with the kids and maybe their mom. The lyric went,

"I don't believe that East is East and West is West
and being first is always best
but I believe in Love
I believe in babies
I believe in Mom and Dad
and I believe in you"

Don Williams straight forward delivery of a simple beautiful song. The gentle Celtic cowboy. I wondered if he was clan related to Hank Hiram Williams.

But I could no longer...not in the dark night believe in... believe in her. Maybe later but now my answer to what in life I should be 'gitten' after was closer to Tom T. Hall's song that followed, claiming "Faster horses, younger women, older whiskey, and definitely more money."

I sped through the tri-state borders of Wyoming, Nebraska, and the Dakota country; spent the night there and at first light drove fast southeast through Nebraska's corner between Iowa and Kansas into Missouri toward St. Louis. Crossed the wide Missouri River, by the Arch into the humid Illinois country, redolent heartland of a hundred river valleys. Finally crossing the Wabash into the trees and rained green pastures; back home again in the foliage of Indiana, the heart of the heartland.

I drove straight to my parent's home in North Terre Haute. They were glad to see me...of course, but my father could not conceal for long his contempt for my Japanese vehicle. He thought its purchase was a betrayal of American union labor. He actually refused to even look at it. Remembering his behavior now reminds me of a cat killing terrier I'd later own. Ol' Nick while accepting the addition of a kitten in our home always refused to look at it.

Mom and I shared a salad and iced tea. Dad said he'd already eaten. Mom tolerated my terrier in her house about the way Dad was tolerating my truck in his carport. As pre-arranged I phoned McMurtry collect. Hurriedly he said we have an emergency hearing, a court appearance Friday at 1 pm. Amazed he got it so fast, I was trying to ask how as he interrupted saying, "Aye, And he's a Notre Dame man and a fellow ex-marine." McMurtry at his best if he could hook in theologically, politically, ethnically, or in this case militarily. Finally the luck of the Irish in a good way. "Stay out of Terre Haute these next two days... don't let Anne know you're there...still might be warrants out for you and pick us up early Friday morning at the Sky King landing strip in north Vigo County. Phone me Wednesday and Thursday at high noon California time for any updates..." and he hung up. I'd hide out on the farm for two days and help the Brawlesons prepare to move.

Me and Digger dog crashed early in my old bedroom; Mother charitably ignoring his existence. Retired, my parents still 'git up' before sun-up...waking me for a great breakfast of biscuits and gravy, oranges, juice and black...Black coffee. "Black as the eye of despair", Steinbeck would say. My folks always seemed in better spirits at dawn. Surreptitiously Mom snuck Digger some sausage gravy.

I had to ask them to tell no one I'd returned...not for these next two days and especially not Anne or my sister's family. Mother's eyes snapped, "of course." Dad sighed his displeasure, saying, "When will all this be over? When will it be like you and Callahan use to say...'all she wrote'." I looked down and said nothing. "Probably never!" is what I thought but did not say. Hadn't thought of my childhood pal Callahan much. Hadn't thought of Callahan since he became an agent for the (FBI) Federal Bureau of so-called Investigation. Us Leftys called it the Federal Bureau of Intimidation. My father thought Callahan's slang expression was a way of closing the door on a subject. Closing the door behind you to concentrate on what's ahead. I've always thought American slang improves the Kings English. Maybe the she in 'all she wrote' referred to Greek mythologies three female 'fates' (Clotho, Lachesis and Atropos) who spun, cast and inflexibly lopped off destiny's options. In the spirit of that idea I became incapable of answering my mother's questions about California or Dad's questions about the long drive I'd just finished. At Dads suggestion my mind had become lock-stepped disciplined in focusing exclusively upon the immediate future.

My long sojourn in the San Joaquin had to be filed. Its bachelor squalor and brite colors of sadness, a sacramentum of some other script than mine. Already it seemed, in time, so desolate in terminal obesity and [÷] doubtful authenticity. Longings overlapping eye lids of labile existence. Beside myself most of the time, I'd moved in minor keys; unaligned in the opiate of my religion slowly healing Hells gnashing wounds within my dark coat. Paced to where I might whup the demons was 'all she wrote'.

I took my leave quietly and abruptly. Kissed both parents forehead and whistled Digger toward the truck. Drove down 46 without being spooked by the wreck site, through that corner of Clay into sweet Owen County. Every glade, hollow, meadow, and tree line an old friend.

Stopped in Freedom for gas. Old Marie still ran the gas station. She dragged herself outside to pump from old equipment for every single vehicle that pulled in her station. For all seasons she wore frayed gingham dresses and a denim jacket. Recognizing me, she became animated and nearly tearful. "God bless you boy, have you come home to stay?"

"I have. And how are you Marie? How's things?" "It wuz an awful wet winter, but now", she looked around at the trees and skyline, "we're havin summer early." Indiana seasons overlap, causing permanent Hoosier complaint when weather doesn't match the calendar.

"It's good to see you…" I began when she interrupted by hailing down a slow passing car. A faded Ford coupe pulled up alongside me and the gas pumps. It was Frances Volk and her adopted son Larry. Frances was a Slovenian war bride and a widow. Larry was an adopted

Native American as dark and silent as a remote claybank. They were our closest neighbors southeast through three miles of high forested hollers toward the west fork of the White River. Good friends and neighbors. We saw them weekly at mass. Larry came over to my window side, said nothing but shook my hand resolutely. Then he stepped back and just smiled; my, my he just beamed that silent, eloquent, welcome home smile. "C'mon Larry", Frances hollered "we'll afford gas later. Come visit us Tom." Her back tires threw a few rocks pulling out on to the pavement. I recalled she used to say "See you at Church."

Good people. It would be grand to pastor a church or churches near here. I'd include all my friends somehow…catholic and protestant.

Driving into our valley I gloried in its beauty. Gloryville Farm on Gloryville Road…I liked to think its first settlers had so gloried they gave it the name Gloryville. But, I knew the cynical history was its W.P.A.[1] residents had little glory in their pockets: hence the name.

And myself…its residual resident owner was similarly short of glory in his pocket, i.e. cash. I needed to get on a payroll soon. As soon as my legal situation was resolved…or at least clarified I would phone the Indiana Bishops office and pursue an assignment.

The sculpture of David Lewis still stood guard by the front gate. He'd sculpted the 'Agnus Dei' a militant lamb with a pennant on a stone slab bordered by the letters 'O.A.M.G.D.' for ' Omnia Ad Majorem Gloriam Dei'; 'All to the Greater Glory of God'. I'd commissioned David's work by bartering two sixty pound Suffolk lambs for it. He used the lambs for models; making the 'Agnus Dei' significantly Suffolk looking.

My pastures appeared unkempt, with sage on the hill and the old corral falling over. The last time I saw it like this I wanted to run away. Now I wanted to grab hold. I could cut that stand of sassafras to build a new corral. I'd lime the hill pasture come June…and mow the yards and pastures. The big meadows would require a lot of mowing. My oldest Morgan mare would pull a sickle-bar if I could borrow one from the Amish. The wood fences, sheds, and barn still gleamed white from three years ago. A young pastor from 'The Church of God of Prophecy' had spray painted everything before collapsing in feint from

1   W.P.A.: Works Progress Administration of Roosevelt's New Deal.

fasting. Reviving him I expressed thanks for his work, that I admired his fasting (he was trying for the big forty days and nights) but that he should keep better hydrated. He lived and is still a 'tentmaker',[1] that is, a full time pastor and part time painter.

As I parked the truck Digger and Clover started speaking and greeting each other in deep whining canine words of welcome and glee. Correct protocol. Clover greeted me first then ran off in circles of joy with Digger.

On further investigation I found the livestock satisfactory, that is, farm fat and cared for. Seventy some head of cows and calves. Forty-nine head of Suffolk ewes. All last year's market lambs sold. This year's calving and lambing just beginning. 'Synchronicity'[2] I thought, or rather hoped. Next I examined my Suffolk ram, 'Jacob' and prize winning bull, 'Welsh Nation'. Two years ago Nation may have been the biggest two year old black bull in the world at 2,000 lbs., but I couldn't afford to place him in the Guinness Book of Records.

'Jacob' approached me to be handfed. That ram was one of my favorites. As a long yearling[3] he had resisted the dogs bringing him in with the flock for shearing. Charging the sheep dogs he stumbled into the steep dry creek bed by the bridge. I jumped in after him. My back to the clay bank I saw the fire in his eyes deciding to charge me. More agile in those days I easily dodged his charge as he buried his horns and head into a tangle of roots in the soft clay. Stuck...he bleated like a baby lamb. Speaking gently I held him tight to the bank stroking his bare neck and wooly shoulders until his bleating calmed and subsided. Then I untangled his horns setting him loose. He backed up against the opposite bank and considered charging me again. Still speaking softly, I walked away down the creek bed to find a gentler slope. Climbing out of the ravine Jacob followed me at a slight distance. Since then he's always been hand tame.

Walking back from the west pasture I could hear my own footsteps. I listened to them carefully. When it is quiet and peaceful enough to

---

1   'tentmaker': St. Paul's word for apostles who work for a living.
2   Synchronicity': stretched notion in Jungian psychology. Like things supra-coordinatively falling favorably in place.
3   long yearling: almost two

hear your own steps you can trust them. That is, trust their direction; the direction they are taking you, the direction you have taken. That day my steps sounded steady … not heavy or light. I walked my farm re-discovering the mystery of the place.

At noon I phoned McMurtry. Nothing new. Plans remained the same for Friday. I phoned Benny Williams about bringing the horses home. I phoned the James family about calving and lambing shares. I was home now and responsible but I assured them I would honor our agreement for all the work they'd done… Visited a little with the Brawleson kids after school. They liked hearing me say something positive about their father and mother in the same sentence. Their Dad told me our timing was good as he was ready to move before school was out…"This weekend O.K.?" he asked. "Sure", I answered. More synchronicity I dared to hope.

However, Father Brawleson seemed a bit spooked and in a hurry to move. I joshed that I'd help them this weekend unless the Friday court put me back in jail.

"Ats all right", he said and then cryptically, "we know who you are, now, man." It was too cryptic and I was too disinterested in anything other than what I had to do next… to try and understand him. Later his children would alarmingly tell mine how their father had discovered volumes of our "family secret." He had pried around the closet floor and found boxes of filed (S.W.P.) Socialist Workers Party documents, convention position papers and policy statements. Must have been pretty exotic for Brawleson. God knows what sector of the last centuries cold war propaganda provoked him the most.

"Dad says you guys are a danger to the guvmint" his kids told mine. Bethany Kate defensively sprang to long intellectual formula… explanations of marxist and socialist politics. The Brawleson kids heard her out then said, "You guys just think because you read a lot you're smarter than most people!" Eliot's response to that cue was like Edward G. Robinsons to Humphrey Bogart in 'Key Largo'. "Yeah," he said. "Yow… we read a lot and Yow . we are smarter than most people!"

Thursday Jack McMurtry phoned at 11:45. "Things are set for

tomorrow at 1 pm. I intend to fly into Terre Haute at 10 am. Please be there at Sky King promptly or early to pick us up. Kathleen is looking forward to seeing you and the children. I am asking the court for their immediate release to you for the weekend." Then warned again, "stay out of Terre Haute until tomorrow."

To spend the excess adrenalin I felt forming toward anxiety I applied my double bladed axe to the stand of sassafras trees. A full day's work spent the adrenals, cleared my mind, produced few blisters and many near perfect poles for the new corral.

Friday morning I arrived early at the Sky King Airport. After about an hour McMurtrys piper cub landed unsmoothly on the tarmac. I always think of small planes as jalopies of the sky. Kathleen was jittery from the rough flight. Jack spoke comforting to her and instructively to me as he made and paid the airport arrangements.

We made Kathleen as comfortable as possible in the little back seat of my truck. I suggested brunch.

"No, no," Jack announced (it sounded more like an order than an announcement) "No meals until we finish in court." Then in the same breath he grabbed rice cakes out of his valise, offering them to me and his wife who groaned what she needed was a milkshake. To that, Jack pulled out a bottle of Perrier for her. Nauseous, she silently shook her head no.

Jack began, "We need to make a phone call to…" Kathleen interrupted, "I'd settle for a cup of coffee and maybe …" she implored, "just a bite to eat."

"OK", Jack snapped, "but nothing for us" nodding at me as he munched on another rice cake.

I told them I knew a nice place, near the courthouse, that had an inside phone we could use. We'd be able to park there and walk to court.

"Good!", he said while offering me another rice cake and Perrier. I accepted both.

At the Saratoga Café I prevailed upon Jack to put away his rice cakes and Perrier. We all three had coffee and Kathleen was allowed to nibble on a sweet roll. "Digestion must always be distinct from battle,"

Jack proclaimed as he asked to use the phone at the bar. Motioning me over, he said, "I'm going to ask Anne to let the children speak to you. She'll probably refuse and we'll have current news to report to the judge. If she lets them speak to you… well .. it'll be good for them."

Her phone was ringing. She answered. He officially introduced himself as my attorney and witness to my request to speak to Bethany and Eliot. Quickly and quite volubly she replied SEE YOU IN COURT!, then slammed the phone down.

We returned to Kathleen at our table twelve feet from the bar. "Did you hear that?" he asked.

"Couldn't miss it," Kathleen answered.

We took our time. Jack went over ad nauseam for Kathleen and me the contingencies of the courts processes. Then slowly we strolled to court. I took a seat in the south corridor reserved for witnesses. Jack and Kathleen went in to the courtroom. No sign of Anne, her lawyer or the Prosecutor. They entered court through the main east entrance.

After twenty minutes the McMurtrys burst out the door – jubilant.

Kathleen kissed my cheek. Jack shook my hand and said, "We've won. All warrants dropped. The judge scolded the prosecutor and said he and the court owed you an apology. (I never ever received one) More importantly he ruled the children's visitation with you to be immediately placed under Indiana Guidelines beginning this weekend, that is, tonight at 6 pm until Sunday 6 pm and every other weekend with three uninterrupted weeks this summer. And… receiving our petition to modify custody you know…change the bloody thing (he translated) the judge set a date…the seventeenth of next month to decide that matter." I didn't even get the chance to see her…to see Anne.

Walking back to the Saratoga, Jack put his arm around my shoulder, stopped me and said, "I'll probably not be available to fly back here next month. Get yourself a local Methodist lawyer. It will be a different judge and I'm told he's a Methodist."

"Most of e'm are", I answered. "Do we have a chance?"

"Look at today!" Jack was walking again, still basking in his victory. "Take your three weeks of summer as soon as school is out. Acclimate the kids to living on the farm again. Strengthen your rela…naw, hell just maintain your close relationship with your children. Kathleen and I are impressed it's the best and closest father-kids relationship we've ever seen. Just maintain, you know, conserve it. The judge will speak to your children *in camera*, that is to say, in his private chambers. They'll convince him, if you haven't, that they should be at their farm home with you."

"I'm sure they will", Kathleen added.

XXV

We had a pleasant luncheon at the Saratoga. I took pleasure introducing Jack and Kathleen to Syrian hummus and kibby. I ordered wine. Jack refused it muttering it was much too early. Kathleen and I enjoyed it. Thank God Jack brought her with him. Alone he'd have me walking everywhere and eating only rice cakes and drinking bottled water. With our baklava and coffee Jack proposed we walk to the River Park he'd heard about.

"Fairbanks Park", I replied, "was not as far as the Eugene V. Debs foundation. If you ever run for national office Jack you'll need labor support. It's about six blocks from here. We can walk through 'Indiana States' campus…"

"Let's go there first", Jack interrupted. "We've got all afternoon." He got up encouraging us toward the door.

Jack intended to witness the visitation exchange himself to assure and confirm "it went according to Hoil."

Kathleen and I kept up as best we could with Jacks long strides across I.S.U.'s campus. Then cut across Lab Schools' large playground to Gene Deb's old homeplace. I told them the story about "Kissy-kissy Eliot." We laughed together up the eighth street steps of the Debs Foundation.

I hadn't been here in years. I usually liked to point out the brass mail box on the front porch. Over the decades Debs had received letters in it from socialist and labor leaders throughout the world; including Lenin, Luxemburg, and Trotsky. Knowing that would mean little to the McMurtrys we went ahead in and toured around the place coming upon a new wall mural by John Draska. The same ex SWPer and spouse who had cheered my presentations at Unitarian meetings but refused my phone calls after I brought them comradely greetings from Farrell Dobbs. They had become respectable faculty liberals. Recently they had declared their shock and sympathy to my ex, that "wasn't it awful I'd become a 'conservative Preacher man'."

Since the sixties whenever accused of being a Communist, knowing full well the rubric indicated by the accuser included many things I was not, and sorely tempted to qualify myself more accurately, I had learned instead to grit my teeth and keep on truckin to demonstrably calibrate what kind of communist they condigned and deserved. Kind of like St. Paul when he was Christian bated in Antioch. (Acts 11:26)

Similarly since the eighties when accused of being a conservative I claim it with traditional revolutionary credentials against muling and puling liberals. The principal diagonal in mathematics from lower right to upper left. These ex socialist libs thought my putting marriage before their principle of personal freedom was reactionary. I thought their narcissistic principle of personal freedom merely the libertine right to fuck around. At its worst the abomination of home wrecking.

Wandering away from the wall mural I discovered a display documenting some of Debs private letters. Many were to his brother Teddy, Theodore Debs, some were to his pal Jimmy, James Whitcomb Riley. One was to Rose Karsner, several to her husband David Karsner, and one to my mentor Jim Cannon. James Patrick Cannon, Revolutionary Socialist grandfather of American Communism, Anti-Stalin Leninist loyal to Trotsky; Socialist Presidential Candidate and longtime leader of the Socialist Workers Party. Author of books on labor history, marxist theory, and political leadership. In the mid-sixties I would sit for hours on the floor of his house in L.A. listening to him speak about the importance of principled organization and principled leadership for the Proletariat, the working class to prevail. "Keep faith with the working class, keep faith with your class, son and we will prevail. In truth we are the only social and economic force that can prevail against the Capitalist."

To me and to many Jim Cannon was the ideal of political leadership. To Rose and David Karsner and to Gene Debs writing them he was…"the other man", in a marital crack-up. Old Debs ministered to his comrade David's grief, counseled reconciliation and return to her husband for Rose, then comradely corrected Jim for behavior that morally violated the faith and natural trust working class men and women…working families everywhere must have for their leaders.

The vanguard must reflect their highest values.

That was it! I looked for a chair. Gene Debs did not concede marriage and family values to the bourgeoisie. The working class deserved it's just share of those universal values as much as air and water. Our species require it no matter the relative material conditions. These fundamental moral values are evident in the caves of Lascaux, Holy Writ, and the very DNA of moral fiber. The only *'freedom'* that the source of morality, i.e. God is concerned we have is the 'freedom' to do his will. Foremost of which is to follow the Commandments and raise children up in ways pleasing to God.

In so far as socialist solutions advance this central phenomenon, the working class follows its leaders. When liberal idiocy, or lumpen influence, no less than nationalist treachery substitute alternative life styles and/or flag waving the socialist cause is lost again to the idolatrous market of selves. Atomized selves, not souls inevitably degenerate to settle for informed pathological togetherness instead of collective solidarity. I found a chair…and couldn't sit down.

Not since Jack London wrote of our discovering Avis Everhard's note in the oak tree had I imagined a document leaping from obscurity to such relevance. In his Novel, 'The Iron Heel' Jack London describes a fascist stomp-down in America after the Revolutionary Left lost its chance (temporarily) to prevail. Avis, the widow of his Everhard protagonist is being executed. Before her execution she leaves a letter of fidelity to her husband against the oligarchy in the hollow oak tree near their Wake Robin Lodge. She did not "dream that for seven long centuries the tribute of her love" for her husband and their resistance to the Oligarchy "would repose undisturbed in the heart of the ancient oak". Seven hundred years!

It has taken almost one hundred years for the sins of the Soviet Union to totally demoralize its best operatives. Soon the greatest Socialist achievement in history will roll over dead. Marxian Socialism was scheduled for the advanced industrial countries of Europe and the Americas where a vast and skilled working class could implement it. Not! Definitely not in the sprawling backward wastes of Czarist Russia. The Bolsheviks seized power there because (1) they could and (2) because they presumed first Germany then the rest of industrial Europe was soon to follow them. The industrial resources and Proletarian might of Western Europe would consolidate with Russia to build a world socialist order abolishing the class system with cooperative commonwealths.

Didn't happen. Stalin got stuck with the untenable task of "socialism in one (backward) country". Stalin ran it and probably only Stalin could have ran it like a Red Czar. Declaring war upon the majority of Russians i.e. the Peasantry (who *were* starving the cities), industrialization was forced upon the country in a blood bath which delivered lights and bad plumbing throughout Russia. Incidentally this unsurpassed industrial strength it developed defeated Hitler more than any other force in World War II.[1]

No more ruthless than the average Georgian roughneck or Sicilian Godfather except in scale. Stalin's unprecedented systems of butchery extended to millions of innocent people and (gak!) was done in the name and cause of Socialism. How did the greatest concept of western civilization for social justice sink so low? Sunk so low it caused the best of intelligent men and women (of the third international) to deny degenerate reality and apologize for it. Sunk so low it justified so-called social democrats (of the second international) the world over to deny its socialist achievements and condemn it. And then there was the momentary moral hope of Trotsky (AKA) Lev Davidovitch Bronstein, Jewish intellectual father and family man, who affirmed the socialist foundations of the Russian Revolution, and put his life on the line criticizing its Stalinist corruptions.

Albeit briefly in bed with an adulterous cripple[2], then cut down and killed by a Stalinist ice axe assassin, his heroic if hapless personae pervades the moral dilemmas of our time.

Trotsky's genius and heroic morality has inspired the best hearts and minds of two centuries. His hapless hauteur has also been handed

---

1   "The essential truth about World War II is that it was won by the Soviets on the Eastern Front, where eighty percent of the combat took place and where the Germans incurred ninety percent of their losses.

2   Adulterous cripple: Frida Kahlo wife of Comrade Diego Rivera.

down to his followers producing sectarian litters of snowball-like[1] pigs at troughs of tragic illusion.

No less a Trotskyist I liked the Stalin I read about first in Isaac Deutsher's biography and now in Simon Montefiore's. That is, the young Stalin, the cobblers son, the brightest, toughest kid on the school ground, the seminarian who memorized the entire New Testament, the brave devil may care revolutionary in and out of Siberian exile who even robbed banks for the Bolsheviks inspiring and unnerving Lenin. After power... reality changed but the publicized myth was no less attractive; the gentlemen diplomat, proletarian charmer and pal of F.D.R., commander of the Red Army defeating Hitler's wehrmacht.

What flaw, what sin led this man to betray the Revolution, the Socialist cause so badly it would die in Russia a slow demoralized death? Liberals in self-congratulatory schadenfreude blame Lenin's revolutionary successes. This justifies their total lack of success while rhetorically blathering otherwise.

Trotsky's followers insist bureaucratic castes almost identically replaced capitalist class enabling them to conserve their marxist schemata with the intention and appearance of integrity. All of which still falls far short of reality.

By the evening of November 8, 1932 the fifteenth anniversary of the Revolution three years after Trotsky's expulsion and exile, Stalin and all Bolshevik leaders still lived in modest plain quarters and received state wages no more than the "maximum responsible worker" of say a steelworker, truck driver or mechanic. Their (tverdos) hardness, that great revolutionary virtue, "coexisted with a rigid code of party manners: Bolsheviks were meant to behave toward one another like...gentlemen". "Divorce was frowned upon more severely than in the Catholic Church".[2] Promiscuous military men were called sluts. Proletarian poets like Demian Bedny were criticized for profanity.

Nadya Alliluyova, Stalin's wife was said to love him very much. And General Secretary Stalin loved her. Recently opened Russian archives include multiple notes and letters of their tender regard for

1   snowball-like: "Snowball" was the lily white ineffectual hog of George Orwell's 'Animal Farm' satire.
2   Simon Sebag Montefiore: "Stalin: The Court of the Red Czar" p.44

each other. They missed each other when apart for even short periods of time. They mutually loved nothing more than to be with their daughter and son together.

It was not however an easy relationship. "They were both passionate and thin-skinned; their rows always dramatic."[1] He had a workaholics schedule. She was always ailing. Both were oversensitive. She nagged him in public. He flirted with ballerinas. It was gossiped she was nuts. Peers described her as beautiful, witty, loyal, honest, and sincere but also aloof, troubled, hysterical, depressed, and chronically jealous." Seems pretty normal to me!

Montefiore concludes "despite their turbulent marriage and their strange similarity of passion and jealousy, they loved each other after their own fashion."[2] His narrative continues while "Nadya prided herself on 'Bolshevik Modesty' wearing...shapeless dresses draped in plain shawls, with square necked blouses and no make-up"[3] on that night (November 8, 1932) she made a special effort.

In their modest apartment, "she twirled for her sister, Anna, in a long unusually fashionable black dress" and had "indulged in a stylish hairdo instead of her usual severe bun."[4] She dressed to be lovingly noticed by her Stalin, the General Secretary, her man.

That night, at table, even though she sat opposite him, he drunkenly flirted with another man's wife: "a brash film actress, Galina Yegorova, wife of Alexander Yegorova, a Red army commander. She was known for her affairs and risqué dresses. Among the other plainly dressed women she was said to look "like a peacock in a farmyard."[5] Nadya try as she might could not tolerate her husband's attention to this woman.

She left the party and shot herself with a small Hauser pistol. Discovering his suicided wife and her hostile suicide note around 3am; according to Montefiore "Stalin was poleaxed." Grief-stricken and humiliated he wailed, "She's crippled me!" "Nadya... Nadya how

1   IBID
2   IBID
3   IBID
4   IBID
5   IBID

we need you, me and the children."[1]

"That suicide altered history", claims the Stalin's nephew Leonid Redens. "It made the Terror inevitable." The man of steel "was in a shambles, knocked sideways" exploding in "sporadic fits of rage" blaming everyone – anyone else other than himself before crumpling into despair.

Then declared he was going to kill himself. "I can't go on living like this"[2], he said.

The Terror itself was a complex political phenomenon. Under and above the tsunami of socio-economic forces personalities shaped it. The traumatized loss, wound, and guilt of Stalin certainly did. Stalin is said to have never forgotten the guests and the part that each may have played that November night. He is said to have replayed that night over and over again in his wounded mind. Many of the guests that night were later induced to liquidate the others.

In Freud's opus "Civilization and its Discontents", I'd previously thought he went too far asserting that wounded and/or uncontrolled libido could cause war. Wars have no single cause. Economics, greed, capitalist markets, national chauvinism, racism, imperial bullying all contribute to a list which fundamental Jewish, Christian, and Islamic theology would call sin. Add to that the sin and wounds of infidelity and home-wrecking. I know how that too smolders toward violence.

Unlike American meta-freudians who twist his formulae into liberating the libido Freud himself called for its disciplined control and sublimation. He valued the super-ego conventions of Fidelity and Marriage to protect the tenderness of children, women and men from the ravages of its opposite.

The Catholic Church carefully defined sin in unjust wars centuries ago and yet has managed to support most of e'm. The bride of Christ has been in bed with the war makers. So have bourgeois Protestants. Only a remnant...make that remnants remain. Religious and Political remnants of conscience and consciousness in relative human purity remain... unjoined together. That was my calling! Maybe I could contribute toward Allah's unifying process. Our Father in Heaven's harsh

---

1   IBID
2   GARF 7532C – 149a Staff gossip and document 7

and dreadful[1] love to rear and reconcile his people. Not to help God. He does not require our help. We need His. But to clarify, to declare His will to the world.

Had I reached a nearness in time and place for thoughts of such importance? Or was it mere propinquity to peripheral consciousness; not part of the basic processor, moving around with those nerves which run outward from the brain and spinal cord spilling into tissues of personal advantage? I hadn't even seen her.

Lost in my thoughts as we left Gene Debs home, we walked to Fairbanks Park and then back to my truck. I could tell Kathleen was exhausted...I suggested she freshen up and rest a bit at my folk's house.

Mom and Dad as always hospitable, were glad to see us, meet Jack and Kathleen and...hear about court. Kathleen was shown into the guest room for a short nap and Dad took Jack outside to look at the trees he'd planted. I talked mainly with Mom, clearing plans that the children and I would stay over that night and leave early, *early* in the morning for the farm. Jack waived off any offers of food or drink. After her nap Kathleen joined Mom and me for some coffee and spice cake. Jack kept talking to Dad in the kitchen like he was running for election. At 5:30pm we drove cross town to test the courts visitation order.

With her mother's money Anne had bought a big house downhill from Ohio Boulevard. Earlier she'd described it as the kind of house, Karl Marx would have liked to own. It sat on the northwest corner of 17th and Ohio. Spookily I recalled and told the McMurtrys I was born on this same 17th Street miles to the south near its end by the railroad tracks.

Promptly at 6pm the three of us knocked at her front door. Without flourish the doors were opened just enough to nudge the children out and then close. Not a word nor a meeting of the eyes. But the kids were raucously in my arms and kissing Kathleen and Jack. Both McMurtry's wept. I almost felt guilty I didn't. Incredibly I saw Jack swell with satisfaction and pride of accomplishment... the only pay-

---

1   "harsh and dreadful love": Dostoyevsky's reflection upon God's holy commandment in 'Conversations and Exhortations of Father Zossima part VI of Brothers Karamazov.'

ment he expected or wanted. I thought this bad tempered Mick lawyer had the soul of a saint.

We drove out to their airplane which the children enjoyed climbing around on. Especially Eliot, who liked sitting behind the throttle saying 'May Day' 'May Day'. After roaring in laughter with Eliot, Jack leaned over and whispered to me, "When you celebrate our victory tonight, don't get drunk!" Kathleen had given Franciscan brown scapulars to both children and one for me. She also gave rosaries to each of them and one for me. All the way to the airport she had instructed Bethany on ending the sorrowful mysteries.

Later that night, Eliot and I fell asleep listening to Bethany and her Grandma Vi praying the rosary. The soft repetitive verses sounding like a series of soothing rainfall.

XXVI

Sweet laughter and merriment for breakfast with my parents and children. Even Dad could see the children were better with me. We took our leave happily.

On the hour's drive home to the farm, Bethany noticed I had the radio tuned to a country music station. "I thought you only liked classical music and jazz, Papa?"

"Out west I learned to appreciate country ballads and singers." (The lyrics of one John Connolly song ['I don't Remember Loving You'] had accurately described my clinical condition)

We talked about Johnny Cash, Merle Haggard, Charlie Pride, Patsy Cline, Ray Charles, Willy Nelson, Anne Murray, Indiana's Bobby Helms and Don Williams popular song…'I Believe'. Bethany wanted to argue a bit in favor of the classics me and her mother had taught her. I assured her appreciating the best of country songs need not challenge our pantheon of Prokoviev, Brahms, Bruckner, Beethoven, Messian and Ives -Miles Davis, John Coltrane and the M.J.Q. (Modern Jazz Quartet). Bethany just wasn't sure she should like these sometimes "kinda clangy" sounding country tunes.

As we crossed the Eel River near Bowling Green Don Williams' ballad, 'I Believe', came on the radio. I pulled off the road to stop so we could listen carefully to it. In a pleasant, caring, western drawl, Williams sang these words, "I don't believe in Super Stars
organic food and foreign cars.
I don't believe the price of gold,
the certainty of growing old.
That Right is right, and Left is wrong,
that North and South can't get along.
That East is East and West is West
and being first is always best,
but I believe in Love…
I believe in babies.
I believe in Mom and Dad

And I believe in You.
I don't believe that heaven waits
for only those who congregate.
I like to think that God is love.
He's down below and up above.
He's watching people everywhere.
He knows who does and doesn't care.
And I'm an ordinary man
sometimes I wonder who I am,
but I believe in Love. I believe in Music
I believe in Magic
And I believe in You.

Eliot cheered "Hooray for da' Country music". Bethany still wasn't sure…but she sure liked Don Williams ballad. "We must get it for Mama," she said. Eliot carried on "Hooray for da' cowboys and da farmahs in da San Wahkeen and Indiana."

I promised Bethany we'd get the Don Williams record album that included that song for Mama at Honey Creek Mall on the way back Sunday. And then as on cue for Eliot, (Disc jockeys seemed to be coupling these tunes) Tom T. Hall comes on the radio singing repetitively his solution for life's problems; "Faster Horses, Younger Women, Older Whiskey and More Money."

Eliot whooped it up, 'Faster Horses, Younger Wimmin, More Munee'

over and over. We laughed and sang all the way to the White River Bridge. It was still a rickety old Covered Bridge and Eliot imitated little Jess (from our favorite movie "Friendly Persuasion") making echoey scary sounds until we reached its endpoint of light. Quantum tunneling into a new sunlit chapter of our time. The complexity of neutered to hideous possibilities constricted to the straight way. "The way of those upon whom God has bestowed His Grace. The way of those whose portion is not wrath and who go not astray." The Grand Exordium[1] would rule our Valley. His values we could clearly discern would rule our lives here. Axiarchists!

We greeted the dogs and the wonder of the place, then went inside.

1   The Grand Exordium: the first prayer, the first words of the Holy Karan.

The Brawlesons were partially moved out. They left a note saying they'd finish up next Saturday.

Bethany went straight to the record player to aesthetically immunize from the doses of clangy country music she'd endured for me and Eliot. My record collection had been left intact. We spent a restful half hour listening with Bethany to the Czech Philharmonic complete Beethoven's 7th Symphony. Then Bethany proceeded to rummage through the records chattering knowledgably about each one. She wished to affirm her appreciation to me and be instructive to Eliot. I reminded her how the great Duke Ellington said, "There are only two kinds of music: (1) music that sounds good and (2) whatever you want to call that other stuff."

I'd gone to the bathroom when I heard Bethany and Eliot yelp a frightened surprise. Rushing to them in the kitchen I was also startled by the dark, somber, silent image filling up the window. It was our neighbor Larry Volk, leaning on the sill saying nothing. He was like that. Indian silent he'd walk three miles through the woods to visit us and just quietly lean on the window sill…til we noticed him. We liked and trusted him. Modern people found him creepy. Eliot fondly referred to him as 'Injun Joe', (from Tom Sawyer) or 'Injun Larry'.

I smiled and opened the door for him. He joined the kids at the kitchen table and I poured out a half cup of coffee. He gulped it down as I knew he would and said, "Need help on the corral?" He'd seen my pile of sassafras from top of the hill.

"Yessir" I answered, "sure could use some help." Halfway to the kids' room to help them change into work clothes I heard the fridge door open and shut. Now Larry didn't exactly have refrigerator rights… but I let it go. Got Bethany and El in blue jeans and was going out the front door when Larry stopped me to say, "Got to make two calls…can I use…?" he motioned toward our phone. I nodded sure as I took the children out to the smokehouse where I kept my tool chest. By the time I'd put two hammers, a poke of three penny nails, a small crowbar, my old axe and a wad of bailing wire into a five gallon bucket Larry caught up with us at the corral and we all set to work. The children held ends of the poles while we nailed and wired then to sturdy locust posts.

Two hours passed when Bethany announced "Company Papa" and we saw Galen's old truck swing into the lane. Larry ran to open the second gate for him then they rode together up to our corral project.

Galen got out with his arms full. "I got goodies!" was his welcome greeting. Larry had noted our nearly empty fridge and phoned his mom and cousin Galen about it. The kids squealed with delight as Galen demonstrably presented his goods. "I got a chocolate pie with homemade meringue from Larry's mom. I got a dozen brown eggs from our hens, a full side of bacon from Uncle Gale Abrill, store bought tomatoes, and mom...my mom sends her love with this pan fresh cornbread and a half gallon of our own best buttermilk. Larry and I also saw a case of cold beers in his backseat.

We had a great weekend. Home again. Home to stay. We reveled in it. Nearly finished the corral. Got a little drunk with Galen and 'Injun Joe' after the kids were asleep.

Took Beth-El to the stone veneered Methodist Church in Freedom Sunday morning. Young Pastor John was glad to greet us and many of our neighbors provided a caring welcome.

It was a fair service. Eliot no more than me struggled against dozing. Bethany however beamed in evangelical ideal-illusory fellowship. "To think", she spoke later in the day, "that we're all Christians together... there."

It was a partisan remark for me against the unserious liberal crowd around her mama, but I also knew the unreality, the unlikelihood we could count on these Christians being *there* for us.

Pastor John or Prester John[1] as Eliot insisted on calling him introduced us to his new visiting fiancé. She and Bethany immediately took

---

1   'Prester John (also Presbyter Johannes) legendary Christian Patriarch said to be an ecumenical descendant of the Maji; firing centuries of imaginary unity. A symbol of the Church's universality, transcending culture and geography to encompass humanity in times when ethnic and inter-religious tension made such a vision intellectually and physically but not spiritually distant. Imagined from the 3rd century "Acts of Thomas'. Not getting his tongue around the correct pronunciation, Eliot's typically clipped and rapid thought exceeding vocal musculature to articulate was sometimes... strangely in sync with other dimensional time. COCU indeed.

to each other. This beginning a long line of women drawn to Bethany as a "motherless child".

John informed me that Indiana's Bishop Armstrong had set up a series of summer educational-pastoral training programs for the licensure of new ministers.

"It's a week long program held at De Pau University; all expenses paid for you under my sponsorship, but you should phone the Bishops office first thing Monday morning." He gave me the Bishop's office number. "Leave them your phone number and our District Supervisor will contact you. His name is Millard Stilmore."

Sunday nite, the children cried all the way from my truck to their mother's door. They were not prepared to return to her. It was my responsibility and I had not seen to it. Indiana's — like most state guidelines require the non-custodial parent to return their children (1) on time, (2) properly bathed and clean, (3) properly dressed, (4) well fed, *and* (5) emotionally prepared (i.e. psychologically accepting of their return) for the exchange.

I agree with all that. I hadn't got used to it… yet. I got home to a raging complaint of a phone message. She hung up with her threatening slogan again of "I'll see you in court."

Early Monday reached Bishop Armstrong's office; I left word and my phone number for Superintendent Millard Stilmore. "Millard Stilmore" sounds like the name of a bird dog.[1] I also asked the female voice at the Bishop's office if they could recommend an attorney, a family law attorney for me. The voice said Melvin P. Rueblood was the brother of Reverend George Rueblood and she would recommend him. 'Stilmore and Rueblood!' – what's with these Anglo-Saxon Methodist names?! As good a referral as I was likely to get. I phoned and got an appointment at 1pm Tuesday the next day. The easy early appointment made me fear Lawyer Rueblood was probably not…in

---

1   Millard Fillmore: Thirteenth President of the United States. Also name of English Setter in James Street's novel 'Goodbye My Lady'. Made into a great movie with Linton, Indiana's Phil Harris, Walter Brennan, Brandon de Wilde, and Sidney Poitier. I think it was Poitier's first film. The segregated conditions of the deep south so bad in the fifties where it was filmed, that Poitier refused to even mention it in his autobiography 'The Measure of a Man'.

great demand.

By noon Supervisor Stilmore phoned. Brisk and businesslike he asked how early I could "meet with him the next day." Then added "at my home", giving his address in Woodridge an upscale suburb in east Terre Haute. In the habit of rising at 6am (unless hung over) on the farm, and being approximately one hour from his address…I replied, "eight am." "Well… (he stretched out the word) then you are more of a morning lark than a night owl." "Well… (I stretched it out too) I've achieved the farmers early to rise, but I'm still working on the early to bed part."

My remarks I thought deserved at least a chuckle. They didn't earn one with Stilmore. He replied quite neutrally, "Eight am will be fine." Then "God be with you – goodbye" and he hung up. Later on I would learn he didn't like my remark identifying myself as a farmer. Supervisor Stilmore was a pro, against part-timers and tentmakers. He hued to the ideal of professional iteneracy in ministry.

I was Cannonite[1] prompt for our eight am appointment. Not slightly resistant and a little late, not over eager early or nervously-compulsively on time. I pulled into Stilmore's drive a minute or so before eight and strode with prompt composure to his door. He greeted me cheerfully and hospitably. He was dressed in a dark three piece suit wearing what was unmistakably (in Terre Haute) a high collared 'Packard' dress shirt.

Without asking he served me a mug of black coffee, then poured one for himself. His eyes seemed to question O.K.? Mine blinked O.K. "Morgan", he asked with words now, "What is your commitment to Christ's ministry?"

"Heart and soul", I answered.

"Good answer!" Almost bantering now in what John Wesley would call chaffing good humor, Stilmore continued.

"What do you know of Philip William Otterbein? And…what do you know of the Evangelical United Brethren EUB uniting with the Methodist Church in 1968 creating the United Methodist Church

---

1   Cannonite: From Jim Cannon SWP leader known for his insistence on disciplined punctuality.

UMC?"

"I know very little", I answered. He continued,

"You might read up on it a bit. Otterbein's theology is doggedly Germanic without the lift of even Swedish Methodism, but where people are looking to justify a difference, he's handy. The Otterbein judicatories were more populist than ours. The church we are assigning you may be providentially close and convenient to this farm of yours, it is also convenient administratively to us."

I was happy to be so simply accepted and happier yet that a church assignment could be close and convenient to the farm. Then Supervisor Stilmore asked if I could arrange to be at De Pau University in Putnam County all of next week and accept the assignment of Pastor for Birch Lane United Methodist Church when I returned.

"Yessir", I answered to both questions. Stilmore then described the location of Birch Lane as "way out in the country triangulated between Coalmont, Clayford and Hectorsburg."

Hectorsburg was a hamlet west of Spencer, our county seat and just south of the Vandalia hills. Clayford and Coalmont were in adjoining Hayes County southeast of Brazil. I reckoned it was less than one half hour from our front gate and mid-way between the farm and Terre Haute. Perfect! I was delighted. A bit too delighted for Stilmore.

"Birch Lane is a big church with almost two hundred families, half of them regular attenders… generous in collections and pastoral pay." Then quite gravely he said, "It has been a troublesome parish for us since 1968.[1] Hostile to Preachers. Angry about what they think they lost in the merger yet not remembering what it was. You will face a great deal of disunity. You are described…" he opened a file which I presumed was mine. "Your work, your ministry in California is described as unifying disparate elements. We will pray the holy spirit assists you with unity at Birch Lane. Remember legal, administrative unity is already structurally there. You'll just have to patiently herd the troublesome flock, more fully, into the fold." He went on…

"It says here", he said, holding my file forward with one hand while he adjusted his bifocals with the other. "It says here that you requested

---

1   1968: The year of merger for the Evangelical United Brethren and the Methodist into the (U.M.C.) United Methodist Church.

a 'country conservative church'. What does that mean? Country conservative?"

"Traditional!", I answered. "Rural and traditional. Not fickle, high falutin bourgeois. Home centered working people. Not loosey goosey liberals looking for loopholes and excuses for modern immorality."

"Hmmm… tell me about your churches…your people in California." I described briefly as best I could the conservative country people, the rural traditional people of Knights Ferry and Coulterville.

"How old are you?" he asked, looking but not saying he was somehow amazed. He saw my age in the file before I could answer and grunted, "I think conservative in California means something different than conservative in Indiana. You are from here, aren't you?"

"Yes, yes…" protesting, "I don't mean narrow minded right wing reactionary racist politicals. I mean culturally conservative, socially conservative family oriented, seriously spiritual men, women, and children."

Still looking slightly amazed, old Millard Stilmore just shook his head and said, "I think you'll find or relearn" he shook his head some more, that "conservative in Indiana especially in the countryside means more times than not just stupid maybe stupid and illiterate."

Now I liked Stilmore even though impeccably undishevelled he seemed in many ways the Reverend Mr. Black. But his hostility to the countryside was like Maxim Gorki's toward the Peasantry. An opinionated attitude I found held by most U.M.C ministers who felt safe only in the suburbs.

"Check in with me", he stood announcing our adjournment, "after you've finished next week's seminar." He smiled broadly, if a bit paternalistic as I shook his hand and said goodbye.

Our meeting gave me a lot to think about during lunch at the Saratoga. Hummus, Syrian salad, beer and Kibby. It was early so I saw no one I knew. No friends to visit, no lawyers to avoid.

My one o'clock meeting with Rueblood was three blocks east on Wabash. His office was in the old Tribune building upstairs above the Liberty Theater. Up the stairs, not the elevator I reached his office on time and was shown right in. He sat behind his desk, not rising, holding out his hand and staring at mine.

"You still wearing your wedding ring?" he rather demanded than asked. Stopping to look at my own hand I weakly (for me) replied, "Yeah, I guess I am."

"How long you been divorced?"

"About two years." He shook his head exactly like old Stilmore did. I wondered if there was such a thing as a Methodist headshake?

This Rueblood seemed generally cross, a condition I've always found infectious.

"As I told the divorce court...I took marriage vows to God *not* to a pack of lawyers."

"You actually said that in court!" Rueblood's head had stopped shaking. It was now sort of bobbing up and down but still disapproving.

"How long you been a Methodist minister?"

"Not long... little more than a year."

"How long you been a Methodist?"

"The same."

"What!?" Rueblood was exasperated. "What then is your religious background?'

"Irish Catholic (and remembering Dad's side)... Hardshell Baptist."

Defensively I thought I should share my nearly two decades as an Archdiocesian and Director of Catholic Charities and Social Ministries...and did so.

"Well sir, you're representing Methodism now. You're got to git this extreme fundamentalism, and dogmatic Catholicism out of your system."

His head switched from bobbing to shaking sideways again. It provoked me.

"Protecting the fundamentals and universal, that is, catholic nature of the faith is what drove John Wesley out of the Anglican Church whose very existence began with justifying an illicit divorce for the King! Are you truly a Methodist, Mr. Rueblood or merely a throwback to Anglican compromise?"

"Look man," he did not stand but half leaned out over his desk. "I know the Judge. Yes he's Methodist but he will expect you to be the soul of moderation. Your reputation precedes you. People think you're some kind of a radical...kidnapping your kids. Or...let me put it this way...immoderately, carelessly, recklessly, allowing yourself to be accused of such a thing. It sets a bad example. A ministers actions could encourage other men to defy the courts. Willy, nilly the church might be seen as encouraging or agitating people against law and order."

"Isn't that what the church did in the civil rights struggle? Encourage the breaking of unjust laws. Moral conscience is required to stand fast against such things as racism and home wrecking."

"You expect Judge Farley to order your wife, I mean your *ex* wife back home to you?!"

"Of course not, however the old Methodist Discipline[1] might."

"The new one wouldn't..."

"You're right, you're right...I only wish to expect Judge Farley to be persuaded by your moderate counsel how the children, my daughter Bethany and my son Eliot are happier living with their father on their family farm. That his work on the farm and his ministry near the farm is more stable and more conducive for the rearing of little ones than their mother's conference hopping and day care centers."

Now quietly, Rueblood began, "not bad...that sounds not so bad... but your tone is still wrong. Your public presentation of ethos and personae is still all wrong. Not Methodist."

Just as quietly I raised both arms palms open to gesture "What!?"

"See", he spouted, "even your physical expressions are wrong. You appear militant, not Methodist. Judge Farley perceives, and I think correctly...he perceives militancy as akin to mindlessness. Dogmatic Catholics and country Protestants not giving up and not getting along with the required give and take of modern complex society. He'll be studying your appearance and demeanor...your atty-tude more than

---

1   Methodist Discipline: by-laws of church behavior – midcentury revised. The old refused divorce without proof of contract violation; not granting remarriage to guilty violators of contract i.e. divorcers not divorcees. Reflected early US laws. New Discipline reflects present US no fault divorce. Both old and new consistently campfollowing establishment consensus!

anything else."

"Is there no criteria?..." I began. He interrupted bitchily and teacherly, to tell me what I already knew! "There is no criterion in family law except one phrase. 'What is in the best interests of the children'. We must orchestrate every impression to the Judge that you are Methodist moderate, unobtrusive, soft and gently reserved. More considerate to her than she'd be to you. Capable of compromising what you think is right in order to make the Judge look good. Judges do not like to look bad.

Catching his breath... "He knows she is local faculty; her position accountable to College and Community. You, on the other hand are some isolated and independent farmer made worse by thinking God is on his side. You gotta appear humble pie and keep your mouth shut. I'll do the talkin. Remember the proverbs, 'He keeps his life who guards his mouth'."

I read Proverbs recently but could only recall a few. I recited;

"A good wife, her husband's crown. A shameless wife is cancer in his bones."

"She's *not* your wife! *She's not-no longer your wife!* You've got to git that out of your head. The Judge won't miss that atty-tude that psychologically you're still entitled...still laying claims on her. It stinks of olde school catholic thinking... marriage vows forever and obedience; all that til death do us part stuff."

I knew it was a stretch to expect the so-called 'family law court' to even resemble a legal entity. No case law. No precedents. No criterion. Just a free market brawl of atty-tude management with the Judges personal prejudices and predilection for re-election (i.e. what would cool not sully his electoral reputation) ruling. All this atty-tude instruction from Rueblood was intended to help my case. But with all his animated and voluble insistence on my being moderate and quiet... so quiet as to hide myself so the lawyers semi-divine provisories could prevail... started to smack of perverse quietism. I began seeing Rueblood as Madame Guyon[1] in drag, ethically antinomian and heretical. Yet, I remained kinda *quiet*.

Rueblood concluded, "I think the best we can hope for is a second

1   Madame Guyon: Quietist heretic condemned by Innocent XI in 1687.

chance. It would be like Farley to rule for your ex with warnings and the next time around (ka-ching $ I thought) give them to you."

Remembering another Proverb, I concluded, "Mr. Rueblood 'Hope deferred makes the heart sick'. I want to win this as soon as possible."

He said it might be months not weeks for a hearing. He was still shaking and bobbing his head both ways as I left.

His secretary confirmed the farms mailing address on my way out the door. For billing, no doubt; [$Ka-ching$Again] I swallowed the thought with disgust. Years ago, I had signed a petition that was as they say half joking and whole earnest that called for the re-legalization of dueling. The final solution for lawyers and lawyering.

Yet with Rueblood it was more than lawyering. He knew more about some things than he should and less about others than he should. I wondered how many currents of Hoosier gossip we were dealing with here. The bliss of California anonymity practically guarantees no one knowing you well enough to gossip much about you. I'd better phone McMurtry.

I couldn't reach Jack McMurtry all that week. He and Kathleen were on vacation. I did locate Birch Lane….rather spookily. Driving west of the Vandalia hills I had always been drawn to the deep forested roads that lay south of the pavement. Always meant to explore them. Never took the time. Now I took the time. It was moonlit warm that night and I slowly drove wherever I seemed called to… like a tourist might if he was from somewhere else. Beauty is missed when we don't tour and travel our own home country.

I drove mainly south, but a little west turning on roads whose expanse of moonlight or mystery of night appealed to me… when BAM out of the dark foliage appeared this welcoming bright refuge of light in the darkness. A white clapboard Church built long and narrow into the woods. Like Welsh Longhouses in the Black Mountains near Abergavenny it seemed radically as one with the soft night, peacefully reclusive with a serious reserve, a serious reservoir of spiritual strength, in, of, and from the wilderness, an aesthetic barracks for saintly respite; heavenly barricade for earths idea of how to get there.

Out of the truck I stood astounded in light of the place. I'd heard

Preachers and Priests speak of the call... Could this be it?

A small sign loomed up from the grass. It read Clayford U.C.C. United Church of Christ. Guess not. Wrong Church. It was not Birch Lane U.M.C. United Methodist Church. I found Birch Lane Church the next morning. In the light of day Birch Lane appeared a bit earthbound and pedestrian. At least when compared to the mystical night church near Clayford. Two old clumps of birch trees hung about the churchyard as survivors of a previous grove. The Church itself was structured large and squarely in the middle of a vacant country road corner surrounded on three sides by a large cemetery. A white rock lane expanded almost big enough for a parking lot up from the corner; the lot slightly elevated not quite big enough to be called a bluff. It appeared almost ponderously unwieldy; unable to heave its human burden heavenwards.

But it was to be pastorally mine. My ungainly barge of a separated lifeboat from the barque of Peter. My flock of souls to serve, protect and care for. And it was gracefully and gratefully close to my Gloryville Farm.

XXVII

The weeklong seminar was to convene at 8am the following Monday in De Pau's historic but small assembly hall. I'd arranged for Galen to stay at our farm and care for the livestock. Sunday evening me and the other country preachers began to arrive at De Pau's guesthouse. I arrived at nightfall and there was an atmosphere of pleasant confusion as to who was who. Most of the country men were young in their twenties. The suburban instructors were all my age in their forties or fifties. Probably because of my age the latter were less than confidential in their remarks around me. Several times I heard them refer to the younger men as 'hicks'. Lawyer Rueblood was a perfect introduction to these suburban snobs. They liked to joke about taking the hicks to town so they could see the elephant. "To town" was Indianapolis and "the elephant" was the rescue helicopter on top of the Methodist Hospital roof. By the end of the week I'd forgotten this mockery until our field trip to Methodist Hospital. When we reached the roof all the young country preachers *did* run to see and touch the helicopter. Senior Methodists snootily shook their heads at each other allowing that "every crop of hicks do the same thing all summer."

Next morning in De Pau's historic assembly hall our week's seminar began with three assignments. The first was an essay review to be written on William Hordern's book, "Living by Grace". The second was to be a sermon reflecting what we learned from Hordern, this week's discussions, holy scripture, and a "heartfelt" experience of our own. The assigned sermon was to be preached from the Breeden Memorial pulpit Saturday morning. The essay review was to be typed and due Thursday. We were all scheduled for an hour of pastoral counseling Friday. And thirdly we were to take...to submit to taking the 'MMPI', the 'Minnesota Multiphasic Personality Inventory psychiatric written exam... Now! They began passing it out. Whoa! I raised my hand and stood to be recognized.

Since there had been no introduction, I introduced myself... including that I had worked as a mental health professional almost twenty years. I then described "the MMPI as a penetrating psyc. exam, but very pliable to interpretation, that is malleable;...bendable to its interpreters. I encouraged patients and practitioners to use it properly in caring therapeutic settings *not* in personnel, that is, employer-employee evaluations."

The chairman or presider, perhaps more accurately to be called the assigner as he had announced the assignments but not bothered to introduce himself. This assigner seemed non plussed for a second, then asked me, "Do you question this conference being a caring therapeutic setting?"

"I dunno, so far you haven't cared enough to introduce yourself!"

Lines were drawn. Sympathy from my fellow conferees. Hostility from the arrogant instructors. Senior Minister Dr. Acuff took the floor apologizing for *"not properly"* (attempting a humorous and cynical tone to *properly*) introducing our conference chairman this morning the Reverend Jim Webb. "We've been very busy... my staff," he motioned for them to stand, "are all dedicated to organizing, evaluating, and improving our program here to be the very best educational experience for you in preparation for your Pastoral assignments. Of course, this setting" he waved his arm around toward circular windows showing the De Pau Campus, "is caring if not exactly *therapeutic* (that tone again). Our responsibility is to maximize the effectiveness of your ministry in this *modern* world."

He spoke the word *modern* as too many Baptists pronounce Gawwd. Too revered, and too self-righteous. Acuff was from the deep south. I never met an Acuff who wasn't. He had a Doctorate from Duke and was chairman of the Religious Studies Department at De Pau. I later learned he also chaired the Methodist Bishops Human Resources (i.e. personnel) committee.

He continued, "You men have been chosen for assignment to some of our remotely located churches. We are not evaluating whether you got the job; we are evaluating how best to help you do it."

I interrupted, "Whose property will be the interpreter's evaluation?"

Now flushed, the Reverend Doctor Philburt Acuff replied; (preciously pronouncing every syllable) "The property of The U-Ni-Ted

Meth-O-Dist Church!" He then sat down. Reverend Jim Webb stood and announced a fifteen minute break.

A scramble followed. Actually two scrambles. One at the rostrum with the instructors. One at the back of the hall with my conferees. These country boys had rarely encountered a union but knew double-dealing employers enough to recognize the need for one.

Surrounding me they all asked, "Should we take that thing? Should we submit to the test?"

"If we refuse, we must refuse totally and together," I advised.

"Then we should refuse together with *solidarity*", said this very young man in a military shirt. His name was Jason DeVries and he hailed from the Florida pan handle. *Solidarity* was political code and I looked at him expectantly. "Yeah…", he answered the look, "my older brother is a Vietnam vet…was active with the Vets against the war. Two or three others spoke up strongly in support of Jason. All were against taking the test. Only half were game enough to formally refuse it. These guys Jason started calling' fraidy cats' which of course made them more afraid. We ended our brief huddle with an agreement I proposed that in solidarity we would take the MMPI but unanimously protest its appropriateness for a personnel file. Jason would speak for us and referring to me he said, "Dr. T. will write it up for the conference record." The nick name Dr. T. stuck as it was based on Mr. T., a popular black man enforcer on the A-Team television program.

Yet there were questions as to how they should take the test. "Take it honestly", I said. "Tell the truth consistently. The MMPI is structured to catch deception and inconsistency. Play it the way you would employers like that nodding toward the rostrum. Be as honest as you can. Kiss their rears as much as you can stand." They all laughed in solidarity with Jason and me as we returned to our seats.

Jason made our formal report. Dr. Acuff, Reverend Webb and the rest stared at us in Cheshire cat like solidarity. The MMPI test forms were passed out and taken. I wrote up our formal objection and protest. We all signed it and turned it in with our finished test forms.

That night at a pizza joint Jason and I drank beer with our pizza. The other young Preachers timidly did not join us except one big guy named Arthur Price. It turned out I knew some of his relatives in Riley, near Terre Haute. He had accompanied them once to my father's bar on the 'south side' of town. "Better keep that quiet", I joked as the old Methodist Discipline forbid the ministry to anyone whose family was in 'the liquor trade'. Arthurs mother had been a Metzger and he'd been raised in the Missouri Synod of the Lutheran Church. He told us he'd attended and flunked out of Concordia Lutheran Seminary. He said the flunking was due to girlfriend trouble. He said he didn't want to talk about it. He said he wanted to talk about his cousin Steven Metzger. "Steve" he said, "was pastoring a small Lutheran Church in Hectorsburg. I heard you say you have a farm near Freedom, Indiana. That's close to Hectorsburg, idn't it?"

"Sure", I nodded encouraging his story.

"Steve's having a rough time of it. Dr. Acuff has counseled him some. Acuff teaches pastoral counseling at Concordia."

"How could we not be surprised at that" was our droll reply.

"I thought your calling on Steve in Hectorsburg might help him… and helping Steve just might help you with Acuff."

"I got trouble with Acuff?!"

"He was staring daggers at you all afternoon!"

"I'll handle Acuff. How can I help your cousin?"

"He's half nuts and whupped, whupped… whupped. His fiancé ditched him for some pot-smoking patriotic type. She ran off right after he accepted assignment to the Hectorsburg Church. She'd expected something, how shall I say, less modest than tiny Hectorsburg. He's a Concordia Ordinand! I'm just a flunky yet the Methodists have trusted me with a Church twice the size of his at Hectorsburg."

"When did you become a Methodist?"

"Well…" Arthur stammered, "not…not long ago."

"Let me guess…", I said. "The church of Christ Uniting C.O.C.U. according to Philburt Acuff."

Jason amplified, "Coo Coo, coo coo."

"Hey!", Arthur Price defended, "I know I have a call to the ministry. Old Acuff has been kind to me and my cousin. I'd never be happy in Fort Wayne, Indy, or Da Region.[1] I belong in these knobs and val-

1   Da Region: Urban N.W.IN. Calumet steel mill area. Remote part of

leys. The Methodist Church owns the countryside in Indiana; COCU, coo coo or not. I'm grateful for this chance. I only hope they approve of me."

"Who is the *they*?", Jason asked.

"Why the Hoosier minded hick heretics who've been burying John Wesley for nigh on one hundred years" Arthur declamatorily ranted.

From Florida, young Jason had no idea what Arthur was talking about... I did.

"D'yuh think it might be the weather?" I asked.

"Huh?"

"You know...the riverine humidity; versatile and fickle. Meandering moods and modes always changing; usually extreme like the weather. Humid, damp, colder than Alaska and humid sweat hotter than the deep south. Or...seems like it."

"Yeah...it does seem like it. Unpredictable weather and unpredictable people."

"No forecast for fellowship?", Jason joshed not understanding a word of our Indiana conversation.

"The 'dark and bloody ground'[1] of Kentucky backwardness is clannish...'git offn our land' stuff. Here it seems atomized into very fine particles of commination."

"That's it! I think you got it.!" Arthur, excited went on, "it's 'comminatorius'.[2] Ash Wednesday assinines who can't get to Good Friday, let alone Easter!"

"Charitably now", I cautioned, motioning Arthur toward the shocked at swear words Jason. "Charitably...I love the foliage and home centered families of Indiana. Our working people; family men, loyal wives, mothers, daughters and sons. Farmers and workers. Farmers waning to become workers gaining to become farmers again. Yeomen[3] get bye[4] here. The most affordable animal units per pasture in America... But short of family shelter Indiana is pure schizoidism. Chicago's urban sprawl.

1   'dark and bloody ground': meaning of Native American word Kentucky.
2   comminatorius: (Latin) recital of threats against sinners rehearsed on Ash Wednesday.
3   Yeoman: Small Freehold Farmer who works and fights for his own land.
4   "get bye or go bye": stock dog signal to the left of the flock.

A state of schizotypal self-constructs; dereistic, disordered, deteriorating demented and disorganized."

Jason tried to conclude, "Nuclear Schizophrenia[1]!"

Arthur concluded, "A state of fratricidal disrespect."

I continued, "From the moneyed snobbery of Carmel and North Indianapolis; heirs of the Silver Shirted Fascists of Noblesville, the Capital City founding of the John Birch Society, and the half century domination of the Klu Klux Klan. Indianapolis spread its Copperheaded Confederate sympathy to the majority of County Seats — The Countryside resisted. Abolitionists,

Quakers, Baptists, even a few rural Methodists maintained the underground railroad against Slavery. Frederick Douglas praised Indiana black farmer "Persisters" against the Indianapolis engineered and racist Indiana 'Constitutional Convention in 1850 which restricted black ownership of farm land, barred 'newcomer negroes' from settling within the states boundaries and prohibited free blacks from entering the state after November 1851. Then there was the troopers of the Fifty First Indiana under Colonel Abel Streight who led the "Lightening Mule Brigade" to raise insurrectionary forces in Northern Alabama to help Grant break the back of the Confederacy. There were committees of abolition throughout Indianas countryside just as in the depression there were committees of reds in practically every county and urban working class neighborhood. Gone now...gone blowin in the wind..."

Jason encouraged me, "You're on a roll Dr. T. Keep goin." Arthur seemed to mildly agree.

"After the civil war our people were spray forced out the nozzle of the nineteenth century into particles becoming a virtual atomarium of displaced personaes. Industrial Corporations further fragmented them. Then came the Red Resistance. Gene Debs out of Terre Haute had a mass following of the majority of Indiana's workers and farmers. Most of whom were too practically oriented to bother voting for him.. Churches in the countryside and blue collar districts in town main-

---

1   Nuclear Schizophrenia: process caused by predisposing-precipitating environmental factors.

tained the hope and vision of a… Just Community."

"Hearkening back to Robert Owen and the Rappites[1]", Arthur added.

Jason added, "Indiana gave America and Hollywood James Dean, didn't it?"

"Yeah, he was from Fairmont."

Aiming toward a more negative downshot, Arthur groaned, "And Indianapolis gave us Clifton Webb, a snob for every hero."

"What about the great writers from Indiana?" Jason wasn't done. "My mother loved Jean Stratton Porter and read "Girl of the Limberlost" to me when I was a kid. And Jessamyn West's "Friendly Persuasion" a Christian masterpiece. You guys see the Gary Cooper 1956 movie?"

"Everybody's seen it," Arthur wasn't budging.

"Hey Arthur", I said, "Jason's on to something about the writers from the soil of Indiana's commination's and contradictions. During the worst of Indiana's sundown towns[2], Terre Haute produced Theodore Dreiser, the most celebrated communist writer of the twentieth century.

"Yeah", Arthur returned "and Indianapolis produced Booth Tarkington. My point…snobs for heroes."

"Whoa…" Jason whoaed, "I know that snob. Tarkington…Alice Adams in drag."

"Yep the snob envy spirit of North Indianapolis deprived of adequate social mobility."

"A very pushy little person." quoted Arthur.

"When class peace could have been the solution all along", I analyzed Alice.

"Gee Whiz…" Jason mock quoted Kate Hepburn's last line in the movie 'Alice Adams'."

"My point Arthur…at the point of these contradictions we can min-

---

1   Rappites: Eighteenth century communist idealists who founded egalitarian community in New Harmony, Indiana; later taken over by Robert Owen and Welsh Utopian Socialists.

2   Sundown Towns: reference to signs in Indiana main streets up to 1960 "Nigger, Don't Stay Here Past Sundown"

ister a synthesis. The Holy Spirit, the Baraka, the dialectic can break through to… the straightway, the straight path of those whose suffering God bestows His Grace, the path more straight than the long barrel of a gun our predecessors had to look down when approaching Indiana homesteads…to hear Whosyhere?? Hoosyre? Hoosier??" Arthur and I humorously recited for Jason, who laughed out loud saying he thought the word 'Hoosier' came from 'hussar'[1] the Polish boatmen who first plied riverboat passengers into the state.

"Maybe parallel development", I said "but you can still hear that same rank hoosyere? Hooseyere?? at the doorstep of backwoods Hoosier homes. Rankling the very air with its tones of bitter menace."

"It's the way they say, 'Don't know nothin about that!'."

We agreed. Even Jason knew about the 'Know Nothing's, the 'Know Nothing' nativist political party that flourished in pre-civil war (1850's) Indiana. Opposing Catholic immigration, (mainly Irish and Italian) supporting slavery. When asked about any nuance beyond their native ignorance they would proudly respond 'I know nothing about that!' And…they still do! Indiana is one of the few places in the world where people boast about what they *don't know*, i.e. "Don't Know nothin bout that!" Suggesting that something must be wrong with *you* if you do know something about it.

"But…Indiana's literary and religious life has led otherwise… hasn't it?" Jason was tentatively-hopefully trying to less than assert. He continued, "What about contemporary Indiana writers?"

Arthur and I confessed we didn't know any.

"What about James Jones? 'From Here to Eternity', and 'Some Came Running'?"

Arthur responded, "Jones is a war writer, a World War II writer; not so contemporary."

"It's, that is, his stuff is of our time…this half century. Idn't it T.?"

I liked Jones and said so. "They started making his mid-century novels into movies in the late fifties and early sixties. Actors Lancaster

---

1   Hussar (or huszar): Polish or Hungarian light cavalryman. Regimental or freebooter. Tom Beckiewicz, chairman impresario of Cathedral Arts in Indianapolis has published this ethnic myth of many hussars becoming river boatmen; hence Hoosier-hussar.

and Sinatra gave us a lot to identify with in our own lives and locale. Jones wrote a lot about the dark bends…of people 'around dark bends' of Indiana Rivers but I'm not sure he was from Indiana, Paris Illinois or Paris France. They say he did most of his actual writing in a writer's co-op in Robinson, Illinois and from several whore houses in Terre Haute. So I guess we'll have to claim him."

"Jones! When people hear or think of James Jones from Indiana, they think of Reverend James Jones, the Peoples Temple in Indianapolis and San Francisco and his 'pass the Kool-Aid' finale suiciding almost a thousand adults and innocent children in some bullroar of a Collective", he looked at me then went further "wasn't that Jones some kind of comrade of you guys… trying to heal up the wounded country from the Left. Knitting all wounds, yarns, and work behind the Lefts insertion to form a brand new stitch. Knit stitching people to walk a brand new plank of despair?"

Jason and I looked at each other a little helplessly. I had met Reverend Jim Jones while working for the Archdiocese. I had attended meetings with him of the NAACP and several ecumenical commission judicatories against racism. He was generally considered the foremost active Protestant minister against the sins of racial discrimination. Liberal members of other denominations flocked to his church. Many joined up and stayed. Many more moved with him from conservative Indianapolis to liberal San Francisco, and finally to the utopian jungle and suicidal managed death.

I gruffly answered Arthur fully conscious of my inadequate thought, "Jones was increasingly isolated and ego-driven into madness and despair." I remembered the words of the Lady Pentecostal Minister at the rather antidoron[1] funeral for all those who had left Indiana with Reverend Jones and who would not be returning. Looking as desperate as her congregants she said, "This must have happened so we may ponder and understand it better."

Better understand where Marx stops and Freud begins. 'Civilization and its Discontents'! American meta-Freudians have perverted its central message. Freud's moral grounding as a Jew (albeit an atheist

---

1   antidoron eulogia: bread blessed but not consecrated for non communicants.

one) drew him to clinically document the essential need to discipline human emotion *never* to liberate it. Undisciplined expression of even the most innocent or just emotion leads to disaster. Jonestown was not too Totalitarian. It was not totalitarian enough.

We spoke long into the night about totalities and prayerful spiritual discipline. Most of our country pastor conferees joined around our table and listened. We, as they say closed the place.

XXVIII

(Locum Tenens[1])

Next morning's conference convened at 9am. There were stale sweet rolls and room temperature coffee in the lobby. There was no opening prayer. There was an hour long tepid lecture by Dr. Acuff on our assigned book, "Living by Grace" by Reverend William Hordern. Clearly annoyed by mindless evangelicals who insist on measuring faith by who can stress certainty the most, he drove in the polar opposite direction, achieving a rather unbecoming case for applying Heisenberg's 'uncertainty principle' to theology. That is, the impossibility of specifying value positions under life's sheer momentum of energy and time. The more certain we are of one the less we know of the other. Another Hamlet as modern man disguise; borrowing from 'quantum physics' notion there is no fundamental difference between left and right in order to construct a more perfect parity of cowardice.

Acuff reminded me of Peter Sellers 'Emperor of Me' in Joe Manciwiecz 1964 'Another Carol for Christmas'. Aggressive subjectivism teacherly instructing us how to objectively interpret Hordern the same way he did.

My interpretive review follows:

Living by Grace (by William Hordern)

More a polemic than a thematic presentation on the doctrine of grace, William Hordern develops his argument systematically and, I think with integrity. There are annoying interludes of inconsistency however, and his subjective emphasis interpreting 'justification' while insightful and persuasive is I think unconvincing.

Hordern introduces his book with Luther and Calvin identifying "the doctrine of justification by Grace alone through faith alone" (vs. works-righteousness of the Medieval Church) as the central doctrine of 'The Reformation'.

Will Herberg's observation of Americans "faith in faith" and its

---

1   Locum Tenens: a substitute acting for a doctor or clergyman over a period of time; one holding another's place.

subsequent cultic sincerity is brilliantly interpreted by Hordern as a practical result of certain pastoral abbreviations. The doctrine properly called 'justification by grace alone through faith alone' has suffered the shorthand whereby we speak of 'justification by faith alone'. When 'by grace alone' is dropped from the phrase the impression is given that faith is the primary element in justification.

Faith then becomes something we must perform and crank out. Demonstrating we have certainty the most. Rather, Hordern 'clarifies justification'; affirms the primary aspect *not* to be our faith (let alone our certain sincere performances to illustrate it) but — — God's grace.

It is such practical insights that make William Hordern's book valuable. It is when he moves to intellectually buttress the practical that its value is severely limited. Indeed when confronting substantive intellectual error Hordern appears to join the contemporary chorus that concedes the field and cheers from clinical side lines that all substance is secondary to relationships.

Gene Siskel barely manages movie reviews from such shallows. So it is not surprising to find a ship of sound theology running aground here. In steering wide of the Scylla of conservative civil religions legalism, I think Hordern's book plows directly into the Charybdis of anarcho-liberal moral relativism.

Early on Hordern posits the outrageous choice of "Righteousness (the 'just' in K.J.V. translation): External or Internal?". A straw man of external behaviorism is concocted and bullied about as the exclusive wrong choice; suggesting an antinomian embrace of internal subjectivism as the exclusive right choice. "Jesus would appear to be saying that where the reason for not acting upon ones motivation or desires is a prudential or selfish one, the person is as unrighteous in God's eyes as the person who actually commits the crime" (!!)

At this moment I may be thinking about shooting some of my anarcho-liberal brethren. Some of the reasons I would not shoot them is my fear of God and the Police, to say nothing of several civil disadvantages. Come now… the thought of murder or any temptation to sin *is not* as unrighteous in God's eyes as the murder or sin committed. And Jesus did not appear to say so — no matter what Hugh Heffner[1]

1   Hugh Heffner 'Playboy's' unfortunate interview with President Jimmy

would like us to think the President was saying.

In demonstrating how so-called Christian behavior is negatively paternalistic thus stifling a brother's brother into a brother's keeper Hordern again indulges in overkill. From Mark 10:3-5, 6 and 9 it is observed that Jesus did not think the marriage ideal could be maintained by external laws or social pressures. Quite. It does not follow however that external laws and social pressures are by their very nature paternalistic, keeperesque, and incapable of assisting and encouraging internal conviction. Such is the extreme implication of Hordern's argument and it makes suspect any condition of the heart that is not totally butterfly free. It becomes a kind of Milton Friedman method of reverse moralizing; a "Living by Laissez Faire" liberation from all those old 'Anselmic' regulations.

I am reminded of Judy Collins 'Song of Isaac' whose lyrics include this view of personal relationship:

"I'll love you if I can
I'll kill you if I must
But pardon me if I ask
According to whose plan."

Surely there is no greater contemporary example of pharisaical formalism than that which insists upon the primacy of personal relationship.

Personal relationships to God according to private testimony determine Justification in the altogether — i.e. once and for all — *saved*!

In Conservative or Liberal clothing this error then condones (as Hordern hesitantly suggests) its own sins and that of its milieu. Next it condemns its opposite by cultural commission or (just as savagely) administrative omission.

Fortunately we have an historic prescription for this contemporary malaise. Borrowing from Puritan theology in 1797 John Wesley recommended "the book of James as a powerful antidote against the spreading poison of antinomianism." (John Wesley collected works

---

Carter. After saying "No, he'd never committed adultery". Playboy asked if he had ever lusted i.e. committed adultery in his heart. The President confessed "Yes". Playboy concluded if ones as bad as the other why not go all the way?

VIII p.282)

We might recommend again "that book of straw" to certain contemporary Lutherans.[1]

According to Wesley "the justification spoken of by Paul (1) and James (2) are two distinct aspects of Justification. One indicates (1) Justification by grace through faith and the other (2) Justification at the point of judgment which is made on the basis of "those works which spring from faith". Justification is not a 'once and for all' event but has "two loci — (1) presence and (2) finality."

Final justification or the culmination of the historical process, comes at the judgment event wherein a person's obedience and good works will count and consequently man's moral responsibilities are then integrated, not fragmented.

Enter Anselm again. Hordern gets us…not out of court, but toward the para-legal potential tyranny of a closed juvenile hearing.

From the more dialectical, more developmental view of Justification we can begin to conceptualize Sanctification; a task which Hordern never quite rises to except in some quotes of others and an occasional reference to it as a process. A quote from Calvin on 'the process' is that "No man will be so happy, but that he may everyday make some progress however small."

Hordern concludes his book with several positive examples of Church work projects while apologizing that he is not deliberately proposing them (That would be WORKS). Rather he feels confident they would spontaneously occur from true faith. Quotes from Cox and Barth join him accordingly. The thought here sincerely wishes to keep hope for the Church in God and *not* in the Churches membership. The book unhappily fails in this because of its mechanical separation of externals/and internals, faith/and works, form/and content, criterion/and relationships.

Wesley's progress came from John Goodwin's "Imputatio Fide" where he found the idea to hold in tension these same elements in order to gain both a Reformation doctrine of faith and a genuinely

---

1   Luther proposed purging the book of James from biblical Canon. He called it the "book of straw" for upholding works with faith. Author Hordern is Lutheran.

fruitful affirmation that man has moral responsibility, whereas one without the other lacks essential truth.TGM

The week ended with a banquet Saturday evening. Convened at a local motel, we were seated in a private dining area adjacent to a public salad bar, which divided us from the darkened bar room.

Aloof from the instructors who sat reserved at the head table shaking their heads at the young men joking and jostling at the salad bar… polar coordinates of mind were palpable. A cold front not only between the conferees and instructors but an especially drawn polar curve around us i.e. Jason, Arthur and me. We were viewed as culpable in shifting focus away from the fixed axis of the conference plan. At least we were seen as the point around which such concentration was taking place. All three of our Saturday morning sermons preached against moral relativism, and many of our conferees followed suit. I spoke from my experience of the jail cell in California, Jason of his anti-war work in Florida, Arthur of the cowardice to assert church authority. We all spoke of the disquiet we felt regarding the imperial tone of the conference instructors. A dichroic passage Dr. Acuff called it "reflecting light of quite another color than the one transmitted… tangential to the proposed direction."

In all the Friday counseling sessions MMPI's were interpreted in a kind of cliquish differential calculus; objecting to variable rates of functional change transposed from the dependence of functionaries. In short, they really didn't like us.

As we joined our fellow conferees at the salad bar under the glaring looks from the head table Jason began to clown around. Why not?! One cannot (and should not) lose sense of humor in such circumstances. Especially since the young men getting salad reminded me of the old Catholic joke about how you could identify Protestants at the salad bar… their heads down, lowing like cattle toward the lettuce… hungry beasts after bales of fresh hay…All because they hadn't had a drink from the barroom to cool out and calm down.

About that time an old ghost, an ignis fatuus[1] entered the area obsequiously greeting the instructors at the head table. It was Grover Haltman, longtime chairman of the Indiana Council of Churches.

1   ignis fatuus: foolish phosphorescence

His perpetuity in that office due to his galaxic *humble pie*ty and as layman in the U.M.C. United Methodist Church, by far the largest judicatory[1] i.e. denomination — constituency in Indiana. Representing the Archdiocese I'd worked with him on several ecumenical[2] commissions. My direct Proletarian manner and not so slight anti-clerical bias offended him deeply. His excessively compromising moderation irked me. Over the years as the reason for his having to pay judicatorial respect to a red papist I became anathama[3] to him. Compliant to that role I took pleasure in frequently quoting to him the Hebrew books of Wisdom and Ecclesiasticus which is included in the Roman Catholic canon but Apocryphal to Protestants.

Hadn't seen Grover for years. He'd put on a hundred pounds and had the bearing of an obese chipmunk.

After we had all finished our rubber chicken and washy vegetables, Grover was formally introduced. I guess he was supposed to be our after dinner speaker. But...there were several. All equally and consistently banal. Hannah Arendt's book about good soldier Adolph Eichmann was called "The Banality of Evil." Our evening speakers represented "The Evil of Banality."

After the Council of Churches Chipmunk had carried on for forty some minutes on the biblical injunction "Thou shalt not judge" to include any possibility of moral discernment and/or evaluation, a succession of Reverend others followed.

Reverend Jim Webb was a little less banal and less tolerable in his insistent condemnation of those "who dared to sin in judgment of others."

By God...that is enough, I thought. Jason had the same thought and was already standing. He respectfully raised his arm and was ignored for two minutes. Remembering a legislative gambit from high school speech tournaments, I rose and almost loudly asked, "Will the speaker

---

1   judicatory: literally judiciary court but used by church denominations to describe their administrative offices or bureaucracy.
2   ecumenical: pertaining to organizations or movement toward universal Christian Unity.
3   anathana: literally the gravest ecclesiastical censure.

yield to question?"

And Reverend Webb literally yielded that is to say, he shut up and looked up at Jason. I stood along encouraged by the others. Jason pulled from his quiver of papers the 1964 (N.C.C.) National Council of Churches document condemning racism; racist policies of the government and/or private sector. It had been approved by the Florida council as it had Indiana's.

Jason read the preamble aloud which summarized the many forms of racist policy and behaviors now condemned by the Council as evil and anathema to Christian Faith. He paused then asking Reverend Webb, Grover et. al if they no longer abided by such strictures of the faith? He remained standing. Jim Webb sat down, nodding to Grover that it was a Council question.

Grover stood flushed, but not yet ashamed... to attempt whacking the puck back...to me(!) he asked, "Precisely what objection are *you* making?...any questions might be...held from...might evolve from any premise." He focused on me, yet faltering and stammering just long enough to be interrupted appropriately. A stanza from Kenneth Fearing cued to me:

"Are there any questions?'

Has anyone any objections to make?

Can a politically new approach or a better private code evolve from this?

Does it hold any premise based on faith alone?

Or are you, in fact, a privileged ghost returned, as usual, to haunt yourself?"[1]

Slightly motioning to the head table, then back to himself and us, he asked, "What does that mean?"

"Go Haunt Yourself!" I said and sat down.

Reverend Webb adjourned the evening.

---

1   Keneth Fearing stanza from collected poems "Dead Reckoning" p.31

XXIX

The last memory I have of the conference was Jim Webb shaking hands good-bye, saying "Dr. Acuff tells me you're being assigned Birch Lane Church." I nodded. "Well we've had our differences but no one, not even you deserve those Sons of Birches" he sinisterly cackled and was gone.

Many of the conferees gave me their phone numbers and addresses and asked to keep in touch. I gladly agreed, exchanging my number and address. Especially with my new friends Jason and Arthur. I promised again to look in on Arthur's cousin Steve, the Lutheran Pastor in Hectorsburg.

A lot to do in the next two weeks before my first sermon at Birch Lane. Rueblood had managed to get a custody hearing scheduled the following Thursday. I tried to prepare for it. Attempts at telephone conferences with Rueblood were not helpful. He kept repeating that I just needed to cultivate a better tone... he would do the rest. More annoying he said several times that, Judge Farley has "probably already decided to not rule in your favor until next time...after ample time has passed for you to prove demonstrably you are a responsible member of the community."

Rueblood's lawyering instruction of time made me feel like the destruction of time was preferable and I said so. Long before Skype I could receive a perfect picture of him still shaking his head.

Thursday's hearing went eerily as Rueblood said it would. He greeted me in the courtroom brightly; grateful I was not wearing my wedding ring. As we sat down, he did ask, "Is it in your pocket?" "Yes it is", I lied...just to see him shake his head some more.

There were no other witnesses. I kept it in neutral til the last. The judge spoke neutrally to my lawyer. My lawyer spoke neutrally to the judge. They spoke *neuterally* to each other. Finally the judge asked me to characterize my style of parenting at our farm home. Rueblood critiqued I revved it up too proudly. It all took less than half an hour. Judge Farley said he was "taking it under advisement and would rule shortly." Grinning, Rueblood said we would win next time. "But, he hasn't ruled this time yet", I tried to protest. Then I got the emphatic all knowing, be patient you ape shake of his head.

PART FIVE:

DREAD AND WONDER

The drive home was hot and I rolled the truck windows down. At dawn and before court I'd felt more than a bit queasy. Probably got the 'summer complaint' I sighed to myself. When early summers humid heat first wakes the bugs of Indiana's foliage it also arouses bacteria that find their way to intestinal tracts. The traditional antidote for this Hoosier 'summer complaint' is blackberry wine. I was driving the back country through Clayford and Hectorsburg to call on Arthur's cousin Steve. I stopped at a liquor store on the north end of Clayford.

As the lone young clerk was packaging the blackberry wine, he said, "we're selling a lot of this nowadays." "Uh huh," I grunted as he seemed to be examining me closely, the way a wary gastro-intestinal internist might. He asked, "Are you the new Minister?" Whoa, it wasn't my illness that concerned him but the ministry. How had he marked me for a Minister? Must be my appearance or gait. I'd been not quite unconsciously thinking of myself i.e. casting my appearance as the Humphrey Bogart Priest amid the "Heathen Chinese" in 'The Left Hand of God'. A favorite mid-fifties movie of mine from the William Barrett novel.

The clerk went on… "too bad about the last minister."

"How do you mean?" I seriously asked.

The clerk now seemed to feel he'd been given permission to speak personally. "Well, I kinda got to know Pastor Steve. He was a customer here. I just don't think he was treated right."

In an uncomfortable advantage, I quickly clarified I was the new Minister for Birch Lane not any replacement Pastor for the Lutheran Church. Adding however I was on my way to visit Pastor Steve and was concerned about him.

Feeling final permission now this young man spoke admirably of Pastor Steve and angrily how a committee of church ladies (he spoke the last two words as if categorizing a phylum of reptiles) had done him in. "Gossiping, backbiting, banshees" Looking at me he choked himself down from saying the other B. word. "Prohis, hypocritical, hysterical prohis[1]... they used to phone here and ask if he'd been in? Asked even what he bought and what condition he was in...? I hung up on e'm soons I figured out what wuz goin on. Now Pastor Steve liked his beer. Only sky pilot around here who was open and honest about it. My family's Baptist ministers have to leave the state to have a drink. And yore a friend of his; you know, he's been disappointed in love. That'll drive a man to his drink. Those women stormed in his parsonage. He wuz out - on the couch. Took all his beer outta the fridge and pantry. Probly destroyed it. Took his house and car keys. He had to call family members to get outta town...they say."

"When did this happen?"

"Just did! Day before yesterday."

"Anyone over there now?"

"Dunno. Don't think so. I drive by there every day to git here. I rent a cabin out on the gypsum ground." —

Whoa again...had to ask further about that..."Does the 'New Briton Hunt Club' still ride that ground?"

"Yuh mean those fox-hunting horsemen with all those hounds? Yeah, we see e'm helling through the brush from time to time. Most of e'm from North Indianapolis ain't they? You ain't from Indianapolis are yuh?"

"No, no I have a farm over near Freedom. I've rode with the New Briton Bunch. I had a standing invite in the old days to hunt with them through their Master of Hounds, Tom Chandler."

"They're all rich people ain't they?"

"Most of e'm. Not Chandler. He was the best rider I ever saw sit a horse. He could ride at a dead gallop through close timber where you couldn't thread a needle. Everyone else would lose a kneecap or hit the dirt. He'd earn a twenty dollar cropping fee for everyone that fell off their horse. Had to amount to hundreds per weekend."

"I dunno. I tried to talk to some of e'm before. They weren't very friendly. My Dad says they think their own stool don't stink."

And that is exactly the way my father would describe rich people,

---

1   Prohis: Prohibitionists. The Prohibition Party was on the ballot in Indiana up until the sixties. My Grandma Morgan always voted for them.

even snooty upper middle class people. At the end of my first season riding and hunting with the 'New Britons' we were invited to their terrier and hound bench show gala celebration. It was held at one of their North Indianapolis Estates. Hors d'oevres and drinks were served on the lawn by young black men in starch white high collar jackets. Tasting one of the delicate, subtle, mysteriously wonderful hors d'oevres I realized that if they ate like this their stools probably wouldn't stink.

I gave the Liquor store clerk my phone number to call if he heard any more about Pastor Steven, then drove to the Lutheran Church and Parsonage. Locked up tighter than a drum with two trash barrels still smoking!

When home I phoned Arthur Price. Laconic as always he said, "Yeah, you just missed all the excitement. The ladies sodality got tired of his being hung over every Sunday and blurry eyed in between."

"I thought all Lutherans were beer drinkers?!"

"Not those country girls! Steve said they've been steamed their husbands drink and used him as an example. Worse…everyone of e'm has a divorced cousin and/or girlfriend grass widow they kept trying 'to fix Steve up with'. He would not submit to retreads. Made em' mad!"

"Can they do this?"

"They've done it! In maedadic frenzy!"

"Gynaecocratumenos1 - how's Steve doin…?"

"Scared sober. Might be good for him in the long run. Hurts the authority of the Church in the short run. Wild women unrestrained by their men buckin the Preacher!"

He continued, "They say the Talmud warns, 'Beware of People ruled by women and children[1]'. If you'd make that 'wimmin and teenagers' you'd describe modern America. What you call the superstructure… anyhow."

"Whew."

We said our good-byes. But not before Arthur added, "Dr. T… be careful out there with the Rubes. That mainline liberal mush we met at conference is driving the countryside crazy. Get yourself a gun. Make

1   Gynaecocratumenos: Ruled by women.. John Milton

a lot of housecalls. Pray for discernment. So long."

By the weekend comrade Blackberry and I had whupped the 'summer complaint' just in time for another affliction to come in Saturday's noon mail. We were being taken back to court again. Anne was petitioning for my visitations to be supervised away from the farm and no overnights.

Monday ...I phoned Rueblood. "The 'next time' has come early," I attempted to say as he interrupted.

"Winning the next time meant on our petition regarding her mistakes; not her petition on your mistakes."

"What mistakes?!"

"She'll parade them all from California to the present."

"I thought she couldn't replay what's already been in court."

"This is 'family law' court, man, she, that is, her lawyer can sneak in anything. She's retained Alvin Marlin, Catholic and friend of the Prosecutor. And...and have you paid my office the bill you owe me?"

"I haven't even received a bill yet. You mean from last week?"

"Yes...last week will have to be paid before we can represent you next week. The court date is one week from Friday 10am. Correct?"

"Yeah, yeah...but when will the Judge speak to my children?"

"Probably never. Judge Farley prefers not speaking to wards of the court, that is, children, not even *in camera*...(in his chambers). But we may not get Farley this time in circuit court. We may get Judge Dexter Brolin."

"Is your meter turned on?" I asked.

"Yes it is," he answered.

"Bye for now!"

I phoned Jack McMurtry and got through. "I am floundering amongst Meth-Heads[1]", I told him, trying not to shake my own head in discouragement. Jack dug out the salient points: (1) The children not being allowed to speak with the Judge (2) Her attorney being able to drag out the 'California kidnapping' episode and (3) Rueblood's 'lay away payment plan' for lawyering. He concluded, "God dammit I'll fly in next week. Should get there before dark on Thursday. Too

1 Meth-Heads: Methodist Head Shakers

much hard works achievement could still be lost. And by Christ it will not be!"

First time I ever heard McMurtry cuss. I like to hear a man swear. Sometimes words are a bit inadequate without the special emphasis of a little swearing.

Things went well on the farm. Finished off the calving and lambing. Worked on my first sermon for Birch Lane in the evenings. Researched Philip William Otterbein. Prester John had told me it was customary for Superintendent Stilmore to formally introduce new pastors to their flock. But when I checked in with him he respectfully declined, "You're on your own with those folks," he said. Then informed me to be at Birch Lane next Saturday at 2pm to meet the elders and give the church secretary a program outline for liturgy, i.e. prayers, hymns, and homily. The secretary's name is Rose Vincent. He added, "she's good and loyal. She'll have it typed up with plenty of copies in the pews Sunday morning."

Court came soon enough. Picked up Jack at the air strip. Slept on the floor of his motel room. Went over everything. Got to court with Jack one hour early. Dexter Brolin on the bench. He greeted Jack cheerily and they chatted about his flying in. I sat in the south pews on the aisle, surrounded by prisoners or soon to be prisoners awaiting their time in court.

A particularly Uncle Tomish acting black man sat in front of me surveying the thirty some 'customers' in our section. "Sho is mo flies than buttermilk sittin' round heah" he said. About that time Melvin Philbert Rueblood comes in the side door and approaches the bench. Gak! I forgot to call his office telling them he's off and Jack's back on the case. At a distance I can't hear Judge Brolin explaining to Rueblood his name is no longer filed on the case. Slowly and sheepishly Rueblood seems to understand and then turns to angrily see me sitting in the back section. Stormily stomping up to where me and the existentially frightened black man were sitting looking straight ahead he barked out the order – Tom! Follow Me! – and stomped away without looking back to see the poor old Uncle Tom bowing, scraping, and shuffling after him. This poor black man followed this haughty lawyer through two doors to the outside steps. I'd sure like to have seen old Rueblood whirl around startled to see who was following him. Upon returning the black man complained to me, "I sho didn't appreciate that white guy makin a spook outta me!" I explained he had ordered me to follow and I ignored it. I was sorry he misunderstood it.

"Fust time I've ever been in court. I'm trying to do what theys tellin me to do.

"Did it spook him much?" I grinned.

Grinning back he said, "Man he bout jumped outta his skin when he whirl around and see me."

A quick conversation bench side between Judge Brolin, Jack and her attorney Marlin settled things without a hearing. According to Jack the judge said, "Our courts are tiring and impatient with these people. They should start cooperating and stay out of court. We will not hear any evidence pending Judge Farley's decision and then only evidence occurring after his decision. Then Jack advised "cooperate…cooperate…Out cooperate her. When she screws up…and she will. We'll nail her." And then he spoke that dread antonym of my legal confidence, returning reality to my economic state. "I can't do this anymore without billing you. You do know that?"

"Yeah up, got to" I joked, "these Philbert people are nuts."

Birch Lane Church: 2pm

Pulling up in the sunlight of Saturday afternoon I was surprised to see so many parked cars and trucks. There was approximately fifty people present. "Can't all be Elders", I thought helping my children out the cramped crew cab seat. Bethany took my hand and Eliot hung on to my coat tails up the steps and into the Church Sanctuary. Rose Vincent greeted us at the door, received the file of my liturgical outline, then stooped down with several ladies joining us to make over the children. Men approached to shake hands; Gene Vincent – husband of Rose, Emma and Roy Gossett – who served as sort of Church Warden, Tom Geary – who introduced himself as brother to my friends and neighbors Helen and Forest Keller's son-in-law James, two different grown sons of the Vincent's, then Tim and Peggy Cottom who said they were snowbirds back from Florida for their summer and fall on the farm, Joe and Anna May Mueller – who told me they knew my Aunt Fern in Sullivan County. Anna May said she was the pianist but Ruth Leslie Logan also played and better…she was the organist and pointed to her sitting way back in the Church. Mrs. Nell Mayrose was introduced as the oldest female member of the church, and Margaret Finzal - leader of the M.Y.F.s (Methodist Youth Fellowship) who couldn't pronounce her f's.

More than a third of those present sat in the back and did not come forward to be introduced. It was less a meeting than a chaotic buzz of introductions with snatches of shared information. Little organization. Roy Gossett cornered me for a few minutes saying, "the church had eighty dollars a week budget for an inside and outside janitor. Lawnmower and vacuum cleaner provided. That would include the parsonage (until it's rented). They say you live close by."

"I'd be glad to take over the janitor responsibilities," I answered, then asked "Has the church been swept for tomorrow?"

"Nope," he said. "I wuz gonna do it myself this evening but if you're game, he smiled, I'll announce it right now.

"Go ahead."

Roy stepped up to the pulpit and announced, "Our new pastor has volunteered to begin his service to us by also being janitor, even cleaning things up tonight for tomorrow." There was some applause…even from the back.

Roy shook hands again saying, "A Preacher who demonstrates his willingness to be a servant to his people will do well here." I reminded Roy, "we were all to be servants to God and His Church…*not* to the church membership." He gaped puzzled.

After my perfunctory prayer of dismissal I sped to the door in front of the non-responsive third who'd sat silently for an hour in the back pews. Forcing introductions and handshakes, I first met a big beefy farmer, Karl Mannheim and his wife Barbara, next the Muellers again, a very old fellow with a cane and shell rim glasses named John Bought, Jack Schmitt – a cold eyed disheveled young fellow wearing a T-shirt, and twenty some glum others I can't remember. But there was no forgetting Ed Logan. He and his wife came out last. Ed Logan – an intense black Irishman, sunken eyes half grinning and half grimacing as he introduced his wife Ruth Leslie.

"Yes, our organist", I said, taking her hand. She immediately started prattling about hymnody, as I noticed she wore ten rings on what seemed like twice that many fingers. As he assisted his wife down the steps, before he stopped to chat with the Mannheims, Ed Logan turned his squint back to survey all of us still framed in the doorway. He did so with such withering condemnation it could not be confused with mere mortal hatred. This guy was eat up. His soul seething with more than he or others could explain.

Bethany and Eliot had been running around with some other kids. I turned to find them, when Rose Vincent walked up...a child in each hand. "We were hoping you and your children would join us for dinner?" "We'd be delighted (the kids cheered) except I have to finish cleaning up around here." "We'll help Papa", Bethany said God bless her.

"That's fine then...we'll wait. Expect you around by six. We're the third place due west on the pike. Right hand side of the road. Big Vincent mail box next to a brown eggs sign. Can't miss it. Good bye..." as she gave me the church keys.

"God be with you," I thanked her.

Bethany asked "Good bye is like God be with you isn't it, Papa?"

"Yes, little one", I touched her near perfect face still scarred by shattered glass, "One comes from the other one."

Finding the broom closet, I gave Eliot a new broom for the outside steps and walkway, Bethany a dust cloth for the pews and pictures, and I revved up the old vacuum cleaner. We were done in an hour and a half – upstairs and down. Inspected Eliot's work, washed up, and found the Vincent's place a few miles away by 5:45.

We were greeted at the end of their lane by Gene and his (23 year old) son Jay. They led us into the Farmhouse where (19 year old) son Luke relieved his sister Mary (15 years old) in the kitchen so she could take charge of entertaining Beth and El.

Before long we sat down for an Indiana supper of cucumber salad, fried chicken, roshenears[1], mashed potatoes and Sunday gravy. I was asked to return thanks. As is tradition I deferred to the head of household Father Gene. This seemed to please him and he stumbled through a very improvisational grace.

They all laughed when I told of how Californians who enjoy a range of ethnic restaurants even in small towns thought the Hoosier Inn outside of Stockton and its Hoosier fare motioning toward our table was particularly exotic.

Rose announced to Gene and all that I was preaching tomorrow from a quote of Phillip Otterbein. Gene pensive…said, "Otterbein is an E.U.B. name idn't it?" "Yes", I replied.

"Well…that might soothe some of the savage beasts."

"Now Gene…" Rose said, "not in front of the children" Gene looked around. "The children can't hear me." The children were seated ten feet away at a 'children's table' jabbering with Mary. There was an awkward silence.

"You were speaking of a savage beast, Gene?"

There was some laughter, "It's like, I liken them to ravenging beasts; Ed Logan, the Mannheims, John Bought and the rest. It's all they think and talk about. And Ed Logan…he acts on it."

"Gene, if you could please explain", I asked "a little more specifically."

"Sure it's like when we brought the Ravelette family to church. Ed Logan and I were working at the same Foundry then. It was before he got kicked upstairs to management. Paul Ravelette was a neighbor and fellow worker at the Foundry. We both liked him and invited him to Church. Him, his wife, son, and daughter. His son Tanner played on the local varsity high school basketball team. A quick little guard who could steal the ball. His wife June taught Sunday School with Ed. We'd all see each other at the ball games and visit."

"Get to the point dear…" Rose encouraged.

"Ok, ok, during the sectionals when our team was playing Riverton Parke…Paul gets up and goes over at half time to visit a cousin of his sitting on the other side. His cousin had kids that went to Riverton Parke. Well, like cousins they got to jawing, time passed, and Paul

1   roshenears: Hoosier slang for roasted ears of corn.

didn't come back to the home team side until the sudden death of overtime. And we lost."

I thought sudden death only a football term but said, "yes… yes, I didn't get it."

"Well then Ed", Gene continues "wants Paul expelled from the church for community disloyalty. He and that ham handed Mannheim stare daggers at him. What my mother would call 'gave him the evil eye'. Old John Bought and Mrs. Mayrose do the same and all the rest of e'm. Rose will tell ya. They had poor June half hysterical with tears. They'd go to her Sunday school classes and criticize, if you could call it that, you know poke fun at her lessons. The Ravelettes were treated so rudely they had to leave – apologizing to most of us but unable to stay."

"What," I asked, "in God's name did your minister do during all this?"

"Nothing!" Rose said.

"Worse than nothing…that one, that minister was a big coward, afraid of being bullied himself. We had one who would've stood up to them but he just got too sick. Rumor was they'd poisoned him."

"Just rumor," Rose said.

"The point is Reverend", Genes concluding, "what started back in 1970 when we moved out here, and had been going on since '68 was all the whinging and moaning about the Methodist take over. They were all the time threatening to drive clear to Bellmore to some E.U.B holdout church…I think it was called Otterbein. In the ten years we've been here they've chased away more than a half dozen preachers. I personally don't think it's denominational or theological. I think it's just habitual. They're deadlocked in the habit of bullying the Pastor."

"They are *not* the majority are they?"

"No." Rose, Gene and Jay answered together. "But" only Gene continued, "they're the most active." His wife frowned at him. "No that's not right either. Something like they're the most articulate…"

"They're the most pushy! That's it!" said Rose. "What Gene has told you is true. They were mostly the remnant of the E.U.B. Church before '68. It was called Birch Lane then too. When the Methodists took over they were furious. Many of them left over the years. But these hard core stayed propagating like an evil dream that someday they were going to get their church back… never specifying what it was that was lost, or what they wanted 'to get back'; only what they want to get rid of which is every Preacher sent by the Methodists and most every other modern thing in the world that's happened since 1970."

"Like civil rights for black people," I guessed.

"You got it!" Gene was back, "you should have heard them when Reverend Stilmore was here…you know to hear them…(us) out as to what they (we) expected in a minister. They, especially Ed Logan kept badgering them to guarantee he wouldn't send us a black preacher or a woman preacher. He even asked them to guarantee we weren't getting some kind of queer or pervert preacher. They just forgot to ask about a divorced Preacher", Gene winked then continued…"The only reasonable one of them is Gordon Bruce. He kept asking the one question that seemed to bother Stilmore the most. He asked that in fairness, Birch Lane should get a Pastor respectful of its reformed background."

Rose added, "You'll like Gordon, he never misses a Sunday. He's an Insurance Man, works six days a week but never misses Sunday. He was raised in this Church by his widowed mother when it was E.U.B. He's not bitter like the rest, but he does back e'm up. At least, he will appreciate your respect for Otterbein."

"Let us hope so," I said, as Rose served dessert. It was cherry pie, with an incredible lattice crust. Luke helped serve the strong black coffee.

We said our good-byes. Jay said he'd "walk us out to our vehicle." On the way past the chicken yard, he invites us "back in the daylight so's I can show you our fine domineckers." The Vincent's were proud of their laying hens. "Almost forgot," he rushed back to the house pantry and retrieved a dozen Plymouth Rock brown eggs for us. Then looking at me close… darkly appealed, "You don't remember me, do you Reverend?" "No", I answered, studying his features in the dark light. "I wuz one of the paramedics at your wreck two years ago." My God, in similar light I could recall him holding her hand in the ambulance. "I wuz trying to comfort your wife, Reverend, and in all due respect you seemed kinda crazy, kinda out of your mind. "Yes, I remember son, some would say I still am."

"We Are Brethren"
(Philip William Otterbein)

Sunday morn:

Huge attendance. Approximately one hundred fifty people in the pews. Parking area full of shiny cars and trucks. As was traditional at Birch Lane I greeted people as they came in not as they left. I met Gordon Bruce and asked to speak with him after church. He agreed.

Anna May Mueller stopped me at the Sanctuary entrance. "Ruth Leslie and I are unprepared to play and sing these hymns you've chosen. We're not used to them and the congregation is not used to singing them.

"What hymns is she...are you prepared to play?" Answering quickly, "The congregation knows...is used to singing 'Come to the Garden Alone', you know he walks with me and he talks with me. They also like 'Church in the Wildwood'... you know the old traditional hymns."

"Those hymns are not traditional nor am I sure they're in our hymnal for everyone to follow. They are pop songs from the 1920's. I am not opposed to singing them sometimes. I am opposed to your refusing hymns from our hymnal I've chosen that are conducive to themes in the sermon. Routinely I'll give them to you and Ruth Wednesday nights at Prayer meeting when I give Rose the liturgical outline. We can discuss them at that time. I'm sorry we don't have time to discuss them this morning. *We* will just have to do the best we can with them.

Unbelievably Anna May repeated my statement, "You mean you want me to tell Ruth Leslie we have to do the ones you choose?"

"No, no I'll be glad to tell her." We approached Ruth together. She sat regally at the organ her hands and rings upon the keys.

"I'm sorry about the lack of time to speak about the hymns this first weekend. From now on we can discuss any choices on Wednesday night. Today we're just going to have to do the best we can with the ones I've chosen to frame the sermon."

"Preacher...you know this first hymn," Ruth spit it out..."is a Lutheran Hymn?"

"When we sing it Ruth, it will be our hymn. Time for church now." I went to the pulpit and welcomed our gathering asking for God's grace to be upon all present.

The Introit, our first hymn you will note in the program is on page 110, 'A Mighty fortress is Our God' [Silence] I added, "Please also pray for Ruth and Anna May our stalwart musicians who because of time restraints have been obliged to play some music we are unaccustomed in sharing together. I looked over at Ruth Leslie Logan. She sat silent for another moment and then with a flourish banged out the olde sixteenth century hymn, her rings pecking loud on the keys in additional percussion. The congregation of regulars and guests did fairly well in keeping up with her. I had arranged for Rose Vincent to read from the Preface in the hymnal an opening prayer and the third pre-scriptural prayer. I read the second confessional prayer.

1. Rose, church secretary:
> Almighty Father,
> to you all hearts are open, desires known
> and from you no secrets are hidden.
> Cleanse our thoughts
> by the inspiration of your Holy Spirit,
> that we may perfectly love,
> and worthily magnify the grace
> thou has bestowed upon us
> through Christ our Lord.
> Amen

2. Minister:
> Merciful Father,
> We confess that we have not loved you with our whole being.
> We have failed to be an obedient church.
> We have not done your will,
> We have broken your laws,

We rebelled against your love,
We have not loved our neighbors
and we have not heard the cry of the needy.
Forgive us, we pray
Free us for joyful obedience and justice
through Jesus Christ
All pray in Silence.

3. Rose Vincent:

Lord by our hearts and minds
by the powers of your Holy Spirit,
that, as the scriptures are read
and your word proclaimed,
we may hear with understanding and joy
what you say to us today.

(Rose and I persuaded Jay to be our first reader):
Scripture Readings:

Jay:(Psalm 110) Yahweh's oracle to you is to sit at his right hand and He will make your enemies a footstool.

The Lord shall send the rod of thy strength to rule in the midst of your enemies. Your people shall be volunteers in the day of your power; in the beauties of holiness, from the womb of the morning; the dawn of your first days. Yahweh has sworn an oath which He never will retract, you are a priest forever in the order of Melchizedek.

(Bethany was the second reader):

Bethany: (Isaiah 58)If you take away the yokes the pointing of the finger, and the speaking of wickedness. If you extend your soul to the poor and hungry and satisfy the afflicted soul. Your light shall dawn in the darkness and your shadows become like noon. The Lord will guide you continually; giving you relief in drought. You shall be like a spring whose waters do not fail. You will rebuild the ancient ruins, build up the old foundations. And you shall be called 'Repairers of the

Breach' and 'Restorers of Ruined Homes'.

Congregational Response: "Praise be to God";

(Matthew 23:8 "....and you are all brethren")

Sermon:"We Are Brethren"

Long before the first flatboats plied the Wabash and west fork of the White River bringing Christian settlers to our part of the world... Ten years before the turbulence and dislocations of the American Revolution there was a "great meeting" at Longs Barn six miles northeast of Lancaster, Pennsylvania. Preachers and scattered church members from Mennonite, Amish, Congregational, Methodist, Episcopal, German and Dutch Reformed, Presbyterians, and Baptist groups assembled in the huge barn to hear Martin Boehm, a Mennonite preacher on Whitsuntide, 1766. Whitsuntide, or Whitsunday is the seventh Sunday after Easter commemorating the first of Pentecost. Thus anticipating the inclusion of our Christian friends who are Pentecostals. The first recorded Great Ecumenical Inter-faith meeting in America.

A Mennonite Boehm preached on how former meanings given through European catechetical training and years of churchmanship were being given an experiential reality in America to include a total Christian fellowship. The sermon completed all eyes were on the forty year old Senior Otterbein, German Reformed Pastor of York who moved forward quickly to the pulpit greeting Boehm and the entire assembly with the very audible words, "We Are Brethren".

Martin Boehm later reported "at that moment, the words of Otterbein enlarged our hearts toward all religious persons, and to all denominations of Christians."

Then came the administration of the "Sacrament of Communion". Inspired by the words of Boehm, and Otterbein, distinction of sect or denomination appeared for the time to be lost in Christian fellowship. [1]"For as one, they were seen approaching the Lords Table as sons and daughters of one Father."

Otterbein said "We Are Brethren." But with Mennonites, Amish, and Baptists? Hadn't they from their Anabaptist beginnings in the

---

1   "For as one..." Philip William Otterbein (1726-1813) Evangelical Pastor, Loyal Churchman, Active Ecumenist: P.H. Ackert

sixteenth century been slaughtered by Catholic and Protestant princes who deemed these left wingers guilty of treason to the state and heresy before the church?

Otterbein's response came from his deep conviction "that all believers as members of Christ have part in Him and each one must feel himself bound to use his gifts readily and cheerfully for the advantage and welfare of other members"[1]

One of the pointed questions of all church history the answers to which had augmented both in thought and practice the disunity of Christ's body, now had to be answered again in the light of Otterbein's heritage, thought and practice.[2] Who shall come to the Lords Table?

Otterbein formalized his answer twenty years later in 'The Church Book of 1785', which became doctrinal to German Reformed, Brethren and Evangelical churches. Rule 7 daringly states: "Forasmuch as the difference of people and denominations end in Christ (Romans 10:12) (Colossians 3:11) and availeth nothing in him, but a new creature (Galatians 6:13-16) it becomes our duty, according to the gospel, to commune with and admit to the Lords Table professors to whatever order or sort of the Christian Church they belong."

For Otterbein, "a denomination and the Church were not necessarily congruous." He affirmed the giveness of the One Church, and denominations were churches within The Church (ecclesiolae in ecclesia)[3]

Whatever the reason for denomination, he was determined to keep reaching out to manifest the unity of the One Church with all who would share in any common proclamation of the Gospel. Always cautioning "but we must prevent not add to the formation of sects."[4]

Moving into the eighteen hundreds the warning became increasingly relevant. John Wesley died in 1791, Otterbein in 1813, Asbury in 1816.

Circuit riders on horseback getting scarce. Little preaching in the open air and working fields. The pietist dream of movements being churches within The Church (ecclesiolae in ecclesia) degenerating

1   IBID
2   IBID
3   Creeds of Christendom Vol. III p.307
4   IBID P.540

to separate denominational churches. Competing denominations defensively emphasizing ecclesial authority instead of ecclesiolaic discipline. Not that authority does not require discipline as discipline requires authority. One without the other creates bureaucracy or cliquishness. And, I think, conflict with one leads to crippled formation of the other.

A general shift from unity to forces of disunity in the new nation were disappointing to ecumenists like Philip William Otterbein. He valued the authority of the German Reformed Church based on its declared principles and organization in the Heidelberg Catechism which "ministered to him all his life."[1] Reform, that is, Calvinist but not hyper-Calvinist theology states clearly in Article 13: "No Preacher can stay among us, who teaches the doctrine of predestination as the impossibility of falling from grace, and holds these as doctrinal points."[2] That is, no one saved always saved arrogance. Hence the word Brethren is to connote this position of assurance rather than predestination.

Similarly Otterbein saw the word Evangelical as literally preaching the Christian Gospel *not* the theology of justification by faith (i.e. certainty) alone; also while denying that good works and sacraments are in themselves efficacious for salvation not denying their importance (we need all the help we can get) not avoiding ritual and not recognizing individual interpretation of the bible. Not like Lutheran (sola scriptura) scripture alone authority, but like John Wesley's triune authority of scripture, tradition, and reason.

Loyal to the ordinance of the German Reformed Church Rule of Order including a) "All members should subject themselves to a becoming Christian Church discipline according to the order of Christ and his apostles, and thus to show respectful obedience to ministers and officers in all things that are proper. b) The Preacher shall admonish his people; baptize them and/or their children, attend to their funerals, impart instructions to their youth; and should they have children, the Church shall interest herself for their religious education. c) Every member shall sedulously abstain from all backbiting and evil speaking

1   Paul Herman Ackert "The Evangelical United Brethren Heritage"
2   Heidelberg Catechism Q & A 54

of any person or persons without exception and especially of brethren in the church. d) No member is allowed to cite his brother before the civil authority for any cause. e) No preacher can stay among us who will not, to the best of his ability care for other Churches of whom we stand in fraternal unity. f) Whosoever shall refuse to abide by the verdict of the Vestry (pastor and elders) or on any occasion speak of matters in dispute, or accuse his opponent the same excludes himself from the church."

Such rules reflect the spirit of authority and discipline in our present 'Methodist Discipline' which you may find in the pews with our hymnals and book of worship. Otterbein's life and ministry no less than Wesley's inform the essential nature of our church long before 1968.

We live in a time which has forgotten or despairs of moral and spiritual discipline. It is a time of opportunity for us, for our church, our brethren to set an earnest and opposing example of God to this world of self-serving disrespect and fragmentation. Many of the 'We Are Brethren' aspirations and ecumenical motivations of Otterbein and his Reformed colleagues are now emerging from the underground to speak afresh to us. As the Reverend Arthur Core of the Evangelical United Brethren stated upon the 1968 merger with the Methodist Churches: "The life of Otterbein, his kind of ministry and his loyalty to the ideas of catholicity, to evangel, and to unity in process will afford us insight and encouragement as we endeavor to let the living Christ give more complete manifestation to the Church truly catholic, truly evangelical, and truly united."

Here at Birch Lane United Methodist, we must work to be united in our method to resist the evils of this earth, reach out to others in need, repair the ruins, and with God's grace work together toward heaven.

Let us pray The Litany for Christian Unity; by (Karol Wojtyla) on p.556 of our hymnal: Let us ask the Lord to strengthen in all Christians faith in Christ, the Savior of the world.

The congregational response is: *Listen to us, O Lord*

Let us ask the Lord to sustain and guide Christians with His gifts along the way to full unity.

Listen to us, O Lord

Let us ask the Lord for the gift of unity and peace for the world.

Listen to us, O Lord

We ask you, O Lord, for the gifts of your Spirit.

Enable us to penetrate the depth of the whole truth,

and grant that we may share with others

the goods you have put at our disposal.

Teach us to overcome divisions. Send us your Spirit

to lead to full unity your sons and daughters in full charity,

in obedience to your will; through Christ our Lord. *Amen*

Congregational Creed; Response to the Word: p.7 in our hymnal.

"Together now", I instructed, "and a bit louder please."

I believe in god, the Father Almighty,

Creator of heaven and earth.

I believe in Jesus Christ, his only son, our Lord,

who was conceived by the Holy Spirit,

born of the Virgin Mary,

suffered under Pontius Pilate,

was crucified, died, and was buried;

he descended to the dead.

On the third day he rose again;

he ascended into heaven,

is seated at the right hand of the Father,

and will come again to judge the living and the dead.

I believe in the Holy Spirit,

the holy catholic church,

the communion of saints,

the forgiveness of sins,

the resurrection of the body,

and the life everlasting.Amen.

Intercessory or Thanksgiving Prayers (Congregation Response:

"Lord, hear our Prayer")
    [There were none.]

Invitation:

Minister:	Christ our Lord invites all who love him
	to earnestly repent of their sin
	and seek to live in peace with one another.
	Therefore, let us confess our sin
	quietly before God and one another.
	All pray in Silence
Minister:	In the name of Christ Jesus, you are forgiven.
The Peace:	Let us offer one another signs of reconciliation and peace.
	(All exchange signs and words of God's peace.)
Offering:	As forgiven and reconciled people
	Let us offer ourselves and our gifts to God.
	(Roy Gossett and Gene Vincent pass the plate.)
Hymn:	Doxology p.95 in our hymnals to be sung as the offering is received.

The Lord's Prayer: And now with the confidence of children to…

    Our Father who art in heaven,

    hallowed be thy name,

    thy kingdom come,

    thy will be done,

    on earth as it is in heaven.

    Give us this day our daily bread.

    Forgive us our trespasses

    As we forgive those who trespass against us.

    Save us through tests and temptations;

    deliver us from evil.

    For thine art the kingdom, the power, and the Glory

    now and forever. Amen.

Hymn:??

Sending Forth: "I had planned we sing hymn 435 the old Llangloffan welsh hymn, 'God of Every Nation' as conducive to Reverend

---

Otterbein's ecumenical theme, but in deference to Ruth Leslie and Anna May let's try that old standard on p.361 'Rock of Ages'."
Dismissal with Blessing:

> Go forth in peace.
> The grace of God, our Father
> the love of Christ Jesus,
> and the communion of the Holy Spirit
> be with you all.Amen

In the liturgical act of 'going forth' a majority of the people 'came forth' to welcome me again and 'compliment the message'. Approximately one third of the people 'stood forth' in the back, not leaving but watching Gordon Bruce.

Bruce approached me tentatively *not* timidly. "I appreciated your talk on Philip Otterbein and *our* reformed tradition. Perhaps we can talk soon about how to preach not about, but *like* Otterbein and the reformed tradition."

I had hit not exactly a home run with this fellow. "I am told you work hard…six days a week."

"Ummh," he acknowledged.

"What evening is best for you? Do you ever come to Wednesday evening prayer meetings?"

"No I don't, but I'm here every Sunday!"

"So I'm told and glad to hear it. Since I'm over here on Wednesdays perhaps we could meet afterwards?"

"I dunno…I, well… let's do it", he smiled. "Come by for coffee after evening prayers Wednesday. Everybody knows where I live, by the old school house just north of Coalmont."

"I look forward to it," I said passing on to greet the others.

Bruce walked to the back speaking with the Logans and Mannheims. A rather still moment in ordinary time. Yet a kind of future gained entrance here to my attention, much closer to life, Rilke would say than "that other noisy and fortuitous moment when the future happens to us, as if from outside." Like Rilke's 'Panther'[1] I would have to gather my spirit up for the leap into deed. In the mean time I would

1   Rainer Marian Rilke's 'The Panther'

"hew to what is difficult".[1] As I had hewn to the party line; as my Grandfather had hewn coal from the coal face inside Indiana's earth.

The opposition felt it had lost an important church experience, an experience of their God-consciousness, miscarried somehow, no longer an imminent eternality but a longing for what had already been. A knocked down rather than a knocked up sense of Providence. Unlike the Amish, or conservative christian who wished to conserve important values of the past these folks wished to waller in assorted aborted complaints.

---

1   IBID

XXX

Wednesday Prayer Meeting convened at 7pm, Nell Mayrose presided. About twenty older ladies, then Rose Vincent, Peggy Cottom, Barbara Mannheim, Anna May Mueller and Jane Schouten. Jane was the only 'single' lady in the church and said to be smitten with Gordon Bruce. She operated the local 'beauty shop' and was all smiles and small talk. I'd been introduced to everyone except Jane. Nell re-introduced us all over again. She also noted "it seems the consensuss (her dentures slipped on the s sounds) that we all like the way you led us in the 'Lord's Prayer'. That is, sssaying tressspasssesss instead of ssinss against uss." That roused some spoken affirmation and a little applause. Nell looking very seriously at me said, "That's the way my mother taught it to me *not* the way it's in that red Methodist book." (The U.M.C. Hymnal)

(I decided to tell them my childhood Lord's Prayer story) "It's the way my mother taught me Nell. My father's religious background was Hardshell Baptist, my mother's Irish Catholic." The last word aroused a sound in the group something the opposite of a swoon! I continued, "My father, also a Mason prayed 'forgive us our *debts*'. At five or six, I could not understand debts or debtors. I thought I could understand trespasser, you know someone getting over on you or violatin the boundary rules of God. But I wanted to make sure of the tense of the trespass. I fretted quite a bit about it. Surely the trespass to forgive was in the past tense, that is in trespassed e.d. not in the present tense still trespassing i.n.g. right on you. Surely it's e.d. after it's over, I thought. Surely you're not expected to forgive them while it's still happenin' to you. My exasperated mother with dozens of tasks at hand patiently listened to my long winded question. She pondered the question for a millisecond and quickly replied 'Tommy, you're a wyrd kid. Go out and play'!"

My story amused the group. Mostly mothers they laughed in sympathy with my Mom. Jane Schouten, a maiden lady "owwed" in sympathy with the kid sent out to play.

More seriously I concluded, "The words that Nell's mother and my mother chose I prefer as they do allow for tense. The red books "sins against us" and my fathers "debts and debtors" do not allow for tense."

Jane spoke up, "Yes, I think you guys Moms were right. The trespass e.d. version allows us to collect ourselves, reflect and then forgive."

I had sat down beside Jane Schouten and Peggy Cottom. Nell was going over a prayer list of 'shut ins', people 'hospitalized' and 'afflicted with other problems in need of our Prayers'. Peggy whispered to me that Ed and Ruth Logan's daughter, Carol was on the list. She's at Union Hospital in Terre Haute. Knee surgery, I think, Ed and Ruth Leslie might appreciate you calling on her. I made a note of her name and said I'd see her tomorrow.

As the Prayer Meeting adjourned Ruth Leslie, Anna May and I met briefly regarding the hymns for Sunday. I told them I wished to keep the Gloria Patria and the Doxology ritually in place. The offering hymn or anthem I'd chosen was 'Crucified Redeemer' p428. And 'O God of Every Nation' p435 for the closing hymn. Both were Llangloffan welsh hymns lyricized by David Evans in 1927. The sermon theme was to be about hatred and division giving way to love and peace, as formulated by Whitfield and the Welsh Methodists in their more Calvinist than Arminian Reformed tradition.

Anna May was receptive, smiled broadly, and said, "I guess we'll all have to learn some new things." Ruth Leslie sulked, and said nothing.

Nell and Jane walked me to the door. Jane's eyes glittering, she asked, "Are you off to see Gordon Bruce now?" I nodded yes. She touched her lips modestly as if throwing him a kiss through me.

As I slowed, driving past the old school house up to Gordon Bruce's home, I recognized his closest neighbors place across the road. It belonged to Wayne Trapp, a farrier and friend of mine. I could see his horse trailer and bird dog kennels behind a small red barn.

Years back…Wayne had shoed my Morgan mare and we had hunted quail together along the creek-bottom meadows of Gloryville Farm. Our arrangement afforded Wayne a great place to shoot quail and provided me hours of pleasure hunting behind his expert pointers and setters.

I rang the Gordon Bruce doorbell. It took a while for him to open the door and greet me in his bathrobe and slippers. His house like his yard definitely lacked the feminine touch. Noticing my notice, he regretfully spoke about his "work and all... causing things to get away" from him.

"How long you been baching here Bruce?" I asked.

"More than ten years since Mother died."

"I think Jane Schouten is applying for the position..."

He laughed nervously as he served up coffee in fancy china. The coffee was barely warm and incredibly, – on his own he'd – without asking creamed and sugared both cups into a cloying fulvous slop.

"I'm receiving applications", he said "just not processing them."

"Well...Jane seems an attractive, intelligent Christian woman who knows how to work."

"Umm...I guess you could say we're seeing each other.

Mother always thought, you know Jane is kinda rough..."

He didn't say rough trade because it wasn't in his vocabulary. This Insurance peddler dared to look down his barely bourgeois nose at a working class woman who loved him. And he did so in total expectation that their (his and her) minister would affirm or tolerate such a remark and attitude. I quickly and sternly replied "Bruce, I must caution you to not let class bigotry trump your Christian conscience." He looked completely non-plussed at me, saying, "I think we should talk about your Preaching."

"Fine", I said

"We…" he used the word we as if speaking for a huge constituency. "*We* appreciated your recognition of Otterbein and *our* Reformed Traditions! But we need the feeling too. The emotions! The intimacy of us and our Lord's loving personal relationship...celebrated by God's word and our righteous praise. The intimate love of our Father for us that has saved us and set us free!"

Now I sat non-plussed. Bruce continued, "Many's the time Mother and me would leave Birch Lane Church after a genuine Evangelical sermon and we would be so sure we're saved by a God who personally knew us, who was familiar with our lives, who had chosen us as His special people and who unconditionally loved us, we could hold our heads high above the Sinners of this earth."

All I could think of was a quote from Professor Fullerton. I kept turning it over in my mind. I wanted to remember it precise so I could speak it precisely.

"Bruce", I said quietly and respectfully, " 'Intimacy…intimate worship degenerates into casual overfamiliarity; it's both presumptious and embarrassing to those who see God from a transcendental perspective'. The Church can't be some kind of country club of the saved and self-righteous. It is more like a spiritual hospital for those who are suffering from the sins of this world."

Bruce's little speech of instruction had bothered me… in its time and content. Its intent, his intention was not yet clear to me. He'd spoken his words as if he had e'm memorized. As if he'd delivered these instructions to the pastor many times before. Probably many pastors before. And for what purpose and to what effect? Sure… and that was it alright. Gene Vincent said they'd run off a dozen preachers in less than that many years. He'd delivered a kind of canned sermonette to put me off in the process of running me off.

There was a long lull in our conversation. Moving away from ideology I asked about his neighbor, Wayne. Didn't move far.

"Why that reprobate!" Bruce exclaimed. "He smokes, drinks, chews and is a terrible womanizer!"

"Well, I'm sure against the latter!" I mock exclaimed back. Having drank, smoked and chewed with George I could only emphasize the latter.

"I wish," Bruce went on, "I wish he didn't even live, you know live here…in these hereabouts. He and his sons are terrible moral examples to the community. How is it you know him?"

"He sure is a good farrier and bird dog trainer", I answered. I moved to church history, "Then other than the emo-delivery and atmosphere there was nothing exceptionally different at Birch Lane becoming Methodist from Evangelical United Brethren?"

"It was the way it was done. Everything done from above at the conference… at the Coetus level."

Coetus was a word in E.U.B. history I had avoided attempting to pronounce in public. In deutsh or dutch it translates as conference, or synod a coming together in a judicatory. But its pronounced sound is too close to the English word *coitus*[1]. In clinical point of fact I began to suspect it was the very Freudian element which Gordon Bruce was so militantly opposed.

"You realize Bruce", I patiently explained " 'the way it was done', that is proper congregational involvement and congregational preparation for the merger – or not – would have been the responsibility of the E.U.B. Conference, the Conference which Birch Lane was a part of then not any other conference. At your own (I risked it) coetusing level."

Everything Bruce and I said to each other seemed to daze the other. More dazed than me at this point Bruce shook his head like a Methodist and said, "I've never looked at it that way. I guess we were betrayed as well as took over." Now as he began blaming the E.U.B. bureaucracy as well I began losing my E.U.B. research as leverage for peace-making.

"We just should have gone congregational", he said. "That's probably our only hope in the future…to become a congregationally independent Church."

"Please don't go there Bruce." I appealed he continue valuing the historical reality of the E.U.B. and its reformed Calvinist tradition. I'm preaching more on that come Sunday. "Don't idealize some a-historical congregational indulgence, but help us at Birch Lane live and project a synthesis of E.U.B. and Wesleyan methods of Christian faith, fully united in our Witness to God's Authority and Love. More fully united, more truly united…"

"More truly catholic…" he said in a sinister grin.

"Yes as in my sermon, Bruce." I shook his hand. It was damp.

"Thank you friend for listening… to my sermon at least. Good night."

"Good night," he cooed as innocent as a choir boy.

It was late or I might not have resisted the temptation to drive in and

1   *Coitus*: sexual intercourse [French Latin coition, coming together]

visit Wayne Trapp. To have a straight non shifty conversation about quail and pointers. Driving home my mind raced back to a similar furtive episode. Decades ago working for the Archdiocese of Indianapolis I'd been assigned a 'Community Organizer' task in the southern New Albany deanery.[1] My boss at the time was Father Schmidlin, a vicar to Archbishop Schulte and the Director of Catholic Charities. 'The old man' (Archbishop Schulte) was said not to like Schmidlin and didn't want social service programs or agencies spread around His Archdiocese.[2] 'The old man' did have a soft spot in his hard heart for traditional charities like the St. Vincent de Paul Sodalities. Technically St. Vincent de Paul work was under the jurisdiction of the Director of Catholic Charities. We conspired to penetrate the southern and rural deaneries by effectively organizing Vincentian Groups to demonstrate the value of diocesan wide charities work.

Archbishop Schulte wrote a letter addressed to every Pastor in the New Albany Deanery requesting they cooperate and support our efforts to organize St. Vincent de Paul groups in their parish. I was to hand deliver the letter to each Pastor, plan and implement the necessary organizational and social ministry work. I had great respect for the Vincentians I'd met in Europe, Mexico and state side. Their work on behalf of the poor not only materially assisted millions of needy people it was great for consciousness raising of the existence and causes of poverty.

The first Pastor I called on was Father Dearing at St. Mary's the biggest and oldest parish in the county. I'd been warned he was an old stick in the mud, didn't like Schmidlin and was delighted the Archbishop opposed Catholic Charities work.

He greeted me brightly, didn't invite me into his office, sat me down in a hall chair, stayed standing himself. Pointing to a wall clock he said, "Sorry I won't be giving you much time but I wanted to give you the courtesy of explaining why I'll not be cooperating with you or

---

1   deanery: sub territorial group of every diocese.
2   The only Catholic Charities agencies were in Indianapolis (1) Catholic Social Services: a counseling center (2) St. Mary's Child Center: for afflicted children and (3) St. Elizabeth's Home for unwed mothers; an adoption agency.

any other minions of Father Schmidlin.

"Please", I interrupted "be assured I am no henchperson of Father Schmidlins. I am a Vincentian myself at St. Judes in Owen County. We work with the county home and the rural poor who are virtually without services or assistance were it not for the presence of St. Vincent de Paul."

Stymied, but for a moment, he parried, "Is your pastor young Father Dillon?"

"....yes", I answered "but...this..."

He interrupted "No buts, no this or that. You might as well say the late Father Dillon. He's shuckin' it in, didja know?"

I nodded yes.

"Heh, heh, didja know why? Why he's abandoning his holy and eternal vows to the Priesthood?" He didn't want nor wait for an answer. In a quiet shriek, "He's abandoning his holy vows for a hank of hair and a piece of bone. Some twit!" (I didn't think Father Dearing would use the word twat.)

"I didn't know..."

"Aye that's it m' boy. A hank of hair for holy vows. I would never... It's his generation you know... no   sense of loyalty or obedience to their Archbishop. It's his generation and the one just before it...the poisoners and the poisoned. No sense of authority. Like that Father Schmidlin of yours and his liberal lackeys. Marriage counseling wayward wives instead of affirming the authority of their Marriage vows."

He began to remind me of the Bandit in 'Treasure of the Sierra Madre';

"I don't need no stinking hank of hair. I have my Lady."

He turned to an icon of Mary on the wall. "My Lady. And my Archbishop whom I am obedient and follow totally and agree with totally so I am sorry young man I cannot cross my loyalty to my Archbishop to cooperate with this..."

Now I interrupted, "Father Dearing, I just happen to have a letter here (taking it from my vest pocket) addressed personally to you from Archbishop Schulte asking you to cooperate with us. My instructions from the Archbishop were to hand deliver it personally to you."

He took the letter tentatively, then slightly bent into the hall table light to read it. Growing progressively pinker in the dim light, he finished reading the letter, slamming it down on the table, he blurted out to me, "The Archbishop don't tell me what to do!!"

I remembered the Art Young cartoon titled, 'Twas Ever Thus'.

Once home I found a phone message from Tim Cottom. "Greetings Preacher. I don't wanna speak on the phone. Peg and I need to speak with you as soon as possible. We're home all day tomorrow. Come have supper with us at six. Call us if you can't."

Peggy Rennick Cottom had inherited her parent's farm just three miles east of Birch Lane. She had grown up there and attended Sunday School and church with her two younger sisters. She'd met and married Tim in Florida where he worked construction. They both retired to the farm three years ago.

I arrived at five thirty admiring their neat out-buildings, driving back a long lane over two cattle gates to the privacy of their yard and home. Like most of my parishioners; they were typical of Indiana working class families who dream of retiring on their own place in their own time. Hard industrial work for two to four decades, then getting to your own place in the country. Getting there as soon as you could to rear children with chores or at least to receive your grandchildren on weekend visits. Indiana was still the most affordable place to purchase a family farm or inherit one; as most inherited farms come with an unpaid mortgage.

Tim greeted me in the yard and showed me the thirty some young steers in his west pasture. They were black baldies, half Hereford and half Angus. He explained they buy them as weanlings in March or April and market them before Thanksgiving. "Feed e'm nothing but these pastures of Indiana's native orchard grass." We talked a little about the over rated Kentucky tall fescue grass that was taking over many meadows with endophyte problems.

Peg greeted us at their porch ringing a dinner bell that scared the steers. We sat right down for supper and… God bless them they served wine with the pot-roast and potatoes. And what wine! Some kind of

South American vintage they'd discovered in Florida called Malbec I think. A dark red wine tasting of black pepper and vanilla. Spectacular!

"We knew you liked wine", Peg grinned and Tim laughed a little embarrassed. She motioned for him to speak, "That was all their first gossip...don't you know. Karl Mannheim" pointing toward the road. "Their farm is just south of here he talks to me and Peggy a lot cause she comes from here...you know...back when Birch Lane was E.U.B. not Methodist. They've sent us a boozer", he said. "He's been caught buying wine his first week on the job. Right outa that liquor store in Clayford. He'll probly be as big a drunk as that wet nosed Lutheran."

"More rife with gossip than is imaginable", I thought and said, while beginning to shake my head like a Methodist. "Where do they get off thinking I'll be their cockshy for this...?"

"We didn't mean to hurt you by telling you what they're saying.

Tim and I just think you ought to know how mean they're talking and to warn you how mean they can act."

"Is this the way they've treated previous Pastors?"

"Sure is," Tim agreed.

"Maybe not so quickly," Peggy added.

"I was on my way to call on Pastor Steve at the Lutheran Parsonage as a favor to his cousin Arthur who I'd met at De Pau's Conference of Ministers."

"Before you came...he was all they could talk about. How his drinking was an insult...no I think Karl's word was outrage to the community. And they visited and blabbed with their friends in Hectorsburg... agitating them on against him."

"Just like they've done with our own Pastors," Peggy said, unhappily.

"They always start out..." Tim was speaking angrily now.

"They start out blabbing about the E.U.B. but you preempted that with your sermon Sunday. You know more about Otterbein and the E.U.B. than they do. Ol' Karl complained, 'why he's using Otterbein against us'."

Peggy interrupted, "Karl and Barbara know we drink wine with supper sometimes and beer in hot weather. Karl will tease us about it, kinda chide us for it, but they don't think Preachers have a right to drink at all."

"There's no Prohi,[1] like a previous drunken Prohi," Tim described, Karl Mannheim. "He was an Ironworker for over twenty years. Us carpenters could never drink as much as most Ironworkers. Karl bragged to me once he'd drank ninety beers in one evening. I scolded him the Ironworkers I knew could always drink enough to damn near die." He looked guiltily at Peg for swearing in front of the minister.

"We just want you to know, we've…Tim and I have supported our Ministers and we will support you. We and I mean most everyone at Church were touched by how you cared for those lovely children of yours. Our daughter Gail, she lives in Pensacola, is divorced with two kids. We know how tough it can be. You can count on us and most of the congregation. It's just the Mannheims and their followers. But you know Ed Logan is the worst. He's who I would call their ring leader."

"I thought Gordon Bruce was."

"Naah," Tim put in, "Pegs right. It's the Logans. Bruce is just polite about it. Mueller and Gossett a little stupid but Ed and ol' Ruth Less… they are the dangerous ones."

Deliberately *not* shaking my head, I looked directly at Peggy and asked, "What would you recommend I do? You are the veterans here. Should I ignore them? Confront them privately and/or publically?" Tim and I waited for Peggy to speak.

"I was watching you and Tim out there with our cattle. So many of our people are small farmers, including the Mannheim bunch. Even if they are workers somewhere else during the week. Tim tells me you're kinda the same. You run cattle and sheep… and have some horses. We've never had a farmer-preacher before. I think they'll like that. Just like you talked to Tim out there with the cattle…talk to Karl Mannheim about his pigs, apple trees and rabbits, Roy Gossett about his clover crop and bees, the Muellers about their mules and truck gardens."

"And Ed Logan…?"

"You got me there", she laughed.

"Ed raises nothing but his lawn", Tim joked. "He's out there on his little lawn tractor from Spring til late Fall. He's no longer a

1   Prohi: Prohibitionist

Union Man either. Just a low rung manager on an acre plot out here in the middle of farm country."

"Well now…" Peggy remembers, "They did…Ruth and Ed did raise a mighty fine daughter. Carol is their only child. She's grown up and married now. Lives in Terre Haute, has two little girls and a hard working husband. They did good with Carol."

"She's in Union Hospital now", I reported. They nodded they knew.

"I planned to visit her today, but didn't. I'll get to Terre Haute tomorrow for sure."

Peg and Tim talked on about Carol; how she has a beautiful voice, sings in choirs and is a "music minister" for Victory Tabernacle, a large mega-church in Terre Haute.

Leaving the Cottoms I smiled into that night after hearing Peg's infrastructural referents to Birch Lane families. The hard working, home centered, land locked people of Indiana. No less farmer-workers than the North Vietnamese Army. I loved this place. Especially since that De Pau Conference. Since then… as a Midwesterner, a Heartlander I realized my generation was not only divided by the issues of racial justice vs. racism, peace vs. war, work vs. management but more fundamentally between those grown up children who understood why Dorothy wanted to get back to the farm in Kansas and those who didn't.

XXXI

Showered up after morning chores. An early drought is showing up in a few cases of foot scald in the sheep. Doctored the whole flock with koppertox. Stinking stuff. Have to trim back their hooves and apply the med koppertox directly on the proud flesh. Vally, our young black Morgan mare is overdue to foal. I'm watching her closely. Old mares are typically a month overdue; not ones as young as Vally. Groomed the cockle burrs out of Joe's mane and forelock. Joe is our Morgan stallion. My olde Pal. He'd produced for us what I'd aimed at and Gloryville Farm became known for: tall, black, and typey Morgan Horses. I'd actually sold colts back to Vermont.[1] I'd ridden many a trail with Joe. He'd go over Swampy ground faster than Thoroughbred Hunters of the New Briton Hunt. We were asked to be Outriders at their point to point races and kept advantage of all competitors. He was twenty-two years old now and failing. I'd have to arrange for him to be sent to the killers[2] before winter and that was killing to me...to think about.

But... showered up and on the road to Terre Haute I was feeling better. Too many things to fret about. I was hopeful. Hope is what's needed when hopeless feelings threaten. Otherwise it's not that important.

Finding Union Hospital in North Terre Haute reminds me of my mother. She worked there after my sister and I started driving. We weren't home much and Mom and Dad moved us to the 'North End'. She worked hard for substandard wages throughout the sixties. Fair pay for female non union hospital workers was screwed tight to the bottom of the scale.

But, she loved it. Indeed she thought Heaven would be a lot like 'Central Supply' working with the autoclave machine.[3] "It will be very

---

1   back to Vermont: 'Figure' the first Morgan owned by Stallioneer and Welsh singing teacher Justin Morgan in Vermont. Vermont is origin of Morgan breed. Vermont exports Morgans. Rarely imports them.
2   the killers: slaughter house for aged horses.
3   Autoclave machine: Super-heated steam pressured sterilizing machine for surgical instruments.

clean" she'd say, "and everyone will have a job."

It was early afternoon. Not exactly visiting hours. I took the stairs directly to Carol Logan Lentz second floor room. Nurses deferred to the clerical black I wore. One stooped little nurse with salt and pepper hair smiled kindly and pulled back the curtain revealing Carol on the phone in bed.

Forefinger to lips she whispered audibly to Carol, "Pastoral call." Then asked me to sit down as she left the room.

Carol appeared an attractive young woman around thirty. She seemed tall, that is, she lay long in the bed lightly covered by a sheet. As she took her hurried time ending the phone conversation we had a few moments to study each other. I thought it was mutually appreciative.

As she hung up, she said in an alto voice, "You must be the new Pastor for the North Side Assembly."

"No" I replied, "I'm the new Pastor for your parents church at Birch Lane."

"What… why…the new Pastor? I don't believe we've met. Mom and Dad didn't say…"

"I have a farm near Freedom, not far from Birch Lane, but I grew up in Terre Haute. My parents live here in the north side. It was easy to stop by."

"Thank you…" she said. "Have you been a Minister long?"

"No" I answered, "does it show? How can you tell?"

"No, no. I just meant have you pastored churches here in Terre Haute before?"

She was doing her best to hide the previous negative narratives she'd absorbed about me, or Methodists and/or all Preachers at Birch. I spoke to her about her family. There was a small photo of them on the night stand. We spoke about pain and her knee surgery. I prayed with her, wished her family well, and sent my regards to her parents. Upon leaving she asked, "Were your churches in California, spirit filled?"

I knew what she meant. "Spirit filled" is a code word for Pentecostal practices in Non-Pentecostal Churches. Such also referred to as 'charismatic'. Answering yes or no would be sunk into a sectarian socket. I answered, "Some would say so."

So…maybe the olde heresy is behind all the fever at Birch Lane. Turned on by T.V. evangelists, the kind that light the fires of narcissism sparking off against all those not seen in their mirror. Spirit filled indeed. What kind of spirits is never asked. Opening themselves up spiritually too often without the discipline of intellect or religion. The vacuum filled with spirits; some good and some very, very bad. I've seen both. The beautiful angelic glossolalia and the inflamed imperious selves whose holier than thou selfishness is more consonant with modern American marketing.

Carol reminded me of my kid sister. Not only in their tall good looks but in their Christian charism as well. Both daddy's girls, but strong and competent because of it. The charismatic growth of my sister I had watched with some alarm. An inside joke among diocesan priests had been that too many female parishioners saw them as 'sacramental studs'. The real sick joke to my mind was too many priests were more than willing to accommodate them.

A Father Dave started seeing my sister taking her to Catholic Charismatic Services (I called them rallies). There were some national ones up at Notre Dame and several local ones. Father Dave started presiding at Catholic Charismatic masses. Then they attended some ecumenical i.e. inter-faith Charismatic services. Next my sister started attending these services without Father Dave. And finally she emerged as a full-fledged holy roller herself. She joined the North Side megachurch assembly which then seemed to out join our family…at least too many of our family gatherings.

Most of our family gatherings were at her house, a magnificent olde Germanic hulk of a place near Collet Park. Catholic Worship, the Catholic Mass is radically 'deocentric', i.e. 'God Centered'. Charismatic Services, I think, tend to be 'homocentric' i.e. 'fellowship centered'. These 'fellows' started out-joining our family at our family functions. Frequently even out numbering us at birthday and holiday celebrations.

At my mother's birthday get together many strangers, that is, people we did not know – had not yet met joined us for dinner and dessert.

After cake and ice cream, my wife, children and I were leaving... saying a final happy birthday and good-bye to Mom who sat in the kitchen. Just ahead of us one of the stranger church ladies fairly leaped upon her, hugging her *not* dispassionately exclaiming, "Oh Mother Vi, we just love you! Hap..." At which point Mom broke free of the charismatic hug, and exclaimed back, "Well I don't love you! Hell, I don't even know you. It's hard enough lovin my own damn family, let alone strangers."

Gold bless her! If me mother could only testify at more charismatic intersections.

Next Sunday's service and sermon at Birch Lane went well except for one attempted train wreck. When we reached the first new hymn Ruth Leslie demonstrably refused to play the organ... the congregation sang fine with the new hymn not even missing Ruth's organ. After my fire and brimstone preaching against hatred and division she hesitated a bit but joined in playing the organ for our closing hymn.

Debriefed by the Vincents and Cottoms the sermon was well received by the majority and neutralized much of the minority. Jane Schouten reported Bruce was no longer so critical. "Now he's not yet what you'd call supportive but he ain't so very critical anymore." I was sure I could win most, maybe all of the opposition over. Just as in California, I would preach and teach orthodoxy; taking the personal to home visits and counseling. I kept in close contact with the Vincents and Cottoms and tried to plan a major home visit to one of the opposition weekly. I also initiated an informal progress report to Millard Stilmore and spoke often with Prester John.

Weeks later I called on Roy and Emma Gossett. They both were retired postal employees. Roy took me out past their garden to inspect his bee hives. "They're mostly imported Italian" Roy tenderly described his bees. They were his treasure. "Tending them"... taking care of them...sharing their produce of honey with them and his friends was a source of joy to him. His neatly organized apiary embodied the most ancient art of livestock husbandry. Complimenting his apiculture we retired to their kitchen where Emma served us some of its fresh produce; clover honey on Ritz crackers. Smooth, delicious and just a little salty.

Emma's interests were in gardening and photography. Sitting in their sunroom she showed us several of her photographs. Most were of her garden in a kind of time study of its growth and development. The most striking photos I remember were several she and Roy had taken of a large group of snow bound sea gulls in their cornfield. Years later gulls are sighted along the Wabash but this many then was very unusual. "Snow stormed down from Lake Michigan", Roy said.

"We kinda felt like e'm ol' sea gulls back in sixty-eight", he continued as Emma excused herself, saying, "You men talk politics while I'll get us some coffee."

"Coffee sounds great" I pled, "But I'd like to hear your opinion Emma."

"Got none", she blew back quickly. "We were federal employees right through the war years. New Dealers. Ed Logan thinks he's some kind of Republican. I stay out of it but none of us liked the things back in '68." She stayed in the sunroom.

"Yuh know..." I tried explaining. "It seems I've worked for change most of my life but few changes ever pleased me." Then joked, "It's a wonder those right wingers aren't afraid of you Federales."

We laughed together and went into the kitchen for coffee.

Many weeks passed. The general countenance of oppositionists calmed. I sold some breeding stock that gave me a much needed economic cushion. Beth and El did great on our weekends. I spoke with them on the phone most every night. Their mother retracted her claws.

Vally foaled without complications. I found her at first light lying in a bed of ladino clover. She was in labors pain when I sat down with her in the clover. I stayed with her an hour past sun up til the foal peeked out his head... and then came out of her. A fine black stud colt. His mother massaged him with her tongue and bit through the umbilical cord. He stood shaking off the slime of passage and looked out over the vast green terrain of our Vally Keep. Chortling little sounds of approval he moved toward the warm comfort of his mother's milk. By noon he was running in the pasture with her and it seemed as if he'd always been here. Foals! From kittens to human infants the evidence of being comes slowly. Horses burst into being almost immediately.

'Glory' the dam of 'Vally' I'd kept open (i.e. not bred) for riding and working in the warm weather of summer and early autumn. She was the first Morgan horse foaled on the farm. Dad broke her to harness in an old jalopy of a jog cart. She was still fiery and a lot to handle on the open road but calmed right down on wooded trails. I'd blazed many a trail out of our valley where she was perfectly tractable. That is, until we hit the road home, then it was off to the races. Many's the time my little nephew Morgan Joe would ride calmly with me for hours until we hit the road home. Then he'd hang on my coat tails for dear life. He was a brave little lad.

"The worst ain't so bad once it happens", Tim Holts character says (in the John Huston film, 'Treasure of Sierra Madre') after seeing so much hard work and hope blow away; the windstorm blowing their gold dust back to the mountains. She, my wife (*not*...no longer my wife) was gone. There would be no reconciling of the family on the family farm. Being...quietly at home. Being cognizant, being consciously accepting of life all around and beyond my self...grateful for what I had of it, becoming...being a part of it. Getting shut of extravagant notions of free will. 'Freedom' was just a place on the map or otherwise Anglo-Saxon propaganda. Like the Brits gunships on China, demanding "freedom" for the Chinese people to buy British opium. Willful freedoms a dodge from responsibility or worse. Revolutionary and/or progressive optimism cooing over illusions of a different nature in a perfectible future. Sholokhov's cavalry[1] cantering into each other and off the cliff.

Living alone on the farm encouraged a certain detachment. I'd always admired the ancient sage's refusal to be swayed by the vicissitudes, the fickle chanciness of this ol' world. Maybe I could get there. If history called, I could be Thomas Mùnzer. But, I was not wasting any more time with cyclical apocalypticists and revolution in the next five years nonsense.

The 'Long Haul' perspective always looks backward a little more than forward. It is an old man's perspective. The past being more vividly recalled than the future imagined. I was to be my children's old

1   Mikhail Sholokhov: author of 'Quiet Flows the Don' trilogy.

man. I would become the old celibate Pastor, the Shepherd of my herds, flocks, and parishioners. Forty something going on eighty something I was getting older. I still think the art of ageing well is to get old early.

Old people reflect on their ancestors; genetic, intellectual, and spiritual. Young people waste time with their ambitions. The old order Amish, I think, are the best example for Communist Cuba, which in turn is the best example for all the Americas. The oppositionists at Birch Lane value a past they imagine against a future they fear.

I would gently and demonstrably share their recollections into the present affirming the integrity of a united prayerful community for the future. The rest of the summer went well. Even the sociogram of Sunday morning changed. That is, the seating arrangement ceased to be the one third minority sitting in the back section. Most of 'the people in the back' started sitting with their friends in the larger front section. Emma and Roy Gossett took the lead in that. The Muellers quickly followed with many following them.

During the first cool nights of August the large Mueller clan annually convened a cookout and bonfire. "It's mostly for the young people", Anna May told me. "They invite all their cousins and friends. We allow e'm to stay up past midnight around the fire. They'd like for you to join us for hot dogs, marshmallows, and soda round the fire. They all just like to sing songs and tell stories. Maybe you could say a prayer for e'm, yuh know,…to keep it down after us older folks go home to bed."

I thanked her for the invite. "Tell Joe I'll come round before dark and help him and the boys with fire preparation."

"Really", she almost squealed. "That'd suit Joe just fine. We'll see yuh Saturday."

It never fails. The bias that men of the cloth will not soil their hands in physical labor seems universal. At least it always surprises people positively, when you pick up a pitchfork, rake, axe, or hammer. Thomas Münzer was known through Europe as 'the man with a hammer'. On Saturday Joe Mueller, his sons and I sawed wood and cut brush for the fire. Near twilight we returned to their farm house to clean up. We had just enough time to inspect Joe's yearling mules and Belgian broodmares. Knowing he was a Jackstock man I brought with me pictures of Kentuckiana, the roan mammoth Jennet[1] I'd owned seven years ago. She stood sixteen hands tall and easily won grand champion status at the ADMS[2] national show in Martinsville. My friend Jim Moore curator of the art History Museum in Albuquerque, New Mexico assisted me show Kentuckiana. He is said to have displayed this photo in the museum, captioned: "Tom Morgan and I show our ass in Martinsville, Indiana."

Joe was impressed with the picture and said he'd sure like a jack colt out of her. Confirming that thought with a nod I told him she'd had breeding difficulty and I sold her to a mule dealer in London, Kentucky.

We got along great talking about Jackstock. Joe didn't own a jack so he had to take his mares to Nelson Cooper in Orleans, Indiana. I knew Nelson from the ADMS expositions, so Joe and I shared a mutual friend.

I gagged through the hot dogs, marshmallows, soda-pop, and pubescent-pop songs to manage praying with them before leaving the very eclectic canticle of love from the Methodist sacraments and church rites. As it raided the Song of Solomon, St. Paul, and the prayer of St. Francis I carefully raided, i.e. edited parts of it:

"Let love be genuine and hate what is evil,
hold fast to what is good.
Outdo one another in showing honor;
 be humble and never conceited for
Love is stronger than death
and Jealousy is cruel as the grave.
Floods cannot drown love
and wealth cannot buy it.
Love is not jealous or boastful,
careless, oblivious or irresponsible,
arrogant, rude or possessive.
Love is patient and kind.

---

1   mammoth Jennet: female ass of the mammoth breed
2   ADMS: American Donkey and Mule Society

Love rejoices in the right,
it is virtuous and faithful.
Happy are those whose love
resides in God.
Lord keep our love for each other
on the straight path of virtue. Amen

Joe told me later as the adults were leaving Anna May whispered to him, "these kids will be lovin on each other but it'll be respectful after the Preachers words."

Word or words of social successes spread. Throughout the summer I'd gotten around to 'bout everyone. Except two chief leaders of the so-called opposition. Logan and Mannheim. Their henchpersons, the old and surly John Bought and the young and surly Jack Schmitt seemed less important.

"Ol' Karl will come around", Tim counseled me. He also cautioned, "It's his wife Barbara you gotta look out for. She's more mindlessly militant then he is. She told Peggy she never met a Methodist Minister who wasn't mealy mouthed and lazy. We all know you are a forthright straight talker and hard worker. Karl told me he's heard both Roy Gossett and Joe Mueller say so. Why don't you invite yourself over there and talk livestock with him? He's got a whale of a pig operation goin on."

"Nobody likes importunate self-inviters or Pastoral drop ins" I said, "always seems sneaky."

"Better yet" Tim induced, "Is there something you could ask him, yuh know ask his advice about some farm thing or' nother?"

"I dunno, I'm not much on keeping pigs…"

"Barbara and him used to be 4H leaders when their girls were still home. You got your kids in 4H?"

"They're too young… next year I think it would be good for Bethany, but not pigs. I'd like to get her a Saanen doe."

"Whazatt?"

"A dairy goat. At State Fair I've seen a lot of young girls show dairy goats. Steers too big for them. Sheep too wild. Pigs indelicate…

for young ladies."

"That's it! Ask Karl... about it. He loves giving advice. Being a kind of mentor, he thinks. That's why, I think that Schmitt kid follows him and Logan around like a guard dog for Jesus. But, ask his advice about 4H for your daughter."

I told Tim his was a good idea. Trying it out the next morning I phoned Karl Mannheim. He was cagey and skeptical...at first. Then immediately warmed when he realized I was asking for help...for his advice. "Our girls were in 4H every year. Barbara and I stayed on as leaders until we had grandkids. Jack Schmitt and his sister were some of our 4H kids. But, I think you're right about a goat project for your girl. Our girls always did cooking and sewing. They also showed calves, shoats, and gilts.[1] Until Gracie our youngest got an Alpine doe. Named it Heidi and it made the perfect livestock project for a ten-year-old girl. Where you gwine to keep it?"

"I thought I'd just let it run in open pasture with my sheep and cattle."

"You got sheep?"

"Forty head of Suffolk ewes. Over seventy head if you count the lambs."

"Well..." he sounded approvingly. "Tell you what", he proposed. "My cousins boy Caleb's a mechanic and he's just started working at your new gas station, there at the west edge of Freedom. I'm off to see him here in a minute or two. Meet me in Freedom and I'll buy you a cup of coffee."

"Better still," I said. "Karl come on over to my place. Drive a few miles more...I'll keep the coffee pot on...and show you where I could house some doelings. See what you think."

"Well...", he said again. "Be there within an hour or two."

"That's fine, I'll be working up close to the house. I'll open the second gate for you. So long."

Karl arrived well within the hour, opened and shut the front gate after examining the stone marker. At the second gate he seemed a little nervous about our bull approaching his car. "He just wants his

---

1   Shoats and gilts: Gelded i.e. castrated young boars and young female pigs. A female pig is not a sow until she's borne baby pigs.

---

back rubbed," I grinned opening the gate and shutting it behind him. Getting out of his parked car, looking back down the hill this lifelong Brethren shook his head just like a Methodist.

"Man that's the biggest bull I've ever seen. Is he Angus?"

"Nope, he's Welsh Black. I brought some of the first breeding stock in from Wales and Canada."

"Man, he's a big 'un. How old is he? How much he weigh?"

"Turned three this Spring. He weighed two thousand last Spring as a two-year-old. Throws calves just like himself."

We walked downhill amongst the calves and mother cows.

"They're docile cattle, ain't they?"

Steering him away from 'Rhyllech Memi 9' I explained, pointing her out.

"That one has not read the breed description of how tractable they are. She's OK year 'round til calving time when... she will try and kill you. More cattleman are injured and killed by mother cows than ever by breed bulls."

We steered clear around Memi. She was terrible but nonetheless a great brood cow. She'd been the poster cow for the breed in Wales and Canada with studies on her production growth increments by the University of Wales in Aberystwyth.

Karl Mannheim loved the farm. I'd always claimed it as a significant selling point. That is in selling livestock it was difficult to get buyers to the farm, but once here, the beauty of the place would close the sale. Maybe it would sell ol' Mannheim on my being OK, being acceptable as his minister.

Leaning on the Serviceberry tree, looking out over our valley, he sighed, "Why would you ever want to leave this place?"

"I never ever wanted or would want to...but Karl a man's got to try whatever to save and provide for his family."

"Is that what this Methodist ministry's about? Is Birch Lane Church the whatever?"

Ouch! That cut a little too close to the rough side of home.

"I've heard a lot about God's call to the ministry Karl, but not much about how it comes about. I think I was called to the ministry no more *but* no less than you were called to marry Barbara. And your children were called to earth by your union with her. Holy Scripture tells us God knew us before we were in our mother's womb. Strategic destination from God. Tactical discernment and work from us with forgiveness when we fail. Mine is a failed, a failing family situation. I have a failed marriage. My wife divorced me. I could not prevent it nor reconcile it. God forgives this failing Karl. Why isn't that good enough for you?"

"? ? ! ?"

"As to the whatever: I came to Birch Lane because I was so assigned by Bishop Armstrong. Still and all I consider it a Godsend to me and my children. Thank God I can serve a church…have a church family this close to my family home."

"….whew", he finally said. "Makes sense to me, who

would want to leave this valley. But what were you really doin in California?"

"I pastored two churches as a kind of Methodist Circuit Rider."

"And before that?"

"I was Director of Archdiocesan Social Ministries. I worked for the Archdiocese of Indianapolis pretty much since I finished graduate school in 1968. Has someone told you otherwise?"

'Well… there's been a lot of talk. Yes…a lot of talk",

he said discomfited but still suspicious.

I resisted the urge to roar 'For crying out loud *Who* is talking about *What*! Instead I peacefully invited him on into the kitchen for coffee. He looked around a lot and asked, "Do you keep a liquor cabinet?"

"You want a drink at this hour, Karl?"

He laughed out loud at that. And we laughed together successfully dodging the liquor question. As we took our coffee out on the porch to see my sheep coming in for a drink at the pond, he said almost apologetically —

"It's just that we've heard so much talk."

"Are you comfortable, are you free Karl to speak to me about this talk?"

"No sir, I reckon not. But I think you're on the level. I think you'd best speak to Ed Logan."

Ed Logan again, the great progenitor of the prejudiced. The beget-ter of who knows what bull. Enough! I decided to visit the Logans invited or not.

XXXII

Before Karl left we inspected the low shed sheep stalls on the north end of the barn.

"That'll be fine for Bethany's goat project. I think
I still have phone numbers for dairy goat breeders as far
north as Lafayette. Our Gracie shopped around a lot. You wantin' Alpines?"

"I'd prefer Saanens."

"Lots of the dairy goat breeders keep several breeds. A
close one...over between Cloverdale and Greencastle has Alpines, Nubians and, I think, a few Saanens. I'd start with him. Say, why don't you come on over to our place after church Sunday. I'll find the dairy goat list for you... and I'd like to show you my livestock."

"I hear you raise swine according to the old Purdue formula."

"That's right!", he almost exclaimed. "My sows are not going to be crowded into air conditioned confinement crap and farrowing crates."

"What breed are your sows?" I asked.

Eyes a glint and curious he asked back,

"And what breed would you guess?"

"Everybody these days seem to prefer Hamp and
Yorkshire crosses but under the old Purdue Plan of pigs in pasture and woodlot I'd prefer Large Blacks or English Whites cept' they'd be hard to find... so I'd guess Tamworth. You keep red Tamworths?"

"Dang[1] it all if you don't know swine! Never heard of Large Blacks or English Whites. But yore right. I keep registered red Tamworth boars. Can't afford such sows. For sows I buy the cheapest but quality grade gilts that come thru the auction."

"What is your average litter size?"

He didn't want to answer that question.[2] So he scoffed off something

---

[1] Dang: is an acceptable word instead of damn for Hoosier farmers in the same way that frig is an acceptable word instead of the original F. word for "Christian" teeny boppers.

[2] Preferred natural production is usually quantitatively less than the contrived unnaturally crowded and confined systems.

like, "I dunno. Not really exactly sure, but at least they're farrowed out in the open of Gods nature, not confined in crap and disease."

"I'd sure like to see your swine operation. Haven't seen a Tamworth boar in decades, not even at the State Fairs."

"They're rare alright and expensive."

"You ever keep back some of your half bred gilts?"

"Good idea", he said. "I thought about it. Hey, we'll talk about it. What about Sunday?"

"My children will be with me next Sunday."

"All the better. Barbara loves kids. Why don't you all come for Sunday dinner?"

Remembering Tim Cottom's view of Barbara I asked Karl,

"You sure? Are you sure Sundays alright with Barbara?"

Karl slowed to the thought, "Well...I'll check with her. See if there's any plans. We'll call you tonight."

I received no phone call that night...nor the next day. I talked to Tim Cottom. He said, "Mannheims truck had been parked in Logans drive all afternoon and evening." By Friday Karl phoned...leaving a message that "*We'd* like to have you and your kids over for Sunday dinner after church." There was a strained apprehensive tone in his voice. What's next?! 'Summer s over', I reckoned.

Come September...skeins of geese appear again. Within external and internal skyways. Trebled notes of awareness ringing change in the cloud banked edges of our existence. "Seldom mild", my Uncle Tom Montaigne would warn. "Seldom mild", the seasonal passage. Especially the Fall into Winter.

Literati prefer the hushed and measured syllables of Autumn and Autumnal.[1] In most of America it is called the Fall. It is the season when things fall apart. Even the brisk falling leaves shatter when retrieved. I have written of 'The Autumn Follicle' in 'Glimpses'. The veterinary disease of mammals pervasively stuck in sexual season til deep winter. It is the time when women leave their men. And it is the time when memories of being left cue the virtually identical sensory and soulful injuries of primary experience. Neurologist Oliver

1   David Thomson: In America "those hushed and measured syllables [Autumnal] go to waste."

Sacks has researched the physiological correlates of memory using functional brain imaging "and these images show that vivid memories produce widespread activation in the brain involving sensory areas, emotional limbic areas" [as well as] "executive frontal lobe areas."[1] Dr. Sacks point is that factual and/or narrative (i.e. recreated and/or refined) memory cause the same physiological response.

This has led the mental health industry to counsel subjective reconstruction *reframing* of objective traumatic episodes in order to heal memories painful response. Well... maybe but it strikes me more than a little sneakened.

More hopeful to me is the activation of the frontal lobe areas.

Executive empowerment of the brain to achieve new therapeutic (i.e. contra-traumatic) experience to displace the past traumatic painful memory. The best displacement being replacement of primary experience!

A jihadic[2] struggle from the trenches of past experience. A significant part of everyone's life is a struggle to survive, think through, and retrench from past traumatic episodes.

In the crisscrossed septarium of my soul I yearned to know... too much. But yearning ain't wrong if you're conscious of its limits. "Madness need not be breakdown. It may also be breakthrough", said our late comrade Laing.[3]

I was born in this season, in this time, this time of all the years... the exact time of my parents union.[4] Maybe I was born for this time! A Septemberist for this senescent fragmenting time of forgotten valor and the synthesis of revolution. From the prowess of ancient Celtic septs to septic modern failures.

The Septuagint was made by seventy translators for the library of Alexandria in the second century. Preferred by Jews of the Diaspora and the early Fathers of the Church, still used by Eastern Orthodoxy. It includes the Apocrypha. I've never read it, but intend to...also the

---

1   Oliver Sacks "Speak Memory" NYRB 2-21-13
2   jihadic: as in jihad, the Koranic concept of moral struggle in deeply rooted immoral situations.
3   R.D. Laing: Socialist minded mad psychiatrist according to Clancy Sigal.
4   Their wedding anniversary September, Friday 13th.

Masoretic text, the Masorah: a collection of marginal notes and criticism on the text of the Hebrew Bible in sixth century Aramaic.

Cloudbanks kept coming

PLAIN SPEAK

I would preach the plain and simple truth of Christ's message. Young Issa[1] the carpenter…called to his Father's business in the final conflicts between Heaven and Humanity…between God and the renegade rulers of this world. Between the way of God's love and the ways of His wrath. That God is the loving forgiving kindness we show each other to endure the injustice and wickedness that surrounds us. The Messianic loyalty of Jesus to His Father in heaven the only exemplary loyalty we ever need. Contrary loyalties are at best idolatrous confusion at worst deliberate blasphemy. Neither to be tolerated. If gentle discipline (what the Quakers call 'Friendly Persuasion') fails maximal action then required.

CRITERION

He was probably the only one who ever sued the Archdiocese of San Francisco and won. He was certainly the only Irish Catholic Communist Lawyer who'd done so. He…was Vincent Hallinan, the 'Lion in Court' who'd run for President on the Progressive Party Ticket in 1952 after Henry Wallace had been rekenneled by the Establishment. Asher Harer, Long Shoreman and Bay area leader of the SWP introduced us in Hallinan's office.

Early on he felt he'd been wronged by the Archdiocese. "I was not vengeful", he said, lifting his hand toward heaven…"for Vengeance is His." "Patiently I waited biding time until Providence brought them clearly in range…" He kept his arm high in the air. "But then…when in range" he glared at his desk top as his fist slammed hard upon it. "I struck!"

---

1   Issa: Aramaic and Arabic for Jesus.

SKULLFACE REENTERS MY RADAR
(....the malice of a good thing is the barb which makes it stick.)

R.B. Sheridan

Three years after that fateful October demonstration of us and the Five thousand students mobilized against us, I'm back at I.U. finally finishing my senior year. At 1pm the Sociology Departments Professor Alfred Lindesmith[1] and the Kinsey Institutes for Sex Research Professor Bill Simon[2] and John Gagnon[3] convened their Seminar on Deviant Behavior.

I had presented a paper that day on 'Wanton Violence'. More precisely...on the libidinous cues and cause for so-called wanton i.e. causeless violence. I used literary material and animal behavior experiments as examples and evidence.

When finished my sycophantic fellow students were reticent to

---

1   Dr. Alfred Lindesmith: his very countenance was Minnesota's Rural Americana. We were the only two in the class who had witnessed imprinting behavior in cattle and horses. Dear Lindesmith a quarter of a century after this seminar and much revolutionary infamy I was visiting my terminally ill Aunt Peggy in a very modest Bloomington Nursing Home. Upon leaving a gowned patient jumped into the elevator with me. "Morgan is it you?" he asked. It was an aged and frail Dr. Lindesmith. "Thank God it's you. ;You must be here to organize us. We've got to overthrow these creeps", he gestured toward the male nurse approaching us from the ground floor. As the nurse took him away, he showed the fist of resistance. I was visiting from my hospital job in California. I could not visit him. I prayed for Professor Lindesmith.

2   Professor Bill Simon: a product of Fritz Redl's counseling center for children in Detroit. An SWP activist prior to academic credentials. Author of the "Existential Sleuth". I met Allen Ginsberg at Bill and his wife Marlene's home. We traded Poetry Readings. According to Bill, Ginsberg told him I was the least dogmatic marxist he'd ever met. We probably hadn't talked long enough.

3   Professor John Gagnon: brilliant academic researcher for the Kinsey Institute. As Aldous Huxley empirically explored and experienced (i.e. tried out) every drug he researched in his book "The Doors of Perception", Gagnon similarly researched deviant sexual behavior. Shel Sklare and I joked John's opus might be called "The Apertures of Appreciation" rather than the less respectful "Whores of Deception" title we'd hear from other graduate students. Bill and John both found anti-libertine, anti-libertarian, anti-liberal views too puritanical. Bill said, when the history of the sixties is written there should be a chapter titled 'Sexual Revolution and the Renegade Morgan'.

respond until they saw which direction the three faculty were headed. Simon led with a kind of back handed compliment.

"After two generations of intellectual travelers from Marx to Freud found liberation there Morgan has more accurately discovered discipline. When the great Rabbi of Repression Sigmund Freud, speaks of sublimation or discipline it sure seems like another form of repression albeit a creative one …to me. However Morgan has correctly applied Freudian theory here with clinical examples of violence caused by the lack of sexual control rather than the icey hands of over control. Comrade Morgan you have done Cotton Mather[1] proud. Gagnon grimaced and Lindesmith grinned throughout.

Cocky from the coup and kudos at seminar I strode out of Ballantine Hall toward the Library at around 3:15pm. Going down the steps from the old library annex toward its east entrance taking pleasure in Octobers foliage, I was confronted - [WHAM] - with a situation of such opportune glee - [BAM] – *there* it was – there he was, Skullface himself. Walking jauntily toward me, down the east entrance steps. Smiling he was… in fraternal not quite likely recognition of me, that is, in my smiles which were radiant in grateful retribution.

I wore a herringbone sport coat and regimental tie — dressed up for my seminar presentation. Why – to him I must have looked like any frat rat dressed for a smoker. We met…standing an arm's length apart.

Frangibly polite he spoke in brittle tones, "You have me at a disadvantage…"

Interrupting, I said, "Yes I do."

Extending his white hand, he asked "You are?"

Taking his hand much more than firmly, I answered, "WETBACK!", easily pulling him off balance like a sixth grade Indian Wrestler. Enjoying the surprise in his pinking face I jerked hard toward the ground banging his face into my skull.

"WETBACK WETBACK you COWARDLY SCUM."

Remember "WETBACK!" A couple more jerks of his face into my fore skull and he began to bawl. A final low jerk sent him to the ground. Sorely tempted to instruct him further with a few kicks to the head, ribcage and groin area, I resisted, just jumping toward him like I

1   Cotton Mather: early puritan leader and nemesis of secular humanism

might. That sent him rolling down some steps to the north. He gained his feet, staggered and was easy to knock down again. I warned him, "One word from you now or ever again and I'll bury you in Dunn Meadow." He limped away across the meadow toward his fraternity house. I later regretted not making him sing the sweetheart of Sigma Chi while he was bawling.

My frontal lobe, indeed my very forehead had thus activated a therapeutic displacement, a contra – traumatic primary experience.

LEGAL LEFTOVERS

My legal situation seemed like the wife who served so many leftovers she couldn't remember the original meal. Somebody was trying to serve me papers. Twice a week or so a deputy sheriff would cross the county road bridge to stop at our front gate. The dogs would bark. The deputy would slowly open, drive in, shut the front gate, and drive the one hundred yards to the second gate. He'd honk his horn and holler up toward the house. That would provoke a kind of pack fury in the dogs; two stock dogs, four hounds, and Digger, the J.R.T.

I once had a long phone conversation with Bill Koehler foremost expert in America on Guard Dogs. I'd read his book[1] "The W.R. Koehler Method of Guard Dog Training". I remember his saying "a pack" of dogs regardless of breed was more defensively threatening than any one particular breed of guard dog. The deputy would whine and holler but never came in the second gate. I did not wish to receive any papers whether they were from my ex, Rueblood for his money or anybody else. Methodist Judge Farley had taken my case into advisement perpetuity.

Sometimes the Deputy would come on Saturdays. The children and I would lock the doors and hide in their bedroom closets. He never got past the second gate.

(GIT OUT! GIT OUT! GIT OUT of Here, Tom!!)
The Mannheim Visit
After church Sunday Karl Mannheim very neutrally confirmed our

---

1   W.R. Koehler: The Koehler Method of Guard Dog Training

invitation saying, "dinner at 3, come over as soon as you can." I noted

Barbara had not been at church today and asked if she was alright. Karl looked away saying, "she's fine, but she woke up a little poorly and … she has a lot to git done today." He added the last with a wink, nodding toward dinner I presumed.

My little girl and little boy helped me for an hour or so with the janitor work. Then we cleaned up and were off to visit the Mannheims.

The Mannheim farm house, like our own set way back off the frontage road. A long lane crossing two cattle gates led up to their home and outbuildings. I was surprised at the cattle gates as swine were their main livestock. I was surprised the wide piping would deter pigs or their parents from crossing it.

After Karl greeted us with a wave to park in the graveled area between his barn and storm cellar I asked him about the practical structure of his cattle gate.

"They're spaced a little wider…works perfect for the hogs.

Best thing we ever done…puttin' them in. I mean the grating instead of a regular gate. Before we put e'm in…us and ever body wuz wastin' time openin' and shuttin' gates."

"Ummh", I thought and said, "I like slowin' the traffic down coming to my place."

"Ummh", he said "We've heered a lot about that!"

"I reckon you have Karl Mannheim. Will you please tell me what you've heard from whom?"

Turning abruptly away Karl said, "time we looked at the stock before we go inside."

We looked at the new litters first. Tiny baby pigs nursing their mama sows in ample saw dusted pens. The children loved hearing them squeal. The babies were mostly red and snoutish like their Tamworth papas. Most of the mother sows were spotted.

"Are those sows from Spotted Poland stock?" I asked.

"Confound it!", Karl answered "Howju know such about swine? I guess yore Grandpaw and others back in the day would have said they are select spotted from Poland-China stock. But nobody talks that way these days. Jest calle'm Spotted. But I know…and I guess you do.

But I'm real partial to the old black Poland-China breed. These cross spotted gals is as close as I kin git to it. But howju…?"

"I worked for Veterinarian Doc Archer all through junior high summers and Saturdays. Never missed a day and in the sixth grade Boy Scouts I earned a merit badge in Animal Husbandry."

"*You* in scouts. Heh, hey the Reverend wuz a Boy Scout! Whereabouts?"

"Terre Haute Troop Nine. We met at Montrose Methodist Church on Seventeenth Street; four blocks from where I was born. Good experience. The Liffick boys, Tom Davis sons, Jerry Reynolds, Joe Withrow…good bunch of guys."

"You go to Camp Krietenstein?"

"Every summer I was in Scouts." With these Oppositionists I threw as wide a net of normal name dropping as I could. I figured any ordinary referent they might recognize would auger against whatever sub-human categories the likes of Logan were spreading.

"Well…up" Karl sighed, "we think scouting is a good program. We…Barbara and me were 4H leaders. Our girls were active as I said but they always envied their city cousins in Girl Scout uniforms comin' round, sellin' all them cookies."

He chuckled on about Girl Scout cookies as he led us to the boar pens. The Tamworths were impressive, long and lean. They had the long snout remnant look of wild boars.

"My hogs feed on hickory nuts, hazel nuts and roots, the way nature meant them to…"

Agreeing with his implied argument, I admired Karl's operation and stated my disapproval of the newer confinement systems. I was telling him how my father was persuaded to start a similar operation with registered Hamshires and black baldy cattle back in the early fifties. Dad almost bought an eighty acre farm west of Hymera, but mother outvoted the rest of us. Dads dream and mine were definitely not hers. I dreamed about that place or one like it for years… I then realized I was talking to myself. My kids had heard the story before and Karl was even less interested…nervously looking over at the kitchen door of the farmhouse.

I stopped speaking. Karl rather tensely announced "it's best we go in now." He led us up to a side entrance to their sunroom. Looking a bit stricken, he said, "It's just that Barb gits het up sometimes making Sunday dinner and all."

As we sat down in the sunroom, Bethany politely asked if she could help Barbara in the kitchen. Before Karl could reply, we heard a shriek of surprised recognition,

"Dang You Tom! You know I don't want you in here!"

The shriek came from the kitchen or farther in the house but was continuing fast toward us... when we glanced through the double windows to see Barb charging toward us with a broom held aslant and flailing ahead she threatened, "Git out, git out! Git out of here Tom!"

As she rounded the corner to us, I stood. The children ran to grasp my pockets and pant leg as she whirred... not at us but past us broom banging the door and a yowling ginger colored Tom cat out the door.

We weren't under attack but we'd sure witnessed one. Barbara wasn't 'having kittens' she just wasn't having this yeller Tom Cat in her kitchen. She apologized profusely, scolding Karl for not sitting us in the front parlor.

"I didn't know you were all out here. That Tom, that

Tom Cat will be the death of me yet. We raised him from a kitten. He's always where he shouldn't be. Why last year he almost got caught in Karl's cider press."

The children laughed first, then Barbara, Karl and me. Karl grinned too much and didn't say enough. I think he enjoyed seeing me startled. A funny one upmanship. It seemed to give him an imagined edge. He presumed it gave him the upper hand somehow. Maybe the whip hand.

After dinner, which was fair and served with big carving knives; baked chicken never greasy enough for me but there was lemonade, a great salad and lovely mashed potatoes. We, that is, "us men" as Eliot said went out for a constitutional while Bethany helped Barbara fix the whipped cream for strawberry short cake.

Karl showed us his cider press. "That yeller Tom Cat won't escape next time," he said. It sounded cruel instead of funny... the way he said it. And I think he meant it so.

Ever darker cloudbanks.

DON'T KNOW JACK SCHMITT

Not once but twice Karl Mannheim had mentioned Jack Schmitt. First he had referred to him with that sinister twinkle as a good...*kinda* ol' boy. Jack was in his mid-thirties. While Karl sat beside Barbara he spoke of Jack more conventionally as "A fine young man." Barbara said they'd "kinda raised him; sponsoring him in 4H and taking him to church on Sunday. Seeing that he wuz baptized and saived. His own family...his parents ran with a rough neck crowd", she said. "He wuz sweet on our daughter Gail, for a while and...they've remained friends. He married Gracie Harris, a girl we definitely approve of."

Barbara and Karl both encouraged me to drop in on Jack. I asked why Jack does not bring his wife and children to church? He always attends alone sitting with the Mannheims or Logans. Barbara excused herself from table and Karl shook his head saying, "there's just been so much talk."

I stopped in on Jack an evening later that week. He was working in his garage. Two small children played at his feet. Seeing me walk toward them across the lawn, Gracie appeared out of nowhere scooped up the children and disappeared into the house.

Jack did not seem alarmed but continued concentrating on a small engine at his work bench.

"Evening Jack."

"Greetings Preacher, what can we do for you?"

"Just stopped by...Barbara and Karl thought a Pastoral call ... would be OK with you."

"Yeah, I heered you ate dinner there after church. With all the talk, weren't you afraid we'd pizen ya."

"I reckoned on trusting the Mannheims regarding poison if they could trust me with those big carving knives."

"Yessir I wuz surprised to hear it."

"Why surprised Jack,? Like you and Gracie they are part of our church congregation."

"Just how do you figure that, Preacher?"

"You are all on our membership roster."

"You keep a roster?"

I said nothing…hoping some silence would pressure an explanation.

"Yuh know" he began, "kittens can be in the oven that don't mean they belong there."

I smiled, "That's a great old saying but I don't think you've got it quite right."

"How's zat?"

"It's an olde saying but I heard it best from Malcom X. He would say, 'Kittens can be born in the oven but that don't make e'm biscuits.' About black people being enslaved, then released into white racist society."

He smiled a little, saying "Better yet. That saying just suits me. I hear yore a friend of Wayne Trapp."

"He shoes my horses."

"He's trash!"

"I dunno. He's a good horseshoer and bird dog trainer."

"I oughta know," he said now fiercely. "I was born to trash.

My folks were adultrous all around…would divorce and then remarry. Neither could keep a job or stay sober. Both used drugs and never paid their bills. Sat on their ass and got welfare money to squander and waste. And you Methodists are for that…for coddling the welfare addicts. Pro-choice abortion for kids like me they conceive and decide to cancel. My mom had multiple abortions. Many's the time…"

His voice broke, almost emitting a sob. Jack Schmitt's very character had become a dark cloudbank but he was also plagued by the same within himself. Our conversation reminded me of Clancy Sigal's "Short Talk With A Fascist Beast" in the collection 'Man Alone' by the Josephsons.[1]

"You're doubly wrong," I tried to say gently. "The Christian Church whether Methodist, Catholic, or Evangelical Brethren must care about *not* coddle the poor. And especially the poor according to Jesus 'the least of our brethren' you just described stuck in sin as well as

1   'Man Alone': 1961essays on alienation collected by Mary and Joseph Josephson.

poverty. But the only welfare system I ever saw that worked was in the Soviet Union where employment was constitutionally guaranteed under the biblical aegis, 'he who does not work does not eat.' Employment...work there a constitutional right. Sin... especially the sins of exploitation and sloth causes poverty and poverty causes sin. By the love of Christ both should be eradicated."

Jack talked. He talked on and on... about "upper class liberal elites who look down their nose at us common country people. You modern Methodist Preachers think we're all a bunch of hicks. You all have a lot of education, but that's just 'book learnin' to speak in ways that's hard for us rednecks to understand."

"Wow" I said settling into a folding chair. "I'm not sure where you get all this. I think some of it is true. But you need to rifle in on reality better; no scatter shots around. You'll injure the wrong people."

"Like you for instance?"

"Yeah, like me. I'm probably the "reddest" redneck you know... and the best educated. I've gone to good schools, studied hard, read good thinkers and always listened to serious intelligent people especially the older ones. I have no truck with silliness, yappers, big shots, or bad women. I care about the good book, good faith and God's grace to good people—applying 'book learnin' to the practical common work sense I got from my parents and family. There are degenerate and shallow city slickers and bigoted rubes in every church around, but there are good people too...with God's grace the bad and the good can get better. You can't condemn wholesale what you've only experienced retail.

"You're good Preacher..." he sounded cynical. "We've had Methodist preachers who've resisted before. In time they all leave and go back to where they come from."

Interrupting "Well Father Schmitt I respect you as head of your family which apparently you see some need to protect. But you'd best respect mine. We come from here and we're not going anywhere! What is it you want for our church in Birch Lane?"

"There ya go claiming it already as part of your own after you been here a few months."

"What is it you want for the Church, son?"

"We want to own it and run it ourselves. A Community Church run by its own people not by any bishops, bureaucrats or uppity preachers." (A view not far from my own anti-clericalism.)

"Have I been uppity to you or anyone in the Church?"

"No, not yet."

"My job is to pastor...to shepherd the flock. That includes its discipline. Anyone I may have to discipline...it will be out of active concern, that is, love for them, the church, and our shared faith. It won't be uppityness–."

"So you say...and threaten?"

"So I say and promise!"

At church when I had tried to speak with Jack he would just grunt commonplaces. Underneath the commonplaces were these vapid complaints, personal without substance; a kind of terrorists soap opera.

The dull and hoary ambience exuded by these characters and their cornball complaints; the utter banality of it I began to experience as evil incarnate. Yes, the evil of banality! As noted, Hannah Arendt saw the banality of evil in Eichmann, the good soldier and concentration camp guard. I see the evil in banality itself. Banality requires near total divertissement and distractedness in unconscious repression of the depth charged concerns of every human heart. The mind not taking charge, responsibility or even recognition of the deeper currents of being which then erupt pathologically.

I tried again.

"Why accuse me of being pro-abortion or against a community church? You, the Mannheims and Logans, the previous Brethren would not get a majority vote on any question now. Why not try to be respectfully persuasive on these matters instead of so hatefully accusing and rejecting."

"You bleeve in abortion? Are you as they say pro-choice or pro-life?", he smirkingly asked.

"I am precisely and militantly anti-choice. Idolatry of choices people substitute for the only freedom God cares about... the freedom to do His will."

"The constitution...", he started.

I finished "concerns entitlement and property. Stick with–the–

Bible son. Agape. Cooperation. I was raised in the Catholic Church whose theology not unlike the Calvinist theology of the Reformed Presbyterians systematically refutes the liberal sop of bourgeois abortionist feminism in most of the mainstream Protestant Churches."

"Ed Logan says Cathlics are agin abortion only because the Hierarchy tells e'm so. It's not from their hearts response to Gods word."

"I know Communists against abortion. Quakers and Amish, Baptists and Mennonites, some Methodists and Campbellites. Only God knows their motivation and that should be good enough for you, Jack."

"But it's just their own positions not that of their church or organization... right?"

"Who cares?! You just said it should be a heartfelt conviction. Look....give a person credit for taking a moral position. If it becomes an organizational or collective church position...all the more. I worked for years with the Catholic Charities program 'Birthright' where volunteers not only counseled women with troubled pregnancies to bring their unborn child to term but also raised money to help them care for the new born or helped them see the child adopted to a good home if they were unable to properly care for the babe. These people had the advantage of a heartfelt conviction and their Churches formal position supporting them."

"Yeah, yeah, but which came first?!"

"Does it matter Jack!? No, no I guess you're right we can analyze it that way. The church existed before the people were born so it came first. But that's the same with all of us."

"How ju figger that?"

"Well, which came first... Gods word in the bible or Gods word in the church?"

"Huh !...?"

"Historically, which came first the Bible or the Church?"

"The Holy Bible, of course!", he answered militantly.

"You'd be wrong Brother Schmitt. The Church existed for a long time before the Church convened councils selecting and not accepting certain books and manuscripts in circulation. The early Christian Church collected these books up and men made the decision to call it the bible and make it the official word, the words of God."

I went on…

"The word abortion does not appear in the bible. The decision for it or agin it is man–woman–human interpretation."

He blurted, "It says in the Ten Commandments 'Thou shall not kill!'"

"You a pacifist or a vegetarian Jack? You buy and cook steer killed beef at the store every week don't you? You believe in lethal force defending yourself and your family? Just wars? The American Revolution throwing out the Brits? The war of the rebellion defeating the southern slavers? Quakers and Amish interpret this Commandment against any and all violence. I admire them but don't agree with them. But yours, Ed Logan and my interpretation against abortion is a man made one."

"Then how do you interpret?"

"You think… historically and contextually. Before the Jews, before Christian and Islamic influence the entire pagan world practiced primitive abortions and infanticide."

"Infanta whut?"

"Infanticide. Another word that's not in the bible. Leaving unwanted infants to die on the hillside. Usually baby girls. They left millions of e'm to the pagan Spirits and the vultures."

"Jews, Christians, and Muslims…the people of the Book…interpreted the God of holy scripture to forbid such murderous injustice; some say causing our global population problems. The point is that intelligent, prayerful, God fearing people didn't need a cookbook bible telling them exactly what to do. Sola scriptura is the Lutheran limit. Otterbein and Wesley maybe the Pope agree that the triune authority for Christian conscience is (1) Church tradition; His story (2) Holy Scripture and (3) interpretive reasonable thinking."

"You not agin a Community church?"

"No. I am agin a Community church not connecting with other community Churches. Would you be against a community church connecting with others to say…better oppose the aborting of unborn infants?"

"No, no I guess you got me there", he said.

"That's what Bishops and Presbyteries are for… and to provide pastors pay, so the Preacher and the preaching don't become private property of the churches membership. So the people get sermons they need not just the ones they want."

"Is that what yore tryin to do? Gimme an example."

"The best example I can think of is back in '61. The Civil Rights Conflicts, especially in the south was on the NEWS every night. Most of my (Terre Haute) city's restaurants were privately owned and as segregated as down south. People were divided and confused. The churches were as silent as they were segregated. Not worrying about his paycheck or job security Pastor Winterhalter at St. Benedicts began his Sunday sermon with the words "Segregation is a God Damned thing; a God damned *sin*!"

"He swore like that, right from the pulpit?"

"Yes he did. God bless him. Would you like to hear a sermon that began 'Abortion is a God Damned thing'?"

Jack Schmidt broke into laughter saying, "So's segregation and racism. I work with some black guys at the clay plant. Good church going Christian people."

I was pleased and surprised to hear him say it. His generational branch breaking off from the racist trunk of the tree. Probably from the anti-racist bias of the media. Just as previous decades of media silence had sealed down home racism, the opposite was significantly healing the country. Propaganda works.

I remember thinking, no way Ed Logan can conserve this young man as a hateful ideologue. We parted on good terms with each other. More smiles than suspicions. Even Gracie and the kids smiled from the window when I waved good-bye.

XXXIII

Wesley's Horse and the Warfarin Wedding

I'd been speaking every week or so with Prester John. He'd counseled sternness with the opposition minority at Birch Lane. When he called last night he asked, "What color was John Wesley's horse?" Replying I didn't know incited John to explain "Hey I know at least one thing about horses more than you. I've just read he rode a black mare, which became the model for a century of circuit riders. We're celebrating the centennial of circuit riders along the west fork of the White River this month. We'd like you to ride in on one of your black mares costumed as the frontier circuit rider John Wesley. We'd like to do it Sunday week[1] in the evening. You could issue a brief homily, shake hands with everyone, especially the children and ride off into the sunset across the river bridge. One of the Abrill boys has a movie camera and he'll film the whole thing...The autumn foliage will be out, and we should have a lot of visitors. I've sure been busy T." he said. "I'm marrying someone this Sunday whom you know."

"Whozat?" I wondered.

"Jim Warfarin, an ex-catholic like you."

Annoyed at the ex-catholic bit, I responded,

"No ex, John. I'm that part of the Reformation that still considers itself Catholic; like John Wesley after Ireland."

"Sorry T. I should have described you as former Roman Catholic Operative. That sound better?"

"It do" I joshed. "But what about Jim Warfarin? Hey...he's a married man with eight kids!"

"Not now. He divorced over a year ago. He's marrying Delilah Thompson Sunday. It's not til 3pm. Maybe you could come."

"I'll not be there John. You must know I don't approve. Ol' Delilah over the hill was his neighborly romp in the hay, years ago when I was marriage and family counseling his whole brood. She was married

---

1   Sunday week': Hoosier for 'a week from Sunday'

then too...I think to an over the road trucker."

"I think he really loves her...Tom. I..."

"What the Sam Hill does that have to do with anything! We're talkin bout the sacrament of Christian Marriage they've both been violating for years. I don't know the trucker but I know the Warfarin mother and children. I am sure they are traumatized. Their wounds now further plundered by John Wesley's church rewarding adultery and home wrecking with a church sanctioned marriage ceremony."

"I'm sorry you feel that way..."

"Feel! feel! Indulging feelings is what brought on your divorce, mine and Ol' Warfarin's. Emotional sentiments of the heart and hard on whose very boundlessness has unleashed the contemporary flood of trauma and misery. His children used to ride with me to mass at Saint Judes, his wife slaving away in their unfinished basement making a big Sunday supper while Ol' Jim popped over the hill for a quickie at Delilah's. Tell you what - why don't I ride my black mare into this Warfarin Wedding disguised as John Wesley or Reverend Morgan and object to the lot; the entire execrable egregious blasphemy!!"

A whole lot of silence followed. John was too taken aback, and I was too out of breath to say much. Finally John said,

"I think we'd do better to talk about the movies."

John and I had always enjoyed conversation and moral analysis of popular films. Reminding him I'd said...

" 'From Butterfield 8' in 1960 to 'The French Lieutenant's Woman' in 1981 American film had progressively (as Lincoln Steffens' prophesied) both caused and reflected popular behavior. Especially adulterous behavior which we were called to take a stand against and fight. Not just being perpetually plaintive as the perfidious plaintiffs march over us...but to resist them. It is the grand resistance of our time."

"I saw 'Butterfield 8' on T.V. last week," he said. "Did you catch it?"

"Yes, I did."

"Seemed dated, that is outdated somehow."

"Sure it did. Over two decades old. No one is now touched by a John O'Hara story of ill reputes. Lawrence Harvey's home wrecked because he couldn't keep his heart separate from his camp following courtesans. The Academy Award scarlet womans performance not tragically believable in Elizabeth Taylor's death because the heaviness of such feelings now so commonplace..."

"I thought the uses of Eddie Fisher were eerie. Like some cinematic preview of what he was going to get. But, Thomas...torn souls become murderous when they resist tragedy, because tragedy is insoluble. Doesn't your soul need a rest... wouldn't you like to stop fighting? If you could find a new love, a new wife like I have..."

He continued for some time describing the beauty and peace he found in his new wife. I didn't wish to argue. He had no wounded unhappy children. Not really listening to John I found myself thinking about how celibacy was probably the preferred lot and sacrifice for a Minister. I also thought of the Saudi Revolutionaries and Salafis I had known literally selling out their souls jihadic struggle for the peace of princely homes and new wives. I wondered if it was less traumatic if the wives were concurrent rather than sequential. Another point for Einstein's sense of time, that is to say it [time] exists so everything doesn't happen at once.

In splendid feminine intelligence, Hannah Arendt has written "... the heart begins to beat properly only when it has been broken or is being torn in conflict, but this is a truth which cannot prevail outside the life of the soul and within the realm of human affairs."[1] Arrant – Arendt wisdom! Sometimes life doesn't even budge for truths within the soul. Or, as the Amish say, "One shouldn't expect heaven on earth."

"Moreover", Hannah Arendt continues[2] "to drag the dark and hidden issues of the heart into the light of day can only result in an open and blatant manifestation of those acts whose very nature makes them seek the protection of darkness."

There was no integrity, no consistent ideology, let alone theology in the so-called brethren opposition. Nor could I see much in the Methodist establishment they were opposing. There seemed a kind of Nietzschean weariness about both. A "weariness that wants to reach the ultimate with one fatal leap"; "a weariness that does not want

1   Hannah Arendt "On Revolution" Chapter 2 'The Social Question'.
2   IBIB

to want anymore." An infectious weariness that creates [false] gods and [fantastic] other worlds; "a coefficient of resistance."[1] Previous Pastors, the Superintendent, or the Bishop should have resolved these differences when they were recognizable issues years ago.

I would ride my black mare and be the archetypal circuit rider. I would be the Reverend Mr. Black for my children. And Logan could howl I was wasting my time and their resources with the Methodists. Tough.

The circuit rider Sunday was just prior to Rosh Hashanah. Between the Jewish New Year in late September and the Islamic New Year in early November we had a very crowded Christian calendar.

Due to her conference affairs and schedules, the children's mother asked we agree on visitation dates different than the Indiana Guidelines.

She wanted to be "free" on Saturday nights and Sunday mornings. I "could have the children for church every Sunday morning, Saturday afternoon and evening." She would have them every Friday evening and Saturday morning. I agreed immediately. The kids could be on the farm every weekend and with me in church on Sundays. The agreement was good for me. I didn't want to think about how it might be good for her.

On the "circuit rider" Sunday evening I rode home on the mare ahead of the church bus which carried Beth and El. The church bus caught up with me on Gloryville Road at the beginning of the flats about one hundred yards from the old iron bridge.

Bob Loots was driving the bus and he slowed to greet the circuit rider as all the kids hollered for a horse race. We started together, the bus on the graveled road, me and my mare on the grassy shoulder. I gave Glory the spurs and she quickly jumped out, taking the lead which we held all the way to the bridge.

The children were cheering and ol' Bob laughed as he stopped safely on the west side of the bridge. He stopped a lot more safely and easily than I did as Glory had her blood up, was home geared and wanted to fly across the bridge. I dismounted, led her across the bridge, remounted, and had her walk slowly while talking with Bob as

---

1   "coefficient of resistance" Jean Paul Sarte 'Search for a Method'

he drove slowly up to our front gate.

Inside the gate I helped Bethany and Eliot mount and we talked and laughed across the meadow, all the way up the hill to the barn. The three of us rubbed Glory down and took turns walking her out before releasing her back to pasture.

First of the week Rose Vincent phoned to remind me next Sunday was Missionary Sunday. That is, the Sunday sermon pulpit was given to a visiting missionary to speak of mission work and be given the entire Sunday collection for that work. There were several "Missionary Societies" in, out, and around mainstream Protestant and Evangelical denominations. The Mission chosen and all the arrangements for the Missionary's visit was the responsibility of the Adult Missionary Sunday School Class.

"You recall that Ed Logan is chairman and teacher of that class. He's made the arrangements for a Missionary Perkins to stay at their home Saturday and Sunday evening."

"Where is Perkins missionary field?" I asked.

"I dunno but I think Ruth said it was France."

"....France?!" Not many pagan babies to save in France, I thought and almost said.

"Another thing...", Rose added. "Ruth Leslie traditionally on Missionary Sunday passes out a questionnaire to the congregation and guests for them to evaluate our church, our services, and our..."

"Don't tell me", I interrupted ". . our Pastor!"

"Yes", she nervously laughed. "They (the ubiquitous they) usually say cruel things but it gives us the chance to say nice things."

"How long has this tradition traditionally occurred?"

"Ever since Ed has taught the Adult Missionary Class. I'd say about ten years."

"Well..." I thought and said, "I'd rather they evaluate than evade. Evading issues, any substantive issue, if they have any I'd like to know."

"You know..." Rose advised "it's mainly their memories...personal and emotional."

"I know..."

Mission Sunday

After the first hymn I welcomed the many guests and introduced Ruth Leslie who passed out "the questionnaire" and introduced Carl Perkins, "the Missionary", who sat way in the back with Ed Logan. Ed stayed in the back. Carl Perkins came forward as Ruth Leslie described him as "a real man of God who spent all Saturday with us and is prepared to tell us all the truth about many things."

Carl was a fat man by anyone's count. Squeezed into an expensive suit, his neck laying over his collar from the front and both sides. Worse…he had a squeaky little voice one couldn't imagine trusting, let alone coughing up contributions.

I expected some proselytizing against the priest-ridden and/or atheist French. I was prepared to try and give some critical support to his message. I was not prepared for an anti-Catholic anti-communist non message.

"In America", he began "We have our God-given freedom from our forefathers. In France they don't have that. Our American Revolution was led by men of God and Property. The French Guillotined and bloody revolution was led by rabble and violence. They can be an irrational and violent people. Massacring the saintly protestant Huguenots throughout the country; making a saint out of a mental health case, encouraging people to worship a cross-dressing nineteen-year-old Joan of Arc. Heating up peoples hatred to establish the first Communist Party, the Paris, France Commune. The worst of both worlds combining now with priests who work for a living and Preach Communism. (The French worker priests!)

Into this queer quagmire we have delivered the calm of the gospel from America. Many of our converts look to the United States for our Freedom and our bible Christianity. Why I think our ministry does more for America than the Embassy diplomats." And on and on ad nauseum. Elmer Gantry without the wit of Sinclair Lewis.

When it ended, there were few questions. Perkins was not interested in questions. He was interested in the collection. As people filed downstairs for Sunday School classes Ruth Leslie and Perkins carefully counted the take; her ringed fingers clicking in the collection plate. She had passed over to me the stack of returned questionnaires to read.

Most of the friendly comments were signed. Most of the critical ones…unsigned. The latter more outrageously amusing than abusing. There were several that complained I dress "too severely". One said they didn't like my Quaker looking boots?? But some were *finally*… substantive. They were alarmed I was not preaching from the 'King James Word of God'. One accused me of Preaching from a French Catholic Bible.[1] That one I figured was Ed Logans via Perkins identification of my Jerusalem Bible. I frequently hand carried the large Liverpool edition of the Jerusalem Bible to the pulpit with a zippered bound King James translation. I'd read from both.

Finally the so-called opposition engaged a substantive issue. The authority and translations of holy scripture. I could speak to that objectively, reasonably without the fearful tread of backbiting and calumny. I looked forward to preparing next Sundays sermon.

THE MASONIC GRIP

At the next Wednesday prayer meeting Tom Geary attended. He came alone without his wife or family. After many intercessory prayers for the community, I read from the Epistles, the second letter from Paul to Timothy.

I advised those present as Paul did Timothy "to think through what is said and the Lord will show you how to understand it all." That the time is come when "far from being content with sound teaching some people will be avid for the latest novelty and collect themselves a whole series of teachings according to their own tastes; turning away from the truth to fables and false notions." (2 Timothy 3-4)

Paul then identifies a coppersmith named Alexander who has caused him great harm. Noting the Lord will repay Alexander for his works, but that all should be "on guard against him because he has

---

1   The Jerusalem Bible: a French translation indeed in 1956 by the Dominican Biblical School in Jerusalem; La Bible de Jérusalem was translated directly from Hebrew and Aramaic sources when possible rather than from the secondary Greek translations…but into French…then in 1966 into English from the French by Christ's College in Liverpool and Upholland college in Lancashire.

been bitterly contesting everything that we say." (2 Timothy 15)

"Like Paul", I said we can count on the Lord to stand with us, "strengthen and deliver us from false notions and bitter gossip so that Gods whole message might be preached for all to hear."

At that point Tom Geary rather abruptly stood and motioned me forward. I turned the meeting over to Nell Mayrose and followed Geary over to the side where we could speak privately.

More than a bit edgy he mumbled something about, "a Coppersmith...I think we've got our own Coppersmith." Then he asked, "Preacher was your Dad a Mason?"

"Yessir" I answered. "A Past Master of Blue Lodge 86 in Terre Haute. A Scottish Rite man."

"I knew it!", he smiled. "I'd heard it."

"What...?"

"Well, right after Church Sunday, Ed Logan comes up and gives me the grip, saying that it is my duty as a Mason to close ranks with him and run you off — away out of here. I came tonight to tell you but I wasn't one hundred percent sure until you read that scripture about bitter gossip and the Coppersmith."

"That's what scriptures are for Tom Geary. They are given to us inspired by God, and are 'profitable for doctrine, for reproof, for correction and for instruction in righteousness'. (2 Timothy 16) Paul says it is how as men of God 'we may be complete and thoroughly equipped for' every good work. Why in the bowels of hell does Ed Logan think I should be run off?"

"He says...Ed says", Tom Geary looked down slightly embarrassed "that you have been sent here as an agent of Rome and as an agent of Moscow." Then with a grin, "He says you have been sent here by Rome and Moscow to take over Birch Lane Church."

"Do you think he really believes that?"

"He says he got it on very sound authority."

"Did he mention exactly how he intended to run me off?"

Now laughing a little, "No but he seems determined... gives me the creeps. I think he might be dangerous Preacher. I wanted to warn you about him."

"Not to worry. I'll call on him at his home this week. Thank you for your concern and I'd appreciate your prayers in this."

"You bet! You can count on me Preacher."

Cleaning up after the Prayer Meeting, I looked into the Sunday School classrooms. In Ed Logan's Adult Missionary classroom there were many stacks of literature arranged as if to be disseminated. Some were from Reverend Perkins Ministry. Most were Chick Young cartoons, that is, comic book form eight page religious porn. They reminded me of those vulgar 'eight page bibles' as they were called of sex porn passed out to boys from under the counter by gas station attendants back in the fifties. This equally vulgar religious porn by Chick Young was rabidly and hatefully anti-Catholic.

I scooped it all up in a cardboard box and put it permanently out of circulation.

On Sunday, I preached against 'know nothing *ism*' and the means to forgiveness through conviction. The secretive-nativist 'U.S. Know Nothing' political party was spawned in 1850's Indiana and dominates a certain mentality to this day.

Residents of many regions brag about what they claim they know. Indiana has Hoosier residents who aggressively brag about what they don't know. "I don't know nothing 'bout that', still the phrase rudely ending too many Hoosier conversations. The phrase itself and the aggressive ignorance behind it historically linked to the racist, anti-catholic, anti-semitic, prohibitionist, xenophobic "Know Nothings."

"Christian polity requires a tolerance toward the views of all of God's children. Forgive me" I confessed, "if I am not at all broad minded when it comes to Klu Kluxers, Nazis, and Know Nothings. Their propaganda will not be tolerated in our Church as long as I am Pastor.

After Prayer Meeting Wednesday I found a box full of anti-Catholic hate literature. I have removed it to oblivion. In the future all literature brought into the church must be approved by the Pastor and/ or his delegates. Equally so with missionaries visiting our Church. In all due respect to Reverend Perkins ministry I thought some of his remarks were erroneous, confusing and disrespectful.

It is disrespectful to the people of France and to those of you with French family names to infer and generalize the way he did."

"Hear, hear," Gene Vincent stomped.

I continued, "The people of France are no more this way or that, than any other people. Their Revolution of (1789-99) accomplished great things as well as violent tragedies. The Paris Commune of 1791 established a cooperative authority of the working class for the first time in history. It was destroyed by the terror and reaction that followed. The French Revolution of 1789-99 had nothing to do with the St.Bartholomew Massacre of Huguenots which was in 1572 or Joan of Arc who lived between 1412-1431. These events separate by two hundred and three hundred years. It is insulting to demean Joan of Arc who the people of France and others throughout the world venerate as a saintly young woman and military hero who helped drive the Brits out of France just a Americans, Asians, and Africans have all had to do. And as far as the French Worker Priests are concerned… American ministers have a similar tradition. You've heard us called tentmakers like St. Paul who also worked for a living. I'm a livestock farmer as well as your Pastor. Others are auto mechanics and school teachers. It's a good tradition.

Now about that questionnaire…tradition or not. I was not properly consulted prior to its occurrence so that will not happen again. Some substantial issues were raised. I appreciate that but we don't need such a questionnaire to address them. As far as personal critiques and commentaries, that is, rank gossip will not be invited again or hinted such is formally approved. I am formally announcing today it is not approved. Whatever you think of my boots or anybody else's…keep it to yourself. It's none of your business.

As to preaching from the word of God. Let's clear up the confusion." I held up the King James translation in my left hand and the Jerusalem translation in my right explaining their history and difference; approving of both. (I did not go into the royalist bias of the King James let alone his mischief of having the entire English speaking world address God, and the Messianic Jesus as if they were upper class henchmen of the English King, that is English…*Lords*.) "The revealed Word of God does not depend on any one translation", I concluded.

Old John Bought rose silently in the rear. "That is not the issue!", he declared solemnly.

"Please…" I invited him forward. He walked forward slowly. In his eighties he moved with dignity and gravitas. He examined my two bibles, then dramatically held his bible high and open for the congregation to see. "See the difference?" he croaked. "The Preacher is not preaching from the word of God! It is *not* delineated in his bibles."

Delineated? What the…!? I respectfully approached John. He pointed in his bible to what he was calling delineated. He was pointing to the words of Jesus the publisher had printed in red ink.

"God help us", I both prayed and spat "John do you really think these words are less sacred when printed in black ink?"

There was laughter from most of the congregation, but also a threatened undertow from some that I might be ridiculing John. "The old buzzard", I thought but did not say as he looked panicky toward Ruth –less who was emoting a great silent gush in his direction. I did say, "Sorry for this confusion John. I'm glad you are following my spoken words with the words in your bible. I assure you the words I read in black ink from the 1611 edition of the King James are the very same words in red and black ink in your bible. The 1966 edition of the Jerusalem Bible has changed 'not one jot or title' of meaning in God's word. It is a translation that more completely explains nuance of meaning in context and detail."

John shuffled back to his pew. Ruth-less stood to applaud but quickly sat down deciding her applause might be misconstrued for me.

Ed and Ruth Leslie always left church in a hurry. I got to their car first that day.

"I'd like to make a Pastoral call tomorrow evening if the two of you will be home."

Ed coldly replied, "Seven?"

"Seven pm", I answered. "Thank you, I look forward to it."

The children and I drove over the hill to Tim and Peggy Cottoms place. They had invited us to an early Sunday Dinner. They were all smiles greeting us and chattering about today's church service.

"You nailed e'm today?" Tim laughed. "And then old John demonstrated your point."

"I liked the way you were patient and respectful to the 'ol goat," Peggy added. "Really to all of them.. I think they'll give up their ghosts now."

"Even the Logans?", I wondered.

"Not Ed Logan!", Tim rejoined. "He's another case, another character all together."

"I'm meeting with him… with them tomorrow. We have it appointed. I'm making a Pastoral call at seven pm."

"Whew. I dunno. Be careful," Tim warned.

"The traditional method of correction would be to follow my Pastoral call with a return call of elders or reps of the church in addition to myself. And thirdly a call from the Supervisor or Bishop himself. That is, before expulsion…"

"Expulsion?!", they fearfully both wondered aloud.

"If Monday doesn't work, will you and Gene Vincent accompany me to the Logans for a Congregational correction?"

"No way!", Peggy almost shouted, more directly at Tim, than at me. "Rose won't let Gene go either, I'm sure! They've been at this for decades. People like that don't change. They just get more so and that Ed Logan is mean and dangerous!"

"Easy Peg," Tim calmed his wife and said to me, "Let's have the Vincent's over after dinner. See what Gene and Rose think."

"He's telling people I am an agent of Rome and of Moscow, sent here to take over Birch Lane."

I then related the masonic grip story Tom Geary had told me.

"Unbelievable!", was Tim's reply.

"No, all too believable!", was Peggy's.

"The Logans deserve a chance to correct themselves. Otherwise I will pull, that is to say, purge their membership."

"Have you prayed about this, Tom?" Peggy asked with palpable…

fear.

"Yes Peggy, I have and I'll continue to…I am no one's agent here except my own understanding of the Gospel and the responsibility to teach, preach, and protect it. There are influences from Moscow and Rome imprinted in my soul. Also Terre Haute and Freedom, Morelos and Modesto, Berlin and Bloomington but Logan is attempting a red-baiting, catholic baiting pitch to arouse deeply entrenched bigotry to condemn. The biblical 'thou shall not judge' is more precisely translated 'thou shall not condemn'. We all have to evaluate."

"And you can count on our prayers at your back," Tim punctuated, with Peggy adding, "Backing you up."

Tim phoned the Vincents who joined us an hour later for sweet potato pie and coffee.

"I got the recipe down south," Peggy explained.

There was solidarity with the Vincents.

"It's the same old story," Rose spoke sadly.…"Except now we've got a Preacher who will stand up to them!", Gene directed toward me.

"Yes, finally" everyone seemed to agree a bit more daunted than dauntless.

This apprehension was viral and my children suffered a little from it. The Cottoms had encouraged Bethany to claim one of the weaned kittens among their half feral barn cats. Less confident than usual, Bethany timidly approached the kittens…shyly asking one… "would you like to be my friend?"

A black and white female; it did finally come to Bethany. She named it Judith. I wanted to call it Chary.

PART SIX:

NO FALTERING DIFFIDENCE

XXXIV

Monday a.m.: Lengthy phone conversations with —

Prester John: supported the procedure I was following in the Methodist Discipline i.e. 'cease and desist calumny or withdraw from officially in any way representing the church.' The organist position and Sunday School teacher position officially represent the Church.

Supervisor Stilmore: supported same but seemed more anxious about 'the property'. As in many of the Brethren becoming Methodist churches there was a lot of cloudy generalities about why who owned what and when. "There is precedent for property being seized and long term expensive litigation. We must pray", he said "that we not allow them to do anything illegal."

Jason De Vries: ardent as ever and always slightly amused he encouraged me to "peacefully purge the philistines and come on down to Florida. We'll get you a pulpit in the sunshine. I'll see to it."

"Florida sunshine is especially appealing when the Hoosier chill in October turns toward the dark night of November. Someday maybe I'll vacation and train two year old colts or greyhound pups in Ocala but you know I can't leave. My children and I cannot leave these environs… our farm." "That farm of yours", he said, "must be sumpthin'. I'd love to see it. Invite me for a holiday and I'll deliver cracking good reconciliation counseling to your ex. I know your heart bro and I would make it known to her. Quoting proverbs, I answered "The heart is deceitful above all things and beyond cure." I thanked him for the offer and later agreed to it. "Just pray for things tonight. OK?" — "OK!"

THE ORANGE HEART OF THIS HIBERNIAN
(Me mother use to say, "Irish need the church more than others. Outside the Church they go wild." Knowing more than a few feral

celts inside the church I paid mother little mind. Today I thought of mother's words.)

I arrived at the Logan's promptly at seven pm. Theirs was a modest cottage home on a corner double lot surrounded by crop ground. A white rock half circle drive nudged up close to their side porch where I parked. A soft light fell on the evenings neat appearance of the place.

Ed Logan greeted me at the door with a warm handshake and the first smile I'd ever seen on his face. Ruth Leslie too swept in from the kitchen with gracious smiles and words of welcome. In fact, both seemed the very soul of hospitality. This was going to be more complicated than I'd thought. Ed and I sat down on leather covered chairs in their den while Ruth asked what I'd like to drink as she returned to the kitchen. She then brought out big glasses of iced cola for her and Ed and served me a piping hot strong mug of black coffee. Too hot to drink, I sipped at it's edges.

"That's the way everybody says you like your coffee," she said.

"Yes mamm," I answered. Before I could ask after their daughter, Carol, they asked after my children.

"They're both fine. Bethany is excited about 4H next year. Karl Mannheim has been helpful advising me about a dairy goat project for her."

"Yes — , Karl and Barbara were both 4H leaders for their girls."

". . And how is your daughter Carol?" I asked. "I trust she has fully recovered from her hospital stay by now. I hadn't heard. ."

"Why she's just fine. Busy, busy. Her and her husband are building on an addition to their house. Two new bedrooms for little Ellen and Gerry." She fetched a picture frame of their grandchildren off an end table to show me.

"Two strong and healthy looking young 'uns", I commended the tow-headed grandchildren.

There followed a brief awkward silence as Ruth retreated to straddle the archway between the kitchen and narrow dining room. Ed remained smiling. His hospitable smile more apparently attached to his regular glower.

"What is your blue lodge, Ed?" I asked.

"Nineteen…in Terre Haute." He answered.

"Grotto?"

"Yes."

"My father was Past Master of Lodge 86."

"I know…" he said.

"Then where do you get off leaning on a fellow mason with a lie about your Pastor, my fathers son!"

Ruth lurched from her straddling into the den side of the dining room. Ed kept his cool, still smiling, but speaking from a deeper glowering place.

"There is no lying about it. I spoke truthfully about what I had been told."

"That I was an agent of Moscow and Rome sent here to overthrow Birch Lane?"

"Yes. And if you knew who had told us…"

I raised my left hand, "No matter. What matters is…do you really believe such a thing?"

Not glowering, but serious, he expressed, "Can't say I do and can't say I don't. But until I know different it is my responsibility to make this known."

"My dear Ed Logan. My fellow Irishman, you are dead wrong in this. You have your responsibility perversely upside down. Until you know different; until you know for certain about some ad hominem gossip it is your responsibility to *shut up* about it."

An undefined silence followed; not awkward, not hostile, just undefined.

Ed asked, "Did you or did you not give Roy Gossett Soviet literature?"

"I loaned Roy my favorite book on bees and apiculture by Naum Ioyrish, a Russian beekeeper. Its title is, I think "Bees and People."

"I know. I've seen your book. Roy showed it to me."

"Then you know it's a history of beekeeping down through the ages. The biology of bees and the curative properties of honey in nutrition and medicine."

"I know it's propaganda for the USSR and the Pope."

"The Pope...?"

"I just glanced through it. In its first pages it was already about the Pope and you know it!"

"I know the book well. I've read it and referred to it. The only references to a Pope I can think of is in the Introduction. I recall there's a report to Clement VII in Rome about the considerable harvest of honey in Russia; 'house' bees being passed down from one generation to the next. That would have been in the early sixteenth century Ed; the early 1520's. How far back does this conspiracy go?"

Another silence. Neither the Logans, nor me could think of what to say next. I finally said, "Hey guys, let's pray. Let's pray the prayer that Jesus taught us. I led them, "Our Father, Who Art In Heaven

Hallowed be thy Name, Thy Kingdom come

Thy will be done on earth, as it is in Heaven.

Give us this day our daily bread and

Forgive us our trespasses as we forgive

Those who've trespassed against us.

Lead us not into temptation, but deliver us

From evil. For thine art the Kingdom, the Power

and the Glory. Now and Forever.Amen

"I have always thought this prayer brings an atmosphere conducive to peace making. To what Jesus calls the Peace that passeth all understanding. Now, Brother and Sister Logan let's try to forgive each other and be Peacemakers. Please ask me anything about myself, my ministry, or our church. Ask or tell me anything and we'll try to think it through to Peace." Then for humor, "Even if it's papist properties of bolshevik beeswax."

Ruth started to speak. A cold look from Ed kept her quiet. Ed did speak, "All this changes nothing. We have been and will continue to do our Christian duty as we see it. And you will have to do the same."

Not exactly Iago, but close. This schemer had been here before. He would follow his duty requiring the Preacher to follow his. The resultant lines of conflict provoking a crisis where the Preacher would flee or be rescued away.

"Not this time!" I said. "I will not be run off! I will require you and Ruth to give me your word that you will cease and desist this backbiting gossip or I will terminate your membership."

I think Ed was preparing to say 'Can't do Preacher' with a bitter smile when he suddenly processed 'expulsion of membership'. The smile and all countenance of cool restraint was gone. Brakes off, the glower was back and volubly protesting, "Memb, Membership! Why we've been members of Birch Lane Church for Forty Years and you've been here barely four months! You can't do that."

"It's done! As non-members both of you are welcome to worship with us as guests anytime. However your position as Organist Ruth is now terminated as is Ed's teaching position at Sunday School. Good night."

I saw myself to the door as they yelled now, at each other. I had outrun his expectations. When you run at trouble instead of away from it you always gain ground. When you run away from trouble; trouble looks at you like a greyhound looks at a jackrabbit.

Tuesday and Wednesday I kept my support network well informed regarding the expulsion procedure. That Ed and Ruth Logans membership could be reinstated at any time if they would simply agree to cease the libelous gossip. Reverend Stilmore sent them an official letter saying the same. I shared copies of Stilmore's letter to the Vincents and Cottoms. Wednesday eve I read it aloud to the Prayer Meeting.

The buzz was immediately more sympathetic, indeed, more fearful for me. I did not assess the situation as over. The Logans were bound to up the ante. Ed from way back, ol' Ruth-less right in your face, but... perimeters were clearly drawn, consequence in the hands of fate...of His Providence.

The maximum goal would be exorcism of all the larcenous ghosts. The Logans reinstated after their inevitable and hopefully unsuccessful storm. Peace then...within respectful parameters.

Stay Left – Keep Right

"On the way back to God's country... Keep to the main-traveled road till you come to a branch leading off – keep to the right" (Hamlin

Garlands "Main-Traveled Roads": stories of the Midlands of America.)

In "Shepherds Quake"[1] I quoted Jacques Maritain's "Peasant of the Garonne"[2] saying "There are no more dreadful revolutions, than revolutions of the left carried out by men of rightist temperament." As if, there were any other kind?! Lenin, Trotsky and Stalin. Fidel, Che, Peng Shu Tzi,[3] and Chou En Lai.

Flanking the foe just as war steeds of the Koran, leverage enemy virtue against its own vain incursions. Political power is then improved coming out of the more righteous gun. No mater whose gun. Levin, Tormey and Wald[4] et al broke the Barnesites neonatal narcissism with the Proletarian Tendency being defeated and Barnes then appropriating their direction. The dialectic striking fiery hooves toward future raids at dawn.

"The pure men of the Left detests being, always preferring in principle the words of Rousseau, 'what is not to what is'.[5] The pure man of the Right detests justice and charity, always preferring injustice to disorder.[6]" Uttering these words Maritain asserts his intention "to be neither right nor left in order to keep his sanity."

In my clinical opinion this illusion of neutrality is no safe harbor from insanity. Evil prowls especially on that undefined plain. Indeed I think all "exasperated complexes of secular ideals"; the rights free market, the liberals sexual freedom, and lukewarm centered self-righteousness can do nothing politically "but practice ruses in the service of passion".[7] However across the political spectrum those issues joined with Revelations from the Holy Land of Moses, Jesus, and Mohammed could strike terror toward the sins of caste class exploitation and sex-

---

1   "Shepherd Quake" from 'Glimpses' Part III Intinction.
2   "Peasant of the Garonne" (Logophobia in Our Cockeyed Times) by Jacques Maritain who also noted "there are no weaker governments than governments of the right run by leftist temperaments, e.g. (Louis XVI) I would add e.g. (Barack Obama)
3   Peng Shu Tzi: Leader of failed 1928 Chinese Revolution
4   Levin, Tormey and Wald: leading factionalists of the 'Proletarian Orientation Tendency'
5   "What is not is the only thing that is beautiful" (Jean Jacque Rousseau) "The real is never beautiful" (Jean Paul Sartre)
6   (Jacques Maritain) Peasant of the Garonne 'Left and Right'
7   IBID

ual immorality. One must be prayerfully both Left and Right. God's Grace merits no shades of gray. And then we can agree with Maritain that "there is no greater evil than to leave justice and charity without (moral and spiritual) witness"[1] as regards the temporal order itself.

Theologian Reinhold Niebuhr I quoted at the beginning wrote that "adequate spiritual guidance came only through Left political and Right religious convergence."[2] Niebuhr believed in the redemptive mission of the working class that stood apart from bourgeois decadence and idealism. An informed political and religious consciousness was required to redeem the total human enterprise.

In Graduate School I'd read his "The Contribution of Religion to Social Work" (1932). He urged social workers to learn from the vital political and religious consciousness of Communists who understand justice requires struggle demanding "beliefs so intense they could not be generated or confirmed by mere empirical reason." "Communist vitality alone however lacked the transcendent perspective" required from which it could itself be criticized and held accountable. Religion had to include struggle and necessary violence within its conception of love. Ideals were never enough. Bourgeois idealism substitutes longing and yearning for action and conduct.

In ultimate fraternal agreement Reinhold's younger brother Richard added, "I think liberal religion is thoroughly bad. It is first-aid to hypocrisy. It worships the God whose qualities are human qualities raised to the nth degree."[3] Sentimental and romantic; Our Father In Heaven as a permissive Suburban Daddy.

Beyond injustice mortal souls inevitably confront evil. While my faith in God has faltered at times…evidence of evil always sends me back to my knees. Seeing men and women succumb as St. Paul said to "the law in their members" that war against the law in their minds and soul requires more than an idealists or magical resource. It requires a moral interpretation of life which allows us to cope while in Paul's words still "perplexed, but not unto despair." Religion is the assurance

---

1   IBID
2   Moral man and Immoral Society 'Reinhold Niebuhr'
3   (Fraternal Correspondence) Reinhold Niebuhr Biography; Richard W. Fox

of God's Grace to console us in the face of brutal suffering and/or banal absurdities.

Conscience in consciousness. To paraphrase the Niebuhr brothers (Reinhold and Richard); Only an orthodox religious conscience of self-examination, penance and forgiveness that recognizes the roots of evil in the human soul and society can be trusted to discipline political and/or spiritual leadership. Only religion can provide an assurance of grace to make sense of the whole range of human experience; personal and political. Grace as both God's gift and as factual experience of morally disciplined human life.

Events required, I keep Right. I would keep to the right as an authoritarian Pastor protecting the Authority of the Church and preserving order in the congregation against the unbridled, unprincipled peddlers of disorder. The undisciplined, soon to be unrestrained opposition of Loganites, or Brucites or whatever they would call themselves had to be disciplined. I would have to be the man with the hammer.

And yet I was not eager for the task. I would do what was necessary … but as Trotsky taught his bolshevik cadre "it is important to distinguish between necessity and virtue." My primary responsibility to minister to all the people at Birch Lane Church included the task of loving them, especially when they weren't being lovable.

Of all the Priests and Ministers I knew…and I knew plenty… I liked a few. My favorite was Father George Rados, an Orthodox Priest, married, school teacher, A.F.T. union family man and Pastor at St. Georges Anitiochan Orthodox Church in Terre Haute. I worked with him on projects for the Palestinians. His Bishop had advised him on his first assignment "to love your people as Jesus did. From that they will learn to love God and each other."

All summer I had called on and cared about my peoples concerns. Their mortgages. Their wee children and adult children. Their marriages. Their frail and elderly parents and grandparents. Their jobs and/or lack of them. Their medical bills and school problems. Their gardens, crops and livestock. Their questions and doubts about their faith in life or facing death. And, then of course…the opposition. As.

Margaret Finzal the (MFY) Youth leader asked,

"Why do they stand out, against you so, Preacher?"

God love her she and her husband were working poor as Jobs oxen and she had such difficulty speaking. She tried to speak in sentences without the f. sound which she couldn't pronounce. I tried to explain the opposition. She looked sad in her skinny almost attractive manner. She said,

"That Karl Mannheim - if he had a brain halffff the size of his ffffat stomach he'd know better!"

I finished my poor supper thinking about all this. The cupboard would get bare toward the end of the week. I'd save up on groceries for the weekend when the children were with me. I walked out on the porch to look at the late afternoon cloudbanks turning Dunn colored as my Irish clans[1] name.

Geese were flying south and sidewise to the wind like pacers do. Someday I'd like to raise pacers and trotters for the races if the Methodists would quit lobbying parimutuel gambling tracks out of Indiana. All my life I'd heard old timers brag "Ingianny was to harness racing; Standardbred Pacers and Trotters what Kentucky and England were to running horses; Thoroughbred racing." They'd usually add… "and we don't need to rent a midget to ride them. Imagine a stuck up jockey boy on the back of Ingiannys Dan Patch or Single G!" At twenty I was in Europe for a year. No one I met knew of Indiana except horsemen in Paris, Stockholm, and the Hippodrome in Moscow.

Thinking of horses I decided to hitch Glory for an evening drive. It was a great way to enjoy the landscape and Glory needed calming on the road. On the farm every hour had its own tone and color. The Gloaming color of evening hours the most appealing. Roan light streamed through the trees then turned russet as a winter apple 'round the white eaves of the farm house.

Hitched to the buckboard Glory pulled across the creek branch by our house and on down the lane still dappled by disappearing cloud shadows. At the gate I could see, hear and feel the wind wandering through the field corn across the road. A dog barked away west on

1   Me maternal grandmother was Katey Dunn and her father Thomas Francis Dunn my namesake.

the wind and tree frogs began to call from the forest toward the rivers eastern basin. The west fork of the White River runs low down and deep under tangles and trouble there.

Hamlin Garland wrote of Midwestern landscapes as coulés ('Up the Coulé'). Our narrow valleys made by "post glacial floods cutting tremendous furrows in the prairie so deep that the undisturbed original levels rise as high ridges on either side of fertile meadows." The coulé or what Hoosiers and Kentuckians call hollers becoming gullies or arroyos out west. To live in such a place forms a kind of neural fortress in one's mind.[1] See "Vally Keep" in my 'Not of Our Time'.[2] Our Vally Keep, long and hazy blue-green; at its end veiled by clouds come to earth. No other climate or place claimed my heart like this valley veiled toward the river deep as the wellsprings of my life here.

Out the gate Glory snorted as Roy Gossett hailed us from his pickup truck. He parked beside our lane, got out, and stepped up and into the wagon seat beside me. He was carrying the Naum Ioyrish book on bees.

"I'm sorry about the book", he said.

"Naa…don't be…"

"Them Ruskys know a lot about bees" he continued, "I bragged about the book when I showed it to the Logans. They've acted real bad about it…"

I thanked him for returning the book and neither one of us said any more about it. I drove east into the veil of evening. We shared a silence not uncommon to country men and friends. Forget about the blues; any bit of melancholy was spartanly disciplined into quiet tones which forbid words.

It's part of what made the pulpit important. These people looked to the pulpit to provide the gift of words to accompany holy scripture. Words sacrally safe from indulgent complaint and brave enough to be uttered in Gods presence. Otherwise… shut up about it.

Sharing an evenings stillness with another heighten its splendor. The fall…falling sunlight had burnt frost off the brush that had grown

---

1   See Oliver Sacks "physiological universals" and nerve storms in his research, "Migraine" Vintage 1999.

2   "Not of Our time" Glenhill Press, 1989

up around the fence line. That left a singed kind of Chisholm plaid coloration. We could hear quail speak out their familiar name along the fencerows.

I'd purchased tuned sheep bells from Switzerland at the state fair. Hearing them along the northern slope while looking east way down the valley one could imagine those rivers the Holy Koran promise run beneath the ground of our being.

The cool breeze from forest and field accompanied our turning around west toward home. Roy Gossett rode along in the chuckling sound of the buckboard with me... without a single remark or question. We shared a reverence for the life around us.

Upon leaving, he said, "You know I'll have to side with them... somehow."

Nodding, "I know" I thought "Somehow on. Till nohow."[1]

We said goodnight.

Gossetts quiet reverence reminded me how I loved these people, the sweet, the sour, the bright and the stupid. Even the dangerous! They were the salt of the earth I'd known.

I remember discovering Hamlin Garland at the Readmore Bookstore on Seventh Street in Terre Haute. It was the summer of 1960. I was going away. His was one of the books my girlfriend Sharon gave to me. I'd never heard of him, but he wrote of my people; the yeomen working poor farmers of the Heartland.

Garland thought these free soil farmers of the Midlands invented the modern (i.e. Twentieth Century) 'American Idea'. 'To be their own boss', that is to not "haf to be under some other boss." His characters say, "I'm my own boss and I'm goin to stay my own boss if I haf to live on crackers an' wheat coffee to do it." An absolute overturn of all the ideas of nobility, special privilege, and social mobility spawned by big shots of the feudal past and capitalist present. Their consciousness had "pierced the conventions of society and declared as nil the laws of the land – laws that were survivals of hate and prejudice." They were "the native spring", "uttering the feeling that it is better to be an equal

---

1   From Samuel Beckett's "Westward Ho"

among peasants than a servant before nobles."[1]

Heartlanders despise the notion of class forces protecting the privileged living off the labor of others. They despise it so much they tend to bridle and deny its very existence.

Generation after generation; every decade of the twentieth century brave families worked, fought, and failed to save their farms. Garland describes them, "They are fighting a losing battle and must fight til God gives them furlough."[2]

One of our yeomens last century stand was the N.F.O. (National Farmers Organization) 'Withholding Actions' in the sixties and seventies. My Uncle Tom and I played a role in that.[3] In every Patrilineal and Matrilineal gene path, there is an ancestral trace of the land that was lost. And all that was lost with it. My kinsmen and women on both sides were militantly working class who still held on to a piece of a farm or yearned to get back to one. Grown up children who understand why Dorothy wanted to get back to the farm in Kansas.

These were the men and women of the Great Heartland Narrative. Right out of Hamlin Garlands midwestern 'Main Traveled Roads'. *Their* tragedies surrounded by the glories of God's creation as opposed to tragedy in town and city without comfort or Glory forcing refugees into each other's refuge. People forced into each other. Full of each other and talking about it. "Personality contagion",[4] interactional infections; the homocentric swamp of lost souls gossiping graves, that prate and sough away into oblivion.

I cooled Vally out and hung up the harness. Came inside, showered and turned in early. Propped up in bed I tried to read some. I'd been reading Samuel Beckett with some difficulty. I'd always considered the Absurdists too absurd, but Beckett's Irishness interested me. Literary critics had either bitched or praised him for his celebrations of indolence. The 'Beckett bums' and all that algorithmic euclidian tedium did not encourage me. Yet Beckett strove I think to describe

---

1   Hamlin Garland 'Under the Lion's Paw'
2   IBID
3   See Glimpses: 'Adagio for Uncle Tom'
4   "Personality Contagion": See Mary Baker Eddy's Christian 'Science and Health'

the relations and relationship bomb of sociograms imprisoned in urban asylums. In developing his art of "non relations"[1] escaping into silences and maximum minimalness he describes the pathological processes of personal contagion.

After our enjoyable silence Roy Gossett had said, "....I'll have to side with them somehow."

"The law of somehow"[2] involves the necessity of an unstable context

. . with its own laws of functioning. Recounting nothing but its own internality of *how* it needs to be. Creating a double bind that is always provisional and shaky. A precarious gap between modes of possibility. The worst might never happen but there is an acceptance that it might and/or part of the worst is only constrained by the inevitable shakiness of "somehow."

"Somehow on. Till nohow on."

"All of old. Nothing else ever. Ever tried. Ever failed.

No matter. Try again. Fail again. Fail better."[3]

Not failing to find the straight path, but failing on the straight path... an aesthetically moral path of failing. Beattitudinal! As in the comprehensive, beatitude, Blessed (or happy) are they who do the right thing and are not suprised when it fails. It still counts!

I think that's what Sam Beckett was getting at all along. Not the *stock punctilio* that his 'fail better' was to encourage the old try-try again-any more than Fantan O'Tooles tennis arms perversion that he was concelebrating disaster.

Beckett was exploring life's inevitable-unavoidable failures; to fail not miserably..but to fail aesthetically. That somewhere at the heart of the gales of grief and love there is a humiliating consciousness of peace in human frailty. Beckett did not have to fly far to find it. It's always thole bloody close for all of us.

Yet.. no referents for Samuel Beckett. No more twain relating or passive diminishing of possibilities. He proceedes from words to their

---

1   See Samuel Beckett and the Philosophical Image (Relation and non-relation) Anthony Ullman

2   IBID

3   Samuel Beckett's 'Westward Ho'

disappearance (in action?) aiming towards an end scene reckoning of everthing.

Pascale Casanova enumerates the three scenes or three "observing functions" of Michel Foucault to illustrate Beckett's endgame. "1) The models gaze as she is being painted, 2) the spectators contemplation of the painting *and* 3) the painter as he is composing the picture." The entire picture looking out at a scene for which it is itself the scene. The task of acceding from "somehow" to "nohow" is that proceeding from words to their disappearance and withdrawal of meaning. That is, "it is impossible not to know anything, but it is possible to know enough to know no knowing."[1]

I dunno. He describes the swamp but no clear trail out. Like Americas medical industry. All diagnosis. Effective treatment remotely accessible. Beckett comes from the 'Ascendancy'.[2] His art ascending somewhere beyond work and struggle.

Still…I hear he fought with the 'resistance', the French underground against Hitler's occupation. I guess that "Waiting for Godot" did not apply to the Nazis. He actively assisted their departure. I intended the same ("somehow") patiently waiting as long as possible, then acting accordingly and decisively as other options become not at all necessary ("nohow!")

---

1   Pascale Casanova 'Samuel Beckett – Anatomy of a Literary Revolution'.
2   Ascendancy: Protestant upper class, the British Empire imposed on Ireland.

XXXV

Donnybrook Fair
It surpasses Parnassus
they gape and they stare
at the free for all brawl
of the Donnybrook Fair

(18th Century Irish Ballad)

We got to church early Sunday morning. I unplugged the organ, recoiled the power cord, tucking it into the recessed shipping compartment low in its unvarnished backside. After carefully resealing its plastic cap I joined Beth and El on the front steps.

A cold nip in the air, I'd dressed the children in light winter coats. We stood side by side to greet everyone early or late. The Logans arrived on the dot punctual with aggressive smiles, shaking hands with everyone, including me like they were running for election. I followed them inside.

Inside they separated quickly. Ed darted to the left toward his regular place in the back pew. Ruth Leslie scurried toward the organ. There were fifty to sixty people already seated. Twenty more still coming in.

Ruth started playing the organ which made no sound. She became more exercised to no avail; her jewelry slapping upon the keyboard. She jumped up and ran around to find the organ unplugged with no power cord in sight. Flushed and feint she rebalanced enough to begin screaming in shrill ear splitting shrieks, "He's cut the cord!! He's cut the cord!! The preacher has cut the cord of our organ!!!"

The congregation froze in attention to this storm. Anna May ran to Ruth's side, helping her as if she were lame to limp-skip across the Sanctuary to the other piano. Anna May kept saying, "It's OK Ruth. It's OK. You can play my piano. You can play this one." And Ruth began plunking anew on that piano.

I approached respectfully, placed my right hand on the piano keys and said, "No Ruth. Please. The Church of Christ[1] gets by every Sunday singing acappella, we can manage today without the piano. Please take a seat with the congregation."

She immediately slammed the pianos' key cover down hard on my right hand. Ow! Knuckles cracked but did not break.[2] Jumping off the piano stool, with arms raised as if assaulted, she yelled "Gittim John" to a figure I barely glimpsed to my peripheral left. It was olde John Bought, his eighty-six-years staggering him toward me with fists flailing the air.

I stood stretched tall, my hands deep in my suit coat pockets and allowed Johns aged paws to feebly pound my chest. Bethany Kate ran up from the pews and solidly held her father's left arm. Olde John quickly exhausted himself and gasping for breath fell over backwards on the floor. Ruth began screaming again, "Now look what he's done! He's killed John!! The Preacher's killed John!!! He's killed John!"

I took the pulpit. "John has not been killed", I announced. "He's just been acting like a teenager and lost his breath. Brother Gene (I nodded to Gene Vincent grinning in disbelief) will drag him outside for some fresh air."

As Gene dragged olde John out the side door, I asked, "If Mr. Logan has nothing further to add or to cause we will proceed with our service." Ed sat quietly with his Cheshire cat expression. We sang our hymns acappella and prayed our prayers in unison, the congregation following acapriccio, i.e. at my pleasure in tempo with their Preachers performance. The Logans left before my sermon. No one else did. John Bought revived and went to his Sunday School class.

I preached about the laying on of hands to invoke the Holy Spirit and when forbidden otherwise between brethren (Acts 26:21).

Monday and Tuesday were quiet and uneventful. Wednesday was not.

---

1   "The Church of Christ": A denomination from an early Campbellite split. "The Church of Christ" denomination does not allow musical instruments in worship.
2   I broke that hand in the fifth grade hitting Henry Thornberg, a sixteen-year-old. I think she damn near rebroke it.

Wednesday Prayer Meeting

We were studying 'Acts of the Apostles'. I always tried to provide an exegetical — historical framework for the scripture we studied. 'Acts' and the 'Gospel of Mark' were originally two parts of one book about the history of the early Christian community. When around 150 AD Christians wanted the four Gospels bound in one codex, these two parts were separated. But, it is clear Mark wrote both.

A Syrian from Antioch, Mark accessed sources in Aramaic, Arabic Greek, Latin and several Semitisms of Hebrew. He recorded the Council of Jerusalem which reprieved all Christians from the minutiae of Mosaic Law save abstention from 1) Fornication — adultery, 2) anything polluted by idols, 3) blood and meat from cruelly slain animals. The Council decided by the Holy Spirit and it's elected delegates "not to saddle you with any burden beyond these essentials". (Acts 15:29)

The early Christian community was described as faithful to apostolic teaching, to each other, to the breaking of bread and to their prayers. "The faithful lived together and owned everything in common: they sold their goods and possessions sharing out the proceeds among themselves according to what each one needed." (Acts 2:44) "They went as a body to the Temple every day but met in their homes for the breaking of bread; sharing their food gladly and generously" (Acts 2:46)

Spiritual doctrine is carefully formulated using Jewish history to warn against the resisting of Grace. Imagined directions to the new converts reminded me of conversations with Clancy Sigal in 1960 London. "As you become more and more radicalized" (i.e. Socialist minded) he said, "You will become increasingly conscious of your relationship to and responsibility for society." God consciousness of His grace and wrath does not dodge but only deepens Clancy's message; determining the very hours of the day. Prayer related God consciousness! I tarried to explain my experience of it. Nell Mayrose and the older women knew exactly what I meant. Jane and Margaret and the younger ones weren't so sure.

The nuances of rearing children, getting along with a spouse, enduring custody court without murdering anyone … and the farm; the care of colts, cattle, and the lambing season — "sacred functions", James Hart[1] called them that "auger in tandem with the rest of your life… toward a healing continuity." Contradictions and problems of caring prayerfully solved in gently enhanced cognizance, extant of scale and aspect. Gods grace most accessible in those hours we register notice. In furloughs before and after work and struggle. Not instead of them. Tragedies of intelligent moral men and women rejecting God consciousness i.e., falling away from or failing to pray and cut off from Gods counsel and the subtle signals of Providence. As a rule single people are less interested than families. Just prior to marriage in 1965 and worn out with bachelor and bachelorette bolshevism I turned to the family life of Trotsky and Victor Serge, one of his most articulate followers. When Thermidoran police took Serge away from his family in 1927 his tearful seven-year-old son told him, "I'm not crying Dad because I'm afraid, it's because I'm angry."

The spirit of massive cheerleading chicanery overwhelmed all the 'believers in humanity' of post-revolutionary Russia. Serge's book "Memoirs of a Revolutionary" record this spiritual malaise as best he can with secular words.

The Thermidoran dis-ease of a morally degenerating revolution afflicted the humanist mind with immediate malignity. Cancers of confusion caused the bravest most intellectually and morally advanced politicals on earth to perform a kind of perverse bolshevik bushido. The feudal samurai code of loyalty and courage preferring death to dishonor expanded stupidly to preferring death and dishonor to secular socialist irrelevance. False confessions of dishonor in order to be executed *somehow* relevant. Bereft of spiritual insight, no worse…the worst of the best of them militantly in denial *till nohow* on and of spiritual dimensions. Musing more contemplatively than cognitively… what words flowed into my spoken narrative I cannot clearly recollect but I do remember concluding…"Not accessible to God consciousness; all the more vulnerable to evil spirituality. Mortal relevance is perception of the barely perceptible straight path of Providence revealed to prayer in the midst of life's scrimmage. God's clemency

---

1   James Hart in his Introduction to 'Not of Our Time'

for our inclement time."

On cue six hostile men burst into our meeting. Karl Mannheim, the Gordon Bruce, Ed Logan, Jack Schmitt, a meek Roy Gossett and a youngish roughneck I did not know stood glaring at... me. They had been listening outside our door. Our meeting room was behind and adjoined the Sanctuary. Catholics would call it a sacristy, Methodists frequently call it a vestry; at Birch Lane it was called the backroom. There were approximately thirty women present amongst our fifty some folding chairs. Barbara Mannheim, Emma Gossett and Anna Mae Mueller were markedly absent. I'd been speaking from a small desk pulpit placed on the front table.

Karl Mannheim strode half way down to the front. The rest stayed glowering by the door.

Speaking more to the group than to Karl, I said, "Welcome men. Please join us in our bible study and prayer meeting. Come sit with us. There are plenty of chairs. But…please do not continue hanging back there hostile like. It is distracting to others who wish to concentrate on Holy Scripture and prayer."

Then Karl spoke. "Preacher," he said "by whose authority are you conducting this meeting?!" His lips curled in a pathetic attempt at snarling. "Well Karl," I tried to patiently reply, "if you were listening you heard us invoke the Holy Spirit of Our Father in Heavens blessing which I think should be authority enough for you. But technically I guess you could say I have been assigned here , employed by Bishop Armstrong's authority in the Church and who is legal proprietor of this property. Now, (much less patiently) by whose authority do you presume to bust in here and disrupt our meeting?!"

"Well *Preacher*,' he spit out the word the way my ex pronounced *Reverend*, "it's all well and good for you to talk to us that a way… hidin behind that pullllpit."

The way he pronounced pulll - - Pit immediately cued a barely conscious behavioral response from me. I picked up the desk pulpit and sprang the yardage to confront him. He stood hands on his hips pushing his big belly belligerently forward.

"And that's what it's for Karl!", I said thrusting the pulpit hard into his midsection. He didn't go down, just grunted and stepped back a little. The second whack I drove the point of the pulpit straight under the sternum to his solar plexus. Then he went down groaning. The other tough guys ran to his rescue fussing about him like worried women.

Roy Gossett had joined Nell Mayrose on the aisle as they looked askance at the hostiles. "All you boys had better leave now", Nell said, "and take Karl home to bed. Roy saw that they all left... sort of quietly.

Nell and I adjourned the meeting slowly, reading Holy Scripture and encouraging prayers for peace. There were many volitional prayers, partisan to their Pastor but troubled about what was happening in, at, and to their church. A chill spirit of collective devotion had set in after the violence. Devout eye contact and near embraces[1] expressed upon leaving.

Driving home I realized the near perfect cue Karl had given me. My favorite pastoral scene in the history of cinema was Trevor Howards parish priest in "Ryan's Daughter"; a movie that captured me mothers temperament in Irish storm. A mob is abusing Ryan's daughter for collaborating with a British soldier. Not approving the collaboration or the abuse Father Trevor intervenes to protect the young woman. A large man attempts to push him away. Father Trevor hauls off and bloodies the man's nose. The man protests, "Sure and you can act that a way hiding behind your priestly collar." "Aye and that's what it's for" says the priest punching the man again and harder.

Prestoral Counsel

Thursday brought a long visit with Prestor John. He came 'round after chores in mid-afternoon. We spoke of how certain group behavior was difficult to categorize. How like Freud's cigar, it was sometimes just a cigar. I described for him my experience of Barnesites behavior. Their political content virtuous; their organizational form repulsive. How their organizational machinations mowed down orthodox Marxists ability to understand or categorize them. The S.W.P. (Socialist Workers Party): host of their parasitic infestation paralyzed <u>with the notion</u> that organizational differences either belied political

1   near embraces: country hoosiers do not hug

difference or were insignificant. Its political integrity thus vulnerable to (organizational) infringement, infestation and infection. Prokaryotic: simple green bacterium without a nucleus splitting and reproducing by personal fission finally overwhelming its host for cultic and/or police spy purposes. The Logan and Bruce led oppositionist at Beech were definitely not *theological* or *ideological* but blindly *habitual*.

"Are you sure they're not being agitated or influenced by someone from the outside... maybe someone from your past?" John asked. I had to laugh. That question was the gateway invitation to outright paranoia.

"I'm told they've acted the same way with previous Pastors. It's just earlier and a little more so with me. I think they are acting habitually. They're in the habit of it."

"You did say, a little more so." Prestor John looked pensive and was encouraging me to be so.

"What . ?" I thought aloud! "The F.B.I.? The Barnesites? Jack himself!? I don't think so. They've bigger fish to fry. I'm a small (mixing my critter metaphors) duck in a smaller pond."

"What about a relative?" Ahh John...he had experiences in detecting a judas goat. I resisted the idea.

"My family has always been solid, that is, tactically different, but strategically loyal to me and to each other. My catholic relatives all seem to think I'd make a good Minister. My Protestants relatives are of course, a bit miffed I'm not their kind of Protestant.

"What kind of Protestant would that be?"

"Almost all backwoods Baptist or newly mega-churched."

"Look out for the mega-churched," he warned.

The most mainly mega-churched would be my sister. The child of my parents. She was still palsey with my ex. And...she was a neighbor to Thatch. My mind whirred. No way. Stirring stench with these people could endanger my children. No way. She loved my children as I loved hers.

Changing the subject a bit Prester John said, "Properly categorizing these Birchers and sons of Birch Lane I find less interesting than categorizing you. Has anyone fraternally observed your theology as

Jansenist. Don't get me wrong..." he continued. "Our United Church must include all varieties of theological thinking"

"Wasn't Jansen some kind of heretic?"

"Ohh the Roman Church declared him so bout' fifteen years after his death. He was the Bishop of Ypres and his ideas flourished through Louvain University, Paris intellectuals, and the seminary education of Irish priests in France. A kind of Catholic Calvinism. You strike me as a kind of Irish Catholic Calvinist. Sometimes as an Islamically informed Irish Catholic Calvinist."

Not eager to attract labels but flattered by some of these I remember saying, "I do think we've left St. Augustine too far behind, and his influence on Jean Calvin, who in spite of becoming a coldblooded lawyer (he assisted the slow burning execution of Michael Servetus) his thoughts and writing upheld the dignity and importance of work positively influencing Marxist thought. I.F Stone has described Fidelistas as Calvinists of the thrid world. Economic work creates economic value. Moral works create moral value. Luther wanted to wiggle out of both; even outlaw the 'Book of James'."

"See..." John exclaimed, "I wuz right. Heresey or not you are in good company with Blaise Pascal, Georges Bernanos, and marxist Graham Greene."

"At least now you can stop baiting me with Edmund Burke. You were burkeing me with all that Burke talk."

A religious studies scholar at IU John had earlier pestered me with Edmund Burke.

"You should read him," he'd say. "He thinks like you. A secret Irish catholic sympathizer both conservative culturally and a leftist critic of the British Empire in America, India, and Ireland.

The only thing remotely interesting to me about Burke was Gibbon had described him as "the most eloquent and rational mad man that I ever knew." He was so secret an Irish catholic that he called himself an Englishman and took the oath of abjuration against the church and for supremacy of the English King. In 'Das Kapital' Marx nailed him as a sycophant bravely critical for the highest bidder. In the pay of the English Oligarchy against the French Revolution just as in the pay of American and/or Indian colonies against the English Oligarchy. "An out and out vulgar bourgeois always selling himself to the best 'natural' market."

"Well he *was* a providentialist, and a traditionalist like you", John would say.

"Goes to show", I'd return, "no one is ever completely wrong."

Critical of social contract theory Burke did claim that "society is indeed a contract, but a partnership not only between those who are living, but between those who are living, those who are dead and those who are to be born. His sense of providence however seems limited to positivist propaganda for the winners, even apologizing for the injustice of class divisions rather than discerning revolutionary providence overthrowing them worldwide.

We had become slightly jocular. Turning more serious John posed the question, "Why not call the law on these outlaws?"

For years I had counseled family members to not render Caesars law on one another if they ever expected to restore love after a quarrel. "I would not call on Caesars cops and deputies against members of the Christian community. It would be like second international social democrats rendering national armaments against each other."

"It's your...It could be your funeral," he said getting up to go.

"I don't think so. They'll wear out, give up, or leave. They are learning I'll not wear out, give up, or leave."

"Is that an Irish thing?" he smiled.

"Maybe...probably. Not sure. What I am sure is an Irish thing is having 'one for the ditch'."

Taking a jar of *shine* from the old wooden ice box I used for a liquor cabinet, I poured us two small glasses. We drank a toast to Revolutionary Providencialism.

Finishing his glass, John shuddered his approval asking, "You call that moonshine or white mule?"

"Depends upon the kick. This jar is technically pear shine."

"From where?"

"The Kentuckian who runs the feed mill shared it with me."

"Good stuff," he said still smiling. "Not too sweet. Plenty strong."

Under the influence of more brethrenly shared 'shine' we both relaxed beyond alert repartee. Prester John was deep into pastoral psychology. In the past we had discussed Freudian discipline in 'psycho analysis' and Jungian imagination in 'analytical psychology'. Even my essentialist emphasis in "Daseinanalyse' seemed overtaxed with morbidities to John. His pastoral emphasis was not on the wounds of negative experience but on those positive experiences which centrally define ones character and can affirm ones life direction. He was required this semester to be "pastorally counseled" himself. So far he was not very happy about it. That is, he and his 'shrink' were not in agreement on clinical goals. His description of it reminded me of my required analysis the last year of internship at Carter Hospital.

My assigned shrink was a pro-shah Iranian I could not take seriously. I would speak of Mosaddegh, the Tudeh Party, and revolutionary Iranian students I had demonstrated with at UCLA leaning forward from my chair as he backed his half way cross the room. Then he would lean forward clinically analyzing my aggressive hostilities and I would back up half way cross the room. He finally concluded…"There are basically two types of people in the world (1) those who want to be loved and (2) those who want to be feared. The trouble with you Morgan is you want to be both."

We laughed. John said, "your memories are so full of enmity Thomas… but you do make them amusing."

"If we can't be amused by what has happened we'll never be amused by what will happen. As for enmity I guess me Mother and I suffer from our share of Irish Alzheimers."

"Irish what?!"

"Irish Alzheimers…wherein you can only remember grudges!"

We laughed again, but John protested for more seriousness. Not… just because he was struggling with the ideas of pastoral psychology but…I think he truly wished to help me prepare for the approaching inevitable showdown.

"Seriously Thomas, what life affirming stories do you most recall? Say…from childhood what experiences most centrally defined your character development?"

"I dunno John...early on I reckon I preferred animals to people cept, of course, those people who knew most about animals like my father, grandfather, some uncles..."

"What about your mother?"

"Me mother? Me sainted, hard as nails, mother, I have loved and love more than any human being on earth. Don't look for any knots between me and mother!"

"Who did the disciplining?"

"They shared it. There was a lot of it! Mom when I was small — Dad as I got bigger."

"Corporal?"

"As if any other kind is significant."

Prester John was more than ten years younger than me. Coming of age not in the militant sixties but in the irenic idiocy of the seventies. The sixties experience knew that violent means to sins of war – avarice, pride, envy, sloth, rage, gluttony and lust were best prevented by equal corporeity.

"And the earlier the better!"

He continued, "What experience of your parents discipline most influenced your respect for authority and values of punishment and reward?"

I told John my kindergarten story.

At five my family moved away from the railroads, factories, and saloons of Seventeenth Street to the country. Or what seemed like the country past Twenty-fifth and Hulman City limits to Indian Acres. A house and garage on two full acres with yards as big as meadows.

It was late summer and I hadn't yet met the neighbor kids when enrolled in a kindergarten off west Hulman Street on Dad's milk route. I was peer anxious to make new friends. The kindergarten was ran by two older maiden ladies in a big 'ol house at the edge of Farrington Grove.

After the first two hours of blissful pack socializing with my new pals, all the boys and girls were herded into separate bathrooms for a five minute pee break. The maiden ladies accompanied the girls. No one accompanied us boys as we stood mystified before the large white urinals not knowing what to do with or on them. We'd never seen such things before.

The kid next to me unzipped and had to pee so he decided to pee on me. Dumbfounded that a classmate and new friend could or would do such a thing I just stood there in my dampening clothes. The kid then yelled over to the dozen or so other boys, "hey guys come on over here, this Tommy kid lets you pee on him." All the boys came over and proceeded to piss all over me. Aghast I stood perfectly still becoming progressively drenched in piss.

Our maiden teachers were more disgusted than prone to discipline. They seemed equally appalled at my pissy appearance as they were at the behavior of the boys who caused it. They sent me to their private bathroom with a towel and a ladies bathrobe. I spent the rest of the day alone in their office bathroom, and bathrobe. I did overhear them speak of phoning my mother."Was she upset?"

"Very tight lipped. She said little but kept asking the number, that is, how many other boys…how many other boys were involved."

Dad picked me up in his milk truck around 2pm. He was kind but disappointed. Arriving home he went outside, leaving me inside to face me mother's wrath. I saw a wet willow switch in the sink… which she applied to stripeing my bare legs until she tired and had to rest. Catching her breath, she said, "tomorrow when you go to bathroom with those boys I want e'm all knocked down. Break heads, crack bones… whatever it takes. You'd better not leave a single one standing. Your dad and I have raised you better than this…we've raised you to stand your ground. Now…" she gasped catching her breath again, "if you don't knock every single one of those little trespassers down and out you'll get an even worse whippin when you get home."

Still tearful from the switch, my mother reached out and comforted my tears saying, "We'll forgive e'm later."

The sting of the switch did not keep me from sleeping that night but I felt it going to sleep and waking up the next morning. I felt it going to kindergarten and I felt it for the two hours biding my time until the bathroom break.

Finally inside the bathroom I knocked heads and kicked ass for the full five minutes. Not a single one of those bad boys were left standing.

They squalled and some screamed. I was amazed they seemed as surprised today as I was yesterday. The maiden ladies were definitely more surprised and shocked by my violence than their previous pissing predations. They phoned my mother exclaiming her child had exploded with some kind of aggressively violent seizure!! Calmly my mother only inquired as to how many boys were actually whipped and knocked down? She then smiled for days from the full accounting.

"My Gawdd..." said Prester John pronouncing God like a T.V. protestant. "My God...experience not only conditions behavior, I think it must even shape neurological function. Your experiences are so different than mine. But Thomas, you must not be a prisoner of your experience. Do not allow the beasts of past trauma drive you back into the darkness of violence. Violence so palpable and near now... near to your ministry and to your life."

I knew John had read Ciardi's 1970 copyright translation of Dante's 'Divine Comedy'. I'd read the 1961 issue in 1961. The decade difference determined much of what we remembered. But we both loved John Ciardi's translations of the master poets view of 'the catholic other worlds'.

"As religious men John, we know the aesthetic wisdom Dante displayed is beyond trauma and beyond reason. 'The long way round' and sometimes through darkness to ultimate light.

Moral-spiritual consciousness of ones total experiences. No short cuts on the 'arduous road' of experience."

"Salvation, Thomas, must grow out of understanding..."

"And total understanding can follow only from total experience[1]..."

"And just how Thomas, do you think Dante and/or all the poets and religious thinkers in the world can discipline and shape their thinking to approach such a totalitarian task?"

"Devout labor! With devout labor. The presence of God's love

---

1   John Ciardi's Introduction to his translation of (Dante Alighieri's) 'The Divine Comedy'.

must be won by 'devout labor'[1]. Labor Omnia Vincet!"[2]

"And violence?"

"No stranger to labor!"

"My call to the ministry" John continued, "was a call away from not precisely violence, I guess, but harshness; a call away from the harshness of this old world. A kind of reductionist choice. You spoke once of a kind of call that came to you at the Episcopal Church on Kirkwood in Bloomington?"

"In the fall of 1969. The sixties were ending. I'd finished graduate school the spring before. My wife Anne and I moved to Gloryville Farm that summer. By September the Indiana Department of Mental Health refused my previous hospital assignment on political grounds. I hired on as a Community Organizer for the Federal Poverty Program in Bloomington and was being red baited in the local press. Right wing pressure on the board to terminate my employment."

"No community support from I.U.?"

"Yeah. Friendly professors kept asking me to come speak about how wonderful the Federal Poverty Program was. Bloomington National Bank temporarily froze our checking account. A vice president stumbled out to explain their policy spilling 1962 newspaper clippings out of a file. I cornered him a fraction of an inch close and blurted, 'A Communist can't have good credit?!!' The bank backed down. I went to Nicks[3] for several brews then crossed the street to the unlocked doors of Trinity Episcopal Church. Typically Anglican its interior had more of a catholic atmosphere than many of the hurrying to be hip post Vatican II Catholic parishes. I knew the place as my friends Dick Lonnigan and Guy Bloomberg had attended there. Anglican or not it was Christ's Church. Its doors were open and I desperately needed at least a glimpse of God's presence and grace to think through the direction of my life's situation. I prayed. Reflecting on my situation; 1) I had stayed in Indiana after an idiot prosecutor had been prevented from throwing me and my co-defendants Rolphe and Jim

---

1   IBID
2   Labor Omnia Vincet': 'Labor conquers all things'.
3   Nicks: Nicks English Hut – venerable Bloomington bar on Kirkwood Avenue.

into prison for being revolutionary socialists. My co-defendants had lit out for California. I had not. I loved Indiana; (if not all of Hoosierdom) its foliage, and farms, its home centered working people, my family and friends – moreover I bridled at the idea of being chased out of anywhere, let alone my home area.

2) Degree certified I was learning that middle class jobs unlike Proletarian ones (from the Steel Mill to the construction site – restaurant counter, vets office or farm work) required more than just 'doing your job'. They required a certain procurement service as well. That is, you had to pimp for the place, institution, or set up. Believe in and be loyal to its bureaucracy. I was gagging on that. Prayerfully pondering my situation, and slightly panicked I wondered what possible place I could find in the economy. Academia seemed sewed up, Indiana's mental health industry had locked me out and I couldn't imagine pimping for any establishment, government or private institution. My hands in prayer dropped to my knees. I stood to deflect these thoughts I deplored. My eyes still closed; I slowly opened them. Aggiornamento! Time and space whirled in mad cognition. As R.D. Laing advised Clancy Sigal, "Madness need not be all breakdown. It may also be breakthrough." The interior of Trinity refilled my interiority. 3) In principle, I could procure for the Church. To be a part of its Propaganda – a pleasure.

There was a phone booth on the corner just outside the church doors. I remembered a Father Carthy pastor of St. Stevens an Episcopal Parish Church in the black community of North Indianapolis. I'd volunteered there as a teacher in their Saturday 'poetry workshops' for young people (junior high and high school kids). He'd mentioned being a board member of 'Episcopal Social Services'. Through Directory Assistance I reached him right away. He said E.S.S.[1] had no budget but C.S.S.[2], of the Archdiocese had a huge budget and was always hiring. I phoned them and arranged a job interview the next day. The rest is history. I was employed for a year as school counselor for the parochial schools in West Indianapolis. Soon promoted community organizer and then Associate Director of Catholic Charities. I finished my career in two

1   E.S.S.: Episcopal Social Services
2   C.S.S.: Catholic Social Services

decades with the Archdiocese as Archdiocesan Director of Social Ministries; also teaching classes at St. Mary of the Woods and St. Maurs Benedictine Seminary."

"This Aggiornamento you called it, this epiphanous revitalizing of your life's direction and career you consider your call to ministry?"

"Yes I do. A bit reductionist too, I reckon, but I think that's the way it works. All the work I mentioned is Christian ministry. It is not pastoral ministry. In the catholic church thats reserved for the roman collars. That's why much of my anti-clericalism and most of my catholic anti-clericalism is based on envy for the priesthood."

"....of Melchizedek?!"

"I suppose...I suppose that tracks. It's just that I'd been critical of priests, *not* popes for so long I thought I'd better shut up or try and do it right, that is, better."

"And your politics?"

"Empyrean versus Imperium! As always".

Prester John finished his last glass of shine. Shuddered, and pushed the empty glass across the table.

"Too many for the ditch, Thomas. I've enjoyed our time."

"It was valuable to me."

Ventilating to Johns pastoral countenance *was* valuable to me. I enjoyed it. And I knew that John had enjoyed the shine... watching him carefully find his way down the lane. His new wife was quite upset with our drinking. To this day we are militantly unforgiven... The first and foremost feminist issue... Prohibition!

XXXVI

The Filth of Time

Saturday night the children and I watched the movie "Lawrence of Arabia." I deliberately rented it to instruct them on good manners. Our capacity for which we were soon to be tested.

When King Feisal (Alec Guiness) reports how the Arabian Army is respecting the Geneva accords regarding prisoners, the US reporter (Arthur Kennedy) asks if that is Major Lawrences doing?

Feisal responds: "Why would you think that?"

US Reporter: "Well, in Cairo everyone says that Lawrence abhors the shedding of blood."

Feisal: "Yes...with Major Lawrence, 'Mercy' is a passion. With us it is merely good manners. Time will tell which is the most reliable motive."

In subsequent scenes of the film Lawrence becomes outraged by the cruelty of the Turks and massacres an entire column of them screaming in his attack "No prisoners!"

We may be treated rudely tomorrow I warned the children. We must not be provoked to rudeness ourselves.

Up early, working at my desk, the children sleeping soundly in their bedroom. The phone rang. I answered. No one spoke... then hung up. Unusual.

Before waking the children I love looking at them. My brave little son and beautiful daughter. Looking at Beth, I remembered a poem I'd written about her as an infant. Returning to my desk, I rifled through its drawers until I found it. Got both kids up, got e'm dressed, fixed oatmeal, fried bacon and eggs; then read the poem to them at breakfast.

<u>Bethany's Brow</u>
 Her eyes entirely as blue
as the Irish Sea,
her ashen hair like
the hillside soil.

She is a frowning beauty
who already loves her mother
and still reflects His presence.
She comes to us from Him.

We drove off to church. I preached that day on Providence from the books of Wisdom (Wisdom 14 – Psalm 127 – Job 38 and 9) with credits to Prester John and Arnold Toynbee.

(Wisdom 14) "….taking ship to cross the raging sea its building

embodies the wisdom of the shipwright but your Providence, Father, is what steers it."

Virtue in the book of Wisdom (Hebrew *sedeq)* is an accord of mind and act with Gods will as manifest in precepts of the law and injunctions of conscience.

God is not the cause of evil, dis-ease or death which do not proceed from any independent principle. Human beings have spoiled Gods order and invited evil disorder and death; the negation of Gods creative act.

God bestows the grace of the straight path even through the sea, a safe way over the waves.

"The meaning behind the facts of His Story towards which the poetry in the facts is leading us is a revelation of the God of History who works through time to achieve His design."[1]

History then can be seen as a kind of vision – dim and partial, yet true to reality as far as it goes – of God revealing Himself in action to souls seeking Him…[2] History's contribution is to record how providence is discerned and/or denied yet always sustained.

Selfishness, individual and collective, violates the path of God's Providence and succumbs to "self-destruction and/or self-stultification."[3] Thus stupefied to idolize the ephemeral self-institutions, and technology. Thus terminally vulnerable to the "huge spiritual force of the discarnate Personality intent on exploding and destroying what hope God has created in the human being, because he himself is denied

1   Arnold J. Toynbee 'A Study of History'
2   Arnold J. Toynbee 'Movement of World Revolution'
3   Thomas P. Neill 'Toynbee and Dawson on the Meaning of History'

the power to create. How many of us have an inkling of the might and the cunning of Superhuman envy, despair and hatred towards God by this fallen angel who cannot generate and will not serve. The evilness of the Evil One exceeds our power to imagine and to fight."[1]

Similarly hateful is the Enlightenments inspired resentment of progressives against religion. Religion which knows why humanity does not progress. "Religion which is never lulled with vain hope that any good things won may not be disputed, not need to be defended and remade forever."[2]

We must lead lives with prayerful effort conducive to the discernment of God's providence; the straight pathway of those "whom He has bestowed His grace, whose portion is not wrath and who go not astray."[3]

Yes…yes twentieth century philosophy has discerned that 'existence precedes essence'. Men think because of what they do – not the other way around. But, modern consciousness has clogged around the above insight like a crick 'round a muskrat hole. The Prophets presumed a broader context than the existential hangover allows. Our species can engage infrastructures with Histories of superstructual knowledge and a capacity to say Amen.

I didn't have to end, "say Amen." Everybody present said Amen. I was learning if a Preacher could emotively connect with his people and not waller in it but move on to the moral message… they'd get it. They would comprehend at a relatively deeper level than mechanical sense or intellectual drift. It's the way one talks to horses and children; or counsels adults. Emotively even but cognitively beyond.

That day those present in congregation thundered Amen because they noticed as I did the empty back pews. The Logan, Mannheim, Gossett, Bruce and young Schmidt men were not present. They had convened a reception committee for me outside.

I made them wait. No sense providing an audience for their mischief. Gene Vincent asked if he and others "should stick around…?" walk out with me as I left. I thanked him for his concern but thought it

---

1   Sigrid Undset 'Amid the Encircling Gloom'
2   IBID
3   The Exordium from the Holy Koran

best I face them alone. I took my time. I would have to outflank Logan again and witnesses would find that extreme. There was always some "friend" or "supporter" who would suggest or push things toward the center[1]; the centrist center of compromise long after hostilities had crossed the line and integrity required action not ambivalence. When the center holds centrist ambivalence becomes a cover for collective cowardice. Dante's "dark center drain bearing the filthy sediment of sin". This centrist conduit drains "the filth of time."

To decisively cut through this crap. To constitute the setting indispensable for the proper turning of consciousness required a careful diachrony of the time to act.

As I saw my children into the back seat of our truck, the six man reception committee plus one came 'round the corner towards us. Before locking the truck doors I reminded Eliot to *not* unlock the door for anyone but me. "Ouch!", he remembered California.

Again Karl Mannheim took the lead. He was twice the size of the others and he might be looking to compensate for last Wednesday. All the others kept an irregular distance behind him. I spotted Ed Logan way to the back. The young Schmidt stood closer to Karl beside a strange youth I did not know. This stranger was fattish, brimming with fight, wearing an Amex coal cap that matched the blackheads across his face.

Karl said, "We'll need to take your keys now, Tom." His eyes were serious, not unfriendly. I returned his look, nodding toward his midsection, which had to be bruised. "You OK Karl?", I asked. He nodded he was.

I walked past him through the others to confront Logan. He panicked just a little bit. Looking him in the eye with all the murderous looks I could muster said, "So you've arranged to call me out; here in front of my children.

Unprincipled as ever, Ed Logan. You hide behind these good, young, stupid and compromised men. You want a fight? I'll fight you right here–Irish to Irish–by the cemetery where it'll be handy to bury you."

His Irish up, but inadequately Logan turned and shrank away. The

1   Like Gary Coopers "friend" at Church in 'High Noon'

young black headed stranger started toward me. Karl stopped him. Roy had wandered off. Bruce was yelping. No one was listening. I returned to my truck, got in, and started the engine. Bruce still babbling, Schmidt, and the black head boy stood blocking the front of our truck.

Eliot said, "run over e'm Papa." It occurred to me as well, but not seriously tempted I waited a few seconds. I was seriously tempted to rev the engine loud to see them jump, but I didn't. Roy was yelling something at 'the boys' and Karl had Bruce's attention. Soon they all walked gloomily away.

We drove off undefeated; obstructions scattered. But...they'd be back. I knew it disconsolately. My Leninist idea of the pastorate longed for a catholic hierarchy with doctrinal authority and administrative muscle. If I called on Supervisor Stilmore or went over his head to Bishop Armstrong they would call the cops. Leaving me the lame leader sucking up to the state for protection. Not very Thomas Münzer!

Militantly organizing the majority of peaceful parishioners against this threatening minority would be like sic'ing loyal family dogs against a pack of pit bulls. In time... in the fullness of time, as Pastor I would have to dispatch these wolves in sheep's clothing. In the meantime, in this Dantesque centered down 'filth of time' I would have to 'mark time'; *not* 'kill time'. I would 'stand by', 'sit tight', 'hold my horses', like Grant at Galena, poised for the right time prayerfully dwelling in faith for the grace of Gods guidance.

The sociogram at Birch Lane was terminally bent. Ahh *sociograms*... the rhetoric of twentieth century sociology... soon to be forgotten in the next century; and consigned to conscripted college departments.

The next week started well until Tuesday evening. Rose Vincent phoned to say Nell Mayrose had cancelled the regular Wednesday bible study and prayer meeting. At first Nell said "she was ill...not feeling well". Then confessed she "just didn't want any more trouble."

"I told her" Rose continued, "that was giving into the bullies. That you, our Pastor would want us to continue normally and *not* be scared off!"

"Well I think he, our Pastor", Nell answered "is beginning to act as rough as they do!"

When Rose Vincent said she offered to fill in for Nell this Wednesday she reported being abruptly interrupted. Nell told her she was "the official convener for the prayer meeting and wanted them cancelled until peace was restored in the church!"

I thought that sounded close to asking me to leave to restore peace and said so. "That's where they're headed." Rose confirmed. "You won't leave us now, will you Preacher?" she asked. "Not now with everything in such a mess."

I assured her again I would not be run off. "We'll let Nell cancel this week. Next week we'll reconvene if we have to do it ourselves."

"Good plan", Rose agreed… weakly. And we hung up.

More of the last two weeks and Rose would be begging me not to expel old Nel. Attrition was being borne not so much by the Pastor, or his opponents as by his people. Relationships, like all human constructs are terminally fragile. Enough pressure and they fracture. By contrast the ease of disposition, habit, and the underlying customs of the countryside live longer as excuses of 'the heart'. Unless…there occurs a profound moral turning point. I would pray for such a thing. And then recall that most orthodox of spiritual warnings. 'Be careful what you pray for.'

The dumbass illusion from Bourgeois Enlightenment that religion and sexual morality is fleeting superstition with no sustainable practicality for modern minds requires an abjuring ignorance from the loyalties, longings, flaws, and work of ordinary human beings. I prayed God give me, give us the grace to deal with this lot that Providence had given us. And I prayed my forgiveness of those, especially the Logans, who had spoken and acted against me. Bring it on. I was ready for it.

It came in a series of evening phone calls, round about dark. All like the one last Sunday morning. The phone would ring. I'd answer, "hello". No one would speak. I'd hear them breathe into the phone, then they'd hang up. Wednesday evening. Thursday evening. Friday evening same thing. Then Saturday evening with the children playing on the floor beside me it rang. This time a voice I did not know... a young sounding voice...said, "Preacher you ever hear of a SHOTGUN!" Then came the intimidating sound of someone racking a shell into a pump gun. A ringing TRSK SCHSSK! Unmistakable and again quickly TRSK SCHSSK! Then silence.

I spoke into the silence. "Since you've pumped two shells, without firing...you trying to scare me with an empty unloaded gun...you moron! Who is this? Identify yourself! What's this about?"

"You'll know soon enough Preacher!" For a second I thought I'd identified the voice. That boy with the blackheads and Amex Coal Co. cap! Then I wasn't sure. It was a young voice like Schmidts. But...I was pretty sure it wasn't Schmidt.

It didn't really matter *who* it was I had to think clearly now about how best to protect my children from an idiot threatening me with a shotgun. I immediately phoned their mother and was surprised she answered on a Saturday night. Gak! He's probably there, I thought, then decided I couldn't afford such thinking.

   "We have an emergency, Annie. I will deliver the children
   back to you at daybreak, at first light. Please be there."
"I'll be here. Can we talk?"
"No."
"Tell the children I'll see them first thing in the morning with fresh baked cookies. Near six...?"
"Yes, goodnight."

I explained things to the children as best I could by bringing out of its boot my Beretta – break action – over and under double barreled 12 gauge shotgun. I'd bought it used from Poff's gun store for $150... ten years ago. They said it had belonged to a Navy man who brought it from the Mediterranean. Beth and El had seen it before but still admired its walnut and steel beauty. They remembered my shooting the heads off young roosters for Sunday dinner. That way the bird wouldn't flop around after it was killed. I never liked that flopping around... and always used steel, not lead shot which rarely remained in the fried chicken. I explained to them the shotgun was a neutral instrument that could be used for good or evil. And that their father, with God's help was going to attempt using it in a good old fashioned way of defense and... instructive discipline.

Bethany led us in a prayer she'd found on our bookshelves. It was Jimmy Steels prison prayer from the 'Wolfe Tone Weekly' in Tim Coogan's

1966 book, "Ireland Since the Rising"

O, Sacred Heart of Jesus!... we prayed,

Look down on us today.

Make us strong and fearless soldiers,

Ever ready for the fray.

'Gainst thine and Irelands enemies.

Wherever they may be,

O, Sacred Heart of Jesus!

We put our trust in Thee. Amen

We left the farm sleepily before 5am. I kept the shotgun handy but felt certain we were up and moving too early for whatever they had in mind. The long barreled Beretta lay between Eliot and me. He liked to think he was truly riding shotgun.

Daybreak brought little winters light to the town as we drove into Terre Haute. Turning off 25th on to Ohio Blvd. past the prosperous places, downhill one block from Seventeenth Street and Anne's shabby blue mother's mortgaged manse.

The children were hanging on to me but looking forward to their mom. We met at her front door. And mutually seemed to open it together. The inside rooms redolent with fresh baked cookies. The kids kissed me goodbye and ran past her toward the kitchen. She stayed by the door, wrapped in her robe and smiling at me. Every cuckolded spouse knows this moment. The zombied ex love of your life before you. All phony froideur absent. Smiling... inviting all the old illusions and some new ones. Dawn light in Terre Haute had a kind of Gallic-glow. It touched her swept back hair. I imagined her blonde, not brunette...like Jean Paul Belmondo's – Jean Seberg in Goddard's 'Breathless'[1]

She asked, why I looked at her so? In Sartrean sulk I responded,

1   'Breathless': Jean Luc Goddard's New Wave 1959 film said to determine American female romantic style for decades. Seberg's last line of the film, an

"You make me feel like 'the far side of despair'."[1] As I was leaving she asked, "What's that mean?...the far side of despair?" Turning on the steps with all the wrenched recoil from unfaithful unreality I answered, "like puke".

I had more than two hours to make the one hour trip to Birch Lane. I intended to be slightly late in order to peg the reception committee I felt sure would be forming outside again. I had considerable to think about...to think through each tactical step. I drove west down Poplar around 9th Street to Saint Benedicts; the church of my kin and childhood. My mother dutifully never missed mass there twice a year; Christmas eve and Easter morning. The six am Mass was dismissing early. I found a kneeler, lit a candle, and prayed the Our Father and The Exordium. Everyone faces east at Saint Bens except the priests. The light there, at times, has hauntingly loomed into what lay ahead... unknowable yet certain at the same time.

In good stead
the light shone safe
this side of dread
Chthonic inclines
calmly sped
the very shape of time

What cut it was the shotgun threat of violence irrespective of my children's safety. My dissenting members had crossed the Rubicon to act like and thus be treated like enemies...almost.

I would decisively enjoin this threat and discipline all associated with it...but not exactly as enemies. I thought back to the sixties and how SNCC[2] preached to secular lefties.

Tic Toc Restaurants were a large chain of racist segregated restaurants in Tennessee. John Lewis was the Nashville leader of SNCC in charge of picketing the Tic-Toc's. Indiana's Y.S.A.[3] had David Fender and me accompany Leroy McRae, our National Secretary to speak at

---

incognizant "What's that mean, puke?"

[1]   "Human life begins on the far side of despair" Jean Paul Sartre 'The Flies'

[2]   SNCC: Student Nonviolent Coordinating Committee

[3]   Y.S.A.: Young Socialist Alliance, headquartered in New York.

SHOTGUN PREACHER

Fisk University and meet with John Lewis. They spoke together about how Gandhi's notion of *satyagraha* (i.e. non-violent action and inner certainty) would not be violated by (in Leroy's words) "twelve big pounders forming an educational committee to discipline white hoodlums attacking the non-violent demonstrators." Leroy explained how it could be arranged to escort the racist bullies behind the restaurant where the educational committee could educate them properly into the ground.

John seemed to like the idea of discipline and spoke of how peaceful SNCC demonstrators were not allowed to slouch or smoke. "But,…" this sharecroppers son who'd been beaten to the floor at Tic-Toc, with his Calvinist scowl warned, "these white hoodlums must not be condemned as racist, Klan, Nazi, class enemy monsters,… they must be disciplined as your ill-informed cousins".

I had plenty of cousins, well informed and ill-informed. I knew exactly what John Lewis meant. I wasn't sure David and Leroy did.

I didn't intend to harm anyone this morning. I did intend to scare the meaness out of e'm. To Pastorally deliver the fear and terror of God's wrath. For them to cease this disrespectful rebellion or "be cast into the fire and smoke of hell". With word and act I would preach from the Book of Daniel.

I knew many of my reverend friends suspect my pastoral gait…my ministry to merely be – in Prester John's words "a refuscent saraband from socialist consciousness." I preferred to think my syncretic certainties were spiritually informed.

My friend Antonio Valcarcel was a Puerto Rican Nationalist and Revolutionary Socialist. He found Indiana and Mid-Western culture intriguing and studied its people as a measure of Americas future. "The shotgun" he'd say "would be the essential revolutionary weapon for America. It is primarily a defensive weapon. And the conservative nature of the American people would only take up arms defensively. To defend, that is, conserve their prosperity, their jobs, their union contracts, their right to organize and their family's safety. Protracted and unjust corporate-government infractions would ultimately face the burning charge of collective steel pellets."

At close range or distance the spread of shot from a shotgun results in many wound tracks in the target. It is less likely to penetrate walls and hit the wrong target with its low penetration and high stopping power. The shot spreads further upon entering the target, and the multiple wound channels of a defensive load are far more likely to produce a disabling wound than a rifle or handgun.

I both loved and hated shooting quail. I'd probably feel the same way about parishioners. The first recorded use of the term *shotgun* was in 1776 Kentucky. It was noted as native to the "frontier language of the Midwest" by James Fennimore Cooper.

Many of my Portagee neighbors in the San Joaquin were armed with "Luparas" (from the Italian word Lupo [Wolf]). Those sawed-off shotguns we saw in the Sicily of Godfather I, II, and III. John Moses Browning, an employee of Winchester Firearms is the American most responsible for the modern development of the shotgun; used by cavalry in the 19th century and favored by Allied-supported anti-fascist partisans in World War II.

In the sixties I preferred Beretta handguns. I didn't even know they made shotguns. My Beretta shotgun was one of my prize possessions.

The shorter barrel Lupara makes for a weapon easier to maneuver around corners and tight places but my long barrel Beretta made for a tighter spread pattern and increased accuracy. The longer barrel swings more slowly but also more steadily. I would swing this long barrel steadily in their direction without taking aim or actually pointing it at them. "You never point a gun at someone unless you are prepared to shoot them": an olde, old country adage.

And this disciplinary confrontation was now required within the hour as I drove south-east toward the county line. It had to be done now. Not doing seemed a serious moral error. I was trying to recall verses from the Book of Daniel I'd memorized last night. Instead I kept remembering verses from Ezra Pounds Cantos I'd memorized years ago...

> "To have done instead of not doing,
>   this is not vanity
> To have with decency, Knocked
> the door open
> To have gathered from the air a live tradition
> or from a fine old eye the unconquered flame
> This is not vanity
> Here error is all in the not done,
> All in the diffidence that faltered..."
> Ezra Pound's Canto LXXXI

PART SEVEN:

THE LAST CANTO

XXXVII

The Baraka with me, timing right on…ten minutes late, parking lot full, everyone in church except that reception committee of eight loafing near my parking place. I swung out of the truck with the shotgun. They did not approach. I swung the long barrel steadily in their direction.

"Come on in boys," I said "I'm going to say good-bye to you today". Only Logan grinned. He was so eat up I'm sure he thought the departure to be announced was mine not his. Quietly they filed up the stairs ahead of me and into the church.

Our appearance and the shotgun caused quite a buzz in the congregation as they jostled in the pews to find their seats. Inspired by an old country song,[1] I demonstrably took out my keys and locked the church doors, looking directly at those just seated. It got very quiet. I could hear my own steps to the altar. I lay the shotgun on the podium, broke it open and loaded two shells. I welcomed the congregation, apologizing to any guests, for the present disciplinary tension.

I described my "Beretta, broke action, 12 gauge shotgun as a neutral instrument that can be used for good or evil. We hear a lot these days about how guns kill." Holding the shotgun high, I said, "If this gun can kill then (pulling a ballpoint from my pocket) this pen can misspell."

There was relieved laughter. Country people are instinctively partisan to anti-gun control remarks and stories. 'It's just part of the sermon' they hoped.

"It's part of the sermon alright," I continued "because last night I received a phone call threatening me and my children's safety with a shotgun. Most of us know who and what was behind that call. It no longer matters why. Only God knows folks true motivation. But… by the word of God and all that's morally sound we know that threatening the

---

1   Country Music Song: 'Coward of the County' where Tommy locks the door on cowardice.

lives of innocent children is dead wrong and cannot be tolerated. And...
sure as hell for the wicked, will not be tolerated by me any further!"

I closed fast the broke action shotgun and swung its barrel up toward
the back of the church. "Now Git!" several of the culprits stood.

"Logan, Bruce, any and all of you who have one whit of sympathy
for them and/or the behavior they influence – git out the door with them.
Git in your vehicles, go home, and never come back here. Never cross
this threshold again unless with penance in your heart and you have seen
me first. My shotgun in rest position I headed toward the back.

They hurried like prancing ponies with bladder problems toward
the locked doors. Roy Gossett stood and looked confused.

"You have keys Roy. Let e'm out of here. Let e'm out of here
before I change my mind they can live. But Roy I'd like for you and
your family to stay."

Roy unlocked the doors, opened them wide and came back to his
seat.

Ruth and Ed Logan were first out the door. Nell Mayrose, her two
sons and their families were fast behind them, John Bought was hob-
bling some to keep up, Gordon Bruce followed with Jane Schouten
and her two grown niece sucking up to Bruce all the way to his Buick
with him militantly ignoring them as usual. As the Mannheims and
Schmidts passed by, I reminded them, "And this goes double for that
young cretin with the bad complexion friend of yours." The Mannheims
look up, but heads down kept moving. Jack Schmidt paused and said
mildly, "I'll tell him."

"And tell him" I slapped the shotgun up vertically, "this ain't rock
salt!"

Three generations of the Muellers left without a word and some
others I barely knew. About twenty in all. Twice more than I'd reckoned on.

I unloaded and booted my Beretta shotgun, while surrounded by
the sixty some remaining and congratulatory members of the congregation. Rose Vincent announced and not weakly *Peace*, finally
restored to our church." She was applauded.

Roy Gossett, in his sad serious manner, spoke quietly to me, "I will miss them". I thanked him for his old school honesty, and told him we should pray for them.

Gene Vincent bragged "I've heard fire and brimstone sermons before but todays was the first break action – shotgun sermon I ever heard." Tim Cottom joked "I'll bet it won't be your last with our Preacher."

Sunday service became kind of an early cocktail hour without cocktails. We did have strong coffee. I visited all the Sunday School classes and met great appreciation. Saying good-bye, everyone said, "See you next week with your children." I said Amen.

I phoned Supervisor Stilmore that night as did Rose and Gene Vincent. Stilmore phoned the Bishop.

The Bishop is said to have responded; "They're really gone?! That young man deserves a promotion." The Supervisor is said to have responded; "He's not that young."

More rewards that night. I just finished speaking on the phone with Bethany and Eliot when my dear friend Mike from California called. I told him all about the last canto. Mike always enjoys a good story. And I always enjoyed his seasonal and seasoned advice, "Morgan you've got to start writing these stories instead of living them."

Monday afternoon Prester John phoned to say he'd been consulted by the Bishop's Office regarding a great promotion for me. "I think they're going to offer you the Associate Pastorate at Memorial Church in Terre Haute. Man, that's the biggest church in the western district! It's bishop- track[1] and would more than double your salary."

I told John I wasn't interested. I've won peace for these people now, I'd like to enjoy it with them and safeguard it. But…the main reason you know…Birch Lane is close to my farm.

"I know…I know, Tom but please don't talk that way around Stilmore. He thinks anything other than iteneracy is settling in to some kind of fat Baptist permanence. He wants ministers as itinerant as Roman Priests. You know about that."

"Roman Catholic Priests, John are celibate if not chaste. They have no families. No children to provide roots for."

John laughed, "Yeah 'ol Stilmore will probably push for celibacy as his wife gets older. His children have flown the coop. But listen…

1   Bishoptrack: on track pastorate to [perhaps] become a Bishop.

do not fail to take advantage of the Memorial offer. It's Terre Haute. You know the city. At most it's a forty minute longer drive for you. Extra money for gasoline and more for your children. The Associate Minister is the youth minister. You'd be good at it. A piece of cake."

"Youth!? I've had a belly full of da' youth, youth movements and so called 'youth culture'. Young people live in no rooted place. They live wherever their mind is… which is usually up their own or someone else's skirt."

"They all wear pants now!"

"I stand corrected…in their own or someone else's britches. I prefer grown-ups – bread winners – working people – Moms and Dads with real issues like mortgages."

"But your intellectual bearing would surely relate better to college students than parents worrying about mortgages."

"I doubt it."

"Please think about it Tom. Think about what it might mean for you and your children."

"John, I've always admired that great celtic actor Archie Leach and his cinematic view of youth".

"Archie who?"

"You know, Cary Grant."

"Cary Grant!?"

"Yeah he had to change his name because of the Brits before he came to America. Anyways in the movie "Monkey Business" he stated his view of youth as 'Maladjustments, mere idiocy, and a series of low comedy episodes'."

Wednesday Rose Vincent and I convened the Prayer Meeting promptly at 7p.m. At 7:15 Supervisor Millard Stilmore strode through the Sanctuary with a grand smile. Surprised…we welcomed him, deferring to him to preside. He announced how "Prayerfully gratified the Methodist Church of Indiana was to the long suffering, patient and decisively brave people of Birch Lane Church." And then with his hand on my shoulder said, "And your stalwart Pastor, the Reverend Thomas Morgan is indeed…(he looked at me and winked) the man with a hammer."

How did Stilmore know ??! of my identification with Thomas Münzer? Probably from Prester John who always denied it. Maybe Bill White? It was perfect spade work from the Supervisor. High on that compliment I listened seriously to his description of not an *offer*, but my "assignment to Terre Haute Memorial."

"Take your time," he explained gently, fraternally ...dare I say almost comradely. "Between Thanksgiving and the new year transitionally visit Memorial with your children. Get acquainted. Pastor Lollard is a good man. Very experienced. He will be helpful. He wants you there. Consolidate your strengths here and physically get away from the Devil."

I never saw the devil in those folks I put out the door. Fact is, I never laid eyes on any of them again. We heard they were having a chaotic time of it trying to organize a '*community*' church out of Gordon Bruce's home.

Regrettably I accepted the Memorial Church assignment. That is, with regret, to leave Birch Lane. They were all so optimistic, so hopeful now about their church's future. They didn't like to hear about my leaving but seemed proud their pastor was being promoted. Without schism whether it was historical, theological, political or just pain in the ass personal Birch Lane Church regained a spiritual solidarity; the iconic cognizance of prayerful community. It's tough loving sanctity revered in the region. Ringing out to others as clear as it's church bell on Sunday morning. I would miss these home centered, hardworking, country families. It would prove a poor trade for the bourgeois civility of Memorial.

Pastor Lollard was a stout little fellow who denied any historical connection with John Wycliffe. He had pastored the Methodist Church in Spencer Indiana in the early sixties when British Prime Minister Harold McMillan came to see his mothers' church. I remember that time and thought well of my fathers home town folk who were little impressed with the likes of P. M. McMillan. Lollard apparently was very impressed and had several pictures of the event in his office. He seemed equally impressed my ex-wife was PhD. Faculty at St. Mary's.

He bragged outright how many faculty PhD's of Rose Hulman and I.S.U.[1] were members of Memorial. I did not mention my primary relations with that milieu was to be divorced from it.

The children and I visited Memorial for a Christmas service in late December. Earlier that week there had been a hard freeze. Galen and I decided to try our hand ice-fishing on his remote pond. He supplied the fishing gear and bait. I supplied the four wheel drive truck to get us there and enough Tulamora Dew[2] and Guinness[3] to keep us warm.

Later I had bachelor cleaned the truck out adequately I thought. Yet I'd overlooked an empty Guinness bottle on the floor of the back seat. As the children careened up out of the back seat – they kicked the Guinness bottle out on the church parking lot.

The tarmac surface of the church lot was expertly engineered with a slight fall for drainage. The rolling Guinness bottle followed that design accordingly across the lot and on to the patent leather shoes of a very tall elegantly dressed church lady — who horrifically stared at the thing in stark disbelief. The lady was Marguerite Crestfallen, chairperson of Vigo County's M.A.D.D.[4]

Eliot and I swiftly retrieved the bottle and introduced ourselves. The lady was speechless to respond.

Inside the Church it was different. The children and I experienced two hundred to three hundred welcomes. All the people at Memorial appeared well dressed, fresh scrubbed and sincerely polite. The music...choir, and congregational singing seemed professional, Lollard's homily palatable and passable.

Bethany and Eliot were thrilled with such collective goodwill and genteel manners. I told Lollard, "My children and I feel we have a new church home." Reverend Lollard beamed with pride of his place and his people.

He drew me aside, "Our church community is in need of your counseling skills. I want you to meet a couple here today that are in

---

1   I.S.U.: Indiana State University.
2   Tulamora Dew: Irish whiskey
3   Guinness: Irish Stout
4   M.A.D.D.: Mothers Against Drunk Drivers; the late Carrie Nations of Feminist Prohibition.

need of some experienced counseling. And I know you have experience with divorce. He went on to explain their divorces were pending. No...no not from each other he explained, but from their respective spouses. They are both members of our church and *both*, he exhaled *full* professors at ISU. They're very much in love and need spiritual guidance through this difficult time."

Adroitly, he ushered me into his office where a near sixtyish couple were sitting. He introduced them as Doctors Jack Skelton and Marie Loudermilk. Then, the Reverend Lollard took his leave, quietly shutting the door.

Dr. Jack hmphed for a laugh, "I'm a Skelton, but not related to Red." He looked to me like he oughta be.

Dr. Marie started right in on how dumb her husband was and how her divorce should be final by Easter. "Sometimes it's just easier to get a whole new outfit than mend an old dress", she said.

Dr. Jack and Dr. Marie were colleagues. They had been colleagues for almost two decades. They had 'fallen in love' at one of the many conferences they'd attended together.

Both of these old dogs had spent decades together in the same academic kennel teaching bean bag courses for the cut and paste degrees of the Education Department. They reminded me of the ol' bromide one used to hear on the ISU campus.

"Those who can – do!, those who can't – teach.

Those who can't teach – teach Teachers."

On New Year's day my name appeared as Associate Pastor on Memorial's suburbanish marquee. It stayed there for a week. The following week two people called on Pastor Lollard to protest my appointment at Memorial and my employment in Terre Haute. They told him I was *not* a liberal but a socialist so far to the Left I appeared to the right of sensitivity.

Lollard panicked. Prestor John phoned. I turned to poetry. One poem I had worked on the last two Paschal seasons I finished. It is called...

Lest Supper

Up the weary stairs
their heavy tread ascends
tired, and terribly unsure
of all that lay ahead.
The place is cold and poorly lit
not yet spring, without a winter fire
stairs creak and cracks in the wall
smell of fish and old wine.
A carpenters hand lain up on the bearing wall
examines the grain where the studs should be;
his dusty feet feeling
for the joist.
An earthly habit,
Not callous of time
Or the misery in mortal looks
That file behind Him.
This man!...like them?...
His political face, his laboring limbs
impend loving glances general fear
and... specific disquiet.
Disciples of disquietude
Matters out of control,
Their disquisition a fulcrum
Of futures undespaired.
Lest supper...
Be misunderstood
The sacrificial body
And its blood.
Consecrate preemptively
our collective intentions
poised to pound the ages
except it grips...
imperfectly slips...apart.
For there is always, at least
one treacherous heart.

Finis

THOMAS G. MORGAN   451

SIA information can be obtained
ww.ICGtesting.com
ed in the USA
V021331211218
948-54598FF